CENTRAL LENDING LIBRARY

Telephone 20109 and 26988

Hours of Opening : 10 a.m. to 7 p.m. every weekday.

IT MAKES THE WORLD GO ROUND

DENIS MACKAIL

has also written

NOVELS

What Next?
Romance to the Rescue
Bill the Bachelor
According to Gibson
Summertime
The "Majestic" Mystery
Greenery Street
The Fortunes of Hugo
The Flower Show
Tales from Greenery Street
Another Part of the Wood
The Square Circle
David's Day
Ian and Felicity
Chelbury Abbey
The Young Livingstones
The Wedding
Summer Leaves
Back Again
Jacinth
Morning, Noon and Night
Upside-Down
Huddleston House
Our Hero
We're Here!
By Auction
Her Ladyship

COLLECTED SHORT STORIES

How Amusing!
Having Fun
London Lovers

BIOGRAPHY

The Story of J. M. B.

PERSONAL OBSERVATION

Life with Topsy
Ho!
Where Am I?

FOR CHILDREN

Tales for a Godchild

IT MAKES THE WORLD GO ROUND

OR

Saint Valentine's Day

by

DENIS MACKAIL

HUTCHINSON & CO. (Publishers) LTD
London   New York   Melbourne   Sydney   Cape Town

Printed in Great Britain
by The Anchor Press, Ltd.,
Tiptree, Essex

PART ONE

PAUL SUNDERLAND, who was twenty-six (what an enviable age!); who was an orphan (but with no memory of either parent, so that he was at least accustomed to this state); who was solvent (again how enviable, if also how rare) and in excellent health, awoke gently, in the bedroom of his adequate if rather hideously furnished service-flat, on an extremely fine morning in May.

In such circumstances—particularly as he was now accustomed to the flat, too—one might suppose, whether he instantly began carolling or not, that he would be reasonably free from black care. For it was not even that he had no occupation; on the contrary, he was an assiduous junior partner in a very sound family firm. Nor had he retired to rest after drinking too much. It would have been quite out of character if he had. The world liked him, moreover; and until of late—however strange this may seem—he had found little seriously wrong with the world.

And yet, though for a moment old habit, and nature, and a hint of sunshine outside, all suggested that he should now relax in complete peace, quite suddenly there was a click in some part of his brain; and peace was the very last thing he felt.

For he remembered. He had reached a tremendous decision last night; late if you like, but with no shadow of doubt. And though nothing could now make him alter his mind—here what was visible of him certainly looked pretty determined—he also knew just how much lay at stake.

Dimly he could still recall those few seconds of calm. And previous clicks; but there had been no click like this. Never. Though of course he had been blind until last night. Yet, again, though last night he had been filled (or so he had believed then) with hope and relief, what on earth could have induced him to hope?

At this point he groaned. If only, he thought, I'd never gone to that party! But he hadn't meant this. Besides, it was as unimaginable now as what he had been like even twelve hours ago.

Or again, if it came to that, as that he should *wish* to be relieved from a condition that was driving him mad. No, no. It was hell, but it was happiness, too; or at least without it there would be nothing

in life. It was agony; but even agony was better than the complete
blank to which, anyhow, he could never return.

Or must he? He gritted his teeth. If she said No—and of course
she would—what was left (here he made a rapid, rough calculation)
but fifty years of pure blank?

He would go on breathing, he supposed. Fellows generally did.
But then fellows—and this marks Paul Sunderland as a true victim
indeed—were all utterly different from him. They took knocks, but
they bounced up. It had even amused him, from time to time, to see
how quickly they started elsewhere. Or they were like his cousin
Roddie—first-rate chap though he was; self-complete and exempt
from all pangs. In neither case, whether flibbertigibbets or rocks,
could they conceive what a thing like this *meant*.

But *he* knew. And that was what set him apart. His whole
record had, in fact, landed him here. At the age of about six, that
is to say, he had cherished a childish passion—but of course he had
done nothing about it, and no one could count that—for his cousin
Rhoda, who was now forty-two. And later in life—he wouldn't
attempt to deny this, for he was human, after all—he had
occasionally looked at a young woman, thought You're rather a
pippin, and passed, still unstirred, on his way.

But that was all. No pursuit. No entanglement of any kind. He
had never felt like it, and hadn't seen why he should. He claimed
no credit. He could even see that it might have made him a bit dull.
Though of course it would have been stupid—well, rotten, in fact—
if he had deliberately egged himself on.

So he hadn't. With the result—though he had nothing to
conceal—that he was without protection. That he was unprepared.
That he had shown no vestige of sense. And had bungled everything
that could be bungled, for three whole months.

Rather absurd—he quite saw that—if it had all happened to
someone else. But then it hadn't. And of course, as the real crisis
approached, one felt ghastly. How else could one feel?

2

ALTHOUGH he had intended to do nothing of the sort, and had even
just been reminding himself (in the midst of other meditations) that
this morning, at least, he would most certainly do nothing of the

sort, Paul Sunderland—owing to his malady—must now go back to the beginning of it all.

A date—it was one of a number graven deeply on his heart—sprang unbidden into the focus of his mind's eye. It was February 14th. Or St. Valentine's Day. The latter point, as a matter of fact, he had overlooked at the time; in common, possibly, with a large part of the human race. But some weeks later, by chance, it had been brought to his notice, in a library book at the club.

"Hullo!" he had muttered. "I never realised that." It was indeed so interesting, in a way, that—although the poor author, of course, was getting nothing out of this, anyhow—he laid the book down. And mused a little. And smiled. For it *was* rather queer. Though (for this was still March) it was no more.

But he hadn't forgotten. The significance grew; whether he knew that it was growing or not. Now, again, it came bubbling right to the top. Was it an omen? He at once crossed his fingers, for luck. It was perhaps ironic. It was at least a most extraordinary coincidence. And back he again went to the same Day.

.   .   .   .   .

It had been quite an ordinary day, so far as he had marked it at all, when it began. Dull, grey, with a bit of an east wind. Nothing special in the newspapers—apart, of course, from the usual threats of complete chaos and disaster. But this hadn't disturbed him. His nerves were all right. For he was healthy, and had plenty to do.

Spilsby, the sallow and perhaps slightly too talkative man-servant whom he shared with the occupants of his own and another floor, had brought him his breakfast. Then he had marched to the Tube. He descended. He had been crushed and half suffocated, but was inured to this, too, as he roared through the bowels of the earth. He ascended. And marched off again.

He turned aside, into Cheesemonger Lane—where cheese is no longer sold, and which, indeed, has become more like a canyon—and entered an office, where he had a room to himself. He worked industriously, undeterred by the fact that the State, after first putting almost every possible obstacle in his way, would then collar most of the results of his toil.

Later still, as on most days, he got into a huddle with some other partners; of whom the chief was his uncle Hayward—another Sunderland, of course, though generally addressed, even by his nephew, as H.B. This character, by the way, wasn't the father of either Rhoda or Rodney; though he had a daughter—Primula, if you can hang on to that—and had once had a wife. She was still alive, and very lively, but as she had now been married to a rich Californian for about fifteen years, she was seldom mentioned, and never, certainly, during business.

So she wasn't mentioned today, though a lot of other things were, until in due course the huddle broke up. Then it was lunch-time, so that Paul rushed forth, also as usual, for a short, sharp, and only moderately nutritive meal in another scene of appalling congestion.

Then he went to a long board-meeting, still in much the same district, where similar obstacles must be faced and if possible overcome; so that the State might again reap where it hadn't sown.

Then, still at a smart pace, he returned to his own office, where Miss Thriplow, his highly efficient if not strictly beautiful or even verdant secretary—though as a matter of fact she was almost precisely his own age—had meanwhile typed a lot of letters for him; all with unimpeachable spelling, punctuation, and spacing, and a complete absence of corrections or erasures.

He read them. He signed them. He said: "Thank you, Miss Thriplow," though without exactly looking her straight in the eye. She withdrew. He instantly hurled himself into a complicated report, in which he was absorbed for the best part of another hour. Or sometimes, as during the morning, he answered his internal or external telephone; politely, and with no waste of time.

But as dusk turned to dark his inner consciousness said Whoa! and he obeyed it, for he had done enough for today. He tidied his desk. He resumed his coat and hat. He called out: "Good-night, Miss Thriplow," as he passed her adjacent cell; and, as there was no reply, assumed, correctly, that she had gone.

He went down in the lift. In a glass box in the main hall an ancient warrior, with medal-ribbons, bright buttons, and a cap with a glazed peak, noted his arrival—over a rather inappropriate pair of pince-nez—and offered him a valediction.

"Good-night, sir," he said.

"Oh—good-night, Banglewick."

"Cold tonight, sir."

"Yes. Oh, yes. Yes, it is. Er—quite cold."

"Parky, I call it, sir."

Paul Sunderland nodded agreeably—for, after all, they had

more or less thrashed this matter out now, and old Banglewick was probably just as anxious to get away—and passed out, through something of a portal, on to the pavement.

And stopped abruptly. Checked by Fate, as he would become aware later on. For the word "parky," which at first had merely struck him as a characteristic, Banglewickian adjective, had suddenly changed not only to a noun but to a proper name. It was even accompanied by a slight sense of guilt. For just as his uncle was called H.B., so Rex Parkinson—theoretically one of his oldest and closest friends—was known, in another circle, as Parky.

And he had had a card from him—or, rather, from Mrs. Parky—about cocktails. If it was for last night, then he had been rude. If for tomorrow, then he could calm down. But if it was for this evening—here Paul Sunderland began de-gloving, unbuttoning, and rummaging for his little pocket engagement-book, as he also moved nearer a lamp-post—then he must either go (and he was far from sure that he wanted to go), or ring up, or write a note when he got back.

For he was polite, you see. He couldn't help being polite. And as he now fluttered the leaves, and saw that it *was* for tonight— "Parky—drinks," he had scrawled—he became aware that it was his plain duty to go.

For the precise reason that he didn't want to. Or for the precise reason that, though he distinctly disliked cocktail-parties, and though Parky was married (which was why their friendship had become so much more theoretical), and though he strongly suspected Mrs. Parky—no, Lulu; he *must* remember that—of regarding him as all wives regarded their husbands' ex-cronies, which was to say as dangerous and demoralising, nevertheless he must *not* be rude.

He would look in, then. They didn't want him. And of course he wouldn't stay. But if he telephoned, it would be making a thing of it. If he wrote, they might even feel—his imagination at this point seems, admittedly, to have gone rather far—that they must ask him specially, for a whole evening, alone. And they would hate that. Or Mrs. Parky would. Or so he chose to feel convinced.

Get it over, then. In and out. And buzz off.

Instead, therefore, of proceeding to his club or his flat, as he had supposed that he was about to do, and purely because an ancient warrior had employed a slightly unusual word, he travelled by Underground, though in equal discomfort, to Sloane Square.

It was colder than ever here, and rather foggy, though the wind had gone down. He began walking, with a reasonably accurate knowledge of his destination, and continued thinking as well. He thought of Parky. Of the past. And how regrettable it was, in a sense, when really good chaps got spliced. And of Mrs. Parky—no, Lulu. And of their children. How many? He couldn't remember. He must be careful—for young parents, he had observed, were sometimes curiously sensitive—about that.

Altogether, in fact, he must be careful. And quick. In and out. Just a word, so that they knew he was there. Then he'd vanish. And *they* wouldn't mind.

He turned a corner. Was this it? Yes; look at those cars. And an open front door. Well, here goes!

3

A COMPARATIVELY brief history of cocktail-parties on this side of the Atlantic—for, of course, they originated, like so much else, on the other—would describe the phase when they were rather daring and dashing, and it was believed that only a professional could use a shaker; the phase when it was discovered that almost anyone could do this, if at the same time with somewhat variable results; the phase when more or less mild intoxication between the hours of six and eight was a social custom with no mystery except its purpose; the phase when all the stuff began running short and rising in price, which marked the return to some very startling concoctions.

And the phase when, although the price had soared to still further heights—with the State, of course, pouching most of it—there was almost a glut of all ingredients but one.

At this last phase, if the sippers had employed more pure reason, they would surely have taken the pledge. But they didn't. As they looked round they all knew, well enough, that if the State didn't tax this it would tax that. There was no escape from it, save possibly through mild intoxication. One must see one's friends, and one could hardly offer them tea.

Or not at that time in the evening, which was about the earliest that they were available, owing to the manner in which they all had to work. Dinner? Very nice, if you could raise the food, and weren't worn out, and went to restaurants for the rest of the week. But these were difficulties. So was the business of cooking and looking fresh. Not to mention the job of washing-up.

No, the orgy was the answer. There was no other way. Buy bottles, borrow glasses, pray that the refrigerator will hold out. Provide, if you are lucky, even some bags of potato-crisps, and other alleged appetisers. Broadcast your intention. Prepare for chaos in the home. And for approximately two hours there should at least be a frightful crowd and a stupendous din, as modern Civilised Man takes his ease.

As the alternative, in the present era, is to see no one at all, it seems preferable, to many people, that they should spend more than they can afford and have holes burnt by cigarettes in their loose covers and carpets than that they should pass from all knowledge or ken. For the race, even if it is its own fault that it puts up with the State, is still a gregarious race.

So Rex, or Reginald, Parkinson, whose old governor was a Judge and had wanted him to go to the Bar, but who had elected, after breaking a number of bones in the Royal Air Force, to put his all into a little publishing firm, and to marry, and—as a reaction, perhaps, from the constant threat of extinction, though it was his wife's idea, too—to become the father of three children in less than four years; this Rex, who was always in debt at this stage, but always cheerful, and preferred life to death; or this Parky, with the assistance of the above-mentioned wife, had sent cards of invitation all over the place, bidding guests to the Chelsea house for which—and quite right, too—his old governor had put up the premium.

Having done this, and having thought of a lot more guests, so that the shower of cards still continued, and having explained to his wife—not that she minded being in debt—that if he asked a sprinkling of authors he could charge everything as professional expenses and thus score off the State (this made her kiss him, but three babies hadn't yet dulled her love), the gallant and literary Parky then set about acquiring bottles and cigarettes.

If asked how, he would have replied that he had his methods; and this was true. While his wife, Lulu, displayed some of her own capability by borrowing glasses all up and down the street, and where this was possible even arranged for a supply of ice-cubes.

On the day itself—and they knew well enough which Saint was involved, for both were as sentimental as they were reckless— Mrs. Parkinson began shopping at 7.30 a.m. (which is possible, if you know how, even in Chelsea), cooked the breakfast, saw her husband off (with another kiss), tied a duster round her head, cleaned the main and indeed only reception room (while Mrs. Bodger, the Morning Help, crashed around in the basement and upstairs), shifted about a ton of furniture, helped and supported the Nannie (who after three years or so was still being told—but of course she *needn't* have stayed—that further staff was going to be engaged as soon as it was available), cooked the lunch, took the two elder children out (Linnet and Crispin—what else could they have been called?), brought them in again, had tea in the nursery (where the baby, Philomel, certainly yelled a good deal, but presently stopped, in response to some maternal singing).

Prepared dinner for the Nannie—it seemed unnecessary for herself and Rex. Had a bath. Dressed, or partially, again with the companionship of the two elder children. Said Nonsense, and that it was a party, when Nannie suggested that they should retire. Won this round, as she had won all others—which was perhaps *why* the Nannie stayed. Set out delicacies in dishes, while popping a few into the children's mouths. Answered the door-bell, repeatedly, so as to take in more glasses and ice-cubes, and on one occasion to get rid of a dun.

Twiddled her hair. Put on her frock. Did her face, as the saying goes; with a dab of lipstick (but of course she must wipe this off again) for Linnet as well. Stood up. Whirled round. Looked amazingly fresh. And dashed downstairs as she heard a latchkey at work.

"Darling!" This was a simultaneous ejaculation, as Rex and Lulu embraced in the narrow hall.

"Mind my face," said the latter.

"How's mine?" asked the former. "Here—use this." He offered his handkerchief, and more lipstick was removed or transferred. "Well? How's it going?"

"Splendidly! How was business?"

"Rotten."

"Never mind."

"I don't. You're looking marvellous."

"I adore you."

"Same here."

"But you'd better wash."

"Yes, I know. Hold everything. Hullo, children! I say—Lulu— are they going to fall downstairs?"

"I don't think so. They can watch you washing."

"So they can. What a thrill!"

High spirits at No. 17, Pelican Street, as the householder washed, laughed, and shouted. As he reappeared, still with the children— but he, no less than his wife, certainly seemed to have the most remarkable power over them. As he switched on more lights— "Blow the expense; this is a party!"—and began uncorking, and mixing liquids, and adding ice.

And then: "Here they come!" he yelled, as the bell rang, and he rushed to open the front door himself. From this stage, indeed, it remained open, as prospective sippers passed in, and piled apparel on the big, battered perambulator that blocked the back part of the hall. Undoubtedly, there was a certain risk that the uninvited might sneak in, and even sneak out with some of the apparel. Yet the Parkinson philosophy was prepared to face that; and it was as impossible for either Parkinson to keep on dashing to the door as it was undeniable that it was the only source of fresh air.

It came in, very likely, with the intention of striking a chill, but was completely baffled within two or three yards. For arrivals were constant, and each supplied further warmth, as the joists of the little house took the strain. The apparel had now completely obliterated the perambulator, and was wedged through the banisters, too.

But there was plenty to drink; and somehow not only did both adult Parkinsons contrive to move through the mob with trays of brimming glasses, but Linnet—and surely this was extremely educational for her—was tottering round, at a lower level, with a dish of delicacies.

Sometimes they slipped, or were swept, on to the floor; but, unless they were trodden on, she at once picked them up. She was a true Parkinson, in her desire to be as hospitable as she could. As for her brother, after he had been personally knocked over several times—an experience which, as another true Parkinson, he took with the utmost sang-froid—this was observed, and he was hoisted on to the host's shoulder. Sometimes he hung on by his father's hair, sometimes by his ear, and once or twice by his nose. Yet he remained there, quite happily, and Parky himself seemed quite content to be carrying a child as well as one or more trays.

What an upbringing! Yet what was wrong, if they enjoyed it, and kept calm? As they did, because they had never known anything else. For No. 17, Pelican Street was a complete republic and always had been, with little distinction between the children and the grown-ups. And it worked, if by a kind of miracle, for one can hardly pretend that it would always work. It was the Parkinson spirit, which goes, so perplexingly, with a constant background of debt. Which couldn't last, perhaps—though nothing lasts—if luck should be overdrawn, too.

But which rose to such heights, on this 14th of February, that not only were the walls virtually bulging with guests, but at a given moment Nannie and Philomel actually appeared on the scene; were received vociferously, to Philomel's clear if rather precocious and Parkinsonian delight; and were still present (though not for long now, and the elder children went, too) when no other than the Honourable Sir Edmund, or Mr. Justice, Parkinson arrived, with his immense upper lip, and said: "Ha!"

At a building in the Strand this would have struck terror into all breasts. Its implication, even here, was unquestionably that his grandchildren were being reared in the most dangerous and shocking manner; with a kind of rider (even though he was a guest) that he hadn't put up £2,000 for the shortish lease of a decrepit house in an ex-slum, nor was still contributing to its upkeep, in order that it should be used for the corruption of infants and the absorption, so far as he could see in large quantities, of excisable liquor.

However, as at practically the same moment his grandson Crispin screamed a welcome at him, his grand-daughter Linnet tugged at his trousers, his grand-daughter Philomel burst into a great beaming, windy, toothless grin, his son Reginald gave him the friendliest nod, and his daughter-in-law Lucinda pressed a small though brimming glass into his hand, Sir Edmund Parkinson found it impossible to keep his top lip drawn down.

In other words, Sir Edmund smiled, and could hardly do less, whatever he thought or might again think when he got home. And it was at about this moment, also—for the front door was still open, and there could be no question, in view of the uproar and other signs, that this was the right evening and the right house—that Paul Sunderland passed over the threshold.

4

HE blinked, once or twice, at the noise and the glare. But though still, in his own view, a mere transient or even will-o'-the-wisp, he wasn't uncouth nor an actual enemy of the species. He disrobed, sideways and slightly entangled with another guest. He hung his hat on what he mistook for a hook, though in fact it was the point of someone else's inverted and half-buried umbrella. He draped his coat on the mounting and slithering pile; from which it passed, almost at once, to the floor.

He saw the children being taken upstairs; but though now apprised, in consequence, of what was at least their minimum number, he saw no reason—since he could recall none of their names —to address them. The bachelor angle, in short. Benevolent, but decidedly detached. Though it did just strike him how queer it was that Parky, or indeed anyone, should have children at all. Then he approached the main rumpus.

The doorway was jammed tight with other members of the species. It hardly seemed, even if they moved, that there would be any space for a fresh arrival inside. But he must try. It was essential, since he was in the house, that he should be seen. So he hovered, peered, oscillated, and hoped for the best.

Nor was he entirely disappointed. The host himself, who had the advantage, for this purpose, of being well over six feet high, suddenly spotted him and, regardless of the conglutination, more or less dragged him in.

"Paul!" he said. "Splendid! Good show! Come along!"

His hair was ruffled, as it would be after shouldering his son. He was rather flushed, as was also natural in the heat and crowd. But the sincerity of his welcome warmed Paul's cockles, too. He was glad he had come. In another minute—for of course they couldn't really talk to each other here—he would probably be equally glad to go. But old Parky was old Parky. An amazingly good chap. And there were memories that even marriage couldn't expunge.

Meanwhile, having been gripped, he was now being turned round.

"Lulu! I say—Lulu!"

"Yes, darling?" Mrs. Parkinson seemed to flow through some solid bodies.

"Here's old Paul!"

"Oh, hullo!"

Mrs. Parkinson flashed a brilliant smile. Why on earth, in fact, Paul Sunderland should have imagined that she disliked him, no third party could have conceived. The illusion, in fact, was entirely subjective; except, of course, that wives like Mrs. Parkinson happen to prefer their own husbands, and wouldn't mind if they—the husbands, that is to say—had never known anyone else. Or, again, it is even possible that she thought *everyone* should be married; in which case Paul might be held to have let her down.

On the other hand—and this was much more the real, warm-hearted, and even broad-minded creature that she was—if Rex liked him, and had known him since they were at school together; and if Paul realised (as it seemed he did) his true place as a mere friend; and particularly if he still avoided asking Rex to stag evenings (as Paul, a great respecter of the hearth, had, in fact, never dreamt of doing), then she would smile at him. And, of course, offer him a drink.

"Here!" she said, instantly producing another small though brimming glass. "Have a drink."

"Oh," said Paul. "Thanks."

She smiled again, and disappeared.

"Well—" he tried to resume.

But even old Parky's attention wasn't quite what it had been.

"Care to speak to the governor?" he suggested. And before Paul could stop him—for though he had known Sir Edmund, if less closely, for many years, too, and could remember his wife, and his other son, Gerald, who had been killed in France, they had never yet found a subject in common—he yelled out: "Hi—Guv!"

But Paul had luck. The huge head made an eighth of a turn, but only, as it seemed, so as to dismiss this interruption. The broad back, unless this was another illusion, was bending gallantly over the nearer end of a sofa. Or over its occupant, though she looked more sprightly than youthful.

"Sorry," said the host, with rather less of a yell. "Seems fixed up. Better leave him. Mrs. Girlie." Or it sounded like that, though in fact she was a Mrs. Gourlay. "Lives round corner. Big refrigerator. Widow."

"Oh," said Paul. At the word "refrigerator" he had looked puzzled, since he was unaware, in his comparatively cushioned and lonely life, of all the planning that had been necessary to produce ice-cubes. At the word "widow" he had undoubtedly done his best to look grieved, if as a mark of decency rather than of any deep feeling. But the look was wasted; and worse. Not only had a surge of sippers wafted Parky away, but it had brought a small young woman right under his nose.

"Cheer up, Paul," she said. "It's not as bad as all that."

He was a trifle vexed. He could hardly explain the origin of the look. Yet he never liked being told to cheer up. Who does, if it comes to that, when nine times out of ten they have merely been looking thoughtful? It was annoying. Yet it was difficult to be annoyed with this small young woman. He grinned.

"Hullo, Bubbles!" he said.

Here was evidence, after all, that he wasn't quite out of the world. That he didn't merely work, and then retire to his club. That the in-and-out policy, though in a sense firmly rooted with regard to this sort of entertainment, couldn't always have guided his path.

On the other hand, of course, the number of people who knew Bubbles Vaughan, and had, within a very short time, started calling her Bubbles—notwithstanding the fact that she had been christened Rosemary—was beyond any ascertained computation. Nor was there a limit—this would have been impossible, since it expanded each day—to the number whom she, also, knew.

She was small, as has been said. She tended to look slightly surprised. Her lips, which, to be quite frank, often tended to put ideas into chaps' heads, were generally parted either in a smile or a mock-pout.

Her surprised eyes were enormous. She was exquisitely finished off. She was twenty-five, and had been carrying on a completely virginal existence from the moment that any possible alternative had arisen. She had a dull father and a dull mother. She was someone's secretary—but neither more nor less—for five days a week. If she could have remained twenty-five for ever—or perhaps twenty-three would have been even better—she would have been completely justified as decorative, amusing, eternally good-natured, and the possessor of a record circle of friends.

But then there's Life (thought Paul). It leaves no one alone. An older Bubbles, though not unimaginable, couldn't possibly be the same. She was balanced (or so he suddenly felt, in a kind of flash) on a knife-edge of Destiny. She would become sprightly—the whole point at present was that she was *never* sprightly—or she would tire, and turn sour.

B

He felt a wave of affection, because she and Life were like that. But without even a vestige of passion.

"What fun!" he added. He bent a little, so as to avoid shouting. "I say—can I get you a——"

"No, thanks. I haven't started."

It occurred to him that she had said this at other parties or gatherings. Or sometimes she said that she had finished. But then why (another thought) should a girl like Bubbles ever bother with stimulants? Though of course lots of 'em did.

"How *are* you, Paul?"

"Me? Oh, fine, thanks."

"Working away?"

"That's right.

"At the old stand?"

"That's it."

"All among the Sunderlands?"

But of course she knew that. This was just her line of friendly talk. A nod would do. Not that she wasn't unique, or at least highly exceptional, in remembering where he worked; and in appearing interested; and in continuing to look at him—when of course she knew everyone else in the room—instead of glancing past one of his shoulders. Yes, he liked her enormously. Though of course everyone else did, too.

"—have you seen him lately?"

Another question; and he had missed the beginning. No, he hadn't. His brain picked it up from where, or so it seemed, it was still lingering in one of his ears.

"Oh, Roddie. No; I haven't. Well, not for two or three weeks." He smiled; thinking of his cousin Rodney, of his cousin Rodney's pleasant if rather non-committal nature, and of his devotion—for his cousin Rodney wasn't associated with the firm—to every and any kind of machine.

"But I take it," he added, "he's covered with oil somewhere. Wallowing in it, and all that, you know."

"Yes. I suppose he is."

"Bet your life," said Paul.

"At any rate," said Bubbles, "he doesn't seem to be here."

"No. Why? Did you think he was going to be?"

Careless questions. He didn't really expect an answer to either of them; though Roddie, now he came to think of it, was godfather to one of those children, and would almost certainly have had a card, too.

A further and not wholly unfamiliar thought. Why Roddie and not me? Thought dismissed as unworthy, and even presumptuous in a chap who had failed to remember how many children there were. A slight look of guilt, as if the thought could have been read. It wasn't reflected, for Bubbles could never look guilty. Why should she? Yet for a moment, dash it all and inexplicable as this might be, she had looked—well, sort of undefended or something.

He spoke quickly, on an impulse.

"I say—Bubbles——"

"Yes?"

He must have imagined it. But that was no reason for being mean.

"Shall we have dinner one night?"

"Oh, Paul—yes, I'd love to!" She was sparkling again. "Only not this week—or next week——"

"I didn't think it would be," said Paul, knowing her life.

"No, don't tease me. I shan't forget."

"Yes, but what am I supposed to do?"

"Ring up, Paul. A little later. Now, if you don't, I shall be annoyed. But you will—won't you? And I'll try to look nice."

Paul Sunderland grinned. The joke was that it was impossible for her to look anything else; but that she wasn't conceited, so that he needn't say so, but could just grin. As for the development of social customs which enabled him to invite a girl of twenty-five to have dinner alone with him and, as was virtually implied, then dance in his arms, this was accepted, without question, by both.

It would also be accepted by the old Vaughans, whether they liked it or not. Furthermore, it was a practice, in the instance of Paul, in which he indulged only rarely. In which he had never indulged with any secondary or ulterior motive. And for which, even if in other instances this, also, had become rather rare, he never expected to be repaid with a kiss.

So these two immortal souls more or less understood each other. Which is to say that, though divided by many deep gulfs and an ultimate and perhaps unplumbable reserve, they understood that they were to have a night out together, at Paul's expense; that he would presently ring up; and that, when he did, time and place could be arranged.

The rarest thing of all, possibly, was his complete assurance that Bubbles's word was her bond. If she had wished to refuse, she would have refused now. When they fixed the date, she would turn up. She would be gay, she would look nice, and they would have fun. Why, in these circumstances, he wasn't madly in love with her must remain a mystery to the romantic; if not to all.

But he just wasn't. Though a number of chaps thought they were. And nothing happened, because she kept the whole lot at bay. What did she expect? What did she want? What was her game? No one knew. She was an enigma—("Well, good-night, Paul—I must tear off to the Twymans'"—and a cavalier instantly appeared, as if by magic, to take her along)—and one only hoped she wouldn't leave things too late.

Darned unfair, though, being a girl, thought the no less chivalrous Paul, as he prepared to forget her, and also to leave as soon as she had really gone. Must get rid of this little glass, though. He put it carefully down. And of course he must at least attempt to express his thanks.

He turned. There was a slight impact. A tinkle, and a wail of woe. He saw what he had done, and that he must be temporarily detained.

5

"I'M *terribly* sorry!" He crouched at his victim's feet. He collected splinters. He looked up. And she looked down. "I say—did it go on your dress?"

"Oh, do be careful! I don't think so. Don't cut yourself—*please*!"

"I'm all right," said Paul, gallantly. He rose, with a handkerchief full of fragments. He was at a disadvantage. This was deplorable, with a girl who looked and spoke like that. He took a violent and almost physical pull at himself. "I say—cuc-can't I get you another?"

Dashed awkward. She must have answered. But he hadn't heard what she said. He had been too busy using his eyes.

Yet with reason, though he now tried to switch them away. And apparently did something else.

"*Don't* put it in your pocket!"

"Oh. Sorry. Must be mad. Did you—" Another powerful pull. "Look here, you *must* have another."

This was madness indeed; for he had left her, when he could have stayed. Of *course* she wouldn't be there, or alone, when he got back. Girls—and all memory of Miss Vaughan was now completely erased—who looked like that would quite obviously be snaffled. Nevertheless, he forged ahead, through the throng and the din, until he reached the host; who was at once conversing with a coterie and officiating at the bar.

"I say, Parky," he announced, "I've broken a glass."

"That's all right, old boy. Glad you're having a good time. Want another?"

"Well, yes; but——"

"Speak up, old man."

"I mean, I'm sorry."

"You're forgiven. I don't suppose it's one of ours. What shall I make it? Parkinson Special? Well, take two, while you're about it. You might meet someone."

"Yes. Well, that's just it."

"What is?"

"Girl over there," said Paul. "Near the door. Rather tall. Fairish hair. Sort of green sort of dress. It was *her* glass I smashed. Who—who is she?"

"Here!" said the host, without immediately answering this distinctly pressing question. "Better let *me* have those bits—unless you *want* to carry 'em around. Green girl, did you say?" He employed his own height. "Oh yes. Someone Lulu picked up. Don't know her myself. Something like Jones."

"Oh." Swift adjustment, during which the name Jones, or something like Jones, seemed to appear in an entirely new light. Miss Jones. Ah! Or Mrs. Jones? Um.

"There you are, old boy. Off you go!"

So Paul returned. And yet, by some marvel—or because though pretty, and even beautiful, she didn't immediately disturb everyone at first sight—the girl was still where he had left her; and even smiled at him.

"That *is* kind of you," she said.

"Not at all," said Paul. "Least I could do." He began looking for Lulu, hoping to regularise their association. He couldn't see her. He turned back; and though still slightly dazed, wasn't an oaf, and had been at parties before.

"Cigarette?" he suggested.

"Oh—no, thanks. I don't smoke."

What purity! But he mustn't dwell on it. He must try again.

"Bit of a jam," he said.

"Yes."

He must do better than that.

"Er—do you know the Parkinsons well?"

Stupid, of course, after what Parky had just said. And rather impertinent. But she was as kind as she was pure.

"Well, no—not really. In fact, it's the first time I've been here. But I met Mrs. Parkinson when we were both having a row in a shop. And then there are the children, you see. I mean, they're rather like dogs—aren't they?"

"Are they?" said Paul, who hadn't observed this himself.

"No, no!" A silvery little laugh, with the most flattering suggestion that he had been witty rather than obtuse. "I mean, if one *likes* them—and they really *are* rather sweet—well, one sort of gets talking."

"Oh, rather. Of course."

And a queer, piercing thought. Did she mean that she had children herself?

"You see, I live near here."

"Oh yes?"

"Yes. Just off the Embankment."

"Chelsea Embankment," said Paul, which perhaps hardly did him justice. Though it appeared, notwithstanding, that he was right.

"Yes," said the sylph. "It was Daddy's house." A shadow flitted across her face. He's dead, thought Paul, and was as racked with sympathy as is possible for an orphan. "And now I've got the top bit. Sort of sliced off, you know. Well, a sort of flat."

"I see." And nothing, after all, could restore the late Mr. Jones. "Rather nice—eh?"

She looked doubtful. Had he put his foot in it?

"Well, it was." She gave what Paul personally regarded as an enchanting little shrug. "But I was sharing it with another girl. Dorothea Brickfield. Do you know her?"

"No," said Paul, with an odd sound of apology, and even regret. "I—I'm afraid I don't."

"Oh, I thought you might. She paints, you see."

Paul tried to look as he imagined that someone would look who knew all about modern painting, but just didn't happen—for some strange and exceptional reason—to have heard of Dorothea Brickfield.

"But she got married," said the vision, again with a slight shadow. "At Christmas," she added, as though somehow this made it worse. "So I'm alone now." Poor angel! thought Paul; but it seemed clear, if inexplicable, that she herself had avoided such a disastrous step. "It's rather dull sometimes." Dorothea was a cad, though he was also the last to wish her back. "Except, of course, that I'm out most of the day."

"I see," said Paul again. He even added, with what struck him as considerable dash and daring: "Like me."

"Yes, I suppose so. Only I do modelling, of course."

He was fooled here. Again he tried to look artistic, or moderately artistic, for he also wished to look manly, as he beheld a studio—but of course it was Dorothea who had misled him—rather than a dressmaking establishment off Bond Street. Yet as he would have been just as incapable of talking about clothes, and might also have been violently jealous of Michael Willoughby—without cause, though this wouldn't protect him later on—no great harm was done.

"I see," he repeated, with an air of respect.

"Oh, well," said the vision—(Had he overdone it? Was she suspecting his utter sincerity?)—"I dare say you despise that; but, after all, quite a lot of it's for export."

Despise? Not the least. Even if it now seemed possible that she designed teapots. Despise? Why, he admired her courage and industry more than ever.

"No, no——"

She cut him off, as she glanced over her little glass.

"I asked for it," she said.

"You didn't!"

"Talking about myself. And when I—I don't even know you."

The sensation of a door being slammed in his face. Yet perhaps, if he pushed hard, he could re-open it.

"Oh," he said, brightly—for it was a fact that he was no oaf—"I can explain all that. I was at school with Rex Parkinson. We were in one or two shows together—I don't mean in a theatre; in the war. I work in the City—quite honestly, and all that. I've got a flat—well, a couple of rooms that are *called* a flat—just off Oxford Street. And my name——"

The remarkable flow seemed to collide with some obstacle. It was quite impossible to pronounce his own name.

"Go on," said the girl. She looked amused. "I'm Bianca Brown."

"Good heavens!"

"Why? Are you my long-lost uncle or something?"

Teasing. And it flicked him; though he knew she was only teasing. Uncle, indeed! And that ass, Parky! But the obstruction had gone.

"I'm Paul Sunderland," he said; without even a twitch.

"There you are, then. Introduced."

"That's right. Have 'nother drink."

"No, thank you. But if you *could* take this glass——"

"Here—I say!—you're not going! I—I don't know a *soul* here!"

"No?" She started something—just conceivably about Bubbles. And stopped. And started quickly again. "Hard luck," she said. "Well. Get yourself another drink. Oh, but look! They're getting up. Let's sit down."

She was observant. More so than Paul; though he had much else on his mind—including the strange effect of that "Let's." The first use, between any couple, of "we" or "us." It can pass unnoticed; or it can be almost staggering in its sudden hint of coalescence. It was the latter that made him just a little slow.

Yet it was true, perfectly true, that Sir Edmund Parkinson had just risen from his son's sofa; and that his width, even if his companion hadn't risen as well, had left quite a perceptible gap.

"Ha!" he was saying. "Well, I must say it's been most interesting —delightful, in fact—after all these years . . ."

Very likely. But Paul's own interest was in the gap now. Let Sir Edmund boom, and look protective, as he forced a passage towards the door. Let him accompany his old acquaintance, if he chose, any distance that he thought fit. Far, far more important that Paul himself, with a certain rigidity of the hindquarters, should guard the gap until his own companion had sat down.

He did this. He joined her at once. He hadn't the least wish for another drink. For though in a sense he had now recovered from the first assault of her voice and looks, he was still reluctant—indeed, extremely reluctant—to lose her.

They got me, he thought. Like a bang. Like a biff. But I'm a reasonable being. Not a maniac. One just doesn't, and can't, lose one's head at first sight. That's a myth. Though she's a jolly nice girl.

And lovely, too. Yes, I quite admit that. In fact, it was what got me, of course.

But I don't *know* her. I was a bit taken by surprise. That was all. Mustn't be tiresome. Or act like a goat.

Triumph of reason; or so he was convinced; or was resolved to

be convinced, as he glanced again, and was a trifle shaken by her
nose. Yet he was quite uncapricornian. And Miss Brown, though
still as friendly as before, wasn't attempting—even so far as a
totally independent and unprejudiced witness might have observed
—to behave like a siren.

No doubt Miss Brown—whose good looks no such witness could
possibly have denied—had a certain experience of young men.
Conceivably, also, her resentment at the recent defection of Miss
Brickfield had tended to reinforce her own prudence.

In any case she was quite cool, as they chattered away. Rather
frank, perhaps—but then girls *were* frank nowadays, in the majority
of examples—about the surface, at least, of her existence. Distinctly
informative, in other words, about life in an upper part, with
certain fragments of background as well.

But not boring. Oh no. Paul liked all this stuff. He even revealed
more of his own story, too. Not competitively; for this wasn't
necessary. She could listen, not merely talk. And so attentively—
this, anyhow, was most unusual—that he had sometimes to stop,
lest he himself should be a bore.

At this lower level, also, and though there were generally at
least two other characters on the seat or arms of the sofa, there was
much less need to shout. They were in an enclave. Not alone, for
the concourse still milled. Yet apart. Lookers-on; when they chose.

Or joint listeners, sometimes, to words from outside; for it even
seemed now that they needn't speak all the time. They heard
snatches and snippets. And sometimes they smiled. As for instance
when the inevitable sprightly guest—not the widow, though, for she
had disappeared—announced that she was getting quite tiddley.

"Now, wait," said Miss Brown. "She'll say 'Well, just a *drop*.' "
She did. And Paul chuckled again.

"Extraordinary idea," he said. "Grown-up people, I mean,
carrying on like this."

"I know."

She understood. That was the remarkable thing. She didn't look
—though he was also aware, in a way, that he had been both—as if
he had been trite or superior.

"But they can't help it," she added.

"Poor devils—I know. It's rather a life, eh?"

"Of course. But quite fun."

She was a philosopher, then, too. A thinker. Quick-witted; yet
deep. He glanced again—astonishing that the same world could

contain that short upper lip and Parky's governor's yard-and-a-half
—and was momentarily silent.

I ought to go, he was thinking. I'll only spoil this if I stay.
Besides, I *said* I wouldn't stay.

He sank back.

They began identifying authors, and authoresses, too; not by
their names, but by other insignia. This wasn't difficult, or at least
not difficult when, even if wrong, there was no proof, and when they
both knew that the host was a publisher. The test, roughly speaking
—and one may regret to report—was an air of intense self-
consciousness. Of pride, but of anxiety as well. I'm Somebody, was
the suggestion. But was this known? And if it were, was some rival
another notch nearer Fame?

They coagulated, because they were comrades. They dispersed,
as their egos clashed. They watched Parky, even when coagulating,
as if he could *make* their books sell; and perhaps would, if they
could catch him alone. But he was at home, at his own party, and
had finished business for the day. So that, whether this would
eventually make them or their agents humbler or not, he had
acquired a bodyguard of ex-members of the Royal Air Force.

"Rather pathetic," said Miss Brown. "Unless we're making it
all up." And then: "Don't stare—but is that one by the fireplace?
Oh, I think it must be. He's got a *beard*!"

Paul looked quickly. Shook his head.

"No," he said. "He's conceited all right. But he's got a blue
flannel shirt. I think he must be an artist. Oh! Sorry."

"Why?" asked Miss Brown, for once missing a point.

But he must explain. He mustn't be even ruder.

"Well, aren't you one?"

"Aren't I what?" She seemed puzzled.

"An artist. I mean——"

"Good heavens!" said Miss Brown. She really had the most
enchanting, rippling little laugh. "Of course not! I said I *lived* with
an artist—" the slight shadow—"or I *did*——"

Paul wasn't, it may be said at once, the kind of character to
become roguish over an unconscious ambiguity, which in any case
he had failed to detect.

"But you said you modelled," he pointed out.

"Well, I do. In a shop. But——"

"In a *shop*?"

"Well, of course! At Michael Willoughby's."

"Oh," said Paul.

"Do you mean to tell me you've never heard of him?"

"No," said Paul. "I mean, yes." But the English language is constantly setting this trap. "Why, what does he sell?"

Lulu Parkinson was bending over them, with the customary tray.

"Hullo, you two," she said. "Why aren't you drinking?"

Paul sprang to his feet.

"No, sit down. Here——"

"This extraordinary man," Bianca Brown interposed, "has never even heard of Michael Willoughby!"

"How shocking!" said Mrs. Parkinson. "But he's a bachelor, poor boy. Here—take this." She had turned to Paul. "I think you'll need it. There!" She had the complete art of forcing a glass into a resistant hand. "And you, too," she said to the girl, "if he's upset you." She performed the same feat again. "Now you can tell him," she said, "*all* about strapless dresses."

She smiled again, looking impish and amused; very pretty; and not the least as if she really despised Paul. Perhaps, he even had time to think, and with a shade more intelligence than some of his earlier thoughts on the same subject, she's more used to me now. Or sees I'm not such a rotten influence on old Parky; though I could tell her a thing or two—and certainly shan't—about *him*.

Strapless dresses? Oh yes; of course. To tell the truth, he *had* rather wondered, from time to time, and again with reasonable delicacy, how the deuce they were kept up. But of course he wasn't going to ask Miss Brown. Though he had been illuminated on another point. She was in a dress-shop.

Mrs. Parky had gone; sucked back into the whirlpool, though in fact it was now a shade less turgid. Other guests, in other words, as well as Bubbles must have left; and for some time there had been a mere trickle of arrivals. Yet with a full glass in his hand— only the second, after all—and, no less relevant, its replica in his companion's, this still wasn't the moment (said Reason) to bring the session to an end.

He said: "Well, now I *have* got it. You must have thought me rather a fool."

"Oh no. Why *should* you have heard of him; after all?"

A tribute to his toughness? Or to his obvious naïveté? Not that I am naïve, he thought—however one pronounces it. Though I'd hate her to feel I was tough. Further dialogue seemed to be called for.

"Is it interesting?" he asked.

"Is what interesting?"

For the first time there was a hint—and he didn't like it at all—that he had lost just a fraction of her attention.

"Your work, I mean. Your job. Well, whatever you do there. Is it amusing?"

"Sometimes." A tiny frown, but he didn't feel that it was for him. "Well, one's got to do *something*, you see."

He had gone too far. He must just guess whether she was hard-up—a ghastly thought, though she didn't look it—or had a conscience, or was being ragged by Authority.

" 'Bianca,' " he said, suddenly.

"I beg your pardon?" A slight start.

"No, no." He was embarrassed. He had been thinking aloud. "I—I didn't mean it like that. It was only—" for the absurd truth was the only way out—"that I was just wondering if you had an elder sister who was a shrew."

It sounded singularly offensive. Either, it also came to him, he must now explain the allusion, or, worse still—I say, how dashed awkward!—she *had* a sister like that.

But she was rippling again.

"Oh, Shakespeare," she said. (Clever girl. Lord, what a relief!) "No, I haven't, as a matter of fact. I'm an only child." (Good! for some reason or other.) "Though Daddy," she suddenly added, "wrote poems, you know."

A *non-sequitur*? Not the least; once Shakespeare had been mentioned. But Brown? Brown? T. E. Brown? No, of course not. He was a Victorian. She was *far* too young. Yet ought he to know? He was distracted again.

And she rippled.

"Oh, don't look like that!" she said. "I didn't mean—well, I can't think why I said it now—that I *expected* you to know. It was just how it came out. Well—" a flash of admirable spirit—"you started it all. But he wasn't famous. Though he was an angel. Poor Daddy."

For another, appalling instant it seemed not only that this beautiful, long, slim, lovely creature might dissolve into soft tears, but that Paul Sunderland—no, he certainly wasn't very tough—might be choked by a sob. But what could he do? He couldn't pat her. Damn Shakespeare, he thought; though in fact he had always hitherto blessed him. He held his breath, with an air of agony. She turned away. She looked back. She was smiling.

"I'm rather silly," she said.

"No," said Paul. "I was rather rude."

"But I have read him, you know. I mean, Shakespeare."

The Swan's stock fairly soared.

"Well, let's talk about him," said Paul. And they did, if this can be imagined, on a sofa at a cocktail-party. They put him through it. They both argued and agreed. Absurd? Nothing of the sort. A most remarkable girl; and perhaps a slightly odd business-man, too. Yet the conjunction, in any case, struck such sparks from the Bard that neither observed the guests drifting away.

The room wasn't empty. Far from it, as yet. The party would end, as the Parkinsons' parties always did, with a joint sortie of survivors—probably at about nine o'clock—to some place where they could pick up some food. It was, indeed, little more than about twenty to eight when Parky, having entertained but also eluded all the authors, came over, still hospitably, with more drinks.

"Now, then—" he began. And then: "Good Lord, what have you been doing? Don't you like it? Do you want some cocoa instead?"

He gazed scornfully at the two glasses, still half-full, and quite warm. His last intention, one may feel sure, was to break a spell.

But he broke it. The girl rose.

"Oh, how awful!" she said. "Look at the time! I must rush!"

"No, no. We're just starting. Here—lemme change that for——"

"No, you mustn't. I mean, it's been wonderful——"

"Aha!" said Parky, though Paul, personally, could have dispensed with his wink.

"—but I left something simmering, and I must *fly*!"

"Oh, well," said Parky; "of course that's different. Paul, then?"

"Er—no thanks, old boy."

"Don't rag them," said Lulu, who had now joined her husband, and was hanging affectionately on his arm. "He's just a bully," she said. "Only, Paul——"

"Yes?" Almost the complete man of business; apart from what he trusted—if incorrectly, for she was more sentimental than ever after a party—that he was concealing from a pair of bright, amused eyes.

"Don't go, I mean—*please*—if you haven't got to. But if you *could* just——" here she nipped the same arm—"just shut the front door. Because I think it's about time. Would you mind?"

"Of course!" said Paul, again tricked (though his meaning was quite clear) by vernacular usage. "But I'm afraid—" his own glance edged away—"that's matter of fact—well, I mean, thanks awfully for——"

Slight confusion. He was submerging Miss Brown's farewell. But he waited a moment. She completed it. She had gone. So had the Parkinsons; yet perhaps he had said all he need. He took himself out into the narrow hall.

He picked up the wrong overcoat, and hurled it away. He found the right one; and even his hat. He turned quickly. She was on the door-mat.

"I say!"

She turned, too.

"Yes?"

"Rather foggy," said Paul. "Are you sure—I mean, can't I——"

"Oh no—please don't bother. It's not at all bad." Dash! "Besides, I've got my little car."

Rather startling. And even annoying, as he recalled once again that the Porchester Leveret which he had on order was still subject to a delay of three years.

"Oh. I see." But he could still be polite. Indeed, he must. "Well, I'll just . . ."

Indication that in addition to shutting the front door—yet opening it first, too, as a matter of fact, for Mrs. Parky must have made a mistake here—he would hover, rather like a car-park attendant, while Miss Brown embarked, and until her engine sprang to life.

The car was small, and distinctly shabby. He put its age at about twelve. So that pathos, rather than surprise or something even unworthier, was now the note. She got in without his help, though he assisted in slamming a second door.

"Of course," she said, suddenly, as she inserted a key and switched on, "I oughtn't to have this."

Another ripple. Was it rueful? He longed for more light. But her starter worked—it would, of course, since (however basely again) he had been hoping that it would falter. The little vehicle was palpitating all over.

"Good-night," she called out.

"Oh. Good-night," said Paul.

She shot off, with a bit of a roar. She was just a tail-light. Not even that; as she swung left, with a toot, into the main road. He sighed. He buttoned his overcoat. He put on his hat. He twisted his mouth. He began walking away.

6

"WELL?" inquired one of the two sections into which it appeared that he had somehow become divided.

"A pippin," said the other.

"Don't be vulgar," said the first.

"Dashed attractive, then."

"Possibly. Yes, I noticed how she bowled you over——"

"Excuse me; but she didn't. That's a gross exaggeration. Please don't talk as if I were sort of amorous idiot."

The second section seemed to shrug its shoulders.

"Nevertheless," it said, "I seem to remember that when you first caught sight of her——"

"I happen," interrupted the first, "to have a normal appreciation for beauty. It isn't so common that when one sees an extreme case of it one just looks the other way. I was rather startled, in fact. I don't hesitate to admit it. But I doubt if she guessed. And I made a pretty quick recovery."

"Oh? Really?"

"Yes."

"Then why stick to her the whole time like that?"

"Because," said Part One, "it just so chanced that neither of us knew anyone else there."

"I see. But you found her agreeable?"

"Yes, thank you."

"Fascinating?"

It was Part One's turn to shrug.

"A darling?"

"I wish you'd shut up," said Part One. "If you'd been listening —and you apparently were—you'd have heard nothing to which even a bishop could object."

"Shakespeare," said Part Two. "Most improving, I'm sure."

"Well, why not? She was intelligent. It just happened to crop up. What do you *expect* me to talk about? Football?"

"Oh no. Certainly not. I thought you did admirably."

"Thanks."

"And, as you say, you quite recovered from what Shakespeare— if I, too, may be allowed to mention him—once compared to the lightning."

"Yes, I did. I'm twenty-six. I don't lose my head. I mean, I can be staggered momentarily—and I was—by anyone quite so good-looking. But after that—well, I just *liked* her. You *saw* how we got on. But I didn't rush her. Or try and flirt with her. It was just—well, a very pleasant half-hour."

"I make it more like an hour, myself," said Part Two.

"Very well. Call it an hour, if you prefer."

"And then?"

"What do you mean?"

"Well, what now?" asked Part Two.

Part One—but the temporary attack of schizophrenia was already passing, and it was really a single, slightly baffled and bewildered young gentleman who was now marching through the streets—was quite unable to settle this point. For it was true that there had been a flash. It was true that he had been attracted. That he had enjoyed the session. That Reason had told him that was all

Reason, indeed—though an observer might conceivably have thought otherwise—had been in complete control even when he had rushed through the hall. All he had been considering was courtesy; a little natural gratitude, perhaps; and what had virtually amounted to an order from his hostess.

Even on the pavement he had been reasonable. A model of calm. But that tail-light, somehow—speeding away like that—getting smaller—taking *her* away, too. . . .

It had just got him. There had been a jolt. A sort of jab, one might say. Not a flash, for that was over; and, besides, in this kind of imagery there couldn't possibly be more than one. But an acute and quite unforeseen feeling.

Rubbish. Absurd! He was making it all up. He shook his head, as if he had emerged from a cold plunge.

He felt nothing. There you were!

"Bianca," he thought. A curiously beautiful name. "Bianca Brown"? At least rhythmical; and better—oh, no doubt of that—no, no doubt at all—than Bianca Jones.

He slowed down. "*I* dunno," he announced to the world. And he didn't. But he saw a taxi, and stopped it.

It took him where he asked it to take him, to his service-flat just south of Oxford Street. And as the service-flat, though it had entire charge of his ration-book, never expected to supply anything but breakfast unless warned in advance; and since there had been no such warning—for he had imagined, until something seemed to have changed his mind, that he would be dining at his club—there was some delay, and also lack of enthusiasm, in feeding him.

Furthermore, when the meal (such as it was) at last appeared, and Spilsby, as usual, resumed his endless monologue on contemporary sport, Paul not only gazed at him glassily—instead of interjecting polite comments—but, though unknown to his partmanservant, was conducting a silent soliloquy, too.

"Ah, Spilsby, Spilsby," was the general line that it took. "Little do you realise, little do you surmise what has come into my life, as I sit here apparently unchanged. Or what hasn't, perhaps. For that's the deuce; I don't *know*. Yet, Spilsby—ah, Spilsby—how fortunate you are, with your simple interests and your freedom from care. And yet, again, on the other hand—ah, Spilsby, if I should be in love——"

"Quite ready, sir," said Spilsby, checking the monologue and stepping back. "Though I'm afraid, sir, your whisky's a bit low."

"Doesn't matter," said Paul—as it didn't, of course, after the best part of two Parkinson Specials and at least the contingency that he had been pierced by an arrow. So Spilsby, who knew well enough why the whisky was a bit low, looked relieved, and withdrew from the room.

But *had* Paul been pierced? If he was still unsure, perhaps not. Yet if so, or even if the answer were in doubt, he was in a condition where he was thinking about it. And that condition, ladies and gentlemen, as may be shown later on, is one where not only are the eyes opened to quite a number of phenomena which a heart-whole chap may very easily overlook; but where the subject, having at least risked infection himself, may—though such a risk never crosses his mind—prove subtly infectious to others.

So much, then, for the main events, omens, and other relevant details on good old St. Valentine's Day.

7

HERE, though only briefly, one must dip further into the past. For it has been said that Paul Sunderland had no memory of his parents; and as readers may already have imagined all kinds of things (for one just can't stop them), such as aeroplanes crashing, trains colliding, great liners sinking, earthquakes burying thousands, volcanoes doing much the same thing, fires, floods, epidemics, and even crimes of passion, this must be cleared up. And so, for it is relevant, too, must the manner in which Paul had been reared.

The precise snip of the shears, then, was nothing more remarkable (alas!) than a car smash. At one moment his parents were bowling along. At the next, owing to an error on the part of the hired driver—who, however, was only momentarily stunned—both were dead. One is shocked. So were their friends and relations.

But though it is true that they might have been spared, it is also true that they might have been mutilated. They were young. They had escaped age; and the Second World War. So far as could be known, they were both translated in a twinkling to another sphere. Or possibly nowhere. But they were together. And it was very quick.

No one, of course—such is the power of hope, even now—would choose such an end to their own story. Yet there have been worse. And without going into all the other possibilities, it is at least a point that Paul himself was barely three.

So that he remembered nothing; or at the most it was again a matter of imagination, based on what he would be subsequently told. And though he didn't know this, at the moment, either, he belonged to a Clan, so that there was no chance of his being removed to an orphanage.

He went, instead, to live with his grandmother—at her house at Greenhurst, a still curiously unspoilt backwater to the north of London—with his own nurse and his own toys. She had had so many children herself that—well, no; one mustn't and can't say that the loss of one hadn't affected her. But there were plenty left. She was a natural matriarch. She was no less naturally kind. And never once—top marks here, surely, to old Mrs. Sunderland—did she look at Paul in a manner calculated to make him howl.

Neither did she spoil him, or not unduly. Nor, again, did he lack plenty of cousins. Rhoda and Rodney were only two of the large bunch; though it was smaller now, thanks to the second war. His future, unless he should choose otherwise, held a niche in the firm. And having finished with the Nurse, having been instructed, up to a further point, by Miss Elvira Crankshaw—a nursery-governess who was still serving the clan, and at that time (though he hadn't known this) had been younger than his cousin Rhoda—he had gone to a preparatory school, a public school, and from the latter (in the same year that his grandmother died) direct into the above-mentioned war.

Which he had survived, as seems clear; to enter the firm and a small flat. With a flying start, no doubt, in the matter of job and prospects. Yet with a distinct gift for business, or for what remained of it now. And with no feeling—apart from piety, and conscience, and all that—that being an orphan had ruined his whole life.

Lucky? Perhaps. But adaptable, too. And the clan liked him—not that it wasn't one of their strange qualities that they all liked each other. So that on February 19th—the interval having been spent in spasmodic thought, speculation, examination of his own emotions, and even, on one occasion, of the Telephone Directory, but as yet in no more positive action—he was delighted when, on entering his Uncle Hayward's (or H.B.'s) sanctum in the City, he beheld another relation, and a very old friend.

"Hullo, Prim!" he said. For the relation was his cousin Primula—half an orphan, in a sense, owing to her mother having passed right out of her life. "Well, well!" But he never dreamt of giving her a kiss.

And then: "Hullo, Cranky!" For the old friend was Miss Crankshaw, which wasn't surprising, since (having guided a selection of young Sunderlands) she had spent the last ten years as his uncle's housekeeper and the child's duenna.

Child, though? As he grasped Miss Crankshaw's hand, he suddenly realised that this was rather a mis-statement. He was, in fact, conscious of surprise, after all. For though of course he wasn't so ignorant as to be unaware of his cousin's age, something had happened. Or he had just observed it at last.

She was grown-up, or as near as dammit. And dashed pretty, too. She had sort of flowered, and fined down, and come on. Amazing. Or rather stupid not to have noticed before. He glanced at her father, who, though he wasn't called H.B. for that reason, had the figure of a lead pencil; and was amazed again. He glanced at the duenna, as if *she* might be in some way responsible. But that was rot, though she was a marvel. No, it was Life.

Would he have felt this, one may wonder, even four days ago? However, he didn't allude to it—top marks, perhaps, here to Paul Sunderland for such consideration or reserve—any more than it crossed his mind to snatch a kiss.

Well, well! he was thinking, though in a different tone from his recent remark. Young Prim! Fancy that! Well, what next?

It then occurred to him that, in the circumstances, he was

perhaps in the way. Or even if not, that he must postpone a talk on finance. He glanced at the door.

"No, don't go," said H.B., "now you're here." He was standing, as was of course correct, even for a daughter and her companion. Yet there was a kind of hint that he wasn't quite at his ease.

"Rather unexpected," he went on. "This visit, I mean. I—ah . . ."

"Oh, Daddy—you don't *mind*! Why, you ought to be *thankful*!"

"Eh?" said H.B., with a marked absence of calm. "Why—why, what do you mean, darling, Eh?"

"Female society," said Primula, with a kind of whirl on her slim legs. "Brightening things up. Bringing romance into your life."

"Eh?" said her father, again. He even backed, as if slightly alarmed.

"Oh, Paul, isn't he tiresome!" Another whirl, and a flashing look. "Of course he's terribly pleased, really—and it's all right, darling—" this was for her father—"you haven't got to give us lunch. But you see, Paul—" round again—"I'd heard of a shop, quite near here. Only they wouldn't sell me anything, because it was wholesale; or something sickening like that. So I thought I'd explore—you see, darling Cranky has absolutely *no* control over me now. And so first of all we went to look at the outside of Mark's office—only I thought perhaps he'd lose his job if we went in. And then—well, why not—I said, 'Let's go and see Daddy.' So I told that *sweet* old man in the box downstairs that Cranky was the Duchess of Whipsnade and I was Lady Uvula Houndsditch—so as to be more of a surprise for Daddy, only unforch'nately he remembered us both, because of that time we came to see the pr'cession and—well, here we are; so would *you* like to give us lunch?"

"Certainly," said Paul, though racking his brains for the right place.

"Prim, *dear*!" said Miss Crankshaw, almost simultaneously.

"I—I— Really!" said H.B., as a kind of jittering accompaniment.

And suddenly Paul's cousin Primula seemed drained of at least the excess of her vitality. A puzzled look flitted across her face, as if she, too, couldn't quite account for her own development. She was wearing no hat, and performed the action, though nothing could have been neater than her hair, of sweeping a stray lock from her eyes.

"I'm sorry," she said. "I was only pulling your leg. I'm lunching with some girls."

Imagination again? Or had that last word sounded rather as though she were saying "scorpions," or even "toads"?

"Oh," said Paul. But he couldn't pretend that this didn't solve certain problems. "I see, Prim. Right you are." And as this, in turn, seemed to suggest rather too much relief: "But perhaps you will, some other time."

Come out to lunch, he meant. And in the plural, of course. Not only from civility, and because Cranky had been part of the leg-pulling plan, and was only a few feet away, but because—even though he suddenly saw how unusual and old-fashioned this was—one must always include Cranky.

And yet why? The child wasn't a child any more. Oh no—(this was Paul meeting an attack from his other self)—I don't *want* Prim alone. I don't mean that. And I'm *devoted* to Cranky. But at the same time . . .

It had been his intention to glance at H.B., to check up, as it were, on his old-fashionedness. But his eyes must pass Prim's, and this was as far as they got. For she was looking at him. Penetratingly. He was only eight years older, he hadn't offered her rusks and milk, but it was exactly as if she had just realised—even as he had realised that she was grown-up—that he wasn't an old man, after all. How absurd! And also faintly embarrassing.

"Oh," she was saying, for thoughts and looks had only taken an instant, "yes, I'd love to. Yes, that would be fun." But he couldn't feel that this statement was sincere. Or sincerity had somehow left it, half-way. "But I expect," said his cousin Prim, "I'm really rather interrupting. In fact, we're off. Come on, Cranky. Let's go."

"Er—" said H.B.

"Oh, darling Daddy, you are sweet!" She rushed at him and enfolded him in a swift embrace; for which, indeed, the senior partner seemed so little prepared that for a moment there was some peril to his equilibrium. But he was against his desk—an article of immense solidity—and didn't fall. She released him, and he was still on his legs. "Perhaps," she said, "it was rather a stupid idea. But now it's over. See you this evening. Oh no, I shan't; I shall be out. Good-bye, Paul. That's an awfully smart tie."

It wasn't; but as she was now trying to leave by the wrong door, as Miss Crankshaw was trying to stop her, and as the tie-wearer (I'd better take 'em down, he was thinking) was already on the way to the correct exit, these were hardly circumstances in which to argue the point. Besides, H.B., after all, had kept his head and pushed a button. The wrong door opened, disclosing his own, much more elderly, secretary, and he addressed her at once.

"Oh, Mrs. Kelsey," he said. "My daughter and—ah—" for some reason he seemed to abandon this part of the description— "have just been to see me. But now they're going. So *could* you take them to the lift?"

"Yes, of course, Mr. Sunderland. How do you do, Miss Sunderland. How do you do—Miss Crankshaw, isn't it?"

"Yes," said Cranky. A very brief look of challenge and apprecia- tion was exchanged between the business and the domestic hench- women, who, in fact, so far as telephonings and various payments were concerned, really knew each other quite well. Then, or at the last moment, Miss Crankshaw glanced at her employer, as if she might be going to defend either her charge or herself.

But H.B. was in a cloud. He didn't see. He didn't speak. Or not until the whole trio had gone.

Then he gave a slight start.

"I—I must apologise," he said.

"My dear H.B.! Your own daughter in your own office. Why not?"

Paul's Uncle Hayward seemed to consider this.

"She's growing up," he announced.

"So I noticed," said Paul. "My word, yes. Quite extraordinary, I must say."

"Bound to happen," said the proud parent, though he didn't sound specially pleased. "Raises rather a problem, you know."

"Oh, I shouldn't have thought so," said Paul, encouragingly. "I'm sure she'll enjoy herself, and—and . . ."

As he couldn't think, or not at the moment, of anything else she either wanted or was likely to do, his voice faded away.

"Very remarkable woman," said H.B., nevertheless. "Really very exceptional indeed."

Who? Prim? What a rum word to use for a chit. Oh, no; I see. He means Cranky. Well, of course!

"Rather!" he said.

H.B. looked annoyed. I'd better get off this, thought his nephew; swiftly and obligingly, and without bothering why. "How's Mark getting on?" he inquired, snatching at a remote echo. "Have you heard? I haven't seen him just lately."

H.B. resumed his business expression.

"Very well, I believe. Or so Rhoda tells me. Of course—well, in a way I see his point in not coming here. Though he could have. He's half a Sunderland. And a nice boy, you know."

"Yes," said Paul. "But half a Medway. You can't have 'em all."

"No, I suppose not. Though he might have bridged a gap."

A tinge of regret here; for if his mother had been a matriarch, H.B. had at least the instincts of a patriarch. And the gap, as Paul realised, lay in the absence of a male Sunderland of about Prim's age.

Yet if his cousin Rhoda had married a man—Charles Medway, in fact, at present touring the remains of the Empire—who was Chairman of a business of his own, why on earth should their son, Mark, enter another?

No reason at all. Or none that Paul could see. And at this dead end, which was reached jointly by both generations, both seemed to recall that they weren't here to talk Family.

"Hrrm," said H.B., moving round to his chair. "Well, yes? Shall we have the others? If we're going into this now?"

His hand made for the bell-push. It, or he, seemed to recall that Mrs. Kelsey might still be elsewhere. Again there was a transient, mystical, worried look on his face. But then he pushed; and Mrs. Kelsey appeared.

"Just see—will you, please—if Mr. Clayton and Mr. Oliver are free? Thank you."

He folded his hands. And Paul took a seat. He had no doubt that his uncle Oliver and his cousin Clayton—of whom the latter was, in fact, slightly the elder—would be here in a moment, and were indeed awaiting this call. He glanced at the patriarch. Amazing, he thought, that he should have had a wife, and that they should have had Prim. Love, he thought. Marriage. Dead passion. Yes, and live passion, too. . . .

Or not? No, of course not. Fantastic idea. Besides, a girl like that—but he had quite stopped thinking of his cousin Prim—was simply *bound* to be engaged to some chap.

Yet he winced. He had quite forgotten the girl's attitude towards Miss Brickfield's romance. Supposing, he was thinking, she's just met someone—while I've been dithering—in these last few days. Oh, lord . . .

His cousin Clayton and his uncle Oliver, both younger than H.B., both married, and each with a son coming along nicely, though still at school, entered together—looking like and unlike each other, as they always did. And Paul, too, was the complete partner again.

"Come in. Come in," said H.B., also in his usual manner. "Now, then . . ."

But the rest of this scene can be cut.

8

Two days later, or as much as a week, by this time, since the Parkinsons' party, the general position was ostensibly unchanged. Paul, that is to say, had continued to think. Not incessantly, perhaps. And quite often in a vein of curious detachment. The Telephone Directory had also informed him—or, rather, had repeated the information—that Miss B. Brown had a number; which he had even committed, if again unconsciously, to his memory.

It had also told him that Michael Willoughby—whom he pictured, for some reason, as both effeminate and salacious—dealt in Robes and Modes only a short distance away.

But he hadn't gone there; either to gaze at the outside (as his cousin Prim had apparently gazed at another building) or—for, of course, this was even more out of the question—so as to force his way in. He had done no dialling, either on the Grosvenor or Flaxman exchange.

He had just existed, if with another picture still recurring in his mind. He had worked. He had dictated to Miss Thriplow, in one sense of that verb, without observing her very closely; though, as he never did, this again marked no change. He had dined twice at his flat. Yet on this third evening, if merely, perhaps, for the sake of variety—or possibly so as to avoid listening to Spilsby—he decided to dine at his club.

He was in its hall, then, eyeing the menu that was exhibited there, when he received a moderate thump on the back. He turned, naturally. And, behold, the thump had been delivered by his cousin Rodney, whom he was delighted, as always, to see.

A little surprised, though; or up to the point that a man may be surprised when his cousin is known to belong to another monastery. Yet of course there was an explanation. Roddie, who was neither covered in oil nor wearing overalls, but was looking tall, clean, cheerful, and distinctive, was keeping a date with an authentic member. And this member, as is not unknown, had thought the hour of their appointment a good moment at which to originate a trunk-call.

"He's here, old boy," said Paul's cousin Rodney, who combined an incredible knowledgeability about machinery with a punctilious pretence that he was a mere fop, or even fool. "I've seen him in a box. I've waved at him. Fellow called Haggerston-Goldworthy." Or something like that, though perhaps not entirely. "Do you know him?"

"No," said Paul, as if it were impossible—and conceivably it is—that any clubman should know another without some much closer link. "But I can give you a drink if you like."

"Better not, thanks," said Roddie. "He might burst out, and then where should I be? Well, how are you, old stiff?" he inquired, affectionately.

"Oh, fine," said Paul. But there was something else that he had been going to say. What? Oh yes; of course! "I say, talking of drinking—"

"Yes, old soak? Don't mind *me*—if your tongue's hanging out."

"No, I didn't mean that. But seeing you reminded me—" his eyes flickered, and steadied—"I half thought I might have seen you last week. At Parky's."

"At old Parky's? Why?"

"Cocktail-scrimmage," said Paul.

"By Jove, yes. Of course. By Jove, I never answered. Dashed rude. But I wasn't here. I was up north."

"Well, 'smatter of fact—"

"Yes? Carry on."

"—we thought you might be."

"You and Parky?"

"No. Bubbles."

"Oh," said Roddie. He looked blank. Not, surely, because his first cousin was violating an extinct rule about mentioning girls' names in clubs. But he looked guarded. Or no, he didn't. Must have been thinking of something else.

"Young Bubbles," he said. "Was *she* there?"

"Well, of course. I've just told you. Why shouldn't she be?"

"Oh," said Rodney Sunderland. "That's right," he said. He pulled out a cigarette-case; opened it; eyed the contents; shut it; and put it back. "Been busy," he suddenly added. "Though if you'll tell me of a party where you *haven't* met Bubbles—God bless her!—" but this was a distinctly offhand invocation—"then I'll— Ah! There's my blighter. More business, you know. Sorry, Paul. See you soon. Love to all."

Even a young gentleman suffering from traces of an obsession could take note, and indeed had, that his late companion was apparently gifted with Second Sight. For the man in the box was only just coming out. Though it might be that Roddie, who habitually drove at fifty miles an hour, had quicker senses and had seen him hang up.

Probably, in fact. And it wasn't the least important. Except that some other impression—— No. It was gone now, whatever it had been. Miss Brown trickled back. And though just for a moment he had given a slight start—by Jove, he was thinking, I said I'd ring up!—he then remembered that Miss Vaughan had said not for another week. Which meant, of course, that he had now as good as forgotten her, too; and might even fail (for this often happens when a thought is thrust out) to remember again when he should.

Besides, there were other cares, or some tension at least, as he sat alone in the long and, for these days, extravagantly lofty dining-room of the Junior Corinthian. And as far as possible from Roddie and the chap with the double name, lest it should be supposed that he wished to join them, either now or later on, and wreck their private discussion. That was Paul, as he ate slowly— not that there was a great deal to eat—and frowned sometimes, and rather wished that he had brought an evening newspaper in with him; though he was also aware that it could hardly be relied on as a drug.

No, he was again musing; the fact is, I'm in a state. Or I *think* so, which is just the same thing. I'm not facing this. I keep dithering and blithering all the time. I keep hoping it's my imagination; but then, just once or twice, when I felt it was, I—I was annoyed. I missed it. I deliberately went back.

But that's not *doing* anything. Or settling anything. And I shall be ill, if it goes on. Which is idiotic; because if I don't know, who does?

Well, no one, of course; and thank goodness for that. But there's

Roddie—(a very swift, covert glance)—without a care in the world; just as I was, until exactly a week ago. No, more. (For such accuracy was of extreme importance.) It was about half-past six, I suppose—and it's after eight now—when I first had that extraordinary sort of jolt.

I mean, *that* wasn't love. Well, of course not. I was just startled. That was all. But it was the beginning—(here quite a remarkable phantasmagoria shot through his mind, though it had certainly had some practice, as he recalled one thing after another that the girl had said)—and what on earth's going to be the end?

Shall I wake up suddenly, and—no, I couldn't bear that. Though I'm dashed—all right, *damned* if I can stand this.

Well, what would Roddie do? He's sensible—I mean, basically; just as *I* was, until I got into this—this mess. (A frightful scowl—to the alarm of a waiter—as he rejected that last word. Mess, indeed! No, that was a cad's line of thought.)

But Roddie would *do* something. (He was back on the main theme.) And so'll I. Yes, I'll do it tomorrow. I'll—I'll—I'll . . .

He had reached this point before. Many times. But the thing was cumulative, for all that. And Rodney Sunderland, whether immune from other arrows or not, had assumed the likeness of a beacon or rock. Look how he had gone his own way in chucking everything for engineering, and had done so well that he was now being dined by an obvious, if also slightly repulsive, tycoon.

If Roddie could do that—and God bless him too—then Paul wasn't so weak but that he could do—what? He was still baffled, in fact. He could see objections to every course. He was doomed. He was just the world's champion chump.

Further evidence of this, perhaps, as he tried to leave without payment; as the cashier coughed; and as he had to return in disgrace. Yet after the rest of a short evening at the Junior Corinthian—owing to the apparent impossibility of addressing even his acquaintances—he walked home, and went to bed. Worn-out, as he believed. Yet having delivered, or so it would seem, such a kick to his Subconscious—with or without the assistance of his cousin Rodney—that it served him the answer, as on a plate, when he awoke.

Well, of course! And quite simple. He would do it today. It was a stroke of genius. Not that he was conceited. But—*phew!*

9

IT was also inevitable that a good deal of gunpowder should run out of the heels of his boots, as he toiled, either alone or with Miss Thriplow, at his tasks. But at the precise hour that he had planned— as if in response to another kick—he rose abruptly, and announced that he must be off.

"But that memorandum, Mr. Sunderland!" said his worthy if still only partially perceived adjuvant.

"Tomorrow," said Paul, half-way to the coat-hook already. "Sorry," he added, detaching his hat and balancing it on his head in a manner sometimes adopted when one is in haste, but also in the presence of the fair sex. "But I—I've got to go somewhere."

The semi-visible Miss Thriplow didn't persist in her protest. Perhaps her conscience was now stilled. Or perhaps, again, she had no violent objection to being released a little earlier than usual. She rose, too. She said: "Well, good-night, then, Mr. Sunderland," and slipped away.

" 'Oo'-'i'," said Paul, who, the better to don his overcoat, was now gripping the hat-brim between his teeth. Then he jerked, tugged, and staggered. Did some buttoning. Replaced the hat, but less asymmetrically, on his head. And was himself out of the room so quickly that he passed Miss Thriplow before she had entered her own.

He didn't pause, though, for further adieux. He shot off at a smart pace. And as the lift was ascending, he ran down the stairs; so that he reached the hall almost as soon as if he had waited for it.

Sergeant Banglewick, with his pince-nez so adjusted that he could peer over one lens and under the other, was outside his box; and, having peered, gave a salute.

"Will you be coming back, sir?" he asked.

"No," said Paul, chassé-ing slightly so as to get round him. Sometimes, it was true, he had a few words with Sergeant Banglewick; about the weather, or his little garden, or his son Perce. It was a kind of custom, off and on. But he proposed to dodge it tonight. And did, though less successful in dodging the Sergeant, as he stepped forward to try and open a swing-door.

For a moment, indeed, there was something in the nature of a collision. Yet there were two swing-doors, and Paul bumped through the other one. He trusted, if again only for a moment (for indeed there was much else on his mind), that Banglewick wouldn't read more into his action than mere haste; that he wouldn't attach such consequence in it as to start a panic in the City.

But then, for he was in the street now, he forgot all about Sergeant Banglewick, his pince-nez, his little garden, and his son Perce; not that he had ever seen more than the Sergeant and the pince-nez. It was the immediate future that filled all his thoughts. His decision—so far as it went. His great plan.

Put briefly, as the Subconscious had first put it this morning, and without all the extraneous matter which had since appeared and rather tangled it up, the great plan was that he should proceed to Michael Willoughby's establishment; that he should loiter— this couldn't be helped, though it was the weak link in the chain; that Miss Brown should emerge, after her own day's work; that he should see her; spring forward; snatch his hat from his head; and . . .

Well, this was where the Subconscious had been so clear, and the subsequent growth had been so tiresome. There was a slight mist now, in fact, over what was to happen next. Yet his note-case was primed. He had no engagement tonight; nor, indeed, until about 9.30 tomorrow morning. And surely, when he saw her, inspiration would revive; and courage, or he prayed so, as well.

Perhaps, now that he was on the brink, it would be infernal cheek to suggest dinner. Or a film. Or, as he had sometimes madly thought, both. No, he mustn't alarm her. There must be no suggestion that he was a wolf. That would be fatal; if also highly unlikely.

But a drink, now. Say at the Berkeley. Or somewhere like that. Why not, in the present era? Chaps were doing it all the time. A little talk. A couple of cocktails. A cigarette—no, dammit, she didn't smoke. But an advance, before they parted. So that it would be easier next time. No compliments. Nothing to frighten her. Just a continuation of last week. Well, why not? But could he ask her? And would she come?

Or would she have fixed something else? Yes. A thousand to one.

Or would she be there? When did she get off? Would he be too late?

He staggered again, at this appalling thought, for it would of course smash the whole scheme. He was screwed up for tonight. Something would crack if he failed. And it would be a sign, too, that he wasn't *meant* to succeed. Just fancy—just imagine another day like this. And—dammit again—there was a week-end coming on.

He must hurry. He dismissed all idea of the Tube, though just now there had seemed plenty of time. Or, rather, he fluttered, drawn at one moment towards its maw, and at the next seeking wildly for a taxi. He was going to be late. He was going to miss her. Every taxi shot past, though he hailed them all, quite regardless of flags. It must be the Tube, then, after all. He reversed. And Fate smiled. Unless, of course—for the old boy climbing out of the taxi that had just stopped was being appallingly deliberate—this was only a pre-ordained trap.

Of Paul's sufferings, as the old boy now stood talking to the driver, a mere hint must suffice. They were acute. They were protracted. Yet still he stood firm. And eventually, though there was a short and rather ugly scene with a rival claimant, he embarked. Furthermore, though the driver seemed disgusted at the destination—on principle, perhaps, for surely the corner of New Bond Street was a fairly central address—he set his vehicle in motion at last.

There was a lot of traffic, and the vehicle strained rather than sped; though Paul assisted it—or at least this was apparently his idea—by perching well forward on his seat. He kept watching the meter, and adjusting his loose change. At Oxford Circus, where there was the jam of ages, he was on the point of leaping out; and was all but hurled on to the floor as they lurched on.

Yet in the end they arrived at the point that he had selected; since of course he must walk the last bit. Why? Never mind. Some good reason, no doubt. And though it was no part of his plan to drop a shilling and two sixpences in the gutter, he recovered them, after the driver had driven off; and rose again; and turned sharp to the south.

Time? More or less, and after all, what he had meant it to be. In consequence, however, of the export drive and the demand for more effort, or possibly for some further good reason, most of the shops were now shut. This was a shock. Was he too late? Had the plan let him down? Or was he secretly and shamefully relieved?

He set his jaw. He wouldn't admit this. He was a man, not a rat. He moved more quickly, so far as cross traffic allowed. He turned right. He pulled up. Yes, there was the name; though it was so discreet that he had nearly shot by. The big private residence, as it had been until the last aristocrat or nabob had abandoned the struggle, blazed with light from a number of windows—which was good, up to a point; but someone had shut the front door.

Oh. Pause for thought. Perhaps it was always kept closed. Or perhaps those lights represented cleaners, and all business had ceased. Or perhaps, again—an ingenious yet distinctly worrying idea—there was some kind of stage-door round at the back.

Should he investigate? No. It might be true, but he might be tricked. He must risk that, though almost convinced now that he had left things too late. He must stroll, on a short beat of about fifty yards. Keeping alert. Looking natural, or so far as he could. And ready to register the utmost surprise.

Yet within a couple of minutes he became aware of something else. That other men were strolling, too. Some were tall, some were short, some were old, some were young. Some had newspapers, at which they affected to glance under a lamp-post. Some paused, and though he was pretty sure what they were really up to by now, took a long time to light cigarettes. Were they wolves? Was this Babylon? Or were they husbands, and even fathers?

He couldn't tell. But though they disregarded him, and he very soon took the same line, there was no doubt that not only were they confoundedly in the way, but he had somehow joined this fraternity, too.

And Paul Secondus was disgusted.

"So that's what you're doing," he said, with a sneer. "Hanging around outside a dressmaker's. One of the pack now. I see. Trying to pick a girl up——"

"I'm not! We've been introduced."

"Well, that's how it *looks*. Except, of course, that you show it much more."

"I tell you——"

"And it's what *she'll* think. A ravening beast."

"Oh, shut up! You ought to know I've never done this before."

"But you've started. That's the point. And once you begin——"

There was another point, though, and a joint jerk, as the two Pauls became one. For an approaching pedestrian had just lifted his hat.

"Good-evening, sir."

Spilsby! My aunt! Now I'm caught. What the devil——

"Oh, hullo, Spilsby. Good-evening. I——"

But though prepared, or almost prepared, to explain his own presence, Paul Sunderland was suddenly let off. For Spilsby, who

wasn't strolling, had already passed on. There he went. Back to
the flat. Whew! And doubts, after all. For had he suspected, or
not?

Well, what was I doing? Reconstruction. I was going that way.
Well, not fast, I admit. But I wasn't *hovering*. And I wasn't outside
the shop. So that's something, too. And I dare say—well, of course
this is the time when he'd be off—even Spilsby can take a walk if
he likes.

Um, thought Paul. But he had been scared. Though it was still
cold, he felt hot. He removed his own hat. He was just feeling
for his handkerchief, so as to wipe some perhaps imaginary dew;
when another figure approached, in slight silhouette; and stopped
short; and addressed him in turn.

"Why, surely—" said a voice. "But, of course! Well, how odd!
Hullo." And there was a visible smile now. "How are *you*?"

Rocky. Very rocky. For it was the quarry herself. By goggling
after Spilsby like that, he had failed to see her come out. With his
hat in his hand he was precluded from raising it. Nor can it be
denied that his conscience was at work, and that of course he *ought*
to admit that he had been waiting for her. But he didn't. Since for
one thing he hadn't the nerve; and for another he was overwhelmed
by deep peace.

It was as if a tooth had stopped aching. He was utterly calm.
Not a trace of that sudden vertigo remained.

"Hul-lo!" he exclaimed. "It's Miss Brown! Good lord! I say—"
Hell might gape, but he had chosen his path—"is this the place—
that you were talking about—where you work?"

"That's right." She hadn't guessed! "And I suppose *you* were
going home?"

"Well . . ." Yet it was no reaction from duplicity that made
him pause. And, indeed, most of the pause was in his mind. "Well,
not particularly," he concluded.

The rippling laugh; which he hadn't forgotten—except, perhaps,
some of its charm. Delicious.

"What do you mean? You must *know* what you're doing in
my street."

"Oh." But for the "my," he might still have confessed all. But
it was a joke. So he could chuckle; and did. Crackling of thorns
under a pot? Never mind. On we go. "No, what I *really* meant—"
for though still bare-headed, which was possibly a sign of slight
nerves, he was twenty-six, after all, and no oaf—"what I was

really sort of suddenly wondering was if it wouldn't be a sort of idea if we had a drink."

"Oh," said Miss Brown, who had seemed to follow this syntax. Paul replaced his hat. He was so calm now—though he might yell if she dismissed the idea—that perhaps, then, he *wasn't* in a state. Interesting. Almost welcome, for the moment, at least. Other incipient subjects have sometimes felt the same way. Yet he was also interested in her reply, which *must* be Yes or No; and then turned out, of course, to be neither.

"Well," she was saying, "I haven't got an *awful* lot of time." His face fell. "But I'll tell you what!" It lit up. "Come round to my club——"

"What!"

"Well, it's near. Don't you see? It's in the mews—and I'll give *you* a drink."

"Oh," said Paul. This was all wrong.

"Don't you want to?" she asked.

"No, no. I mean, yes. I——"

"Oh, come *on*!"

She turned. He should have admired her independence, and perhaps did. Yet it was wrong, when he was a chap, and she was a girl. Besides, he had rather gathered that she wasn't all that well off. There was a silent contest between pride and consideration.

Yet he was still with her. Beside her. And then hastening to catch up, as she turned again, down a narrow passage, to the left. This must, of course, lead to the mews. And either this thought, or another memory of last week, produced an inquiry as he once more drew level.

"Is this where you leave your car?" he asked.

"George?" she replied, unexpectedly. "Well, sometimes. He's rather a problem—though I love him, of course. But as a matter of fact he's not been very well."

"Oh? Oh—I see." George was the name of the little car. A stab of jealousy became sympathy instead. "I'm very sorry to hear that."

"Yes, poor darling." Still the car, though. There had been no need to flinch. "But he's fifteen, you know."

"I say—really?"

"M-h'm. So he's having a little treatment. But I saw him last night. And they seemed to think he wasn't *quite* done for yet."

"Oh. Good. Well, that's splendid."

"It was his valves, poor old boy. Though of course . . ."

D

She gave a sigh, and Paul was now harassed as well; though still, perhaps, rather stumbling after her fantasy. At the next moment, however, he had stumbled in the true sense. For she had cut sharply, and again unexpectedly, across his bows. For an instant, indeed, he had nearly clutched at her arm. But not quite. They were both saying they were sorry.

"My fault," added Paul.

"No, mine. But this is it."

"You mean——?"

But she had already opened the door, and there could be no doubt. The Avocado Club—called into being by the strange laws of this land—had once, clearly, been a stable, and perhaps a garage after that. Unlike the Junior Corinthian, it had, virtually, only one room; longish, low, and with discreet orange lighting. But there was a lobby first, and though there was no porter in the Corinthian sense, there was a tired-looking, furtive, civil, semi-servile, yet patently untrustworthy character, in a blue serge suit, who produced a book, to which a pencil was attached.

"Good-evening, miss," he said. And after a slight pause, and apparent assessment of the visitor's own clothes: "Good-evening, sir." And then: "Here, miss," with a short, black finger-nail on the page.

Miss Brown scribbled. She turned her head.

"It's Paul, isn't it?" she said.

"Yes," said Paul, with some queer prickles. There was a very bright light just here. He didn't waste it. He was studying her. And again there was a strange relief. For perhaps, after all, she wasn't *quite* as beautiful as he had imagined. And though this was hard on her, and though he was a cad, and though she had probably been on her feet all day—well, if it eased the strain, there could be no harm in that.

Or was he mistaken? There was still her aura, and her voice, and——

"Take your hat-an'-coat, sir?"

"Oh. Thanks."

Swift disrobing. There was no visible accommodation for either garment. But he was rid of them. And following again.

"Here we are, then," she said.

He saw the low, longish room. Its sultry illumination. A bar, with a barman. Stools. Chairs, tables, and a banquette. And was conscious of a very lush, yielding carpet. Nor was he so ignorant of civic life in his own times that he had never been in such an apartment before. But he hadn't been here. Nor anywhere with Miss Brown. That made it different, so that he was keyed up and alert.

There were some members, or presumably they were members, of both sexes at the bar. They looked round. And a man said: "Hullo, Bee!"

Paul stiffened. He couldn't help it. "Hullo, Eddie!" she said. But that was all. She was his again. "Let's sit here."

"Oh. Thanks."

She had pointed to the far end of the banquette. But of course he must wait until she was seated herself.

And she was still standing.

"Well, what would you like?" she asked.

Entirely wrong. But it would be rude if he said "Nothing."

So he said: "Oh, anything." And then thought that perhaps this, too, was rude. Or at least annoying, when people said it to him. He made a hasty amendment, though with a slight trace of doubt. "Er—gin-and-lime?" Well, it should be comparatively cheap. Or so he hoped.

"Double?" said the girl.

"Oh, no. No. No, no. No, thanks. Not for me."

Pure humanity, of course. But had it sounded as if he was afraid of it? As if he always got tight if he had more?

She looked at him for a moment. But she didn't argue. She just smiled. She looked away. And of *course* he had been mistaken in the little lobby; though he still felt that other relief. He *liked* her, that was to say; but he was no longer mad, as he must have been. There you were, then. This was pleasant. That was all.

"Oh, Jerry!"

"Yes, miss?"

"Could I have two gins, with lime, please? Singles."

"Very good, miss."

"Let's sit down." This was, of course, to Paul; and they both sat. "Oh, it's lovely," she said, "to relax." She closed her eyes for a moment. The guest noted her eyelashes. Was she going to sleep? No. She had opened them again. "Do you like this place?" she asked.

"Oh yes. Awfully. It seems very—very . . ."

Lack of thought, or of concentration, was the trouble, of course. But she wasn't balked by the gap.

"Well, it's *useful*," she said. "I have lunch here, sometimes—when I'm feeling flush, I mean. And then there's this." Which was vague, but not wholly obscure. "And I don't pay any subscription, you see."

"Oh?"

"Well, none of us do. They don't expect it. They give us cards. Oh, thanks, Jerry." For the barman had just put down two glasses. Paul's hand shot towards his pocket, and he jerked it back. Yet she hadn't paid, either? Free drinks, too? No, of course not. She was being polite; that was all. If she paid, this might suggest—and though in fact it was the case—that her guest wouldn't have any more.

But he didn't *like* that idea of free admission, somehow. He didn't know why; and he was the last person to *want* her to waste money—("When I'm feeling flush." It was almost tragic. Did she get enough to eat?)—but at the same time——

"Well?"

"Oh, I beg your pardon."

She was holding her own glass poised. She was waiting. He snatched at its mate. Time-honoured convention, here and in a million places where the Race dulled or sharpened its wits, demanded that their eyes should meet. That there should be a pause before they sipped. And perhaps that there should be some spoken sentiment, too.

"Well," said Paul. "Good luck and all that."

"Good luck."

"And to George as well."

She rippled. He had been inspired. George was a link between old friends. This might not be intimacy, but he knew that he had advanced.

"Poor George," she was saying. "He *does* have a time. He looked so *pathetic* last night."

"In three years," said Paul, "if there isn't a war, that's to say—well, I'm down for a Porchester Leveret."

"I say, you're not! What a thrill! And at present?"

"Well, I walk."

"What a shame! Well, you must come out—when he's cured—if you dare."

"By Jove!"

"No, I mean it. We'll go for a drive. Only it would have to be a Sunday. Would you be away?"

"No, rather not. Never go away."

"Nor do I." Another link. "Well, hardly ever." But it still held. "Or, I say, do you like music? Or not?"

"Well, yes," said Paul; though rather gruffly, so as to indicate his essential vigour.

Her little glass, which she had only tasted, was back on the little table. She clapped her hands.

"Then I'll tell you what."

"Eh?"

"If it's a filthy day—and now I come to think of it, it's almost bound to be till after Easter—we might drive to a concert instead."

"By Jove! That'd be grand. Or—or I could get some tickets——"

"Wait a moment."

"What's the matter?"

"You mustn't pay," said Bianca Brown. "Well, I mean, if you do, I must pay you back."

"But who's running the transport?"

"No. Please. I—I'm awfully obstinate about that. You've *got* to understand. I'm *not* just a person who takes things. It's a sort of *rule*. We must pay for ourselves, don't you see? Besides, I *like* using the car."

She looked pink; unless this was an effect of the orange lighting again. Paul felt dashed, even though he could approve in pure theory. He had lost ground. He said: "Oh." And then, with a certain resemblance to his cousin Rodney last night, he pulled out his cigarette-case, and thumbed it open. Civilised Man's almost inevitable reaction when dashed. Yes, but where were his manners? The action changed to an offer.

"Won't you have one?"

"I don't smoke, thank you." Blast! He'd known this, for eight days. He had lost still more ground. He shut the case. "But you *do* understand?"

"Yes, of course."

"You're not angry?"

"Good heavens, no. I think it's splendid. I—I quite understand." But was the whole thing right off? And then, abruptly, so that he surprised even himself: "Why 'George'?"

"Oh." But she took the point. "Well, you see, it was Daddy's little car."

"You mean—" rather delicate, this, so that he lowered his voice—"it—it's called after him?"

"No, of course not!" She was smiling. "But *he* called it that."

"Oh, I see."

A father who had written poetry, and called his car "George"? Should I have liked him? But what's *that* got to do with it? I'm rather glad, though (for he had been resisting this trifling criticism for some time; well, it *was* a bit whimsical, you know), that it wasn't her own idea. For piety was, of course, admirable. And quite a different thing. He tossed off his drink with one gulp.

"I suppose——"

But no one would know what Paul Sunderland supposed. A stoutish, jovial, well-shaven, middle-aged man, in a rather tight double-breasted jacket, had approached and was bending over the little table. He also looked as though it were some months since he had last been in bed. He had crimped hair, too. Yet, of course, Paul must rise.

"No, no, sir." The crimped chap checked this movement at once. "Mustn't interrupt. Well, how are you, my dear? Full of beans, eh?"

It was clear that these questions were being put to Miss Brown. But they weren't answered; or not quite on the beam.

"Hullo," she said. "This is Mr. Sunderland. Mr. Sunderland— Captain Dalrymple."

"How d'you do, sir. Pleased to meet you." An extended hand that caught Paul's; and crushed it—apparently against one or more rings—and instantly dropped it again. "Well, dear?" The poached eyes, also heavily ringed, had turned away. " 'Ve you got everything you want?"

"Yes, thank you."

"Right. Fine. Well, come in again soon."

A nod for Paul—with a queer if perhaps amiable suggestion that they were both steeped in vice—and the Captain withdrew.

"He runs it," said the girl.

"Oh, I see," said Paul, again. He would have liked to ask, in a way, if all her friends were like this, and if it was their custom to call her "my dear." But of course he couldn't. And there was no need.

"He's rather awful," she said.

Paul was enchanted.

"But he can't help his hair."

"No, of course not." He wasn't only enchanted, but broad-minded as well.

"And there *are* some fairly awful people about."

"Yes, rather!" How true. And this was intimacy again. Or more like it. Though it was ghastly that she knew. He felt protective; and worried. His mind shot back to the unknown Michael Willoughby. He drew in a breath. Yet it was perhaps as well that she spoke first.

"Oh, and *I'm* awful!" she gasped. "I said we'd got everything— and you've nothing to drink! You'll have another? Jerry!"

"No, look here—honestly——"

"Oh, nonsense!" She suddenly drained her own glass to the dregs. "Then *I* will."

"Well, look here—what you said just now—I mean, I know I'm not a member. But you must—you *must* have it on me."

Had he gone too far? It seemed not. She dimpled and smiled.

"All right, then. I mean, thank you." Companions. Aha! "Only if you pay——"

"That's all right." Paul was pretty quick, too. "Here!" He yanked a note from the note-case without even removing it from his pocket. "There you are. Now we're quits. Here he is."

"Same again, then?"

"Yes, thanks."

The barman had heard; and took the note. Something to be said, after all, for her scruples and rules. It had made them conspirators. He was so pleased that when the barman came back, and—having apparently taken, as they say, for both rounds— planked some silver on the little table, Paul pushed half-a-crown at him, which he at once absorbed.

"Well, good luck."

"Good luck."

And they were off again, so cosily and comfortably—though the room was filling up—in their corner at the end of the banquette.

They prattled. They chatted. They revealed this and that. And learnt this and that, of course, too. Not much, in Paul's case, about the life of a model; for though intensely curious, he was bashful as well. Or he didn't wish it to be supposed, by an innocent girl, that he could even picture her changing her clothes.

So he kept off that, though he was quite amusing about Spilsby— if, of course, with one stark reservation—and about his work, in a depreciatory way. In turn, he acquired some knowledge of the nature of her own quarters. How she was really in the old nurseries and the servants' bedrooms. How there was a separate entrance—

for the division had been made shortly before the war—up an iron, outside stair at the side. How one could see the river, if one stuck one's head out of the window.

Of the dullness of the tenants—though at least they were quiet—who had the lower half of the house. Of the cost of repairs now, and taxes, and rates. And from all this, or amongst it, to a grievance again. To Dorothea—Paul even learnt that her husband was called Hopgrove—who had so basely walked out ("And I don't *want* anyone else") to take vows and go right off to Hampstead.

"Not," said Miss Brown, generously, "that I think *no one* should get married. But we were all settled. And he *was* rather a snake."

"Who? Hopgrove?" asked Paul, as this last point came up. "Do you mean—well, that it's not a success?"

"Oh no. He adores her. And she worships him, too. But he did come there rather pretending that he was only interested in her pictures. He took *me* in, completely, or— Well, I suppose I couldn't have stopped it. But it was a bit unfair. Well, it wasn't quite playing the game. And now, of course——"

She broke off. There was another, younger, taller, thinner, and much healthier-looking gentleman standing over them. Sporting a well-known tie. And a little moustache.

"Brian!" (Paul shot up.) "Am I late? You've come here? Oh—this-is-Mr-Sunderland; and Mr. Cairns."

"How do you do," said Paul. It was all over, then; but it had been jolly nice.

"How-oo," said Mr. Cairns, who seemed a shade short of consonants. "Yes," he said—but they must be inserted, for they are essential in print. "Waited a bit. Said to myself 'Well, it's worth lookin' there.' Came round. Crashed in. And if you want anything to eat, Bee—before this picture, I mean—well . . ."

Clear enough, even without consonants. But where was the pang? This was odd. Paul didn't exactly feel drawn towards Mr. Cairns, though he appeared clean, neat, and well-bred; but it didn't occur to him that he wasn't well within his rights. A date was a date. Nothing was more exasperating, in these days of queues, shortages, and other difficulties, than to start an evening in a rush. An old friend, he assumed. And it was the era of liberty; except, of course, in any relationship with the State.

"I'll go," he said. But there was no hint that he was crushed. "It's been awfully kind of you," he said, "but—well, if you're going to the pictures, I know what that's like." He squeezed round the table. "Great fun," he observed. "Er . . ."

But that was all. There was nothing else. Of course he didn't shake hands. He just smiled pleasantly at his hostess. A shade more guardedly at her squire. She said: "Oh. Well. Then if it's *really* all right . . ."

"But of course!"

He buttoned his jacket. He nodded. He went. The congestion in the room caused some delay in his progress. But he kept on. He was in the lobby. The blue-serge man seemed to remember him; produced his coat and hat from some cache or recess; and was naturally remembered in turn.

"Thank you, sir. Good-night, sir."

"Good-night," said Paul.

The man opened the door, and he passed into the cold air. It was revivifying. But that wasn't all; and though he must still decide where to feed. The point was, don't you see, as he stepped briskly over the cobbles; the point was, and he said it aloud: "I'm cured!"

10

MORE relief, then. Undoubted relief at this stage, as he continued to stride (for he had reached a decision, as it seemed, after all) towards a rather superior pub. Or towards the superior part of a multiform pub, where food was served among ash-trays and palms.

No, it wasn't that he was ungrateful (thought Paul, as he strode). He wasn't even disappointed. He was just calm.

She was extremely pretty. He must admit that. Quite a treat for the eye. He liked her—that was the word—quite a lot. She was intelligent. And friendly. A jolly nice girl. He couldn't pick on a fault if he tried.

Nice manners. Nice clothes; not that he could possibly have described them. Quite a charmer, if one might say so, in fact. But whereas, about an hour ago, he had been palpitating in the most preposterous manner and had been full of the most fantastic ideas, now, thank the lord—and her, too, in a way—he was perfectly normal once more. There you were, then. It was all over; as he had said; but he didn't mind. Possibly—and why not?—they would meet again, sooner or later. If it came to that—and though that fellow had put a stop to any more definite arrangement—it was almost an understood thing.

But he wasn't *worrying*. It was true that she was still here, in a sense; that her voice and face were remarkably distinct. But if he were infatuated, this would be painful. And it wasn't, you see. It was just pleasant. That was all. Nothing more.

For, again, if he were in love—("Pooh!" said Paul, as he neared the pub)—he would have been jealous of that chap with the moustache. But was he? Not the least. Or only to the extent that he had checked the remains of a vague plan. If, for instance, he had been run over—and chaps were, after all—then he, Paul, might have accompanied the girl to their real place of assignation. And, in the absence of Moustache, might have entertained her instead.

But that was only an idle fancy. He wasn't the least racked. On the contrary, he was happy. And free. He could even hope, and he did, that they had chosen a good film. He could even hope, though perhaps with less emphasis here, that Moustache wouldn't just shove her on a bus.

Yet these thoughts, though still calm, hardly proved that he had forgotten her. And indeed he hadn't, as he mused over his meal. She was a little fainter now, which was rather vexing in a way; but there was still plenty to recall and to digest.

Her home-life, such as it was. Rather sad, in a sense. Though she hadn't complained—except, of course, of the perfidy of Mrs. Hopgrove—and a lot of girls were, of course, much worse off.

Her shop-life. Still a mystery. Her club-life? A slight doubt. He had gathered from that appalling-looking manager or proprietor, or whatever he was—and from her, as well—that she didn't go there very often. And he approved. It was no place for a girl on her own. Yet on the other hand her friend Brian had looked for her there; had "crashed in," to use his phrase, so that *he* wasn't a member; and had therefore, obviously, been her guest there before.

How often? No, wait a second. Something else on his mind. *Why* did that bloated night-hawk—whose original name couldn't, surely, have been Dalrymple, though it was quite conceivable that he was a captain; *why* did he grant complimentary admission to the employees in a dressmaker's shop?

Not just from good nature; even if (which, again, seemed not unlikely) he called the whole lot "my dear." No, no; much too hard-boiled for that. But were they bait? Were they houris? Did he count on their bringing men? And on these men, once they were there . . .

"Um," said Paul.

His fork paused, half-way to his mouth. On the verge, and the very honourable verge, of at least dissociating Miss Brown from any part—unless, of course, it were completely innocent—in such a scheme, and of again telling himself that he was a cad, a memory of the very moderate amount of drink that they had consumed clashed with the memory that it was he himself who had, in fact, paid.

A mistake, of course. A most natural oversight. If it had cost him twelve bob, that was all. A mere fraction, in other words, of what he had been preparing to spend. And might have, but for Moustache—dash his buttons!

Yet there was confusion in his soul. It wasn't the money that mattered. He was a man, and it was his *business* to pay. But when she had looked at him—his hand sank, as he again saw the look—and explained that she *always* stood her own share, was this wool over his eyes or—or what?

No, of *course* she had meant it. He *knew* she was straight. It was as true as—(I say, by Jove, how *am* I to find out who he was?)—that her father wrote poems. Only a swine would sit here and give a *thought* to the twelve bob. That was nothing. He had dismissed it for good.

But—this was the jar—if Moustache were paying for her dinner and the cinema tonight, and it now seemed palpable that this was just what he was doing, then, since she was truthful, he must be more than a mere friend. He had gained a position that *allowed* him to pay.

And his haste. His impatience. Why couldn't he wait where he was? Too plain. Altogether too plain.

"I don't *like* it," Paul growled; so that again a waiter looked disturbed, though in fact it was a pretty poor *plat du jour*. But this was all that he said, as he again relapsed into thought. As he finished eating, and walked back to his flat.

Yet presently, as he sat there, in these somewhat tasteless if familiar surroundings, he said "Nonsense"; and the load lifted again. For still—well, what the heck did it matter, anyway?—she was a jolly nice girl. In other circumstances, if he had met her sooner, who could tell what might have occurred? But he hadn't, and was still sensible of relief. He was glad, in short, that he had found out. Or he believed he was glad. For he had certainly given himself rather a tough, if also blithering, week.

As for the car-drive, or the concert, he had written them off. Though if she remembered—but of course she wouldn't—all right.

He felt infinitely better. There could be no doubt that he was cured. All those thoughts were merely the end of a false alarm. In love? Rot. Absurd! He was going to bed. He did. And slept soundly, for nine hours or so, until Spilsby clattered in with his early tea.

Yet during the night, or so it would appear, his Subconscious—which at times was a little indistinguishable from his *alter ego*, or Paul Secundus—must have been at work; for he suddenly set down his cup.

Not because it was chipped, for this was a matter of course. Not because it was tepid, with some tea-leaves floating on top; for this too, might be described as routine.

He had seen a face, though. He had heard a voice. He was slipping again. And however slowly or reluctantly, or against reason and sense, it is not improbable that he would continue to slip.

II

BUT no more action. No plan. No sign to the outer world. No one remarked, nor was it true, that he looked green. He ate. He moved around. He worked. He retired to rest. And three nights later—this brings us to February 25th—he actually and even dined out.

Once, in the dear (though also cheap) dead days beyond recall, any bachelor, in such a flat, would have had a whole mantelshelf of cards. Only rarely would he have spent an evening at home. Or if not cards, then little entries in an engagement-book; the result of meetings and telephone calls.

But though there was a telephone in his sitting-room, the dead days were gone. No regular programme now of little dances and theatre-parties, working up, later on, to huge dances and nightly revels. For Society, as it was once known, had almost ceased to exist. It had taken the knock. It was broke. It was rationed and taxed. Parts of it were in big houses, that couldn't be sold, yet had no staff. Parts were in other flats, where it mattered less that there was no staff, but which only just held the tenants themselves.

Parts, again, which had once luxuriated at a couple of addresses, were in the country now all the year round. No doubt they were still alive, or up to a point. But if they gave dinners—and they didn't often, for they, too, were short-staffed—they could hardly send up to London for guests.

It wasn't true that there was no gaiety in this new, classless world. Where there is youth, it will always be gay. But cards on mantelshelves, save for weddings, or an affair like the Parkinsons', had as good as ceased in a young bachelor's life. People were tired. Or frustrated. Or broke, as was said. They crept into their own warrens, or vast, shrouded mansions, and remained there, whether it was the Season or not.

Down in the basement, or, if they were flat-dwellers now, buried deep in some repository, were most of the plates, dishes, glass, and silver with which they had once served their feasts. But if there was no food and, roughly speaking, no heat in a big dining-room— or, again, if they were flat-dwellers, perhaps no dining-room at all; no cook; no smart clothes; if the custom had died out . . .

Complete it for yourself. It is an exaggeration, of course. Or at least far from a view of the whole scene. For not only were the young still contriving, if but seldom at their own expense, to go out, eat, drink, laugh, dance, and be recklessly merry; not only were a number of the most extraordinary characters going around simply bulging with cash; but although it is still true that Paul rarely dined out—in the old meaning of the expression—it must yet be remembered that he belonged to a clan.

That the clan was loyal. Not yet broke; or not broke to the wide. So that he wasn't surprised, though quite pleased, when, after a gap of some months, his cousin Rhoda—all right, then; her voice, if you insist—came through on his professional line.

"Yes?" said Miss Thriplow, who was taking notes at this point. Then she explained. "Mrs. Medway," she said.

"Oh—thanks. Right you are. No, don't go." He took over. "Hullo, Rhoda," he said. "Can I help?"

It was in his mind that, with old Charles still away, she was in quest of advice. He was even flattered, though it might well be that he was the last resort, at being consulted like this.

"Paul? You sound just like O."

"Like what? I——"

"O. Operator. That's just what they say."

"Oh!" said Paul. "Yes, I see. Still, I meant it, you know. Not that *they* don't. But——"

"Quite. Never mind. But I'm not in trouble——"

"Oh, good!"

"In fact," said his cousin Rhoda, "if you'd stop talking so much, I was going to ask you to dinner tonight."

"Oh," said Paul, yet again. "Is it a party, d'you mean?"

"No, dear. Don't be frightened. You won't have to wash. I just thought it was about time. That was all."

Had he been uncouth? There was a slight pause.

"Or are you busy?" she asked.

"No, no. No. Oh, dear, no. Of course not. Good lord, no."

"You're hurting my ear," said his cousin Rhoda. "Still, I gather you're free?"

"Yes, rather!"

"About eight, then?"

"I say, thanks awfully."

"You sound very jumpy," said his cousin Rhoda. "Is the firm going smash?"

"No. No, no. Oh, no. Not the least."

"Well, that's something," said Rhoda. "But perhaps you'd better get on. And don't change, Paul. Just come round. That'll be nice."

She hung up. So did Paul. And though all vestiges of that childish yet once romantic passion had long, long disappeared, he, too, took the view that it would be nice. For he was attached to his cousin Rhoda, though she had passed forty and had put on weight. He was always glad when these evenings cropped up. It even occurred to him—yet he had tried this, and had invariably failed—that he ought to return some of the hospitality that he had enjoyed.

But she behaved like an aunt, though she wasn't, of course. She said: "No, Paul. Don't be absurd. You come here." And if this always happened—well, it made one lay off. It was like *asking* to be asked there again. The debt, in fact, was a debt that could never be repaid. Not, as he knew, that she saw it like that.

Rhoda, he thought. Well, I *was* a bit young. Though I still think it shows I had taste. Lucky old Charles. And Mark. One of the best. I wonder . . .

Miss Thriplow tapped her teeth with her pencil. Mists dissolved.

"Oh, I'm sorry." He was right on the spot. "If you could just read that last sentence back?"

So Miss Thriplow obliged; and went on obliging, either here or along the passage, until another day's work reached its end. The customary desk-clearing. The descent to the hall. And a word, for he was in the mood—even if there was generally a word—with the grizzled, close-cropped commissionaire.

"Good-night, Banglewick. A bit milder, I think."

"Yessir. Might rain, though, I'd say."

A clear cue for the little garden. But they had had that last night. If not, indeed, every night all this week. Time for a change, then.

"How's your son?"

"Perce, sir? Well, all right. 'E's a good lad, 'e is. Works 'ard. I'll say that for the boy."

Paul laughed.

"And a lot more, if I gave you the chance. Eh, Banglewick? Right. Well, good-night."

The salute. The swing-door. And he was out in the narrow street. Just for an instant he was aware that his little joke hadn't clicked. But it cannot be said that this troubled him very much. Any pleasantry with old Banglewick was apt to be hit-or-miss; and parental pride, though a legitimate topic in a way . . . Well, forget it. He forgot it. Queued and struggled into a bus. And filled in time at the Junior Corinthian.

With evening papers. With tobacco. With old and new thoughts. With some dialogue, for tonight he wasn't opposed to the human race, as it dropped in and took its own part. And finally, of course—though his cousin Rhoda had said not—with a scrupulous wash and brush-up.

Time? Just about right. No. The rain had begun. He was going to be late. He must snatch that cab. He was early. He arrived, in point of fact, at the large block of flats, with nearly ten minutes in hand. He gazed up at it. He was again affronted that this fine and once symmetrical square should have suffered an intrusion like that. That its sky-line was marred. That its railings—though this was really quite another thing—should have been removed, and then replaced with a wire fence.

Civilisation, thought Paul, with a touch of distaste. And Progress. But he had no blame for the Medways. On the contrary, as he also knew, they had shown both foresight and courage—in coming here when it was still easy, and they could sell their old house, and in sticking it out through the whole of the war.

Or "Um," to sum up, as he ducked his head, though this was quite unnecessary, owing to the comparatively low height of the ground floor. And of the other floors, too, for there were eight in this block, and all seemed crushed by the weight of the roof. Yet he was amused by the lift, which slid back its own doors. And having passed along a corridor, with some resemblance to a salt-mine, he rang a bell—though in fact it buzzed—and was let in.

By old Mary, whom he knew—what a link with the past!—Mark's ex-nurse, but still here on the strength. Whether she *did* anything, in fact, except occasionally answer the door, he rather doubted. But she was a friend. And he smiled.

"Hullo, Mary!" For she had dropped "Nannie" a long time ago. "I say, I'm a bit early, I'm afraid."

"That's all right, Mr. Paul. Just go in. That's all right."

"Oh—thanks."

He folded his own coat, and dealt with his own hat, and then—as she had vanished—went through into the big room. The low room, too; and all the lower for having been planned as two rooms. But it was warm. And well-furnished. And about as home-like as it could be, considering its proportions, and the stern resistance, even under a thick carpet, of its concrete floor. Nicely lit. Not too bright. And there were pictures. And even books. He didn't mind being left here alone.

He did some prowling. He heard the latch. He turned round; and saw Mark. He thought again how much he liked him; and how particularly estimable it was, since he was five years younger, never to behave as if he, Paul, were an old man.

"Hullo," said the junior cousin, or first cousin once removed. "Are you coming? Or going? Or what?"

"Coming," said Paul. "I'm going to feed here."

"Oh, fine!" Mark lit up, though he looked tired. "Well, in that case—only just got away from my own little treadmill—I think, if you don't mind, I'll clean up." He went out. He returned. "Oh, I say, did Ma tell you if it was up here or downstairs?"

"No," said Paul. "I mean, she didn't."

"Well, who let you in?"

"Mary."

"What was she wearing?"

"Haven't the faintest idea."

"Well, had she got a hat on?"

"No, of course not!"

"There's no 'of course' about it," said Mark, with a grin; and even Paul, unimpressionable as he conceived himself, must admit that he was exceptionally good-looking. "Haven't you heard? She's become a film-fan—just a bit late in life. If she has the hat on, it means she's off there, and we eat down below. But if she hasn't, then she pretends to wash up."

"Pretends?"

"Yes, that's all. There's a crone who comes in. She stands and watches her. But she wouldn't miss her. They're both mad about the Pools."

Interesting. Not only that the wife of the Chairman of a huge business should subsist on crones, or perhaps only one crone. Not only, for she was in fact far from weak-minded, that she should be so weak with old Mary. Not only that old Mary should blossom, in late autumn, as it were, into a film-fan and football-enthusiast. But that Mark should have such a nice turn of banter.

"Oh," said Paul. He was also reflecting how Mark had grown up under Conscription; and had been conscribed, though the fighting was over by then; and had worked nearly a couple of hours longer than himself today. So that it was rather absurd that he was still only twenty-one.

"So that's that," said Mark, as he turned to dash out. But then he slithered, and stopped. "Hullo, Ma!" he remarked. There was the sound of a kiss—why on earth should it make the guest feel middle-aged?—and his place was taken, as he again shot off, by Mrs. Medway.

No kiss for Paul. Well, naturally not. But a friendly and welcoming smile.

"Ah! There you are. I'm so glad you could come. Something's happened to Time, you know—it just *races*—" but she still tossed back her hair in the old way—"or I'd have rung up *much* sooner. You'll have a drink?"

"Oh, thanks awfully. Can I—ah——"

"Yes, please. Whatever you're having. It's all there—at least, I think it is; yes, that's right—on the table."

"And Charles?" asked Paul, as he prepared to dispense.

"Oh! He rang *me* up——"

"I say, good heavens!"

"Yes—from Sydney."

"I say, good lord!"

"Yes, that's just how I felt. Like a cook getting a telegram. I thought something *frightful* must have happened. I couldn't *think* what to say. Nor could Charles, if it comes to that. I mean, it was thrilling. And terribly sweet of him. But—" Paul heard a slight sigh—"I suppose the truth is, I'm getting old-fashioned."

"Oh, nonsense."

"Well, I am. I'll be forty-two in June."

"I know," said Paul. "But——"

She was laughing.

"Ten for tact," she said. "Though of course you knew. Oh— thank you." For he was back with the glasses. Again there was the conventional pause, as their eyes met. And a pang, though quite a mild one, for Paul.

But she didn't say "Good luck." She said: "Here we go." And then: "Though, as a matter of fact, I *am* a cook."

"Oh, I say! Do you mean——"

"Well, I hate it downstairs. And I'm not an old-fashioned cook. I went to Fortnum's, if you want the truth. And I've opened some tins—Charles would be *horrified*—but— Yes? What were you going to say?"

"Nothing special. Well—only that it's a queer sort of world."

"Paul! Are *you* getting old-fashioned?"

It was his own turn to laugh. And he did. Though perhaps she was right. Or though perhaps—he was suddenly and surprisingly convinced of this—he had been drifting, for months or years, into a rut. He looked thoughtful, in fact.

"And what do you make of Mark?"

"Oh." He looked guilty, for he had been on the verge of this point. Or it was Mark who had somehow suggested the rut. "Why?" he asked. "Has he been ill?"

"Not the least," said his cousin Rhoda. "Though he works like a lunatic. But—" another sigh—"*I* don't know. Ought he to be here? I mean, I'd be miserable without him. He—he keeps me young. But he's old for his own age." Paul nodded, and sipped. "And *you* weren't at home after you grew up."

"No," said Paul. "Well, that's true." It was also true that he had no home, and that at Mark's age he had been abroad with the Armed Forces. His cousin seemed to recall this.

"Oh, Paul!" Her glass slopped. "But there you are. I—I'm so *abominably* selfish."

Ridiculous. She was maternal; and he admired her for that. She was also Rhoda, his first love, at whose wedding he had felt sick. But before he could say "Oh, nonsense" again, here came Mark. So he said nothing at all.

Yet no one could allege that his cousin Rhoda was selfish during the rest of that typical evening. The meal was a banquet, and by no means all cold. She skipped about—nothing could stop her, though the others skipped, too—on a series of trips to the kitchen. Or she presided, but as a listener or a questioner most of the time; so that the guest—though rather ashamed to be talking so much—purged a good deal of stuff from his soul.

Light stuff, for the greater part. But it helped. He was at ease. And then afterwards—and considering that she was really musical, this was patient indeed—she sat, and sewed, while Paul and Mark played duets.

On the piano. As they often did. And they played like blazes that night, from some volumes that had come down from the past. Breitkopf and Härtel. The Classics; with some loose pages. Paul took the bass and, in virtue of seniority, the pedals as well. Mark, who was considerably less out of practice—for there was no piano at the service-flat—took the treble, but did his best to set the time.

Both performers occasionally sang as they played, to keep things going, for there were no words on the score. Both performers, again, though Paul was the worse, tended to forget—but of course this is the devil of duets—that they were supposed to be reading two staves in the same clef. Yet they swayed, and they pounded, and laughed and talked, too. And though it was to be hoped, for the concrete of even luxury flats forms a very poor barrier to sound, that they weren't maddening the neighbours—or that the neighbours were out, or could hear nothing but their own wireless-sets—it was quite an impressive display.

"Darling," said Mrs. Medway, as they stopped abruptly—for a page had just fallen on to the floor, "wasn't that last bit rather particularly frightful?"

"Only," said Mark, as he grovelled and came up, "because we didn't happen to be playing in the same key. Modern stuff, Ma. You ought to like it, you know."

"Good lord!" said Paul. "Were those sharps all the time? Well, come on. Let's have a shot at it again."

Fireworks, now. Even Mark couldn't control the *accelerando*. They reached the end neck-and-neck, with a few extra chords. Paul sat back. It had been fun. But they *had* made rather a row. And it was getting late; though he was still alluding to music as he rose.

"Good old Cranky," he said, as he recalled the origins of his own instruction in the art. "I'd never have gone on with it—though perhaps" (this was for Rhoda) "you're sorry I did—if she hadn't started me off when I was about six. Jolly clever, I must say, at sort of driving things in. Oh, that reminds me. I saw her the other day."

"Did you?" said his cousin Rhoda. Mark was watching him, too.

"Yes. She blew into the office. Or, rather, Prim blew into the office—with Cranky in tow. They—" For some quick, sudden, and inexplicable reason, he decided that he wouldn't allude to what they had done just beforehand. Not that it was a secret, or he wouldn't have known it. Yet it might be sneaking, in a way. Why? He had no idea. Or no time to work it out. "They'd been shopping," he finished off, with hardly a pause. "And I must say—" for it was true, and there could be no harm in this—"Prim's getting astonishingly pretty."

No one answered. Perhaps the adverb wasn't quite the right choice.

"Well, I mean, when I say 'astonishingly,' I'm not suggesting she was ever hideous. But she's come on, you know. I suppose—well, is she at all like Aunt Nita? I can hardly r'member her, to tell the truth. She buzzed off when I was only about— Well, not in *character*, I mean, but . . ."

He was becoming confused. The only divorce in the whole clan, though no secret, either, was still perhaps better left in its grave.

"How *is* H.B.?" asked Rhoda, breaking the silence. "One never sees *anyone* now."

"Oh, fine." This was all right. "Just as thin. Just as sharp. Just as——"

"Have a drink," said Mark.

"No, I won't—really, thanks. I must go. Though——"

"She was very beautiful," said Rhoda. "But too gay. And too young. It was no one's fault. Though I'm told she's got fat."

Paul's face gave him away.

"Yes, I know," said his cousin Rhoda, with a nice, lazy laugh. "So have I. But Charles likes it. So there!"

"Oh, Ma—you're not fat!"

"Thank you, darling." She put out a hand, and her son held it. "Well, not really, perhaps." She stood up, and glanced momentarily at a mirror. "But a little matronly; wouldn't you say, Paul?"

"Are you fishing?"

"Of course!"

"Well, fish, then," he said. "I— Oh, dash it, Rhoda——"

"I know. You're twenty-five. And I'm forty-two."

"Twenty-six, as a matter of fact."

"Good heavens, you've had a birthday! And I was looking the other way. Mark—give me that book. Just behind you, my pet. There, Paul! A bee-ootiful love-story. It'll make you cry. I simply howled. But there's a happy ending. So take it. It's yours."

"To—to keep, do you mean?"

"It's a *present*, you idiot. A birthday present. Didn't you hear me? Say 'Thank you'."

"Well—" but he was really touched—"that's *terribly* kind. And so was the food. And——"

"And I *adored* hearing you play."

"Oh, Rhoda!"

But they were cousins, and friends, and it was all right. They both laughed. "But I must beat it," said Paul. "It's getting late. And if it's raining——"

Mark jerked at a curtain.

"It's stopped," he announced. "Do you want a taxi? Not that it'll come, if I ring up. And the porter's no use. But—all right, Ma, shan't be long—I'll step out with you, for a little breather, I think. I mean, if we both shout at the same time. Or if we stand in the road. Well, they hardly ever run over two chaps at once."

More thanks; and a farewell. They descended in the amusing lift And, as Mark observed—"Only six hundred a year for this joint, now they've raised it," he threw in—there wasn't a porter in view. But it was a pleasant enough night, with a moon in the ragged sky, as they strode together towards the main road.

"I might even get a bus," said Paul, suddenly.

"Why not?"

A further waft of family affection arose.

"Look here—why don't you come and have lunch with me one day? After all, we're both there. I think you ought to."

"In the City?" said Mark. "That's not lunching. It's fighting. I don't suppose we'd even hear each other speak."

True again. And no offence. Not from Mark; with that look.

Of understanding, and an acceptance of facts. He's a marvel, thought Paul. H.B. was quite right; it's a shame that he isn't with us. But I must fix something else. After all, I mean to say—

He saw a bus, approaching a request-stop. It slowed. He shot off.

"Good-night!" he yelled back. "See you soon—somehow or other!"

He dodged a van, but missed any reply. Furthermore, as it turned out, he needn't have run; for the bus, as they so often do, when one runs like this, remained shuddering and at a standstill, while the conductor had a little chat with the driver.

Then he returned, and it set off. Paul glanced through the window. He saw his cousin Mark, not where he had left him or even walking away, but in an illuminated telephone-box. Just a glimpse. Then he was eclipsed, as the bus gathered speed. Rather odd? Well, perhaps he'd thought of something, and had acted at once. He probably would. It would be just like him, of course.

12

HE was still thinking himself—not of Mark now, but, more critically, of his own character—as he disembarked; again walked a short distance; was borne aloft in a more primitive lift that he had long since ceased to find amusing; dipped for his key-ring; and unlocked his front door.

He snapped on the light in the tiny and, as nearly always, rather stuffy antechamber. Got one arm out of his overcoat. And saw some letters on the floor.

This was unusual. Not that Spilsby, or Mrs. Bangham, who flapped dusters and made beds, should have stepped over them sooner than pick them up. But in these days, though the State was now making more profit than ever, it was rare for there to be more than one effective delivery. Then, however, he remembered that this morning he had received nothing. In other words, the first post must have been a bit late. That was the answer. He stooped, and stood up.

A bill. A receipt. The monthly sheet of his pass-book. A long envelope, but with a penny stamp and a triangular postmark, so that he didn't open it, either. He tossed them aside. And—hullo. Who was this?

Small, squarish, white envelope. Illegible postmark. Unknown handwriting, though correct name and address. Even Paul, at twenty-six, must first ponder and turn it over. There was something inside, too—or rather more, as he could now feel, than a mere letter. He suspected an appeal; the extra thickness would be some dashed advertisement—bazaar or something—from a complete stranger. He prepared to resist it. But he tore the flap all the same.

A buff book of stamps fell out into his hand. But there was a letter, too; on blue paper, this time. It began *"Dear Paul."* But he was still puzzled. He looked at the end. He gave a violent start. *"Yours ever, Bianca Brown."*

He moved closer under the light; frowning slightly, as if he were being watched. He wasn't the least startled, as his grandfather might have been, by the familiarity of either expression. It would have been far more surprising, in these days, and after a couple of meetings, if she had employed anything else. It was the custom; and *"Yours ever"* meant nothing. But it was so unexpected—that was the shock—that she should have written to him at all. Why had she done it? Yes, why? Why on earth?

He re-focused, as he also saw the best way to find out. He read. Indeed, he read more than once.

"Dear Paul," she had written, on the blue piece of paper, to which she had added no more than the word *"Thursday." "Dear Paul, I don't know what you think of me——"*

At the first reading he broke off here. For that was just it. He was in precisely and exactly the same state. But then, since the phrase hardly altered this state, he took the rest of the page at a gulp.

—"you think of me, but it was rather a rush the other night and I've only just realised that I went off without paying my share. This isn't the least like me and I feel awfully upset. So here is 5s. which I think is just right. Do please forgive me.

> *Yours ever,*
> *Bianca Brown."*

Quite short, as will be observed. Quite clear. All to the point. Yet Paul read it six times without pause. And each time, so it seemed, it aroused further thoughts. And comments. And queries. And doubts.

Starting at the end, for example, or at the end of the main text, of *course* he forgave her. There was nothing to forgive. Working backwards, it was he himself who had been an absolute cur; first, to imagine that she could ever indulge in even chance or accidental bilking; and secondly to have been so weak, and ill-mannered as well, that . . .

A third point crashed in. Gin-and-lime, he had just recalled, cost two and threepence at his own club. This was ghastly. Any tipping was of *course* his affair. In other words, she had actually overpaid him.

He was appalled. But he hadn't finished. She had felt "awfully upset." He couldn't bear this; and it was all his own fault. Forgetting her principles, for the moment, he felt guilty and mean. He must post the stamps back at once. He must get it right out of her head that he was the kind of chap who took money from women.

Then, however, he remembered her principles. She had explained them, and whether he found them embarrassing or not, he mustn't argue, or browbeat her conscience. That would be tiresome. They must be accepted; and so must the stamps. But—at this stage he stopped frowning at last—of course they must be acknowledged as well.

It was what one did. It was what was done. One must *always* acknowledge payment. With one of the stamps, eh? No, no. Certainly not. The little book mustn't be mutilated. It was a gift, don't you see? He eyed it for a few seconds. And put it carefully away in his note-case.

But then—though that was settled—a doubt still remained. If he wrote, how on earth should he begin? Moustache had called her "Bee"—or was it "B"? Perhaps everyone called her that. If he didn't, it might look frigid. If he did, it might be cheek. But he must be quick. Since already—here, one is afraid, he blamed his cousin Rhoda (which was exceedingly ungrateful) rather than the Post Office—he had missed all collections today.

Or there was the telephone. That was it! He took a step, though still wearing his overcoat as if it were a kind of outsize dolman, towards the sitting-room. And stopped. He was too late, again. Well after eleven. She would be in bed. Or so he hoped. If he dragged her up— Yes, and what should he *say*?

It was terribly important. He could dodge the name-problem,

no doubt, if he sailed in swiftly, and said "You." But what *else* was he going to say? He began mumbling. He shook his head. He was silent; and stumped. For if he just thanked her and rung off, they would be back where they were. But if he went further—and if he didn't, this might well be the last chance . . .

He dropped the overcoat, though not the letter, and paced up and down. This business of "sharing," you know. He'd never met such a girl. He'd met graspers, and girls who just took what they got. But never, in all his experience—which for the purpose of this argument he may have magnified a good deal—had he struck a girl with *this* bee in her bonnet.

"Bee"? Oh, shut up. Don't be such an ass! This has got to be worked out. And tonight.

Um. . . .

He stopped pacing. And even attempting to work it out. The point was that he had never *met* such a girl.

Yet if he saw her—it never occurred to him that this, too, was a trifle odd—he was almost convinced that he would calm down again. It had happened last time—only three nights ago—and he could still remember how calm he had felt. He had felt quite calm at Rhoda's. Quite calm until now. But if she were going to start writing to him—("Cad!" said the inner voice, but he thrust it aside)—it was only sense to look after himself.

And essential, by Jove. For during the lull, as he was now aware, something else had, of course, happened, too. Neither her face nor her voice was so distinct in his mind. They had become blurred. Less objective. The mind had played tricks. It was an increasing effort to peer through the fog. Or it was as if they were on a film, and it was beginning to wear out. There must be a re-take—(Can't you see? So that I know where I am)—and there was only one way to do that.

Or was there? He brightened. For *this* was an idea. Friendship. Aha! Then he could be calm all the time. It involved seeing her, of course; but without all this strain. Besides, he *wanted* to see her. He must!

But the visionary terms that had just come to him, as he stooped again, picked up his overcoat, and hung it on a peg, should be just what a girl like that liked. He wouldn't pester, or plague. That was the last thing he wished. Within reason—tips, for instance, must remain his own job, not hers—she could certainly pay her own share. But he would know where he was. They could have fun when she was free. Or if she weren't—(Steady! There was sudden glimpse of Moustache, and even of the chap whom she had called Eddie, but he clenched his jaw)—then it would still be all right.

"Hullo, Bianca—or possibly Bee. Doing anything tomorrow night?"

"Well, I'm afraid I am."

"Never mind." Tra-la-la!

Or alternatively: "No, nothing."

"Right you are. Then let's meet."

It would be like that. And he would be content, and at peace.

"Phew!" said Paul, just as if he had solved what can never be solved. He re-read the letter. He began to undress. He would do something; and some time tomorrow, of course. But though it was a little annoying that he still hadn't quite got her face—or her voice, if it came to that—it was all fixed now. They were going to be friends.

On this occasion not only did he again sleep until Spilsby arrived, but—whether bewildered or merely worn out—even his Subconscious appeared to take a night off.

PART TWO

I

By the third week in March—yet let no one suppose that the narrator isn't still doing his utmost to get round to the fine morning in May—it may be said, and, indeed, is now going to be said, that Paul Sunderland had achieved much of his aim.

The first fence had proved curiously easy. Still untroubled by anything save a fixed if possibly fatuous determination, he had employed the telephone after lunch—for it was a Saturday by now—and Miss Brown had answered him, from her Flaxman number, at once.

He hadn't stammered. He had found no difficulty in sticking to "You." She had been quite as friendly as he had proposed that she should. "Oh!" she had said. "Paul!" But he had still remained calm. He had thanked her; though without explaining that the stamps had become an amulet, or even alluding (for this he hoped to put right later on) to the overpayment. She had just said: "Oh, well, I *had* to do that."

Then he had laughed, though not the least as if he thought it absurd. And continuing—for although he had looked taut as he dialled, even her voice seemed to have soothed him again—he had said: "I say—what about an evening, one evening?"

"You mean, us?"

"Yes, of course. Dutch treat, I mean—if you insist."

"Oh, but I do. Yes, I must!"

"All right," said Paul, easily, and though he still thought it strange. "But you will, though?"

He might not have written this, any more than he would have written "an evening, one evening," yet the sense was quite clear.

"Oh, I'd love it," she had said.

He was slightly carried away.

"Well, look here—I say—how about tonight?"

She hadn't answered for a second. And then: "Oh, Paul—I'm afraid I can't. You see, I'm going somewhere."

Swift recovery; or he had hoped that it sounded like that.

"Of course; of course. Only an idea. But—well, could we fix something else?"

Was he pestering her? There was another pause. Then her voice. "Yes, do let's. Just a moment. I'll have a look in my little book."

Time, accordingly, to reflect on her more than intelligible popularity. Naturally she would be besieged. He was within an ace, at this point, of remembering Bubbles Vaughan. But then she was back, and the moment had passed.

"Paul?"

"Hullo, yes?"

"Would Wednesday be any good?"

Wednesday, Paul had said, would be splendid. A little later, when he had consulted his own book in turn, he had had to extricate himself from a pledge to his cousin Clayton. Still, it wasn't a party, and his cousin Clayton didn't mind; even if it struck him as distinctly unusual.

"That'll be fine," Paul had added. "Could you meet me at Belloni's?" For somehow he was opposed to the Avocado, and his own club was a pure monastery. "Half-past sixish? So that we could have a drink? And decide?"

"That'll be lovely. I'll write it down."

But she hadn't hung up. He could say something else; if inspired.

"Oh!" That was the inspiration. "Was it a good film the other night? You know. When you dashed off. I mean, last time."

Perhaps she was still writing, for there had been a further brief pause. Yet when she spoke, he had felt a change in her tone.

"We didn't go," she announced. "We—we argued instead. It was rather tiresome. But there! I've written it down. So thanks awfully. Oh!"

"Yes?"

"You don't want me to change?"

"No, no." Never. Please! "Just come round as you are."

She rippled. "All right." She rang off.

A triumph. Only qualified by the problem of her name; by the slight awkwardness—though a little later, as has been said—of telephoning to his cousin Clayton; and, possibly, by her allusion to Moustache.

Not that he hadn't invited it, or, on the other hand, that it was any concern of his. But *why* had they argued? What about? And what was tiresome? Imagination, almost at once, set to work. It rushed to extremes. They were engaged, and had had a tiff. They weren't engaged, and Moustache was out on his ear. But if *that* were tiresome, he might return. She had sounded sad. It was her wish.

Or, again, it was merely tiresome that they should have found the film crowded out. And—very important, this—how *long* had they argued?

Had he insulted her, so that she got up and left? This was tempting, if cruel. Or had they sat on for hours and hours, discussing politics or religion or something—not that Moustache *looked* that type—only to find (which would be the tiresome part) that they were too late? This was considerably less tempting. Paul yearned for them to have had a row. Yet on the whole—for who *could* have a row with her?—he must confess that it was more likely.

Triumph, in other words, became tinged with humility, and with an awareness of the vast number of other chaps. All after her, of course, as he had known at first sight. Except himself, for, though perplexed, he was still calm. Or he was content, seeing that Wednesday would soon be along, to live (as is sometimes said, but in another sense) on his expectations.

That was it. He could look forward. Or back, if he chose. Four days could be managed, easily, like that. He could reflect, but he could escape worry, as he was determined to do. And though it is a fact that he was a little restless by Tuesday evening, when he dined alone at his club, because it now seemed that Providence had contrived to insert at least an extra twenty-four hours into this week, by Wednesday morning he was well over this grudge.

Of course, if she put him off . . . Or if she forgot to turn up . . . But these were only mental precautions—and he knew it—against Fate. And in fact she had done neither. She was there on the dot— Paul himself, for some reason, had arrived rather sooner—and at once, again, he was completely and entirely at his ease.

Conversation had flowed; and on his own part so readily that he was quite surprised by his fluency. But he hadn't interrupted her. Or not often. He had listened, too. Yet there had been no pauses. It had just seemed *natural* to go on. They had also sipped, though not to excess. And presently, still talking, they had entered the nearer part of the restaurant—the section, in other words, where there was still no question of evening dress—and had eaten as well.

Mindful of her principles, and considerate of her purse—for it was quite clear that she wasn't in a shop just for fun—he had avoided extravagance, and had submitted to her choice of water; though, for the good of the house, he had drunk lager himself. Yet even the wine-waiter had smiled, either as a tribute to her looks, or because he guessed—and if he did, he was absolutely correct—that such restraint wouldn't lessen the tip.

What had they talked about? Not politics. Not religion. Not the state of the world. Not even—for apart from the Parkinsons, and the two rather doubtful cases of Captain Dalrymple and Mr. Brian Cairns, there was no one else on the list; not even the personalities of their friends. Yet they expressed opinions, on which it seemed that they almost always agreed. And—what can be more fascinating, if not necessarily or invariably to the other party?—they talked quite a lot about themselves.

This implies that they also listened; as they did, taking turns. And whether or not Paul, on Paul, was amusing (yet the girl either had very good manners or must at least have been temporarily interested), he was simply absorbed when he shut up, and she resumed.

It might be an exaggeration to say that his eyes popped, or that he actually pricked up his ears. But he was extremely attentive. So much so, at times, that he didn't always catch all that she said. For if every picture tells a story, so, in this instance, did every story paint a picture. As he studied them, as his mind, in fact, added further lifelike if imaginative touches, he was sometimes aware that he had fallen behind.

He had been dreaming. He gave a start. He controlled it. He awoke. "Go on," he said. "Tell me some more."

She did; or, again in the most natural way, she passed the ball, and he at once picked it up. Monologues. Duologues. A certain amount of stichomythia, though not actually in verse. And laughter, as a kind of thread, through it all. Afterwards—but, of course, this has happened before—he was vexed that he could remember so little. Vexed that he had missed chances of clearing up points. And remorseful—yes, what *had* come over him, when he was generally rather a quiet, reserved sort of chap?—that he himself should have chattered so much.

Yet he had learnt her age. This had emerged. She was twenty-three, as he had guessed. And—this was absolutely engraved, though he couldn't think how it had emerged, for he most certainly hadn't asked—she would be twenty-four on the fifth of October.

He had also learnt that, in addition to her father having been a darling, she had had no mother since about the age that he had lost his own. To say that he was pleased wouldn't be fair. He was torn with pity. Yet, apart from the fact that it was a kind of bond, in a way, it *was* a relief—for he had been worrying about this a good deal—that if he ever went there (by which he meant, of course, to her own quarters) he wouldn't meet someone, up from the country, who would obviously dislike him.

Or perhaps it meant that he *oughtn't* to go there. No. Rot. Dash it all, they were only going to be friends.

"I beg your pardon?" His thoughts had wandered. He had missed something again.

"I was only saying that I've hardly got any relations, either. Well, only an aunt—though I believe there *are* some others, somewhere—down at Bournemouth. That's all."

She was unprotected. Jolly good. No, it wasn't—poor child. He thought of wolves. He said, though in reference to relations, not wolves: "I seem to have dozens myself."

"Have you really? What fun!"

This was true. Yet, in comparison, it was perhaps a bit dull.

"No parents, though," he added. "They're dead. Years ago. I can't even remember them now."

He wasn't boasting. He wasn't heartless. He was just used to the fact; and had brought it out, if not exactly as a riposte, then as a reply.

But he had been aghast. For quite suddenly her eyes filled with tears.

"Oh, Paul—" She gave a gulp. "Oh, how dreadful! How *cruel*! I—I——"

"It isn't!" Simultaneously he apologised to two honoured shades—yet of course they would understand—and did his utmost to pass it all off. "It isn't, really. I mean, it was." For he was bound to admit that. "But, *Bianca*——"

He broke off. She was smiling again.

"I—I know," she said, shakily. "I'm a fool——"

"No, you're not!"

"I am! I can't help it." The shakiness had gone. "I mean, I'm rightfully sensible, really——"

"Yes, I'm sure you are."

"—but I just howl, now and then—at something sad."

"I know."

"No, you can't. It's all over, you see. You ought to have been angry. Will you promise to be angry next time. It stops it at once——"

"Oh, I couldn't do that!"

"—and I'm *so* glad you called me 'Bianca.' "

"Eh? What?" A rush of blood to the head. "Why?"

"Because almost everyone calls me 'Bee.' It was Dorothea who started it. Not—" though there was still the customary flash of resentment—"that I minded *her*. But then they *all* began. And though of course they mean well—" Paul's nose disagreed—"well, it isn't my name, after all. I mean, Daddy never used it. So do *please* go on. Even—" and she was actually rippling again—"if **I** haven't got a sister who's a shrew."

So she had remembered that, too. And shucks to Moustache. The little, trifling flare-up, indeed—not to mention that most *interesting* information about her tear-glands—had brought them a stage nearer, perhaps. Paul felt so at the moment. Later on, he was less convinced. But this was the point, in any case, where—so as to be tactful, and not to presume, and to escape from such thoughts—he had suddenly asked: "And how's George?"

"Oh. My little car. Oh yes, I told you, of course. Oh, much better, thanks. He's outside."

"I say—is he really?"

But that was a mistake. Or the mistake had already been made. For some time now, in the offing, a small dance-band had been playing softly and a little mournfully. Paul had closed his ears to it. Not that Belloni's, though they had tried valiantly, in the first flush of victory, to insist on their dancers wearing evening dress, hadn't long since withdrawn this rule. Not that he was the least appalled by the conception of gliding round with his guest.

It had meant, though, that it was growing late. Too late to "decide," as he had proposed when he rang up, on any additional form of entertainment. They had talked instead. He had no wish to change that. But now, because of that unfortunate inquiry about George's health, it was only too plain what he had done.

"I must go," she was saying. "Or his battery'll run down."

Bother George! "Oh, I say. It's quite early——"

"But it isn't. I'm sure!" She looked slightly distressed.

"Well, just a *few* minutes," he said.

In point of fact, it was the best part of another half-hour. But there was a threat all the time. And he didn't *want* her to be unable to start. His conscience, indeed, rather took her side in the matter. They went on talking, but it wouldn't leave him alone.

There was a pause. They both spoke.

"I suppose really . . ."

They both smiled. But they both understood. It was the end. They must resume their own lives.

"Bill?" said Paul. It appeared at once. It had been ready since nine. He glanced at it. Noted, without surprise, that it had been bumped up by various permitted, supernumerary charges to nearly two pounds. He planked down two-pound-ten, and waved it away. He shot a sudden, anxious look at his guest.

Had she seen it? Then he must lie. He couldn't possibly take half. She couldn't afford it. And, besides, it was all wrong.

But she was getting up. She said nothing. And again he was relieved, though still slightly bewildered as well. She had made such a *point*—well, never mind. It was a little odd; but then it was odd either way.

They were in the hall, where they had first sipped. He gave his ticket to a flunkey; and, to save time, gave him a shilling as well. Yet her back was still turned, when

"Hul-*lo*!" said a man's voice. "Bianca! By Jove! I say—well, well, well—this is marvellous!"

Paul shot round. Not Moustache. But a good-looking chap. Young and pink, with extremely fair hair.

"Jock! Well, how nice! I thought you were away."

"Aha!" said Goldilocks; for Paul had somehow, and immediately, hit on a derogatory name for him, too. "I'm not, though. I've come back. Now, look here, my proud beauty; when can you——"

Paul moved forward. He couldn't help it. He loomed. The chap stopped.

"Oh," said Bianca. "Paul—do you know Jock Whitley? Paul Sunderland, Jock. Or *do* you know each other?"

They didn't. Any more than they fell on each other's neck. They made noises. They nodded. That was all.

"Look here," said Mr. Whitley, having finished with this; "when can I see you? That's the point." But of course he didn't mean Paul. "Friday evening? Shall I call for you? What?"

"Oh, thank you. That'll be lovely. At least——"

"Right! Don't forget. I'll be there. So—ha, ha!—bring some cash."

"Oh, Jock, but——"

Another beauty, or comparative beauty, who had just emerged from the zenana, joined the group. Said: "Hullo!" Said: "Buck up. They've gone in." And swept Mr. Whitley away.

F

"That was his sister," said Bianca, as she and Paul passed towards the revolving door. He was sorry. Even when she added that she was awfully sweet, he still showed no sign of delight.

However, as they were each in a quadrant now, his demeanour passed unobserved.

"Taxi, sir?" said a uniformed giant, with what had become the customary hint of conspiracy and cunning.

"No, thank you," said Bianca. "I left my little car."

"Round the corner, miss? There's a cop there."

"Come on," said Paul.

He shook off the giant, though he tipped him, too. But there was a policeman all right. He was looking thoughtful. He had the air of having abandoned all other duties—as, indeed, he presumably had—so as to spend the night, if this should prove necessary, beside George. But he came to the alert as they approached.

"This your car, sir?"

"No," said Bianca. "It's mine. Don't you like it?"

"Well, miss—" oh, a very different policeman already—"I wouldn't say that. But you can't leave it here with no lights on."

"But I didn't—oh, dear! Paul! Paul—are you strong?"

"Terrifically," said Paul. "Shall I swing her? I mean, him."

"Oh, Paul, if you *wouldn't* mind—Or perhaps the policeman . . ."

But the policeman had faded away. It was his tribute. Keen, no doubt, as he was on avoiding burglars, on harassing motorists, and on promotion, he, too, was but a man, and had felt the spell. In actual truth, he was still lurking—possibly in the hope of exhibiting his own stamina. But as Bianca switched off the dark lamps, and switched on the ignition, Paul inserted the starting-handle (which at least wasn't buried, for, as the owner said, this was always happening to poor George) and swung like a maniac. By this means, indeed, he not only worked off a good deal of his recent pique at the little scene with Mr. Whitley, but roused the engine to vigorous life.

It spat. It exploded. It was roaring away. The lights came on. And he came round with the handle.

"Are you all right?" he yelled, as he passed it in through the window.

She was saying something. He leant nearer. He heard.

"Oh, but, I say," he protested, if less emphatically than he had swung. "That's miles out of your way. No, you mustn't."

"But it'll do it good, Paul. Don't you see? It'll make some more juice. And I've *got* to start in the morning. Come on!"

So Paul went round to the other door; and thus, for the first but by no means the last time, struck his head with some force against the treacherously low roof of the late Mr. Brown's fifteen-year-old car.

"Oh!" said the present proprietor, as he stifled a groan. "Oh, Paul—are you all right? Did it hurt?"

"Not the least." He climbed in.

"I'm so glad." She released the hand-brake. "Because sometimes it annoys people," she said.

Paul laughed. He was less convinced that he had fractured his skull. And he was driving with her—fancy that!—after a really most enjoyable evening, through the drab streets of London; alone. This was it. This was the idea. Hell take Goldilocks, of course. But he couldn't say that she *looked* as if she were in love.

Nor was he; thank the lord. The point just didn't arise. And never need, if one left well alone. He liked *being* with her; and why not, if she didn't object? One didn't have to drag love into everything. One could be friends. Well, good heavens, there was no harm in that. And she certainly knew how to drive.

He saw a vision, for a moment, of the Porchester Leveret. In three years, perhaps, not only would there be more room for his legs, but—and this might also be more suitable—he would be giving *her* lifts. Unless, of course, by that time . . .

He glanced at her profile. Why *shouldn't* one admire beauty? What else, dash it all, was it for?

"Are you nervous?" she asked.

"No, no. Not the least."

"Am I going the wrong way, then?"

"No, no. Well—" he had suddenly realised where they were— "as a matter of fact, we've just passed it. My turning, I mean." His knees hit the dashboard. "But it's only a few yards. I'll get out."

They had stopped. It was the end, again. It was always the end. Though of course—he opened the near-side door, and put a leg out—not in the sense that it was final.

He began thanking her. For technical reasons, that yet might not be appreciated by light sleepers in the neighbourhood, she kept the throttle open; so that there was a good deal of noise.

"Great fun!" he bawled.

"What?" She checked some of the rumpus. "Oh, Paul—before you go—what did it come to?"

"Oh, please!" But you see? He had misjudged her again. She had only left it till now so as not to embarrass him. And yet he *was* rather embarrassed, as she opened her little bag. "Look here," he said, swivelling on the seat, though also preparing—for she was really the most extraordinary girl—for a rebuff. "Can't we do this? Let it go, I mean? And then next time," he rushed on, "it'll be *your* turn." She didn't answer. "It would be much simpler," he risked pointing out. "And quite fair. I—I might come down your way."

But he wasn't quite sure whether he was alluding to some little Chelsea restaurant, because it would be cheaper for her, or was hoping to be asked to her former nursery. She seemed to hesitate, too. But then she said: "Will you *promise*?"

"Of course!" Another promise flashed back into his mind. "And to call you 'Bianca,' as well."

She rippled. He'd done it. Hit two birds with one stone. Now they *must* meet again; which was so satisfactory that he didn't even attempt to fix a date. He had preserved his pride, but he had respected her own. He had been inspired, once again. And though at this sort of moment, or in circumstances like these, innumerable young men would, nowadays, have leant over and have delivered a kiss; and though plenty of young women, or so one is told, would have received it almost as a matter of course, Paul Sunderland just smiled as he extracted himself. For it would appear, whether this had occurred to him or whether he was extraordinary, too, that he was also pledged to a personal code.

"Good-night!" he called out. "And thanks awfully, again."

"Thanks awfully," shouted Bianca. "Good-night!"

He slammed the door. She roared away. The light sleepers sank back. He was feeling wonderful. Young, strong, fit, capable, ingenious, and—he almost smirked as he strode—completely serene. All memory of impatience or perplexity had gone. The evening had been delightful. He tasted fragments again. And they were still nearly as fresh as at the time.

Yet in the lift another fragment also arose, quite unasked. Or two fragments were suddenly linked. "Almost everyone calls me 'Bee.'" And: "Bianca—by Jove!" Goldilocks. Or Jock Something. His idea, then? Or hers? Mere chance, or had she *asked* him to use her full name? And if she had, did it imply . . .

I'm not jealous, thought Paul. He insisted on that. His sole wish was that they should go on being friends. And yet, though there was a hint that Moustache had dropped back, here was some-one else bouncing right in. Again he had pondered. Used reason. And slept well enough. Yet again, as before, the element of Time played its part. Not only were an image and an echo less sharp, as it raced. But, as it lagged, there must be renewed impatience as well.

2

THE disadvantage, as was gradually brought in on P. Sunderland, Esquire, of what had at first seemed such a brilliant manœuvre was that action had passed out of his hands. If he had been less impulsive, less feeble, if he had accepted payment in cash, then—or so he felt—he could have rung up again.

Not immediately, of course. There must be no suggestion of rush. But he would have been free to do just as he chose. In a few days—well, call it a week, if you like—he could have followed the same line as before. How was she? Had she got a clear evening fairly soon? And, in brief, couldn't they fix something up?

Breezily, you know. Yes, that would have been it. The light touch. The gay laugh. All so simple.

Unluckily, however, owing to his short-sightedness and folly, this would now be the equivalent of claiming a debt. It would be like reminding her—it is perhaps superfluous to explain to whom he was alluding at this point—that he had lent her money, and wanted it back.

This was impossible. And though it could be argued, privately, that she had saved him a taxi-fare—call it half a crown, then—and though he would have done his best to refuse more than five bob for the dinner, so that actually the same or another half-crown ought to put things straight, it was still awkward. Confoundedly awkward.

No, he *couldn't* ring up. He must leave it to her. Anything else would make him sound like a sort of Shylock. And, also, there was no hope on this occasion—though, of course, this was entirely his own blithering fault—of another letter, enclosing more stamps. The original book, by the way, was still safe in his note-case; and considering how closely it resembled all other such books, it was rather strange how often he took it out, looked at it, and put it back there.

But this, of course, was because it was now part of the general conundrum. He may have felt that by re-examining it, and by re-reading the letter, light might burst through the enveloping cloud. For she had touched them, and though it is true that by this time only his own finger-prints could, in all probability, have been discovered, the fact remained that they were a very important piece of evidence.

They proved, for example, that he hadn't dreamt the whole thing. That she was real. Did this help? Not the least. Yet he continued the practice; because it might; one never knew. And cloud was as thick as before.

Paul Secundus piped up.

"You're a jackass," he said. "Go ahead. She's not that kind of girl."

"Eh? What do you mean?"

"Ring her up, and find out. You promised, you know. Go on. It'll be rude if you don't."

"Well, I can't. I never promised to *ask* her next time. Only—and you know that perfectly well—to let her pay. But that's the *point*——"

"Oh, good lord!"

"No, you don't understand. It's—it's all mixed up."

"So are you."

"*Get out!*"

Such exchanges, violent and even passionate as they frequently were, produced singularly little result. The contestants snarled, swore, and spat at each other. Withdrew, yet were imprisoned in the same frame. Became, indeed, one organism again, which performed quite a number of customary actions. Though it also lingered, on at least one occasion, outside Mr. Willoughby's salon.

Quite natural, however, and straightforward. A genuine appointment with a capitalist at his hotel, which was only a short distance away. The capitalist, moreover, had selected the time—which, as it happened, was the same as before; so that it would be absurd not to pass through this street. If she reappeared, that would be all.

No *real* hanging-about. Just a word, or so Paul pictured it to himself; though perhaps he had prepared more than this.

It would indicate, anyhow, that he wasn't a pest. "Hullo!" he would say. "What luck!" Or was that too much? Surely not, if he just explained and dashed on. But it might—or this was the idea—lead to another appointment, and so much more easily than if he wrote or rang up.

Unfortunately, again, though, he had overlooked the approach of spring. Not that it wasn't still bitterly cold, as he emerged from the Tube; but it was no longer nearly so dark as he could have wished. It was dusk. But he felt exposed. The other loiterers were about. He would be seen, and no doubt suspected, not only by them, but by anyone glancing out of a window. This wouldn't do. Dash the spring! He must walk briskly instead. Though of course he could still circle the block.

He began circling it, though aware that this was trifling with chance. And indeed he had no luck, though it was growing darker each moment. Unless it were luck that he was doing about four miles an hour when again the wrong vision turned up.

"Good-evening, sir."

"Eh? Oh. Oh, hullo, Spilsby."

He hadn't paused. Nor had Spilsby. There he went, and it was all right. But really, you know, if he was going to take his constitutional through this particular street at this particular time every single dashed evening, one might as well throw in one's hand. For Spilsby was a talker. He would talk to the other tenants. He would make a story out of it—"Yes, there he is, sir, every evening, regular as clockwork"—and though it would be quite untrue, one just *couldn't* risk that.

No. Ugh! Here—I'm off. The sensitive Paul shot at once into reverse, and though he would regret this afterwards—for of course Spilsby wouldn't have come back again, and he had merely chucked away a golden opportunity—he was at least punctual at the hotel. So punctual, indeed, that he must fill in time washing his hands—capitalists, in his experience, being only too apt to misconstrue even a hint that one was in a hurry—before approaching the reception desk.

As a matter of fact, and though this was also far from unusual, the capitalist was out, and he had to wait half an hour. Yet as a matter of fact, too, after the capitalist had said a great deal about time being money, and had wasted a good deal of both in ordering drinks—and, while he was about it, his own dinner as well—the ultimate interview was quite promising for the firm. Paul withdrew, not displeased, and went off to his own club. H.B., he felt, ought to welcome his report. What was wrong, then? Capitalism? No; Bianca.

There you were. Every reason for being quite bucked. For *knowing* one had done a good job. And yet—Paul gazed thoughtfully at the long, ornate ceiling—one felt anything but a sense of achievement. I could have seen her, he thought. And I ran away.

Yellow. That was the word. And an idiot, of course. Another scene with the *alter ego*, which was again told to get out. Then he laughed, and must pretend that he had just thought of a joke. What do I *want*? he inquired. Well, why *don't* I ring up? He shrugged his shoulders. He was mad. That was all.

This was Tuesday, March 8th. But though insane, he still worked. Habit helped, and the work itself. Or he wasn't always insane. At times, indeed, he was as calm as could be. He hadn't forgotten, but he had got the thing down. He withdrew, in another sense, and was again not displeased. He hadn't seen her for more than a week now. Perhaps, if it came to that, he would never see her again. Well? If he could face this—and just observe, he pointed out, how I *am* facing it—then everything was all right. He believed it was.

He believed nothing of the kind. He had touched off the spring— silly ass to go meddling with it again. He should have left it alone; here, in the office, of all places, where he was busier than ever. And yet, dash it, if he weren't in the middle of dictating, there was the telephone, and the directory, and of course one oughtn't, perhaps, to ring her up when she was at her own work; but he wouldn't mind betting chaps did.

Or would it get her into trouble? It would be ghastly if he did that. He relaxed. He was almost relieved that he had stopped to think. Though, of course, by thinking . . .

" '—your letter of the 9th'?" said Miss Thriplow for the second time.

"Eh? Oh. I beg your pardon. Of course."

He glanced at Miss Thriplow, and though it was important, in a way, that he should restore her confidence in his attention to business, he must yet, for some reason, delay this for a flash. It was a symptom of the disease from which he had just declared himself free that he should suddenly wonder if she, too, had a heart. He had never thought of this before, and of course he couldn't ask. But she was alive. It was a possibility. He was both interested and repelled. It occurred to him, no less swiftly and suddenly, that though he had known for a long while that she was Miss G. E. Thriplow, he had also learnt—from some form, he supposed, such as one was always having to fill in or check over nowadays—that she was called Gladys Evelyn.

Amazing, you know. Why? He was disgusted with himself. He would now, in fact, have very much liked to explain to Miss Thriplow that he regarded her—and this was perfectly true—with almost intense detachment. But as he couldn't do this, he smiled, faintly and apologetically. Miss Thriplow smiled back. She could hardly do less. The flash was over. Its effect had begun.

"Right," said Paul, rapidly, and still quite unaware of the danger that he had become not only to his secretary but to the whole of society. "On we go, then. Hrm. 'In reply to your letter of the 9th instant—' and quote all those drivelling reference numbers, will you?"

"Yes, Mr. Sunderland."

" '—we feel it may be helpful to point out that the permit which you state you are unable to grant was in fact issued to us by your Department on September 27th last, and its receipt was acknowledged by us at the time. Yours faithfully—' because I think that's quite enough for them to take in at one go——"

His telephone-bell rang.

"Just a moment," he said. He uncradled. He addressed it. "Hullo?"

"Oh, Paul—" his expression became curiously and deceptively blank, but he knew perfectly well who it was—"am I interrupting? Do you mind? Shall I ring off?"

"No. No, no. No. No, please don't do that. I——"

"It's Bianca."

"Yes. Yes. Go ahead. Here I am." He tried to pick up a pencil. He hurled it on the floor. Miss Thriplow, ever obliging, went after it. "Oh, thank you. Thank you. Thanks——"

"Paul—why? What for?"

"Something else," he explained, if this could be called an explanation. "I dropped something. Yes? How are you?"

"Oh, Paul, I oughtn't to be talking, either——"

"Why not?"

"They don't like it. But, Paul——"

"Yes?"

"—I've got two seats for *Bohème* tonight. A man was taking me; but he's got a cold. So I just suddenly——"

"Yes!"

"Yes, what?" Had he been too quick, then?

"I—I thought you meant . . ."

"Well, I did. You mean, you can?"

"Yes, rather! Where shall I meet you? Are you changing?"

"Oh no. But I thought—well, it was my turn——"

"Yes, of course." Far too quick. And quite the wrong thing to say. "I mean, I'd love it. What time——"

"Will you come to my little club? Soon after six?"

"Yes, but——"

"Good-bye."

Poor girl. Poor girl. Stitch, stitch, stitch, in poverty, hunger, and—well, no; not exactly. She was a mannequin, not a shirt-maker. But how cruel that she must telephone furtively like that. Hell take Michael Willoughby. But whoops! if it came to that. This was marvellous. Pretty rotten, of course, for the other chap, whoever he was, to have a cold. But he would recover; and, meanwhile, Paul himself had recovered.

He was less exhilarated, perhaps—and this was interesting, too —than back in his normal frame of mind. But he felt tremendously fit. He took a deep breath. He saw Miss Thriplow. She looked away. What on earth had it got to do with her?

Well, nothing, of course. Just as there had been nothing, after all, in that brief, clipped conversation—of which in any case she had only heard half—to put ideas into Miss Thriplow's head. Her whole manner, in fact, and though he had now dismissed all speculation about it, was still the result of his own look. Not that he had never smiled at her on any previous occasion. Nor that he could have explained the precise difference this time.

But it was there. She had been noticed, and startled as well. It had done something to her, not the least in connection with Paul; the unconscious agent of Fate. He was still Mr. Sunderland, who was considerate but remote. Yet, suddenly, it was not impossible that life might hold more than a good job and its accurate performance.

She was a little bewildered. She was wondering, too. The germ, one might say, that her courteous, industrious, but, so far as she was concerned, still entirely sexless boss had picked up at a cocktail-party nearly four weeks ago, and had been carrying around ever since, had leapt the short distance between them at last. I could be loved, thought Miss Thriplow, as she turned the leaf of her note-book. She took Paul's dictation as skilfully as ever. But she was thinking—and considering everything, this was perhaps just as well—of another and distinctly less prosperous young man with whom she sometimes travelled, sardine-like, from Ilford.

3

"THAT was fun," said Bianca.

"I know," said Paul.

"I mean, it's awfully sad in a way—and rather absurd, too. But it's a lovely, old-fashioned, sentimental sort of Wop noise."

"That's right."

"And I'm glad we could see the orchestra. If you know what I mean."

"Absolutely."

"I mean, if someone *very* fat starts singing, or if you think their beard's coming off—well, one looks at all the bows. Or—or don't you?"

"As a matter of fact," said Paul, "I do. As a matter of fact . . ."

"Yes?"

"Dashed queer thing, opera," he suggested. "If they could only bring it off—I mean, the *whole* thing . . . But they can't, of course. Well, how *can* they?"

"How about Heaven?"

"Possibly. But I rather doubt it. Well, it *is* so absurd. But, Bianca, I did enjoy it."

"So did I. It's so short. And I think it's marvellous having no overture. Bang! I mean, and there you are. We had a cat called Mimi."

"Did you really? Did she sing?"

"Well, she was a man, as a matter of fact. But he had tiny hands. And, of course, he *thought* he was singing."

They both laughed. This was fascinating. The whole evening had been fascinating. Though just at the beginning . . .

It was as if he had spoken aloud. He could feel it. She was starting again.

"Paul!"

"Hullo, yes? Hi—mind that van!"

"I saw it." She stopped, so that the other opera-lovers, pouring down Bow Street, swept past them. "Paul—I *must* get this straight.

"Oh, please——"

"No, I *must*. You were very obstinate, you know. You paid for the whole evening last time——"

"But you drove me home."

"That was nothing. And don't interrupt. Paul!"

"Yes?" He sounded bold, but he didn't feel it.

"And tonight you sort of *forced* me to come out again. I *wanted* to give you dinner at my little club."

"But there was such a crowd there."

"I know." She began walking again. "And, of course, it was much nicer where we went." Aha! "But, Paul, I didn't really even pay for the tickets, you know. They were Godfrey's."

This was a point that, while anticipating and enjoying much musical pleasure, Paul had been quite anxious to clear up. He had speculated more than once on the identity of his stricken bene-factor, yet had somehow assumed that it was either Goldilocks or Moustache. But it was neither. And this was the first time that he had ever heard of any Godfrey.

Stupid name, he thought, perhaps a little ungratefully. His conscience instantly tried to put this right.

"How is he?" he asked.

"Who, Godfrey? Why, do you know him?"

"Well, no," said Paul, conceding this fact. "I was only thinking it was rather rotten luck—for him, I mean—to have a cold. Has he got a temperature?"

"No."

A valetudinarian, then. Let's leave him.

"But he's in a temper."

"Oh?"

"And if you ask me, that's all. But he's like that. I mean, he's sweet, really, and he can be frightfully funny, but—well, we got arguing last night. So he's sulking today. And I wouldn't mind that—if he likes it, I mean. But I know just what comes next."

"What," asked Paul, though not over-inquisitively, he hoped, "would that be?"

"He'll ring up and apologise. It'll all start again. And *really*, you know——"

She stopped abruptly.

"Yes?"

"Nothing."

"Right you are," said Paul, though he wasn't quite there. "How are the others?" he heard himself ask, with some slight surprise.

"Who?"

Why on earth had he said that? It was worse than inquisitive. It was offensive. But she was looking up at him, sideways. He was in a fix. He must go on. For a moment, it is true, he had to rack his memory to recall their real names. But he succeeded.

"Cairns and Whitley," he said.

"Oh!" But she was laughing. "You make them sound like a shop. Well, they're around."

"You bet," said Paul, under his breath.

"But you can thank your stars you're not a girl."

"Why?" But he had already leapt at some fearful conclusions. Both fists were clenched. "Do you mean to say——"

"Oh, Paul, no, of course not. *I* can manage them, I mean."

"Oh. I see."

"And it's nothing, really. They're just silly. Well, sometimes, I mean. And you mustn't think——"

"Oh no, I don't!"

She laughed again.

"You didn't even know what I was going to say," she pointed out. "But it's a silly subject."

"My fault." He saw a taxi. He yelled. "Hi! Taxi!" Too late. He said: "Dash!" But the subject was changed.

"Oh no, Paul, please. Of *course* I'm going on a bus. I always do— when I haven't got George."

"But, I say, can't we——"

"No, Paul. I *must* get home."

And I, thought Paul, mustn't be like those chaps.

"All right," he said. They were crossing the Strand. And it was true enough, though there were plenty of cabs tearing by, that they were full, and that there was a lot of wild waving.

"And *please* don't think you've got to wait with me in the queue."

"Oh, I like that," said Paul, as if he frequently did it for pure pleasure. "In fact," he suddenly added, "I'll tell you what. I'll ride back with you."

"Oh no, you mustn't. That's absurd. It's *miles* out of your way."

"But I like it," said Paul, with much the same implication. "Then I'll get a bit of a walk, you see—" the inference now was that walking in this part of London didn't count or was even definitely injurious—"and then— Here! Come on!"

As sometimes happens, or indeed happens as often as not, a whole fleet of No. 11 arrived in a bunch. The queue instantly broke up and began running like mad. Paul seized Miss Brown's elbow— this was the first time that he had ever touched her, but it was anything but a caress—and though he didn't exactly whirl her through the air, their joint progress was both efficient and irresistible. They were on the step or platform. They were on the stair. They were on the same seat. There was a trampling; a surging; hoarse cries from the conductor as he pushed the excess load into the street. Three rapid rings, and the mammoth moved off.

"There you are," said Paul. "How was that?"

"Wonderful. Are you all right?"

"Yes, thanks. How are you?"

They both laughed.

"Wait a moment," she said.

"What for?"

"Here's a shilling."

"Oh, really——"

"Now, Paul!"

Very well, then. He mustn't argue. He had been warned about that. Besides, though he had seen the opera for nothing, he had paid for two dinners, a taxi, and a programme. Quits, then, or he at least hoped she would see it like that. Extraordinary girl, though. What fun this all was. And, apart from a brief moment in Bow Street, how sensibly and calmly he had behaved. No impatience. No madness. Just a couple of friends. And why not, if it was how she felt, too?

"Perhaps," he said, "we could do this again some time."

"Well—" she gave a little gurgle— "I can't promise that anyone else will give me tickets like that."

"Oh, I didn't mean——"

"No, of course you didn't. But I'll tell you what."

"Yes?"

"Well, Paul, just in *case* you think I've forgotten what I told you—or what you've forked out tonight—*next* time—" the bus gave a lurch, so that he would perhaps have contracted a number of muscles anyhow—"you shall see how I cook."

He couldn't answer. It would be so awful if he had misunderstood her.

"Didn't you hear?"

"Yes. Yes. Rather! You—you mean, at your——"

"Well, where else could I cook? Of course. It would be cosy. Besides—what's the matter?"

"Nothing. Nothing at all. I—I'd love it."

"I'm not bad, you know." Good lord! Oh—(you filthy-minded blackguard!)—I see. "I used to do it all with Dorothea." Slight pause, which again it was impossible not to interpret as in reproach for the former and faithless Miss Brickfield. "Oh, and that reminds me—" much more brightly—"I meant to tell you, of course."

A sudden warm sense of intimacy on the top of the cold bus. If she had meant to tell him something, then she must have been thinking of him, too.

"Yes?" But here was the conductor at last. Paul paid, and handed over the change.

"Oh, thank you."

"But what were you going to tell me?"

"Oh. Oh yes. Well, there's a girl called Ariadne——"

"I say—what an odd name!"

"Well, it isn't her name really, of course. She's in the shop, I mean."

"Michael Willoughby's?"

"Yes. And it's *really* the name of a dress she wore once——"

"I say! Do the dresses have names, too?"

"Well, of course!" Another laugh; and Paul had learnt something else. "And it sort of stuck to her——"

"What, the dress?"

"No, the name, of course. Well, she's terribly attractive."

"Really?"

"Yes, lovely. Everyone's mad about her."

"Are they?"

"I say, aren't you interested?"

"Yes, yes, of course," said Paul, in what would certainly have been just the right tone—though he was unconscious of this—if he had been an expert in strategy. "Go on."

"Well, she wants to share my top bit. And she's awfully nice. Well, really *awfully* nice. And I needn't decide just yet, because she's all right for another month. But *I* don't know. What do *you* think?"

Quite a lot. In the first place, that is to say, he had taken "top bit" to be another allusion to some article of apparel. Emerging hastily from this error, he was again interested, but a shade doubtful. He didn't like the idea, or on some grounds he didn't, of Bianca being quite alone. But on other grounds he did. Ariadne, he felt, though infinitely preferable to—well, Godfrey, for example, or anyone else who might snatch her away, hardly fitted in with a vague-ish vista of his own. Guiltless as he was in the loss of Miss Brickfield, he couldn't say that he had ever personally regretted it.

Yet solitude meant danger. He realised that. And besides, it was much more expensive. One should consider that, too. One mustn't just be a dog in the manger; or, to be more accurate, a dog who hadn't yet seen it. It was good, though, decidedly good—yes, by Jove!—that she clearly meant to remain there herself. She hadn't spoken—though, of course, these things happened very suddenly sometimes, and he had absolutely no right to object—as if she were thinking, or contemplating——

"Paul! Shall I? Or not?"

He stalled. "What's her real name?" he asked.

"Oh, Paul, you are funny! I thought you were *really* thinking. Joan Hobson, of course. And the most marvellous hips."

"Oh?"

"I mean, she hasn't got any."

"Really?"

"No, of course not. You do make me laugh."

Paul Sunderland smiled; not quite sure whether he wished to be thought a humorist or not, yet glad, in a way, that he had withheld his advice. He had liked being asked, but he needed more facts. Not now, though. It would be ridiculous to waste time on Ariadne; and in any case how the deuce could he tell? Everything, it suddenly struck him, was a matter of chance. The fragility of the future made him almost giddy for an instant. One mustn't touch it; though one couldn't, of course. . . .

"—rather awkward—" he had missed the beginning, but he

was alert enough now—"having four rooms of my own. Well, even George is rather awkward."

"Why?" asked Paul.

"Well, such a lot of people have got nowhere to live, and can't get a car, and then they look at me, and—well, I don't see why I should marry them just for that. Do you?"

"No," said Paul, at the second attempt.

"I mean, it isn't just being selfish. Is it?"

"Of you? Certainly not."

"There you are, then." She began singing, Musetta's aria, without words. Clearly; softly; but the top of the bus was much emptier now. Paul listened. She took a swoop, and was perhaps a quarter of a tone flat. Why this should have made him feel so remarkably protective and tender towards her, or why, at the same moment, he should have been pleased by this slight flaw, might be a bit hard to explain. But he didn't analyse. He was quiescent. She took the same swoop again, and was dead on the note. He was a shade disappointed. But why?

She stopped. He was going to say something; about their evening, perhaps. But he was being pushed. He apprehended. He leapt up.

"Is this it? Shall I ring?"

"Yes, please. Oh, someone else has. Come on, then."

Down the steps. Past a minifying mirror. On to the rear platform, but there were a couple of other passengers there, too. Into the gutter. And up on to the pavement. The red mammoth, no longer an itinerant nook, went rolling dispassionately away.

"Well, good-night, Paul. Thanks awfully. I hope you'll catch another bus."

"But, I say——"

"No, of course not. No, please. You've come quite far enough."

"Oh."

"But don't forget——"

"Eh?"

"—it's *really* my turn next time. There! *Oh*, it's cold. I shall run." And as she began running: "Good-night!"

As she began running. Of how many young women, alas, would this be as much as to say that she changed in a moment from grace to ungainliness? But Miss Brown seemed to skim over the pavement like Atalanta, or as Paul himself sometimes skimmed in his dreams.

No clattering. No oscillating. No jerking of limbs. She sped. She fled. She was gone.

But he was happy. Alone in the cold and dark King's Road, he was filled with contentment. He didn't even regret—or not yet— the five minutes or so which it might have taken him to accompany her to her door. It had been no part of his plan, if there had been a plan at all, either to clutch or to kiss. He might even have preferred, though, in fact, there was no question of choice—for she had gone, and he didn't deal in such onslaughts—to stand, as he did, with his eyes slightly narrowed, and think of the evening again.

Their meeting. Their meal. The short taxi-ride. Puccini. The walk down Bow Street. The bus. And the things she had said.

Ariadne. How ridiculous! Godfrey—whoever he was. A faint shrug. "Thank your stars you're not a girl." Repellent idea. "*I* can manage them." Well, she probably could. Extraordinary mixture of—the ingredients defeated him. They required study. Much more study. And could have it (one might almost have fancied at this point that he was sucking an actual sweet), because she was going to ring up again, and thanks to her "rules"——

No, wait a second. Dash! She hadn't *said* she would ring up. He ought to have fixed something. What a fool! And if she didn't . . .

His eye caught a wayfarer. He stared. He turned away. How odd. Same chap, with same beard and apparently the same shirt —the supposed artist, in fact—whom they had seen at Parky's such ages ago. Then he was thrown into confusion, because he had just calculated, and it wasn't ages. It was barely four weeks. And yet, in that short time . . .

The panorama of memory widened. The coincidence, as he now realised, was quite unimportant. Yet it led—as he suddenly saw, hailed, succeeded in stopping, and climbed into another taxi—to a decision on which at least he could act. For Parky was a publisher, and, if he didn't know already, could find out about a poet and his poems. And armed with this knowledge—(By Jove, I said I'd walk, didn't I? Still, I wasn't exactly on oath)—he would be in a far stronger position if she mentioned them again. Low cunning? Not the least. He was interested; that was all.

Interested. That was the word. Or amused, if you like. Nice evening. Nice girl. Yes, he liked her a lot. But as for anything else— well, don't be an ass. He decided to yawn, as he rattled along. Perhaps so as to deceive Paul Secundus, or himself. But the yawn passed into a real one. He was curiously fatigued. "I'm cracking up," he muttered cheerfully, for he was still far from depressed. A further thought. That sudden ending was quite a good thing. It meant that it was still his duty to thank her properly.

4

HE wrote on Sunday, when he hadn't much else to do; and because the slight delay, though it might be unobservable at the other end, helped to establish that he was just being civil. At this stage, in fact, he could still taste the sweet. A couple of days weren't enough to start pangs.

Nevertheless, he would write because he had decided to write, so that it would be weak, as well as rude, if he didn't. It was true, of course, that hardly anyone wrote letters nowadays, and he had no wish to appear either forward or eccentric. But then, on the other hand, if he didn't thank her he would be uncouth. And, besides, don't you see, she had written to him (the sheet of paper was still in his note-case, and so was the complete book of stamps), so that she was the kind of girl who not only possessed but would expect good manners.

Q.E.D. Off he went to a rather gaunt and deserted club, for only a few members ever made use of it on Sundays; and having lunched by himself in the long dining-room with the encrusted ceiling, he went through into the smoking-room, where another small table was well furnished not merely with several kinds of writing-paper and appropriate envelopes, but with pens, and ink, and a discreet little lamp.

He switched it on, for, roughly speaking, it is always dark on a London Sunday in the first half of March; and selected a moderate-sized sheet. He dipped. He wrote the date. He wrote: *"Dear Bianca"*. He realised, some minutes later, that this was all that he had written. And, furthermore, that for some reason he had been gazing at a framed engraving of some highland cattle in a snow-storm, though without what one might call thinking about them, either.

He re-focused. He looked down. He wrote three words; and

stopped. So far as they went, they were all right. But they had
raised another point. Or they had destroyed some of his calm.
The simplicity had somehow oozed out of his plan. If he were brief,
it might look brusque. If he ran on, it might seem drivelling. There
was, of course, as he quite saw, a third alternative. A few, breezy,
light-hearted sentences, so that it was neither long nor short. Yet
to judge from the manner in which he was now wriggling his back,
it would appear that there was a difficulty here, too.

"Losing my grip," he muttered, just as two nights ago he had
announced that he was cracking up. It was, of course, a challenge
to his *alter ego*, which reacted at once. "Yes, obviously," it said.
"And, what's more, you know as well as I do that what you *really*
want isn't to thank her——"

"Shut up! I *do*!"

"——but to remind her to ask you round there. If you were more
honest——"

"Good lord! Can't a chap be polite?"

"Just look what you've written." The *alter ego* seemed to mouth
the three words. " '*I do hope*—' Well, what do you hope?"

"I've forgotten. No, I haven't. I was going to say I hoped she
didn't think I'd been——"

"P'ff! What a way to begin! Soppy. Feeble. Ambiguous, too.
Supposing something interrupts her when she's only got that far.
She'll think you're going to ask a favour. Chuck it away. Start
again."

Paul obeyed. It couldn't be said that he wholly agreed. But,
of course, if there were the least possibility that he had got off on
the wrong foot, or was inviting a misunderstanding . . . He snatched.
Crumpled. And took another sheet. He made several more attempts,
with the same critic not only at his elbow but inside him. One
began to see, after a while, why, even in these days when no one
wrote letters, the Committee of the Junior Corinthian still supplied
such quantities of paper and such a vast receptacle for its disposal.

Scratch, scratch, went the pen. Pause. Hammer-and-tongs with
the silent critic; or silent so far as a couple of somnolent members
with Sunday newspapers were concerned. A scowl. Another crumple,
and a fresh sheet. The whole contest took the best part of three-
quarters of an hour—though there were lulls now and then, when
Paul just sat back and glowered at the highland cattle; and the
final version was penned in such an extraordinary attitude—
hunched over the little table, as if to conceal it from some prying

ghost—that not only did it do grave injustice to his normal calligraphy, but there was a blot in one corner as well.

Never mind, though. He was damned—yes, *damned*—if he'd try again. He was stiff all over. Even his legs were in knots.

"Whew!" he let forth, so that one of the members looked round. But he didn't notice, and the crisis was over.

"Dear Bianca," he had written, *"It was all so sudden just at the end the other evening, though I quite see you couldn't stand about in the cold, that I'm afraid I never thanked you properly at all. I enjoyed it awfully, and it was awfully good of you to think of me when you had those tickets. It was really an awfully good performance I thought. I hope you're managing to keep fairly warm in this ghastly weather. Yours ever, Paul."*

And, of course, the blot.

No, scarcely a love-letter. One can hardly call it that. One doesn't, somehow, picture Miss Brown—even if she had shown any other sign of heart-trouble, which she most certainly hadn't—cherishing it and carrying it around in her own handbag. But then, if it comes to that, it wasn't meant to be a love-letter; even if this was just what it was, in a way.

For what did it say between the lines? It said Forget me not. The abbreviated signature was the result of no special thought; for at this stage, and in the present era, anything more would have been stiff. Considering its length, it rather harped on the temperature. Apart from this—and the perhaps excessive use of the word "awfully"—it was all to the point. No, it certainly wasn't soppy; and yet—and yet . . . Well, it wasn't very necessary, either.

Is that, then, the definition? Not at all. The necessity for love-letters hinges on far more than their contents. At the right phase the mere fact that the beloved hand has traced a few stumbling and even ill-spelt words may be all that another party requires. A very blot can be charged with significance. They are not news bulletins. They are tokens. Like flowers; and like flowers they fade. They are cheaper, of course; except, occasionally, when they fall into the wrong hands. But——

This is getting too deep. There is an expression, and not a particularly pleasant one, about playing with fire. Paul was no pyromaniac. Bianca, on all the evidence up to this point, was very far from being dangerously inflammable. Yet, if rubbing two 'sticks together can, as is sometimes claimed, ultimately result in a conflagration, then passing a pen over a sheet of paper can have its effect, too. Not at once, perhaps. But there is a risk all the same. If not for the recipient, then unquestionably for the writer.

At the moment, however, achievement was the word. That's that, thought Paul. It had taken a good deal out of him, and out of the stationery rack, but his main feeling, to be quite frank, was more that of a schoolboy who has just finished an essay than that of a love-sick young man. Such, one fears—and though, of course, twopence-halfpenny a shot is no great help—has become rather a common view of correspondence.

He felt released, though it was he himself and no one else who had set the task. He reached for an envelope. Folded, inserted, licked, thumped, and dashed off the address. Then he rose— it is to be feared, also, that he forgot to switch off the lamp—and though just at first he seemed to hobble rather than to walk, and with a bent back (due, of course, to the strange attitude in which he had won his great fight), he was again erect as he passed into the hall.

Here, for it would also seem that he had either forgotten the book of stamps, too, or still regarded it, for some reason, as sacred, he bought a solitary blue stamp from the porter. And licked again. And posted quickly, almost as if someone were going to try and stop him. Looked alarmed. Looked relieved, or at least fatalistic. Glanced at the telephone boxes, which reminded him for a moment of his cousin Rodney. And thus, resuming his hat and coat, left the premises and descended steps into the street.

Still cold here. Still gloomy. But he had still kept his pledge. At least that was now off his mind. A little air, then, and exercise, in this grey, sombre city. Homewards, since he still lacked any other engagement or occupation. A pipe, perhaps. A book, it might be. A cup of tea presently, even if this did mean listening to Spilsby on the subject of football again. And then—well, Sundays were dull, of course. Particularly in this weather. But one looked forward to them, even if one looked forward to Mondays as well. They were a sort of change, a sort of break, after all.

Thus, Civilised Man, or one example of the species, wandered away through some empty streets, paused once or twice to gaze into shop windows, turned corners, and was passing up Berkeley Street; when a car, necessarily proceeding in the other direction, not only braked in a manner which the prospective owner of a

Porchester Leveret thought rather exceptionable, but tooted, rhythmically and impertinently, as well.

So he glared at it. And then, for a very good reason, he stopped glaring. There you are, he had just time to reflect. One thinks of someone, and then, bless my soul, as long as it isn't the least important, one sort of conjures them out of space. Rather useful, if one could control it. The tiniest pang. And then: "Hullo, Roddie. Good lord!"

"Same to you," said his cousin Rodney, with his head out of the window. He was looking fit, as he always did, though he was in an extraordinarily dirty raincoat. As for the car, well, of course one hadn't recognised it; for though he wasn't in the business, or not strictly speaking, it seemed—yes, there were the trade plates—that he could always lay his hands on something large and powerful, like himself. And on petrol, it was to be imagined, as well.

"I spotted you mooning along," he had just added. "What's the trouble? Thick night with the boys?"

Paul smiled this one off; for of course it was just a joke. But mooning? Was that true? The smile ebbed.

"Yes," resumed his cousin. "Here he comes, I said to myself. The great Paul. The Brain. The leery old fish. Thinking in millions, I bet. I'll make him jump."

He laughed. And Paul laughed. There was no one like Roddie. And of course he was only pulling his leg.

"Like a lift?" he went on. "Or are you leaving cards on the Duchess?"

"No. Look here—come along and have some tea."

Company; that's what I want. I wasn't mooning, but I—I *can't* be alone.

"Or are you too busy?"

"I'm always busy," said Roddie. "Hop in. And don't bleat. You'll get over the shock."

He laughed again. He was a wonder. A marvellous chap. Of course he ragged one; he always had. But this was splendid.

"Right," said Rodney Sunderland, as his admirer got in. "Still at the old stand, I take it?"

"Yes."

"Off we go, then."

And indeed they went off. Necessarily again, or at first, in the wrong direction. But then they turned, on two wheels, apparently.

Turned once more, in the same manner. And thus, with an illusion that the engine itself was trying to burst loose, yet never, in fact, for all its passionate throbbing, with the slightest danger to anyone, they shot gloriously and briefly to their goal.

"Nice bus, this," said Roddie.

"Yes. Whose is it?"

"A bloke's. But it far prefers me. There you are, then, my beauty." He got out, and for a moment, as he patted the bonnet, was like an Arab with his favourite steed. "Shan't be long, old girl—and mind you frighten all the little boys away. Is the lift working?"

"Well, it was this morning."

"Good. My weary limbs have rather had it. Did some reffing yesterday—far too old, of course, but the workers wished it. Sent five chaps off. Blew myself hoarse. Great game. Battle, murder, and sudden death. Fixed a draw all right, and they gave me three cheers. But the limbs—well, they aren't what they were."

Paul interpreted as they rose. It seemed clear that in addition to working harder than most workers, and sitting up all night, very likely, over business and technical detail, his cousin Rodney had then devoted a Saturday afternoon to their health—yes, and moral well-being. The truth, probably, was that he had sent one chap off; or two, so as to be strictly fair. The truth, if it came to that, was that, though a couple of years older, he was a mass of muscle and never felt tired.

But the truth, also, without doubt, was that he had received the three cheers. He would. He deserved them, if anyone did. This was fine. It didn't so much dismiss the memory of Miss Brown, for this was an effect that had least temporarily been produced already, as establish life as a medium for men. And for relations. If Miss Brown had been the pursuer—but she wasn't—she would certainly have been up against this. Part of the clan had just met. Nothing else had a chance.

"Or whisky?" said Paul, in this mood.

"What?" They were in the flat now. "Good heavens, no. A nice cup of char—presently—" the raincoat, which now revealed an almost equally shabby sheepskin lining, was hurled on the floor, with a hat and a long scarf—"but I don't start boozing at this time of day. Do you?"

"No." And perhaps just as well. For a glance at the sideboard

had just shown again that the bottle was curiously, if not sus-
piciously, low. Blast Spilsby. Never mind. He's not bad, in a way.
It's those home wins, I suppose, that got him down. "Cigarette?"

"Got one, thanks," said Roddie. It was alight, too. He was
the type that inhales to somewhere in the region of the ankles, and
then fills the whole room with a cloud. He did this now. Even
James I couldn't have believed that there was any smoke left in
him. He also dropped into an arm-chair; thirteen stone with one
crash. But it survived. That is to say there was a kind of hollow in
it already, but it had withstood this sort of impact for many
years.

"Well?" he said. "Let's have the dirt, then."

Paul supplied it, understanding that this was an inquiry about
the clan. Roddie listened, and supplied comments, or views of his
own. They passed to wider affairs. To the state of business—Roddie,
it appeared, was still in touch with the double-barrelled tycoon
(whose actual name, nevertheless, remained as misty in Paul's
mind as before), and they were making a lot of money, on paper.
Nowhere else, though, he said; which brought both cousins to the
state of the State.

Perhaps they were being profound. Perhaps they were talking
tosh. Paul wasn't quite sure. He wondered—(he had rung for Spilsby
some time ago, they had both suffered his loquacity for a few
minutes, and were now having tea)—if other fellows suddenly
speculated at such moments on the mystery of existence. On whether
they were really grown-up or not. On whether they weren't just
pretending the whole time. On whether they were really here; or
even alive.

On the other hand, this sort of meeting—casual and unplanned
—with one of his favourite relations was certainly just what he
liked. There ought, in fact, to be something corresponding to a
fixing solution (his mind shot back for an instant to a cupboard
under the stairs at Grannie's, where he had once spent hours messing
about with bits of film), so that pleasanter moments weren't lost.
A bit complicated, perhaps. The other chap might object. After
all—no, wait a second . . .

He was still talking and listening, but there was another teaser
as well. A little speck, somewhere on the edge of his mind, kept
dancing about. Advancing. Retreating. Refusing to stay still.
Maddening, because there was obviously a link and a cause, and
the last thing he wanted was to become inattentive. But if it

wouldn't leave him alone, he *must* settle its hash. Not that it was important. But it might be. Or it seemed to think it was. He kept casting back. He tried to drive it out. It bobbed up on the other side, and was as intangible as ever. Dash!

"—could show you," his cousin Roddie was saying, "if you've got some graph-paper, old boy."

Graph-paper? Well, of course not. But he must have missed a good deal. And though he didn't suppose that he would have understood it, anyhow, he liked hearing Roddie explain. He liked technical talk, even when he was right out of his depth. He found it stimulating. Besides, it was his duty to a guest——

The mysterious thought (thinking that it was safe) came too near, and was caught.

"Ah!" said Paul. "That's it."

"Where, old boy? In the drawer there?"

"No. Sorry. 'Fraid I haven't got any. But just remembered. Good lord! Oh, I say!"

"What is it, old stick-in-the-mud?"

"Bubbles," said Paul.

"Bubbles?" said Rodney. He leant forward. "What's she got to do with it?"

"Nothing. Nothing. Nothing at all. It was only——"

"Well?"

"We were going out, you see. And—no, it's nothing. Carry on. I—I'd forgotten——"

"Forgotten *what*?"

"Oh, leave it," said Paul. He wasn't proud of having forgotten. He didn't wish, for he knew quite well now *why* he had forgotten, to be led into any explanation of that. Risky. And misleading. He looked thoroughly disingenuous. "Go on," he said. "Didn't mean to interrupt."

"Oh," said his cousin Rodney. He looked slightly put out.

"Have some whisky," said Paul, leaping up. "Yes, come on. I'll draw the curtains. It's getting quite dark. Just a short one." He told a lie, though it was a hospitable lie, as he brandished the bottle. "There's lots more."

"Oh," said Roddie. He had risen, too. "Well, all right. P'r'aps I will. Though I ought to be shifting, you know."

"Oh, I say—don't do that. Couldn't we have dinner or something?"

Rodney Sunderland looked decidedly contemplative for a second.

"No," he said. "Sorry. I only dashed up to get a few things. I—
I really ought to get back tonight. Though I'll tell you—oh, thanks
—" he had taken the glass—"of a place where the food's not too
bad. Greek Street. Antonetti's. Remember that. Had lunch there
today, 's a matter of fact. But I must be off. Well. Down the
hatch."

He gulped.

"Ah—that's better." He grinned. "See you soon, I expect."
He looked round the room. "Pretty cosy," he said. He picked up
his coat, scarf, and hat.

"I'll come down with you," said Paul.

"All right, old fish. If you really want to."

The lift was still working. They were rather jammed together.
But though Paul was sorry this was over, he didn't seek for a special
cause. Roddie always dashed off, after all. Yet he radiated a good
deal of warm affection, and felt assured that it was being returned.
Of course, he couldn't say so, and didn't dream of saying so. But
there was only one Roddie, you know.

They went out on to the pavement.

"Brrh!" said Paul.

"Well, go in, then."

"No, no. I'll see you start."

"Nice treat for you," said Roddie. He grinned again. Any
possible idea that he had been rattled just now was obviously and
clearly absurd; though of course anyone, heaven knew, had their
worries. He looked rather rakish, with his hat on one side. But
gloriously dependable, too.

He doubled up, and got in. He switched on his lights. He fiddled
and twiddled, and the engine—aware of his virtuosity, no doubt—
began rumbling, and then thundering, as though it were mid-
summer. "Off we pip!" he yelled. And off they pipped. Paul shivered,
and returned to the lift. In another minute he was back in his
warm room.

But again, it must be admitted, he had forgotten all about
Miss Vaughan. For the prick of conscience, though sharp enough
at the time, and, as some might believe, even having its effect on
another living organism, was wiped out as he stared at his own
glass. He put it down, untasted. It was his cousin's word "cosy"—
however inappropriate to this dreary and un-home-like apartment—
that, boring its way inward, had just reached the nerve.

For it was someone else's word, too. "It would be cosy," she had said, in allusion to a certain plan. But it wasn't the least cosy here. This was Sunday evening, of course, when all spirits are at their lowest. But he *knew* what was wrong now. That letter, of course. He couldn't have made a more ghastly mistake.

5

THE small, naked, winged god who goes flying around loosing off shafts—not all of which, as there is some evidence in this record, are immediately recognised or identified by the victims—has, or so it sometimes seems, another occupation as well.

It is also his custom, for he at least takes no rest, to fly back after a while—any delay may be explained by the vast number of his engagements—to examine the effects of the wound. If he thinks it is healing, he doesn't waste a second arrow. He appears to think, and we should be the last to say that he is wrong, that one is quite enough at a time.

But if he suspects any recovery, he gives the first one a twist; often with the utmost ingenuity, too. Instances will suggest themselves to all who have been pierced. There is indeed no limit to the agencies that he employs. On the other hand, in making use of Mr. Kettleworth, Paul's dentist, he at least showed that, whatever his age—and despite his aspect he is in fact anything but young—he was still resourceful, quick-witted, and alert.

He knew, for example, or so one can only suppose, that Paul was due for periodic inspection. He had noticed also, it is to be imagined, that, though distinctly depressed on that Sunday evening, he was better on Monday—owing to business, no doubt; that on Tuesday and Wednesday he was busier still—so busy, in fact, that on both evenings he was confabulating with a partner, at the partner's residence, until about half-past eleven; and that on Thursday, in consequence, which was the date of the appointment, the world hardly irked him at all.

This wouldn't do. It was a challenge that was accepted at once. Off flew the small, winged, naked god. Made his plans; and continued his flight. The result was that Mr. Kettleworth, though usually very punctual, kept Paul waiting. That others were waiting, too. That they had bagged all the best papers. And that Paul, though for a long time he hesitated to sink so low, finally picked up a copy of a periodical called *Style*—it was of course the issue of the previous September—fluttered the pages in a manly and contemptuous manner; and received a considerable shock.

It was Bianca. There was no question. She had been photographed—from about ground-level, apparently—in an empty street, in one of Mr. Willoughby's little numbers. Her name wasn't supplied, but Mr. Willoughby's was. Paul gasped. It wasn't so much that he had been feeling safe here. It was more that danger —for he possessed a most admirable set of teeth—hadn't occurred to him.

Yet suddenly, in this ugly mock-dining-room, surrounded by silent strangers, at about five o'clock on a Thursday afternoon, he was conscious of such a violent psychological twinge that it was all he could do not to get up and rush out.

However, he didn't. He had a conscience. He appeared to subside. Yet the twinge became several twinges. As he was summoned to the presence, took his seat, opened his mouth, and was again informed—though he barely seemed to take this in—that even Mr. Kettleworth could find nothing to do there, he still saw that picture; was much moved by those ankles—for they had withstood even the angle of the camera; detested Mr. Willoughby; was appalled that any girl should be subjected to such treatment, so that any dashed, blasted person could, as it were, stare at her; was horrified by a profession that laid her open to this indignity; and still more horrified at his own unaccountable inaction.

To abandon mythology, and put it all in a fresh way, the line on another graph that represented attraction once more, at this point, crossed the line representing resistance. He left the chair, and Mr. Kettleworth, and Mr. Kettleworth's secretary. He went straight to the club. It didn't occur to him—and why should it?— that another effect of his appointment was that Miss Thriplow caught an earlier and much more interesting train.

But he step-danced by the tape-machine, and sat down and got up, and glanced at newspapers and flung them away, until at last enough time (or so he hoped) had elapsed. And then he bolted into a telephone box, without a thought, on this occasion, of his cousin Rodney, and put in pennies, and dialled, and held his breath.

He heard the ringing tone. There was no answer. She was out. He couldn't bear it. On the brink of collapse, he heard her voice.

In a flash—though of course he should have been getting used to this now—he was perfectly steady again.

"I say, Bianca——"

"Hullo—is that David?"

At the moment, he took even this in his stride.

"No, it isn't," he said. "It's Paul. I say——"

"Oh, Paul—yes. I never thanked you for your letter-——"

"Good heavens, of course not!" But he was delighted that he had written. "No, the point is I've been a bit busy——"

"Oh, what a shame!"

"—but I think it's about time—well, I mean, you did say the other night— Well, I was just thinking——"

He nearly faltered after all, but she came to his aid.

"Oh yes, Paul—of course. How nice of you to ring up! Shall we fix something? Is that it? I mean, here?"

"Ug," said Paul; but as he said "Yes" in the same breath, it was all right. And still more so, perhaps, as he added "Please."

He heard the ripple or gurgle. "Well, just a moment," she went on. "I must think. I must look." But it *was* only a moment. Here she came. "Paul?"

"Yes—hullo?"

"Would tomorrow be any use? Or is that too-——"

"Fine!" said Paul. One might have thought he spent his life ringing up young women, and asking himself to dinner. He couldn't help admiring though he was a little surprised at his own tone. "Friday," he added, so as to remove any doubt. "Oh—" for it was all so simple that he had nearly rung off—"what time?"

"Any time you like," said the obliging Bianca. "Half-past seven? A quarter to eight?"

"Right," said Paul. "That'll be grand."

"And mind you come up my ladder."

"Your— Oh yes; of course." He remembered it all. Outside stair. "I'll be there. Well—till then!"

He was so carefree that it is just possible he was a little abrupt in clearing the line. But it was all right. He knew just where he stood. Not, that is to say, in a telephone-box—though he knew this, too, and was now examining the directory—but on a solid, twentieth-century basis of friendship. For it was the era of freedom (what on earth made him think that?), and though some people, no doubt, rather overstepped the mark, there was of course nothing of the sort in this case.

He was right, too. Miss Brown was as good as she looked. Even if she were also on friendly terms—subject, apparently, to occasional argument—with young men called Brian, Jock, Godfrey, and now David as well, she had spoken the truth when she said she could manage them. Nor was she even opposed (*cf.* Dorothea and Ariadne) to having friends of her own sex. As Paul had said, she was a jolly nice girl.

He still thought so, too, as he popped in more pennies, and dialled another number on the same exchange. *Brr-brr*, went the instrument, several times. And then *Brr*. And another voice said: "Hullo?" Another woman's voice, too; but as there had been a fifty per cent. chance of this, he wasn't seriously set back.

"Hullo," he retorted. "I say, is that—" He remembered, just in time, that he must *not* call her Mrs. Parkinson. "Is that Lulu? Is the old boy around?"

"Someone for you," said the voice, turning aside. "I think it's Paul."

"Yes, it is," said Paul, who could now also hear what at first he took to be a parakeet, but then realised was Miss Philomel Parkinson. And then Parky's voice came along.

"Hullo?" it said. "Do you want bailing out, or something?"

"Not exactly," said Paul. "But I thought perhaps you could tell me something. I—I thought it might be in your line." There was a faint click here, which meant that Mrs. Parkinson was now upstairs in her bedroom, where it was her custom, when she was the least interested, to listen in. As she still had Philomel on her lap, there was also the parakeet noise. But Paul was forging ahead.

"—other evening," he was saying. "That girl I met. Bianca Brown, you know." He blushed slightly, but telephones don't transmit this. "I was just wondering . . ."

"Yes? Go on, old man."

"Oh, Paul!" said Lulu Parkinson. "Are you *still* seeing her home? I wondered what had happened to you both."

"No," said Paul. "I'm not. But—well, *you* introduced me——"

"Do you want the Complaints Department?"

"No, I don't!"

"I should think not."

"But she says her father wrote poems. I feel perhaps I ought to know about 'em. Do you—Parky—do you know who he was?"

"No," said Parky.

"I do," said Lulu. "Oh, Philomel—*please*! Do you want to read them? I don't think you can."

"Why not?"

"Too grown-up," suggested Parky.

"Oh, do lay off, darling. I know *all* the answers. Paul?"

"Yes?"

"They're out of print. I don't *think* they were a great success. But she's awfully proud of him. Oh yes—and something else. Are you there?"

"Yes—go on."

"I've just remembered. She told me. Paul—she's awfully sweet, don't you think?"

"Don't tease the poor lad," said Parky.

"I will if I like. And—Paul—I've got a bone to pick with you, in a second. But she told me—this isn't the bone—that he was really called Alfred Brown——"

"Oh yes?"

"—but when his poems were printed—and I've got an awful sort of feeling he paid for it——"

"Shocking!" said Parky. "I wish he'd paid *me*."

"—his handwriting was so extraordinary—I should say he was rather a pet, you know, but a bit—well——"

"Iiggley-wiggley?" suggested Parky. "Four-ducks-on-a-pond, God-wot?"

"Well, yes. I sort of feel it. And it all adds up. Because it seems— oh, Paul, I'm not laughing at *her*; I think she's *sweet*—but his writing was so awful that the printer thought it was 'Alured.' So he printed it like that. And he liked it so much—can you imagine it?—Alfred, I mean—that he took it over. So if you want to go hunting in the Charing Cross Road——"

"Oh no," said Paul, though he had just thought he might.

"Did you know he was killed in an air-raid?"

"Good lord!" said Paul. He was shaking like a leaf. He had seen death on all sides, but only in battles. This was ghastly!

"Yes," said Lulu. "In a shelter. Near here. She wasn't there. She was at the Post, she said. She thought he was in bed, and— Oh, Paul, perhaps I oughtn't to have told you."

"I—I don't see why not." Poor *child*, he thought.

"It's the queues," said Lulu. "I didn't *ask*, but——"

"My wife," said Parky, from downstairs, "worms everything out of everyone in three minutes, you know. She's got charm."

"Shut up!" said the wife.

Paul was wondering if anything had been wormed out of himself. But what was there to worm—except pity?

"And now for the bone!"

"Oh. Yes. I say—what have I done?"

"You broke a glass here," said Lulu. "No, darling, be quiet. And you, too." This seemed to be for Parky. "Paul's a friend. Paul—did you hear me?"

"Oh, Lulu, dry up!" said her partner.

"I shan't. Paul—do you know whose glass it was?"

"No. But I owned up. Wa-was it valuable?"

"I don't think so. Or not originally. But it was one of a set. We'd just borrowed it. It belonged to Mrs. Girlie." Or this was how the name still sounded to Paul, as he recalled Mrs. Gourlay herself. "And—no, Rex, pipe down!—*she* took it all right. I mean, she only came in about six times to say it didn't matter. But—Oh, darling, *you* tell him."

"Curious case," said Parky, now obeying at once. "The old guv'ner keeps coming, in too. Never been such a business. I don't, honestly, know why they do it all here. Perhaps they're shy. But it's still going on. He used to know her, apparently—before we were all born. And lord knows what he's doing in the law-courts these days, because he spends all his time trying to match it. The glass, I mean. Your glass, old boy. Or the one you smashed. She's a widow, you see. Can you beat it!"

Extraordinary. At that age. Unless he had quite missed the point. "How—how do you spell it?" Paul asked.

"How do I spell 'glass', old boy? I say, are you all right?"

"No. I mean, yes. I mean, Mrs——"

"Oh!" Parky spelt, and one mystery was solved. But this was the bone.

"I—I couldn't help it," said Paul.

Loud, long, unanimous laughter from the Parkinson telephone and its extension. A further background of laughter, from the elder children, perhaps. Fresh, psittacine squeaks from the baby. And then, through it all, dear old Parky again.

"Good lord," he was saying, "*we* don't mind—do we, Lulu? Do him good. Cheer him up. *We* don't care."

H

"Besides," said Lulu, "if they get married, we might ask for her refrigerator."

"But we should never have got it if old Paul hadn't been so clumsy." Or, alternatively, it is just possible, if old Paul hadn't seen a vision; so that infection set off then and there. "The only trouble, old chap, is they're still a bit slow. Can't you come round and smash something else?"

More laughter. Reckless, yet admirable laughter. Bless the Parkys. This might mean ruin. Or, perhaps not, if the old girl was rich, too. Yet, in either case, as Paul knew, they would still be the same. So would he, though this point didn't strike him. For as he emerged from the box, with what might almost be described as a clamjamfry of emotions in his soul, he still had it fixed in his own extraordinary head that Mrs. Parkinson didn't really much like him.

That she couldn't, in fact; not merely because he himself lacked charm, but because he had known her husband so very much longer. In his view, this was axiomatic. It was why he had avoided a direct reply to old Parky's invitation. Or, at least, largely why; for it was also true that he didn't wish to be re-examined, and still less to be cross-examined, on his present relationship with Bianca.

He felt, though, as he shook his head (this was sorrow for the dead past) and then brightened (because he would be seeing her tomorrow), that he had alluded to it both naturally and discreetly. After all, he had only asked what anyone might have asked. Not, of course—(Poor *child!* And she'd never told him. But he was glad he knew)—that he had anything on earth to conceal.

6

ABOUT twenty-four-and-a-half hours later, Paul Sunderland alighted from an omnibus in the King's Road, and though it was dark and drizzling, and though he knew little about Chelsea, he had consulted a map at the Junior Corinthian to such purpose that he found his way without asking it once.

Here he was, in fact; and this was the house. He was a trifle early, owing to having allowed for a slower bus, loss of memory, and other possible misadventures; so that again he must prowl for a while. This also gave him time to reflect on another point. The flowers he had bought—hardly cheap, yet not showy—on an impulse that had since faded out.

The notion had been that it would be a polite thing to do. A little tribute; for girls, he understood, were supposed to like flowers; and a slight return for the hospitality that he was to receive. Owing, however, to the hour when shops close, and to the chance that they might be sold out in the last phase, he had made his purchase at lunch-time. And though Miss Thriplow had said nothing, to his considerable relief, not only had he been acutely conscious of them all afternoon, but on returning to his flat he, and they, had been spotted by Spilsby.

So there they still were, in a jug, on his table. He had, indeed, asked for the jug. They'll need water, he had thought. But with Spilsby looking on, he had been too proud, sensitive, or imbecile to attend to this himself. And Spilsby, who, but for this weather, would almost certainly have been out, had made comments. He had talked so much, in fact, about flowers in general, these flowers in particular, and how they improved the room, that it had somehow become impossible to remove them.

Or it would rouse suspicion if one did, and that couldn't be faced. Sixteen bob down the drain, in other words. And yet, on the other hand, perhaps Providence was right; for of course it would be shocking if he alarmed her. She might have thought, for example, that they possessed more significance than they did. He might have broken another of her rules. So, perhaps, though he had rather counted on her face lighting up, it was better to be cautious, and appear mean.

Or he could try later on. Yes, that was an idea. In fact, so far as he could make out now, he had more or less *got* to go on buying flowers, in order to neutralise Spilsby. This was very important. He had had a narrow escape. It just showed what an impulse could do.

And yet—oh, good lord, where had he got to now? He was going to be late. He rushed back. He took the wrong route. He had to ask, after all, where he was. But he was told—which is unusual—and was directed as well. He returned. He saw the outside stairway, which was at the side of the house. He went plunging and panting up it. He rang.

The door was opened by a complete stranger, but he recovered almost at once. For though a much better representative of the species than Mrs. Bangham—or, if it comes to that, than the Parkinsons' Mrs. Bodger and his cousin Rhoda's alleged crone— she was clearly what is known as a Woman. He was rather pleased, oddly enough. He had been a little worried all day. Not that he himself, and still less Bianca, would lose their heads if they happened to be alone. But other chaps might. And that she asked other chaps seemed clear; or she wouldn't have asked him.

However, this was all right. He smiled, and regained his breath.

"Miss Brown?"

"Yes, sir. Will you come in?"

"Oh. Thank you." And in he came; hat in hand, and undoing his coat.

"Paul? Is that you?"

"That's right," he called back.

"Oh—good. I shan't be a moment. Mrs. Blankett?"

"Yes, miss?"

"Could you help me a second?"

"Excuse me, sir." Mrs. Blankett disappeared towards a sizzling sound, so that it was left to Paul to shut the front door. He did this, with another queer feeling of gratification; though in fact it was a very trifling service. Then he looked round the miniature landing for a hook or a chair. Could see neither. Saw a door, though, which suggested a cupboard. Tried to open it. Failed. And was again twisting the knob, when his hostess herself came along.

"Paul!" she said. "What are you doing? That goes down to the Pottings. Did you think——"

"Oh!" said Paul. "Oh, hullo."

The second ejaculation was to cover the first. He hadn't thought what she would be wearing, and some people might say that a plastic apron over a house-coat was hardly worthy of a Willoughby girl. Yet this was the first time that he had seen her in a dress down to the ground. And the little apron not only spoke of domesticity— which to bachelors has a certain strange if not always permanent charm—but of intimacy, somehow, as well.

Furthermore, though what he had so far seen of her quarters seemed slightly shabby, she herself looked so particularly fresh. Like a flower, he thought, poetically; and was suddenly reminded of his purchase. Dash! Why on earth hadn't he stuck to his harmless plan?

"The Pottings?" he was saying, vaguely.

"Yes. My tenants. Downstairs. Didn't I tell you? He's a civil servant."

"Oh," said Paul. And other civil servants may as well face the fact—though of course they have their compensations—that he took no further interest in the Pottings. "Shall I—ah——"

"Oh, put them anywhere. Here—I'll take them." His coat and hat, of course. "And if you'll just wait two minutes—in there . . ."

An aposiopesis. But she was cooking. He quite understood. He complied with her counsel, and found himself in a room with two windows—but of course the curtains were drawn—a gas-fire, a sofa, a selection of chairs, a gate-leg table laid for a dinner, book-shelves, a small upright piano, and a number of photographs and pictures. The general effect was green, on the whole, and nothing looked new, though it was all clean. It looked lived-in; far more so, he felt, than his own larger room. More feminine, too, as might of course be expected. But not the least disconcertingly so.

No cushions with fringes. Rather plain lamp-shades. Complete absence of the kind of article that one tripped over or broke. Yet cosy—the word returned; not bleak or austere. Could one, he wondered, reconstruct her from this? But then of course he hardly knew her. He had only met her four times. How could he tell? How could he judge? Very queer.

He began prowling again, perhaps in search of more evidence. He even pried, in a sense, though he didn't touch. He examined the music on the piano. So far as he could see, it was of all sorts. He raked a bookshelf with his eyes, and with the same result. Possibly, if he crouched—but, of course, he mustn't do that—he might come on her father's poems. Um. . . . He felt intrusive. A little shattered again. He withdrew. He was gazing at a framed photograph.

It looked thoughtful, self-conscious, ineffective, and gentle. Yet though it was of a man, and not even a young man at that, there was a most curious resemblance to——

Lord! It was the poet. He *knew* it was the poet; just as he knew, in the same flash, that he had written poems here. It was *his* room, in fact, with his furniture, and books, and green curtains. It was explained. She had kept it unaltered, of course. On purpose? Not necessarily. She was pious, but she wasn't rich. She had just left things. Perhaps that was all.

"Dreadful," he murmured, and again turned aside. And then suddenly—and though if the room had been brighter he must have seen this before—he recoiled with another sharp shock. That picture. My hat! And that other one, too. And that small one— good heavens, what daubs! The paint in thick lumps, except, here and there, where the canvas showed through. Crude and raw. Badly drawn, like the work of a child. Representing, in the first case, so far as he could make out, an unmade bed. In the second, either a haystack (but it was mauve) or a loaf. And in the third, with a defiance of perspective that really went beyond all bounds, the yet unmistakable chimneys of the Lots Road power-station.

Whose taste, then, was this? Her father's? Her own? He stepped back, in the faint hope that they might look better from further off. He heard a sound. She was coming in, with a little tray.

"Hullo," she was saying. "Were you looking at the pictures?"

"Y—yes. Ah—" He was baffled.

"They're Dorothea's. I mean, she did them—though they're mine now, of course. Do you like them?"

He must obviously lie.

"Well," he set off, "of course I don't know an awful lot about——"

She was laughing.

"Poor Paul. What a shame! You don't like them at all. All right—say so."

"Well—do you?"

"I liked *her*," said Bianca. "And she gave them to me, you see. And there'd be marks if I took them down. And they're *supposed* to be good. I mean, truthfully, she's got *quite* a reputation. Well?"

Loyalty, thought Paul. The greatest virtue of all. He couldn't and mustn't besmirch it.

He drew in a breath.

"But, of course—here, Paul; here's your drink—she was a skunk to get married."

He took the drink. He was still baffled; or baffled again. Loyalty, in fact, or female loyalty, seemed extraordinarily confusing. He suddenly wondered if Dorothea had pinched Mr. Hopgrove, in the sense that he had been Bianca's chap first. He didn't like this idea. He would prefer it to be wrong. Perhaps it was. Though of course he couldn't ask.

"Good luck!"

"Oh—sorry. Good luck!" He sipped. "I say—this is all rather fun."

"Well," said his hostess, "it *was* my turn." She whipped off the apron, and threw it on a chair; looking even lovelier, if possible, without it. "That was a sign," she explained. "Mrs. Blankett's going to wait on us—or at least she's going to bring the things in. She doesn't always, of course; but she's insisting tonight. I think—" she picked up her little glass again—"you've made rather a hit."

"I say—have I really?" He was enormously pleased.

"'M-h'm," said Bianca. "And she's terribly particular. She doesn't like some of my friends at all."

"No?"

"No. She doesn't say it, but I can tell. And of course I'm frightfully lucky to have her. Mr. Blankett's a postman."

"Is that a help, too?"

"Oh, Paul, you are funny. Of course not. But they're *really* nice people. That's what I mean. I'd trust her—I'd trust her with *anything*."

"I see," said Paul. He was impressed. And a little envious. Not of Bianca, but of Mrs. Blankett, of course. However, as he could hardly raise the subject of his own reliability, as in no circumstances could he hope to take over her job, and as she was now coming into the room, he left it at that.

Yet it seemed, though he had been a fool (as he now saw) over those flowers, that he, too, was still lucky. No strain of any kind, now that he was actually here. He felt at home; that was it. Words came easily, but with no sense that he was talking too much. The slight strangeness of being alone with her like this had existed only in his prophetic imagination; which had been wrong again, as it invariably was.

For she was exactly the same. *She* didn't think it odd. And it wasn't; or not in that way. It was just rather fun. Or great fun, in fact. It was doing him good, and doing no one the least harm. He was aware, because he wasn't blind, that she was a feast for the eye. But whereas some girls, who weren't nearly so pretty, were always conscious of their looks—or at least made one think so—she just had them; without any fuss.

So he was soothed, as he talked. And soothed again, as he ate. And pleased once more that although the main course was certainly delicious—(Clever girl, he thought; she was quite right about her cooking)—she hadn't gone a bust over the rest. That would have been awkward. He would have worried that she was spending too much. But she hadn't; any more (another very good point) than she now referred to the topic of food.

Anyone else, he reflected, would either have bragged or apologised. But not Bianca. She wasn't like that. It struck him that she was an exceptionally sensible and level-headed girl. He began to wonder if she had any faults.

He decided that she hadn't, but he was still perfectly calm. It was just rather interesting again.

She left him once or twice, to assist, or so he gathered, with the dishing-up. On each occasion he prepared to think, about her background and life. And on each occasion he failed, or fell into a slight trance, so that when she returned he was at just the same stage. He bounced up, too, of course, and affected to help. But there was precious little, in fact, for him to do.

"No need to be so polite," she said, once; "or not tonight. Well, next time, perhaps, I'll make you wash-up. In fact, you'll have to, if Mrs. Blankett's not here. But this evening you're lucky. She's even going to do the coffee. And she *can*, Paul. She's awfully good."

Next time. She had said that. And lucky. Quite true. It was just what he had been thinking himself.

"Does she come on Sundays?" he asked suddenly, and for no very clear reason.

"No. Only week-days. And in the mornings, as a rule. In fact, sometimes I don't see her for days."

"But who gets your breakfast?"

"I do, of course. Only there is one thing about my job. I don't have to be very early."

"I see." Was this a flaw? Not the least. He was glad. But he still looked as if he hadn't quite done.

"What is it?" she asked.

It came out. "Do you mean you're absolutely alone here at night?"

"Of course."

"But supposing . . ."

"Supposing what?"

"You were ill?"

"Oh, well—touch wood—that's not likely to happen. I've got a telephone, after all. There's Mrs. Potting downstairs—though as a matter of fact I don't much want her up. And, besides, I've only been alone for about a couple of months——"

"Three," said Paul.

"How do you know? Oh, of course, I told you. And sooner or later . . ."

"Ariadne?" he suggested.

"Did I tell you that, too?"

"Yes. On the bus."

"Well, perhaps. I don't know. I'm perfectly *happy* here, Paul." So am I, thought the guest. "It's only, you see——"

The telephone rang. It was bound to, of course, when it had just been mentioned, and he had forgotten this trick.

"Excuse me," she said. She went and knelt on the sofa. She looked, he suddenly thought, like a child in a long dressing-gown; though it was the attitude, perhaps, that did this. He prepared not to listen. He listened, of course.

"Oh, darling!"

He stiffened.

"Blah-blah-wah-wah," said the telephone, and a good deal more. But in the upper register, so that he immediately relaxed.

"I see, darling." Another torrent. "Very well, darling." A cascade. "Well, no; not exactly alone."

He hoped this would end it. He was rather pleased with "not exactly," though one may not exactly see why. It was hardly flattering. It even suggested that he didn't count as a real character. But it barred inquiry. Perhaps this was the point.

"——wah-wah-blah-blah——"

She was looking round at him, making a face. It expressed impatience. He smiled. She began waving her free arm with a clenched fist. The sense of intimacy was renewed, as the other voice still went on; until checked by the arrival of the coffee. He stopped listening. He was engaged in looking trustworthy, for Mrs. Blankett. He heard a click. It was over at last.

"Oh, dear!" said Bianca, wilting bonelessly for a second. "I'm so sorry, Paul. It was Ariadne."

He wasn't surprised, even if again he had overlooked a fixed law; sometimes boiled down to Talk of the Devil.

"Is she always like that?" he inquired.

"Well, yes, she is. Oh, coffee—good! And that's rather a reason— Well, what would *you* do?"

"About what? I couldn't hear."

"Oh, not that. That was only what she always does on Fridays. A message for Michael about not coming tomorrow. Not that it

matters particularly—and he daren't lose her hips. But I mean—
well, would *you* have her here?"

"No," said Paul, like a flash. But she laughed. It was all right.

"Why, you've never even *seen* her," she said.

"I know. But—" this is clever; yes, this gets me out—"I sort
of felt you didn't want her yourself."

"But she's sweet."

"Well, then, have her." Why on earth did I say that?

"And it *is* rather lonely, you know."

An extraordinary thing happened. There was a lump in Paul's
throat. He couldn't speak. But he didn't have to. She spoke first.

"Oh, I'd nearly forgotten. There—look what I've got!" It was a
packet of ten cigarettes.

He found his voice. "Oh, I say—you shouldn't have done that.
Of *course* I must smoke my own."

"But, Paul, I got them specially!"

"Well, keep 'em for someone else. I—I can't. I—Bianca——"

Clash of wills. He gave way. It was weak to give way. Yet
somehow it had been dangerous—why?—how?—to become involved in a clash. He would make this up to her, of course. And he
would take only one. But——

"Let's come over here, then," she said. "Mrs. Blankett!"

"Yes, miss?" from the offing.

"Don't wait—please—for the coffee-things; if you want to
get off."

"Oh, very good, miss." And a little later, while hostess and guest
were on either side of the gas-fire: "Good-night, miss." And even:
"Good-night, sir."

"Good-night!" they called back. Paul could hear the outer
door being shut. He was in the midst of a most interesting discussion about the Ballet, which it seemed (there had been a little
fencing on his part at first) Bianca found as pointless as he did.
This can be almost as great a link as the other extreme, and no less
so where there is a joint love of music. Or no less so, again, where
the other party is so graceful that she could quite clearly knock
spots off a ballerina.

Yet he heard the latch click, and knew what it meant. That
they were alone now, even more than before. It didn't make him
stop talking, for it was so easy to talk. Moreover, in the middle
of this century of social freedom, it was probably happening all
over the place. He wasn't tempted to move nearer; or further away,

if it comes to that. But at the same time he rather resented the idea
that it was a custom. He hoped it wasn't. Though he might prefer
not to know.

Naturally, he didn't ask. It never occurred to him to ask.
He drove the thought into a distant corner of his mind. Presently,
it might be, it would come out again. But meanwhile, he was comfortable, well-fed, and warm; and it was still surprisingly easy
to talk.

Except, of course, when the telephone-bell rang. It did this
several times. "Oh, bother!" she would say, as she reached for the
instrument. "I'm *so* sorry, Paul. Yes? Hullo?"

He didn't listen inquisitively, but he still had his ears; and it
would be rather marked if he went over and got a book. Once it was
another darling, or member of her own sex; and he was prepared,
though the dialogue sounded both repetitive and obscure, for it to
last, as it did, quite a while. But twice, at least, it was a man, as
he could tell not only from the vibrations, but from her frequent
use of the chap's Christian name.

It was her habit, of course. She was always saying "Paul," and
he couldn't deny that he found this curiously pleasing. But though
informative, up to a point, when employed for other men, didn't it
perhaps imply more than it should? Rather a point; which again
it was impossible to discuss. He wasn't critical—good lord, no!
She could do what she liked. Well, of course. But he wished they
would ring off.

They did, after a bit, and she was once more utterly here. So
was he. And they weren't. Which was fine. And yet—well, who
was Philip, who seemed to be asking her out, and taking the deuce
of a time about it? Who was Dick, who had the cheek to make her
laugh? How well did she know them? And what was their game?

He looked so particularly unreceptive to humour during the
dialogue with Dick that she must have seen, for, to his shame, she
was contrite.

"Oh, Paul—I *am* sorry. It's so rude to laugh. But how *can* I tell
them to stop?"

"You can't," he said, at once. "It was only . . ."

"I know. I think the telephone's hell sometimes; don't you?"

It got me here, he thought. And it was I who was rude.

"I've got no manners," he explained. "That was all."

"Oh, Paul, I think you've got the most marvellous manners.
And Dick Sparrow—yes, that's really his name—isn't it absurd?—

is only a sort of clown. Now, where were we?" She smoothed her dress, again like a child. He was abashed. And he had been flattered. He must *not* be a lout. They went on talking, just where they had left off.

But the last interruption, which was the lengthiest of all—so lengthy, in fact, that he made the great mistake of glancing secretly at his watch, so that he knew now that he must leave in a few minutes—was also much the most disturbing. "Oh, Godfrey," she kept saying," so that he knew who this was; or at least to a certain extent. "Oh, Godfrey, please!" "Oh, Godfrey, don't!" "Oh, Godfrey, you're just *imagining* it." "Oh, Godfrey, *do* be sensible!" "Oh, Godfrey, I can't!" And only, as it seemed to Paul, at an unnecessarily late stage and after much more on the same lines: "Oh, Godfrey, go to bed. I can't go on talking. I tell you—" though in fact it was the first time she had said this—"I've *got* someone here."

This seemed to quell Godfrey. She was left saying: "Hullo?" Then she hung up, and turned to Paul, and was again contrite.

"Oh, Paul, I'm *so* sorry. But some people *are* tiresome." She wrinkled her nose. She bit her lip. "Have some beer?"

"No—honestly, thanks." What did she mean? I can't ask.

"Are you sure?"

"Yes. I ought to go off."

He stood up. He stubbed his last cigarette in the ash-tray. And suddenly he began talking again. She hadn't said: "Don't go." She had said nothing at all. But he'd been damnably offensive, whatever Godfrey's trouble was. Or hers, he felt somehow, as well. Yet he made no allusion to what he had heard. Nor to the beer. And though of course he would remember both later on, this, inexplicably, was almost the best part of the evening.

The philosophical explanation might be that it was the end. That he knew this. And was putting it off. But though he still remained standing in front of the fire, it was somehow as if he also knew that the telephone had done its worst. And because he knew this, perhaps, he was right. He ranged over a large number of topics, and so did his hostess. He learnt a lot—some of it trifling, some amusing, and some (in his own view) pathetic—in that final forty minutes. So did the girl, or she at least had the chance.

But Providence restrained him from reiterating that he was going; and when he went, he went off in a flash.

"Good lord! Past eleven. I say! I must fly. No, don't move——"

"But I've got your things."

"Oh yes, of course."

She was gone. He was on the landing. She was back, with his hat and coat. He jerked himself into the coat, and grabbed the hat.

"Enjoyed it enormously." He tugged at the front door; as it must be called, though in fact it was at the side.

"Wait a moment. I'll turn on my light."

The outside stair was illumined. He stepped forth. He turned round.

"Go in at once!" he said, masterfully. "You'll catch cold."

"Oh, Paul—do look where you're going!"

"Eh? Oh." He clutched the hand-rail. But he still seemed in haste. "Well, good-night, Bianca. Go *in*!"

"Good-night, Paul."

He dashed down the stair into the street. He looked back, and saw the light going out.

He was full of something, and as it made him scamper it can hardly have been food; though he spared a thought for her cooking as well. But he was charged with contentment; enough, he felt, to last for weeks. It was immaterial that he had said nothing about another meeting. He had come through a test, or this again was how he felt, though he couldn't possibly have described what it was. Later—not now—he might go into all that; and when he did there might be points to clear up.

But the main point, don't you see—"Hi! Taxi!" he bawled, and was lucky (but of course!) even in this; the main point—(he was sitting in the middle of the seat, which is always a great sign of mental vigour)—the main point, of *course*, was that his judgment was sound. There had been no disappointment. She was still a girl, but she was still a friend. And presently—oh, hell take those chaps who rang up!—she and he would go on being friends.

7

THIS, then, was the stage, already foreshadowed and indeed actually announced, at which it may be said that Paul Sunderland, bachelor, of the parish of St. George's, Hanover Square, achieved the relationship with Bianca Brown, spinster, of the parish of St. Luke's,

Chelsea, which he had set himself (to borrow a term from the State) as his target.

Not yet, though on our own part every effort is still being made to get there, had he or anyone else reached the fine spell in May. The evening, in fact, when he dined in her upper part (for still, even at the risk of ambiguity or amphibology, we somehow shrink from the word "maisonette") was the 18th of March; when it was anything but fine. Many easterly and north-easterly winds must still blow before Nature worked round to the spell. Not yet, indeed not by a considerable chalk, was it even summer-time in the horological sense.

Nevertheless, within a matter of four weeks and four days, he had met a young woman, he had formed certain opinions about her, he had decided that friendship was what he required, and this was now what he had gained.

By simplicity, it might be, rather than by cunning or guile. and despite patches of indecision as well. The two entities in his being hadn't always pulled together. Often enough they had been distinctly at odds. Yet one or the other, so it seems, had continued to urge him on, and it was this urging that had almost always prevailed.

Inexperience, again, had undoubtedly been a help. It was the war, one might say, that had made him like this. For though a number of chaps, not expecting to live, had become determined to love while they could, there were a few—and Paul was one—who saw the thing the other way. They wouldn't love until they had a fair chance to live.

Perhaps they didn't state it as clearly as this. Perhaps they would have been fastidious anyhow. But, consciously or not, they had put something aside; and this, again, had a double effect. For, in the first place, if you put anything aside, whether good or bad, it is rather apt to stay there. While, in the second place, it is not unlikely, if you *should* change your mind, that you will approach it with far greater power.

Paul didn't know this. It had never entered his head. He would have denied hotly that he was unusual in any way. Yet of course his seriousness and his good manners had helped him along; as far as this, in the particular case. For the girl was a little unusual, too. She had had a shock. There was a slight fixation, on account of the shock. And she was extremely attractive as well.

But love? Oh, no, please not. Not yet, if you don't mind. It spoilt things. Or such was her belief. It was lovely, of course, in poetry and all that. She was as susceptible as anyone to *Tristan und Isolde*. But look what it did. It had removed Dorothea, with whom she had been so safe and secure. And in addition to this, though *all* she wanted was to be nice to people, and meet them, and talk to them, and go about with them—for girls can't live by displaying dresses to rich women alone—as fast as such a person came into her life, he seemed to go crazy as well.

He became what she called tiresome. He had to be managed again. If she wasn't cruel—and she just couldn't be cruel—he returned to the attack. Well, not always, of course; for some of them bounced off with such violence that they at once married another girl. Which would be fine, if they didn't then seem to think they had scored. And almost say it. And make their wives think so, too.

Maddening. Never once had she wanted them back. Or not if they couldn't behave. Yet not only was there now quite a number of wives (whom otherwise she might have liked) going around with that look on their face; not only was there a quantity of young gentlemen who had become tiresome, though with whom she still (if, as they said, it was all her own fault) felt it her duty to be patient. But behind them and beyond them further ranks seemed to loom. Of men who were nice, funny, amusing, and good company, but in turn might go suddenly mad.

Friendship, in other words, with men as well as girls—for as she could never be jealous, she liked girls as much as men—was just what this curious, innocent, if possibly dangerous Bianca still wanted. So did Paul. There you were. And if they were asking a lot, at least they were after the same thing.

Again, if older, wiser, and possibly more disillusioned characters might, without exactly stating which was which, have seen in them a likeness to a spark and some loose gunpowder, they themselves were still immune from this idea. To Bianca, increasingly, Paul was the exception. While to Paul—though several of his relations had noticed how well and cheerful he was looking, and had even commented on the fact—Bianca was just a jolly nice girl.

The nicest he knew. She never teased. She never changed. She was never feminine—oh, of course he was as mad as the rest—in the less charming sense of the word. She was Bianca. Very well, she was a darling, if you like. And a great deal too good to be true. But because he loved her, though he didn't know it (this amazing young Paul), he took his colour and tone from her, too. Besides, they were his own, or in theory at least. If not, at this epoch, in fact.

He was jealous, of course, in a quiet, silent way; but there was a certain difference, after all, in their situation. He had entirely forgotten the other young women—including, one fears, even Miss Vaughan—with whom he occasionally and decorously stepped out. He disappeared from their lives as they disappeared from his mind. And not one of them, which at least suggests that he was breaking no hearts, took the trouble to force her way back.

But when he rang up Bianca—and after the 18th of March he must have averaged four or five times a week—not only was her line rather liable to be engaged (this could be dealt with by trying again), but so, all too often, was she.

"Oh, Paul, what a shame! I'm fixed up, I'm afraid. I said I'd go out with Charles Green." Or better than this: "I'm going to supper with Jessica. You remember. The one I was at school with." Or worse, much worse: "Oh, Paul—no, I can't. I've got Jimmy—" or some such name, known or unknown—"coming in for a meal."

Very different, indeed, from Paul's own cloistered life; as it had become now that he was fencing, in case Bianca should be free, with invitations from even his kinsfolk. "Could I let you know?" he had taken to saying. They didn't mind. They let it slide. They might notice if it went on. But on the other hand he quite frequently turned up. This meant, of course, that another hope had been dashed; though of this they could still see no sign.

Seldom, in fact, had he enjoyed better health; as these carriers, it is believed, often do. Furthermore, notwithstanding any technical rebuffs, there were plenty of meetings as well. There were almost bound to be, if he continued to telephone so persistently, and if she liked him, and trusted him, too. He broke into her week-ends. They went out in her little car ("Oh, Paul, your poor head again! When *are* you going to remember to double up?"), they went for walks in Battersea Park, she fed him, and he entertained her in turn.

More than once, in addition, they did what a lot of people do. Which is to say that they went into a large, dark, tobacconous building, where they sat side by side, while vast shadows performed to the accompaniment of amplified speech. All over these buildings other couples were holding hands or leaning closely together, which indeed was the main reason why they were so full. But Paul and Bianca studied the art-form without such aid. For though Paul had no more wish to be thought a prude than to be thought unusual, this just wasn't a thing that he did.

He also believed, and he was quite right, that it might annoy his companion; though he wasn't pledged to keep his eyes on the screen. Much of the art-form, in fact, slipped right past his mind; though if she laughed it was well worth the price. And this brings us round to another aspect of the phase, which was a slight or apparent modification of her rules.

He was particularly careful to say nothing about this. They were still in force. There was no doubt of that. But even if he didn't actually reckon up—and of course he didn't—what he was costing her in petrol or meals, he did his utmost to see that she didn't lose. Quietly, of course, without pointing it out. But he knew he was better off. He didn't *want* her to pay. And if he confused her a little, sometimes, or even actually prevaricated, he was still—though this, too, he would keep to himself—receiving far more than he gave.

Or *was* she confused? He was never quite sure. She was so honest, and sometimes so firm. Was it possible, then—but, again, of course he couldn't ask—that his good conduct had earned him this boon? That she realised now, though the rules must still be kept in reserve—yes, and even brought out now and then—that with a friend they could be sometimes relaxed?

He wondered.

"There you are, Paul. Three-and-sixpence. That's right, isn't it?"

"Yes, of course. Thanks." He took it, what's more.

For this had become his own rule. Whatever he felt—and he felt pretty awful sometimes—he must never refuse such an offer of cash. He wasn't afraid of her. Not the least. He was only afraid that, if he argued, she might remember some of the occasions when he had got away with a spot of bluff. If he were exposed, she might not trust him any more. Unless, of course, which would be much simpler, she did. . . .

There was something else which he didn't entirely think out, though that isn't to say that he failed to observe it. From the very outset, though he had laughed and been momentarily amused, he had never really much cared for the name George. For her car, that is to say. It was whimsical, he felt. And she wasn't. She was literal, and straight.

At first, it was true, he had fallen in with the terminology. It had seemed to bring him closer at the time. But then he had dropped it. It wasn't his line. And now she had as good as abandoned it, too.

A very interesting point. He had never mentioned his distaste.
That would have been brutal, and horribly rude. Yet two possibilities
suggested themselves. That she was sensitive; but he knew this;
think of her tears about his parents. Or that he, Paul, had more
personality than he had supposed.

Or *had* he been rude? What a ghastly thought. Was it his duty
to say "George" again?

No. Because he couldn't. Or not naturally now. Besides, there
was a little tremor at the back of his mind. If he had altered her
even slightly, it had been damnable nerve. And quite unnecessary.
Yet if he *had*, it was rather thrilling.

He felt guilty. Triumphant. Ashamed of himself. It never
struck him, however, as it might have struck someone else, that
there was even a third possibility. That Time and Paul Sunderland
were dulling a blow. That "George" was a symbolic reminder of the
dead poet. That as it receded, so did some of his power.

There is no evidence, however, that this had occurred to Bianca.
She still spoke of him, fondly, from time to time. And why not?
Even if he was being overtaken—and there was no other sign—she
had still adored him, and nothing could change that.

·   ·   ·   ·   ·

Sometimes, again, Paul encountered her other friends. It
couldn't be helped, and was almost bound to arise. They sprang up
in a restaurant, in the streets, in the Park—("Hullo, B!" from the
men, and "Hullo, darling!", or almost always, from the girls, in a
rough proportion of five to three)—and he raised his hat and, if
they were still strangers, was introduced.

Some looked tougher than others, though all were polite. They
were classless, but then that goes for everyone these days; or is
supposed to, and perhaps does if they are young. Some paused, and
made dates. Some didn't, which he preferred. Thumb-nail bio-
graphies, generally supplied by his companion when they withdrew,
were apt to conclude "but she's awfully sweet" in the case of the
girls; and "he can be awfully funny when he isn't tiresome" with
the men.

So Paul, of course, whether funny or not—yet in practice his
intentional jokes weren't always as successful as some remark that
wasn't meant to be a joke at all—must never, in any circumstances,
be tiresome. Not even, for instance—but there were other instances,

too—when the original Brian Cairns dropped in, on a Sunday afternoon, while he and Bianca were toasting crumpets. And appeared determined to remain; so that it was Paul who left first. And was asked, not the next time he saw her, but nearly a week later, why he had suddenly run away.

"Oh," he said. "I thought I would. Well, two's company, and all that."

"But *I* don't mind, Paul. I *wish* you'd stayed on."

Unanswerable. Flattering? He wasn't quite sure. Besides as he didn't know what he wanted her to explain, it was more impossible than ever to ask. The next time the same thing happened, with a cheerful, rather noisy intruder who never spoke to him once, he hung on like a limpet. But what good did this do? In the end they all three went out to dinner together. Which was absurd. And it was the limpet who paid.

"Paul—" but again this was several days later—"that other evening, when we went out with Toby, did he—well, did he ever pay his share?"

Slight hesitation. But truth must prevail.

"Well, no. 'S a matter of fact, he didn't."

"Oh, Paul!" She was laughing. "He is *funny*, you know. He's got fifteen thousand a year."

Unanswerable again. Yet he was glad she had laughed. He laughed, too. He stopped laughing, because he couldn't think why he had begun. All that money. Supposing . . . But no. Cut that out. If she liked him—he had said this all along—it was entirely her own affair. Paul would seem, in other words, to have missed the point that such a girl would never laugh at a man whom she loved.

.   .   .   .   .

He also met Ariadne, or Miss Hobson, and again in the upper part; on a Saturday evening, this time. He wasn't dining there. It was, in fact, about six o'clock. He had taken Bianca to a Rugby football game, at which she had also laughed. As a former player it hadn't occurred to him that it could produce this effect, and with anyone else—yet oddly enough this didn't occur to him, either—he might easily have chafed at her mood.

But she had laughed repeatedly. It was the scrums that made her laugh. "Oh, Paul!" she said. "Those boys! Look—they're doing it again. Oh, you ought to have warned me. Oh, dear!"

Quite the wrong view of this noble sport. Yet apart from the fact that she didn't laugh so that others heard—which, if she had, might have proved more embarrassing—his own eyes were de-scaled to a certain extent. This might be weak. And yet a phalanx of heaving behinds, after all, was perhaps a trifle absurd. To look at, of course. If you have never formed part of it. Nor seen it, as she hadn't, until now.

Interesting. Even instructive. Though of course they weren't boys, except in a Biancian sense. He began thinking of his own school-days. And then, though he knew nothing about them, of hers. On the way back, in the little car—("Oh, Paul, your head again! You really ought to buy a crash-helmet")—both topics had come up; which was interesting and instructive once more. They had some tea, and though they were both dining elsewhere tonight, they were still hard at it—for as Paul had no sister, and Bianca no brother, there was a good deal of information to be exchanged—when, abruptly, the door-bell rang.

"Oh, bother!" said Bianca.

Paul entirely agreed, though as he was a visitor, too, he didn't say so. He stood up. He stiffened. He glanced at his watch. He heard the latch. He heard "Darling!" It was a girl.

She came straight into the room. She stopped dead. But Bianca had followed. "Paul," she was saying, "it's Ariadne. You see, he's heard about you. And Mr. Sunderland. There! There we are."

It was perhaps inevitable, considering what Mr. Sunderland had heard, that he should now immediately glance at her hips. It was perfectly true. They simply didn't exist. She was like a fish. She even moved like a fish. She was tall, fair, with very bright lips—this, of course, was much less like a fish—and, so far as he could judge, with other pigments as well. She was quite a sight, though he wasn't staring. She was closer to what he had imagined than he would have thought possible. But he still had a surprise when she spoke.

"I saw old George," she announced, in a rich, husky contralto. Mrs. Siddons, thought Paul, though he had never heard Mrs. Siddons. "So I thought I'd pop in."

"Yes, of course, darling."

"Was it all right this morning?" Or a raven, perhaps. "Did Michael blow up?"

But she was looking at Paul now, penetratingly yet myopically. "If you *have* got a cigarette," she croaked.

"Oh, rather. Yes, of course. Sorry. Here." He flipped out his case and lighter.

"Ah!" She was inhaling, almost as deeply as his cousin Rodney, though more slowly, with her eyes half-closed. During the next half-hour, which she spent perched on the arm of an arm-chair, she smoked the rest of his supply. She was rather funny. Quite friendly. She still had no hips. And though posing, so he felt, as rather vaguer than she really was, this still fell short of what he would have described as affectation.

Or alternatively—yes, that was a possible idea—it was an acquired manner that she could no longer cast off. It went perfectly, he could quite see, with her sinuous appearance, though he suspected some basic toughness here, too. An odd life of course. Or was it Bianca who was odd, to be so natural in spite of it all?

His thoughts drifted away. He listened, and mused. He gave a start. For Ariadne was going.

"I must slink, darling," she said; and this was just what she did—though with another of those looks at Paul first.

"You're like someone," she told him. He wasn't sure that he was pleased. "No, you're not," she suddenly added. "I'm wrong."

Then she withdrew into herself, while he was still wondering what he felt. And Bianca let her out; and she had gone.

"Well?" Bianca was back. "Now you've seen her. Don't you agree? Don't you think she's absolutely lovely?"

A cue? Not for Paul. He picked another point. "Extraordinary voice," he said.

"Oh, Paul! Well, perhaps. But I'm used to it, of course. It's all that smoking, you know. What do you think?"

"I think she ought to cut it down."

"No, I don't mean that. But would it be nice if she lived here?"

"Oh," said Paul. He was tremendously flattered at being asked. But he hadn't the faintest idea. He knew, that is to say, that he wouldn't want her himself. He was conscious, also, that he preferred the present arrangement. But the first thought was irrelevant, and perhaps the second was a bit selfish. In any case it would be darned cheek to say it.

So he laughed. And, after a moment, Bianca laughed, too.

"Oh, well," she said; "of course it's got nothing to do with you. It's only—you know . . ." She glanced round the room. She looked harassed, which was so unlike her. Paul yearned for the right words. But there was an obstruction. And though she had paused at the largest of the three Brickfields, she gave a gasp as she caught sight of the clock.

"Oh, heavens! I'd no idea! I must change. I must have a bath. Paul, I'm sorry——"

"No, of course. I'm late, too."

End of another meeting. Too sudden, no doubt. But there would be more. And in a way—for it was quite untrue that he was late—he had even liked being turned out. She wouldn't have done it, or such was his interpretation as he walked up to the King's Road, if she didn't feel that he was a friend.

    .   .   .   .

Sometimes, now, he called for her, openly and frankly, and with no fear of Spilsby—though he did see him once—at her place of employment. By the time he got there it was closed—to the general public, that is to say; for of course, whether Miss Thriplow would have forgiven him or not, he mustn't neglect his own business.

But if she were expecting him, she stayed on. Well, there were always things, so she had said, to be put away. The performance was over, but the stage was still lit. The front door was only shut, not actually locked. He had her permission to enter, and did.

He felt uncomfortable, of course. It was no place for a man. And though the extreme luxury of the *décor* had suffered, in the course of years, from the effect of shortages and restrictions, it was still enough to be distinctly overwhelming. It made him walk on tiptoe as he mounted the stairs, though he had been told that he must always come up. The vast, first-floor apartment, which had once been the drawing-room, made him feel—though in fact it was carpeted all over—as if he had come too soon, or on the wrong night, for a dance.

But she was there, as a rule, and he could take her away. Or if not, there was another girl—it was Ariadne once, who immediately asked for a cigarette, and called him "Paul"—to pass on news of his arrival. They seemed to take him for granted. There was no reason to feel shy. Though naturally it was a relief when she appeared.

She also explained, on such occasions, who the other girl was, though of course she had introduced him as well. But somehow or other he never took this in. He wasn't excited. Quite the contrary. He was now absolutely calm. Yet when she laughed—they were in the street now—and said: "Oh, Paul—you're not listening. Now, *what* did I say she was called?", he didn't know, and she laughed at him again.

"You are *awful*," she said. But he didn't mind that. It wasn't a tone—for she wasn't completely unique—that conveyed any serious reproach.

On one evening, however, when he crept into the salon, he was aghast at the sight of another man. Rather older than himself. Rather sporting in appearance. Looking rather, though at the moment he was in an overcoat and muffler, as if he had spent the morning with beagles and might still have a game of squash.

"Hullo?" said this character.

"I—ah—" said Paul.

Someone nudged him. It was Bianca, who must have entered close on his heels. He was again relieved, though not yet quite composed.

"Michael," she was saying, "this is Mr. Sunderland. This is Michael Willoughby, Paul."

"Oh!" said Paul. "How do you do?"

Not the least what he had imagined. Neither effeminate nor a satyr. Yet tired, on second thoughts. And, though courtesy itself, a little strange and even strained in his manner. My fault, thought Paul. I'm in the way here, of course. But no. Mr. Willoughby must still keep him. He must use phrases and an intonation that exactly matched his get-up—Paul was out of his depth, almost at once—about racing. But it was all put on. One just knew it was put on.

Why? And why bother? It was quite a job getting away. After a while, indeed, it was exactly (Paul felt) as if they were in a charade and had forgotten the word. He was becoming false himself. He was going mad. They were both mad. He couldn't stand this. He was convinced that Mr. Willoughby was in the same state. Bianca saved him. At a point where they both dried up, she said "Come on," tugged his arm, and they escaped.

"Well?" They were outside now. Paul had recovered his identity.

"What an extraordinary fellow," he said.

"I know. But he isn't really. It was you, as a matter of fact."

"Me?" said Paul. "What on earth do you mean?"

"He's got a thing," said Bianca, "about *being* a dressmaker. He thought you despised him, of course."

"But good heavens——"

"I know. And he's terribly good. He hadn't a penny to start with, you know. He's done the whole thing himself—and right through the war; when he was rejected, and thought no one believed it. It *is* rather a shame. And I know he's not married. But he isn't—well, not the least bit like that."

"I see," said Paul. She's too kind, he thought. Yet he felt she was speaking the truth.

"Poor devil," he said. "Though I suppose he's not poor?"

"No. Rolling—or as far as anyone is."

"I see. And how—" for he had always wanted to know this— "how, exactly . . ."

She was quick.

"How did *I* get in? Oh, there was a girl. A sort of friend—though she's married now." With the implication that this was the end. "She took me along. Well, I had to do *something*, you see. And it was reserved—because of Export. Well, Michael fixed that up. Though I don't know what Daddy——"

She stopped. Paul was silent. Since he had learnt about that shelter, he had never known whether to allude to it or not. For *she* hadn't told him, and he mustn't intrude. Besides, he'd probably say the wrong thing. It was a barrier, but he couldn't cross it. Poor child, he thought again. But though she addressed her employer as Michael, that, of course, meant nothing; or not now that he had seen him.

His spirits rose. Speech returned. Here was her car. He banged his head. The evening, which was one of those on which Mrs. Blankett obliged—with just a trace now, perhaps, of Juliet's nurse in her eye, but as Paul thought one look at her and one greeting were enough, he never saw it—was again as cosy and as gently stimulating as ever.

.   .   .   .   .

April, now; and the clocks put on. So that it was daylight, which more than ever revealed the shabbiness of paint and furniture, until after eight.

What else had he learnt? A mass of detail. More, perhaps, than he was consciously aware. For example, and though this may sound dull he had found it interesting, too, he knew the name of Bianca's laundry. He knew, or to a certain extent, where she did her shopping. He knew how she slept; or in what attitude, that is to say, for she had told him. If it comes to that, he had even seen her bed, for she had now taken him all over the upper part.

But she had done this neither bashfully nor with a vestige of provocation. "And this is me," she had said; meaning that this was her clean, tidy bedroom. He had again been interested, but that was all one could say. They had also played some duets, much as he played them with his cousin Mark. Painstakingly, in other words, until they laughed at a wrong note; but with no contact, except by pure chance.

He was rather glad, for some reason, to be told that Dorothea was tone-deaf. Perhaps less so to be informed—"Isn't it marvellous, Paul? I do envy him!"—that Jock Whitley, or Goldilocks, was such an expert that he had tuned the piano.

And she had shown him books of old photographs, as they sat side by side. Yet still this was all they had done. He had seen her as a little girl; and had been touched, but not inflamed. He had seen her father, at various ages and in varying attire; and had made comments, yet still with reserve. Why? Because he shrank from emotion? Perhaps. Yet perhaps it was consideration as well.

"There's grandpapa. Daddy's father. I can't remember him, but I stuck him in. He used to build bridges, you know."

"Did he really?"

"Yes—dozens. He was a—some sort of engineer."

"Civil?"

"Yes, that's right. And he wanted Daddy to be one, too. But he hated it. He wasn't practical, you know. That's how—poor darling— he lost most of his money. Oh, there's Mimi!"

"Who?"

"Our cat. When we had the whole house. Oh, Paul, I *told* you."

"I beg your pardon." Paul bent forward. "Who's that? I say, it can't be *you*!"

"No, of course not. Look at her frock! It's Aunt Boney, of course. Wasn't she fat?"

One might admit this. She was alive. She lived at Bournemouth, as he knew. But why—he *must* ask—was she called Bony?

He was informed. "She was really called Napoleon, of course. Daddy started it—ages ago. She's rather firm, you see. And he wasn't, of course."

"Oh, I see."

"I think I'm going there for Easter."

She turned the page, as if she had said the most ordinary thing. But she hadn't. Blast Easter, thought Paul. Always cropping up when one didn't expect it. When was it? He wasn't sure; but he asked, and was again told. Not only did it prove to be far nearer than he had supposed, but he would be alone, with no work, for four days.

"I'll tell you what," he said, suddenly. "Let's have a *real* evening out. Dressing up, I mean, and—and dancing, perhaps. Can't we? Bianca. Before you go off. It's my turn. Well, work it out for yourself."

The steady gaze, as she seemed to be working it out. But he met it. After all, he must have been here at least half a dozen times, and he couldn't possibly ask a girl to his flat.

"Come on!"

She gave another quick look at his face.

"All right," she said. "Yes. I mean, thank you, of course. Thank you awfully. But——"

"Ah!" For some reason or other he was erect. She seemed just a little surprised.

"Paul—what's the matter?"

"Nothing. Nothing at all. Only it's getting a bit late. I must go."

"I see." It would have been strange if she had tried to stop him, and she didn't; though it wasn't nearly as late as all that. Dash! he was thinking. He was puzzled himself. Why the deuce had he been so impulsive?

But she had shut the book, and risen, too. They were out on the little landing. She disappeared, and returned with his coat and hat.

"Oh, Paul—" He was determined to go, though. He was a man of iron.

"Yes?" Almost sharply, for once.

"I forgot to tell you. I saw Mrs. Parkinson this morning."

"Oh, did you?" No, he was a fool. That was all.

"Yes—here; I'll help you—I hadn't seen her for weeks. Well, it's like that, sometimes—isn't it?—in shops."

"I suppose so," said Paul, turning round. "I wouldn't know."

"No, you're lucky. She's awfully sweet."

"Oh, yes," said Paul. "Rather." And buttoned his coat.

"She sent you her love, too."

"Good lord!"

"Why?"

He didn't know. He was baffled again. He felt exposed. What had she meant? What a message to send, when he *knew* she thought him boring. And what else had old Parky's wife said?

He was tingling. This was ridiculous. But he was dashed if he'd ask. He replied, in fact, with a rather odd shrug.

"Oh, Paul——"

"Wassa matter?"

"—look—you've buttoned it all wrong!"

"Oh, sorry." He laughed, without a care in the world. And Bianca laughed. And he corrected the buttoning without aid, or the offer of aid. "Would Monday suit you?" he suddenly asked.

"For our night out, you mean?"

"Yes."

She considered. He was unaware that he was holding his breath, though he was certainly thinking of the other men.

She nodded. "That'll be lovely."

"Good-night, then." So are you.

"Good-night, Paul."

She switched on the light over the door. He turned, as usual, on the pavement, to see it go out.

"Um," he observed, as he swung into a vigorous stride. It was a complete expression of the whole range of his thoughts.

8

Since he had deliberately chosen Monday on a Wednesday night—on the grounds, if any, that an air of urgency might suggest that he was a pest—it now seemed (though to other persons this logic might be less clear) that he was in for four days' solitude in any case.

For plans, particularly of late, had been much less formal than this. One meeting, in the kind of association that had grown up, had led easily, naturally, and almost insensibly to the next. He had quite got over any reluctance to use the telephone. But this was different. He had seen her hesitate. And he had rather crashed through the Rules. Therefore—if this reasoning can be followed—he must now remove any idea that he was the sort of chap who turned into a nuisance.

This involved lying low; or laying off, as one might say; even if it meant doing both over a week-end. Still that couldn't be helped.

He was convinced he was right. If he overdid things—and perhaps she *had* been having rather a dose of him lately—it would be a frightful mistake. She would get sick of him if he were always around. Obviously. Besides—as he could keep on reminding himself —he would definitely be seeing her on Monday.

Pangs? Now and then; in a mild sort of way. Or little pricks, for which he wasn't always prepared. Something happened, and he thought at once: I must tell Bianca about that. Or, again: I must ask Bianca; *she'd* know. These are signs, without doubt, but he didn't see them as signs. Introspection was out, as it sometimes is at this stage. It never struck him that there was any change in his looks.

This was observed, nevertheless, though without comment, by his partners. They felt he had come on, in some way. They had never thought him a fool, but he seemed much more alive. More alert—though it is also true that he forgot one very important appointment altogether; and didn't seem to mind, which was rather queer. But he was radiating something. They all felt the waves. Though still, because the clan was traditionally discreet as well as loyal, it was an impression that they kept to themselves.

Our theory would be that his cousin Clayton and his uncle Oliver, having a wife, in each case, to whom they were deeply attached, were protected from the full force of these rays. But his uncle Hayward—H.B.—was in a different class. He had been married, and was now single again. We don't assert—for there can be no proof—that it is more than a mere theory. But he kept glancing at Paul. Yes, he certainly glanced. It almost seems, dry and reserved as his manner remained, that down in his own depths something stirred.

Curiosity, perhaps. Or a memory. Who knows? Or something else, that was mixed up with both. Abruptly, in any event, on the Friday afternoon, whether sensitive to the radiations or not, he gazed out of the window—as was his custom if about to deal with anything at all personal—and invited Paul down to Greenhurst for Easter.

This was startling. H.B. was a decided recluse. Generous, of course; the whole clan knew that. But he just *didn't* ask people to stay. Paul remembered the house, for it was in what might be called the Sunderland country; quite near the much larger house— now long since sold—in which he himself had been mainly brought up. He felt sure that it would be comfortable, but that wasn't the point. Why, when H.B. never asked anyone else—and in fact in these days (either because he preferred it, or to please Prim) had become more and more of a resident Londoner; *why*——

But he must answer; and of course he must accept.

"Oh, I say—" a whiff of sentiment from the past stirred Paul, too—"that's awfully kind of you. I'd love to. Of course!"

Easter was solved, what was more. There you were. He had been worrying about nothing.

"Only Prim," said H.B. "And—" he was still gazing out of the window—"Miss Crankshaw, of course." He turned at last. "I'm afraid it may be rather dull."

"No, no. I shall look forward to that."

Ambiguous, perhaps. There was another odd glance. Of regret? But Paul's mind had shot off. He was worrying, so it suddenly seemed, after all. He had just remembered Bianca's words; how she had only *thought* she was going away. What if she didn't? And he did? He had been too quick.

But he was still well-mannered. He didn't immediately make an excuse. Nor did he propose to. He had accepted, and that was that. On the other hand (this was another example of his keen grasp of logic), it meant, of course, that he could now ring her up. That he almost must, in fact, in case by any chance . . . Well, he'd got to find out. Why not?

He dialled twice that evening, but without success. And again, though with the same result, after lunch on Saturday. But at the fourth attempt, after tea, he at last heard her voice. His own rules, he still felt, must restrict him to one question. He may have sounded a little terse. But he got the answer all right. She was definitely going to Bournemouth herself.

He said: "Ah!" She said: "Why did you want to know?" He should have foreseen this, but for some reason it took him aback. He decided—there had been a pause, though, for a second or two—to explain that he had only just wondered.

"But why, Paul?"

He twitched. He couldn't think why he had twitched. The hidden obstruction dissolved.

"Oh, well—" he sounded perfectly natural now—"I've been asked—well, I'm going away, too."

"Oh, are you? I say—do you mean somewhere near me?"

"No, no." But he divulged all particulars, and they continued to converse. It was like old times; after sixty-eight hours.

"I was wondering what had happened to you," she was saying, about ten minutes later. "I thought perhaps—well, you did rather rush off the other night—you'd gone to bed with a cold."

"Oh no," said Paul. "I never do that. I say—are you doing anything this evening?"

"Oh, Paul, I'm afraid I am. In fact, I'm just going off."

"Never mind," he said, gaily. He flung all principles to the winds. "How about tomorrow?" he asked.

"Oh, Paul, I'm so sorry. It's all filled up. I'm going to the Zoo in the morning, and to a concert in the afternoon. And then I'm going to supper at Dorothea's."

"I see." He was less sure about the two former engagements, but the third—though he was rather surprised—seemed quite sound. His mind which, in a flash, had been to Regent's Park, the Albert Hall (though this was pure speculation), and right up to Hampstead, returned and advised him of something else. He mustn't keep her, if she was just going. No, no. Of course not. "Well, I suppose—" he began.

"Oh, Paul—wait a moment. About Monday, you know. We haven't settled anything——"

"Yes, we have," said Paul, emphatically. "You're coming out with me, of course."

" I know." He gave a violent jerk of relief. "But you never said what time, or where."

"Oh, didn't I?" How extraordinary. He must be clean off his head. And dash it, she must have been *waiting* for him to ring up. How shocking. Good lord! He began babbling at once. "Look here, I'll call for you—I'll pick you up—I'll——"

"Oh, but, Paul, you needn't——"

"—about a quarter to eight——"

"But——"

"Please! I—I meant do that. Is that all right?"

"But I could easily——"

"I *want* to," he urged. And was inspired. "If I hire a car, it'll cost just the same. In fact, it'll be cheaper than taxis and tips. It *is*, when one does it like that."

Strange argument, perhaps, to use with a girl. But it worked. She had given in. She had even laughed.

"Oh, Paul—well, in that case——"

"There you are!"

"—I must fly now. But I'll be ready. At a quarter to eight. And then I can give you a drink."

Another laugh, as she rang off, with those characteristic last words. And Paul was smiling, as he emerged from the little cabinet at his club; for there was no question, even if he had suffered a quite inexplicable mental black-out (so that he shook his head, too), that he had staged a come-back with vast presence of mind.

A car, of course. From that chap in the mews. And dinner—no, not at Belloni's this time; but somewhere where *everyone* danced. He'd got it, in fact. The obvious place. So obvious that it was, of course, what he had meant all along. He even believed now, though it was still disgraceful if he had really left things so vague, that it had been implied, more or less, in his invitation.

His amnesia no longer troubled him. Nor did anything else. He felt refreshed. He didn't care twopence what she was doing tonight, or who was taking her to the Zoo or the concert tomorrow. For not only had that recent talk again filled his personal tank, as one might say, but when Sunday was over—don't you see?—it would be no more than a dream. The true reality would be Monday.

With this profound though perhaps incomplete appraisement of the situation—for Monday, of course, must in turn go the way of all days—he went straight back into the telephone-box; consulted the directory; was placed in communication with the restaurant at the Serene Hotel, and chartered a table, for Monday evening, for two.

He also spoke to the mews—but this was in person, and on Sunday—and was successful in hiring both a car and a driver. On the Monday itself he was not only the very spirit of industry and efficiency at his office, so that Miss Thriplow was kept hard at work, too, until the last moment, but found time—though this was at lunch—to consider the concept of offering Miss B. Brown an orchid.

He even entered the flower-shop. But then he turned and came out. The concept, it had suddenly struck him, though harmless and well-meant, might possibly be received in the wrong way. It might give an impression that was completely false, and at the very outset of the evening as well. She had stretched a point, he was aware, in coming out with him on this sort of scale at all. He daren't risk it. He re-entered the shop. But there was a slight queue. He re-emerged. It wasn't that he was afraid of her—good heavens, no. But he must be careful; and perhaps the queue was a sign.

So there was no orchid as he drove to Chelsea, in the hired car and a black tie—he had hesitated here, also, but again she might think a white one a form of excess—and went bounding up the outer stairway, and rang the bell. Yet as she opened the door, after a slight delay (during which, it must be admitted, he went through torment lest she should have forgotten or have been taken ill) instead of greeting her with the customary "Hullo" or "Here I am," he let out a loud, startled gasp.

He had never seen such a sight. He couldn't have described it for a fortune. But she had done something to her hair. And look at her neck. And what she'd got on. A sort of—well, no. He was just dazzled. He could only gape. Until he realised that he was gaping and stopped.

"I say," he observed, finally, "you do look a treat. I—dash it!—I ought to have turned out in tails."

"Oh, Paul, don't be silly. Of course you're all right." He was much cheered. "But you really like it?" she asked.

She revolved, with perhaps a trace of professional skill. He had a little difficulty, for a moment, with his lungs.

But then he recovered. "Yes, rather!" he said. "By Jove, yes!"

She looked pleased. She rippled lightly. "Well, come on. Here's your drink."

"Oh, yes. I mean, 'ks awfully." He followed her into the sitting room and took the glass. But he only held it. "I say," he remarked, "I like that scent."

"Oh, Paul—is it too much?"

"No, no. Not the least."

"You're sure?"

"Absolutely."

"That's good." She smiled again. He was calmer, and ventured a sip. "It's Michael's," she said, "as a matter of fact."

"Eh? What is?" He hadn't got there.

"The scent, I mean. He sells it. And so's the frock."

"You—you mean——"

"Oh, good heavens, I don't dress like this. He lent it me. He does, when he's in a good mood."

"Oh."

"What's the matter?"

He didn't like the idea. Women, it has been noted by those who have studied them more closely, have no objection to wearing each other's clothes. In this case, moreover, there was no evidence that the dress wasn't brand new, and still to be sold. Yet men, gross as they are, seem more sensitive on this point. Paul had blinked. But then, again, if *she* did it, it was all right. I'm a juggins, he thought. And perhaps he was.

"Nothing," he said, quickly. "I only wish——" He broke off.

"Wish what?"

He must tell her, if her eyes were as big as that.

"Dashed stupid," he said. "Went into a shop. Thought I'd turn up with an orchid, perhaps. But——"

"Oh, Paul, that was sweet of you—but of course not!"

"No?"

"No."

They were friends. All was well. And, besides, if one came to think of it—using reason, of course—she was still the same girl, even like this. She would still be the same girl, even— Whoa! Steady, there. His foul mind had gone a great deal too far.

Yet not really, you know. It had had a thought, but it was quite pure. Because *she* was. So there you were. Now get out.

"Have another?" he heard her saying. It would appear that he had drained his glass. He was surprised. But as he shook his head, for of course one was enough, he suddenly realised that she had had nothing herself.

"I say," he exclaimed. "Aren't you drinking? Why not?"

"I don't need to," she said, "when I'm like this."

"Like what?"

"All dressed up." She was a child. He nearly told her she was a child. "And going out to—oh, Paul, you never said! *Where* are we going?"

She looked so eager and effulgent that even the Serene seemed to shrink. He supplied the name, because he must, but as if apologising for its squalor. He even added: "I say—do you mind?"

"Mind?" She clapped her hands. "Oh, Paul—" An abrupt change. "Oh, it's *kind* of you, but—" Good lord! Was she going to back out? "Oh! I'd nearly forgotten. But that makes it a *bit* better."

"What are you talking about?" He might well ask, at such a welter of moods.

"I've got you a little present," she said. "It's here." She was at a pigeon-hole in the writing-desk.

"But, Bianca—" He was aghast. It almost looked, for a moment, as if he would drag her away. But of course he didn't; though he was just behind her as she turned round.

"Here it is," she said, offering him a cellophane cylinder. "The man *said* it was all right. *Is* it, Paul?"

A cigar. He could read the brand. It was more than all right. It must have cost her—well, heaven knew what. Less, perhaps, than the orchid. But he hadn't *bought* the orchid; though he had gone and told her about it, which made things much worse.

He looked down at his hand. He was baffled again. One just *couldn't* outflank her rules.

"Is it, Paul? Or is it awful?"

"No, of course not. It's terrific!"

"Oh, that *is* a relief."

"I mean, *thank* you. But—but you *shouldn't*——"

"Oh, Paul, I *had* to do *something*."

"Well, you've done it," said Paul. He looked up, and met her eyes. If he grinned, it was perhaps the grin of a groggy boxer against the ropes. Yet though put to shame, he was still on his feet.

"I must say—" he began. But she had spoken, too. He gave way.

"Bag," she was saying, with her back to him now. "Key? Yes, that's right. I'm afraid my rabbit—" he rushed forward to help her into a sort of cape or jacket that she had just picked up— "isn't quite the same class as the frock. But still—oh, thank you, Paul—I shan't be wearing it, you see. So you won't be disgraced. Shall we come?"

"Oh yes. Rather." He placed the cigar carefully in his pocket. Followed her. Overtook her, so that he could open the outer door. Let her pass him again—"Give it a good slam," she said; and he did, and in some way this was a great help—and once more followed, down the stair, to the car. The hired driver saluted; the effect of beauty, no doubt, for he hadn't done this before; and executed a slam of his own.

"Lovely," said Bianca, as they began gliding away. Paul agreed; but as she was now singing softly and, as he hoped, happily to herself, he made no comment. He preferred to listen, it seemed.

.   .   .   .   .

Thus—though presently she stopped singing, and conversation was resumed—they arrived at the Serene Hotel. Where once, before the war, you could have eaten and drunk two or three times as much for the same money. Where once there had been two bands, and a cabaret as well, and the so-called guests were all much of one caste. Where today, on the other hand, the redistribution of wealth —not to mention privilege—had rather altered this state of affairs; so that Americans, Europeans, Asiatics, and the kind of native who had discovered how to avoid paying income-tax, though combined, had not quite coalesced.

Yet where, nevertheless, and despite the Musicians' Union, there was still one extremely good band. Where, despite the Catering Act, there were still lots of waiters. And where—possibly to please the Americans, who liked to go back and report that the British were all wearing boiled shirts at Uncle Sam's expense—there was still compulsory evening dress.

Paul and Bianca, however, were not only children of the new era, so that the Serene Restaurant before the war was a mere legend, and even its utility china seemed perfectly natural to them; but they hadn't come here except, in a sense, to be alone. The background was just a background as they sat at their little table. Even when they danced—and it was impossible to do this at the Serene Restaurant without a certain number of collisions—they were yet apart, in the same sense, from the throng.

Noises. Faces. Clattering. Music. They heard and saw them, and if they hadn't it would have perhaps been less fun; yet their evening remained a duet. They talked incessantly, and though it is true that they had a bottle of champagne ("Oh, Paul, you mustn't!" "Of *course* I must. They'll chuck us out if I don't."), they never finished it, for they both forgot it was there. As for the cigar, it was stupendous, though a slight drawback in a way, for Paul wanted to dance, and must still smoke.

He took a risk. She had no brother. She would believe him, perhaps, if he explained that re-ignition improved them. Or perhaps she didn't; but a gift from Bianca was a gift. She only smiled, as he laid it down, and they both rose.

Extraordinary, he was thinking; though he was still talking, too. Fantastic, I mean, how one can do this in a crowd—as if it meant nothing at all, and it doesn't of course—and wouldn't dream of it anywhere else. Interesting, in fact. But I don't think I'll say so.

She weighs *nothing*, he thought. By Jove, I'm dancing rather well. I suppose, though—or was it the *alter ego* that chipped in here?—she must have done it with hundreds of chaps.

He looked down. She looked up.

"Paul! Why are you so grim?"

"I'm not." And he wasn't. He wasn't grim when the band-leader suddenly bowed to her; though the past tense was perhaps a help, when she said: "I used to think him *divine*." He wasn't grim now, when (as was of course bound to happen) a young man—with white tie, and carnation, too—came and supported himself by his knuckles on their table.

This, he was informed, was Bill Buckley—for there was the usual scrupulous introduction—who certainly supported himself on his knuckles for some time. Yet again it was perhaps a help that, when he ultimately withdrew, she should say: "He's rather awful, you know."

"How?" asked Paul, though he was quite prepared to agree.

"Weak," said Bianca. "And sort of stubborn as well. I quite *like* him, I mean. But he gets so *cross* when—oh, never mind. Forget him. Come on—here's our tune!"

Impossible to be grim, at an invitation like this. Their tune, though it was of course no more theirs than anyone else's, was being played constantly that evening. And it was a good tune, or seemed a good tune at the time. And it was rather stimulating that she should regard it like that. Away, then, with Mr. Buckley—(I may be weak, Paul reflected, but I don't think I'm stubborn, and we've *never* had a row)—and, as a matter of fact, later on, with another young man; whose partner, however, held on to his arm while he sought to chat, and then fairly hauled him off.

Away, also, with a girl, not nearly so good-looking as Bianca seemed to think, whose sole object—though in Paul's view she could have been quicker about it—was to announce that she was going to ring up.

But all these were mere incidents, as they danced and talked, or sat and talked, and as the evening still went with a swing. It would be pleasant if it could last for ever, though it couldn't, of course. And in some ways, though he was no kill-joy, danced vigorously, and fully appreciated that, but for the Serene, he might never have seen her in that sort of dress, he felt occasionally that their quieter evenings were best.

"Oh, Paul—" she began digging in her decorative bag—"I suppose this is rather an awful thing to ask you, but I thought perhaps—well, perhaps you'd understand. I mean, you're in business."

"That's right. Come along."

"Well, you see . . ." And at a small, round table in the restaurant at the Serene Hotel, of all places, Paul Sunderland found himself studying a letter and a buff form from the Chelsea Inspector of Taxes.

"Daddy," she was explaining, "used to get the bank to do it.

But the man there—well, he was rather sickening last time. He—"
she wrinkled her nose—"kept calling me 'young lady'."

"How disgusting!" said Paul.

"And 'my dear.' So you see——"

"Absolutely," said Paul. "Well, *I* shan't. I'd never do that."

"I know. That's why I thought . . ."

He was frowning at the letter. He looked up.

"I say—those dashed Pottings don't seem to pay you any rent
at all!"

"Oh, they do, Paul. But it's the taxes. So I don't *get* very much."
She had moved her chair, so that they were side by side. "The
absurd thing—" she went on. "Are you listening?"

"Yes—go ahead."

"Well, it seems if they were paying a lot more I could turn
them out—or that's what the man said. And then—though it sounds
rather horrid—I could let it again, for about double. But—well,
even though their lease is coming to an end, there's a law or
something. And he's a civil servant, you know."

She spoke, and indeed there was some reason for this, as if
alluding to a species of vampire.

"But do you *want* to turn him out? Is it a freehold, by the way?"

"Yes, it is. Oh, Paul, I don't *know*. They're terribly dull. And I
couldn't be cruel. But supposing I had some babies—why *shouldn't*
they have the garden? *I* did. When *I* was a baby."

"But," said Paul, "if you got married—I say, you're not thinking
of anyone special, are you?"

"No, no. Of course not." She even wrinkled her nose, and it was
all so swift that it was as if a shell had passed the end of his own,
and would explode, if it ever did, out of hearing. "Yes? Go on."

"I was only thinking, if you did, you'd be moving yourself."

"Oh no! Paul—I *couldn't* do that! I'd hate it. I don't want to.
I *adore* where I live. I only meant—oh, isn't money *awkward*! But
if you *could* just explain."

He did his best. As a Sunderland, he was well equipped to
explain. She was attentive and almost appallingly frank. Yet as a
Sunderland, and though more than flattered that she should have
turned to him for advice, he was shocked by this disclosure of her
resources. It seemed clear that she must be subsisting from hand to
mouth; that it was essential that she should find a successor to
Mrs. Hopgrove.

He thought of the cigar, and was deeply disturbed. Of those

Rules; another constant, and, in the circumstances, preposterous expense. Of her little car, which no income like this should support. Of what might happen if she were ill, or lost her job.

In all this it is just possible that the Sunderland point of view overlooked how the bulk of the world lives. It is even possible that he was rather exaggerating a situation which, doubtless, could have been very much worse. Yet Paul was rattled, and because he was rattled he became confused.

"Look here," he said, suddenly—for though she didn't seem to have noticed, he was keenly aware that he had just contradicted himself. "Could I take these away? And look into it all? And let you know? You see——"

"Oh, Paul, that's an awful trouble. I never meant that!"

"I know. But——"

It was the Pottings whom he was determined to do down. He mustn't say so, for he had no standing. But, dash it, just think of them hogging that garden—and swindling Bianca as well. He would start in tomorrow. With the firm's solicitors, of course. He had never *heard* of such a state of affairs!

"Yes, Paul?"

Rent Restriction? Never mind. I'll have a shot. And they won't be homeless. They can always requisition a block of flats.

"Nothing." He thrust the documents into his pocket. "Let's dance."

"Oh, Paul, have I been a nuisance?"

"Good lord—of course not! I'm enjoying myself. Come along."

Nevertheless, it was the last time they circled the floor. For when they returned to their little table, after about a quarter of an hour's exercise, a waiter asked Paul if he could get him anything. This, of course, is how the Serene either increases its receipts or, alternatively, makes room for fresh arrivals. It was a hint, in fact. And Bianca had heard it, too. She would have no more refreshment. She didn't even sit down. She said: "I *think*, Paul—if you wouldn't mind now . . ."

And of course she was right. She had her work. So had he. He quite understood. Yes, of course.

But he must pay. The mere thought was enough to produce the bill. Golly! Or dashed lucky he'd cashed another cheque. He ladled out notes. A book of stamps fell on the plate. He snatched it up quickly, but Bianca wasn't looking. Girls don't, as he should have remembered, at this stage.

On the other hand, as they left the restaurant, she asked: "Was it frightful?" And again, whether this was strictly in order or not, he was pleased; because it meant they were friends.

"Corking," he said, cheerfully.

"Oh, Paul!" She stopped dead. "Oh, Paul, we must *never* come here again. I feel *awful*——"

"Bianca—*please*! I—I was being funny."

"Were you?"

He grinned, with a supreme effort. She believed him. She smiled.

"I'm sorry," he said. He could have almost wept.

But he didn't, for whatever reason he could almost have wept. He went to the cloak-room instead. He came out. They were re-united. They sighted the car. A last tip to a magnifico who had done nothing at all, and—well, obviously—he would take her home first.

They didn't say very much on what seemed a much shorter drive. There was, indeed, an illusion, so far as Paul was concerned, that it was over at once. He leapt out as the car stopped, so that the driver sat tight.

"Well—" they both said.

"Thank you," they both said.

They both laughed, and they both said: "Good-night."

He watched her climb up, with his hat in his hand. He saw her open the door. He heard it shut. The driver, whose experience hadn't prepared him for so swift and sudden a separation, was much encouraged, and remarked that it was a fine night.

Paul pivoted slowly.

"Eh—what's that? Oh yes."

He replaced his hat, and re-entered the car.

Pleasant evening? Extremely. But he wouldn't run through it all at once. For he had learnt lately, however base his ignorance of another aspect of the whole affair, that to savour such memories slowly, and one at a time, was the best way to make them last out.

9

IF Easter had originated in this country, and in a simpler manner than is in fact the tortuous and confusing truth, it might be thought that its mobility was an attempt to outwit the climate.

For it is a festival. It is, or should be, a sign of spring. Without fine weather, it must always fail in its full purpose. But the English climate is not only notoriously unreliable, but, as has been observed, can be pervicacious as well.

Announce an open-air fête, and you know what it does. Plant your seeds; there will be no rain for weeks. Send your skates to be ground, because your pipes have all burst. The result is an immediate thaw. Every year it provides portents, or countrymen say so; and then, because they have said so, it lets them down. And since, of all seasons, the spring is the most longed-for, it positively delights—all the evidence of centuries confirms this—in supplying fragments, and then whisking them away.

In brief, it is an old tease. And it does almost seem that, in the matter of Easter, our remote ancestors showed cunning. They would catch it out, they would keep it guessing, they would for once take it off its guard. They would pick a different date every year. The climate may or may not fall into this trap. And if it does—well, just consider the number of fine Easter Sundays that are immediately followed by a drenching bank-holiday—it soon finds its way out.

Yet but for this arrangement—which, incidentally, causes a good deal of perplexity and inconvenience to the human race, too— who can doubt that our climate could *ever* resist a four-day blizzard to coincide with a fixed Easter?

The point awaits proof, while the Church still holds out. We may be wrong; and there are strange exceptions, of course. In any case, in the year with which we happen to be dealing, though the festival was to fall latish, or about the middle of April, the climate seems to have decided to hedge.

It had run through its almost complete repertoire in earlier months, regardless, and certainly not for the first time, of public demand or expectation. There had been warm nights in January, thunder and swarms of butterflies in February, dead calm and electricity cuts in March. But now, whether it was exhausted, or sulky, or bored, there was only one word for it. Dull.

It wasn't particularly cold, but it was far from mild. It wasn't pouring, but continued to look as if it might drizzle. There was little or no colour. Spring seemed held in suspense. Take it or leave it, was the general climatic suggestion, as long as you don't bother *me*. Thus Easter approached, or the human race approached Easter. But it was of course impossible that the conjunction should be postponed.

Paul Sunderland saw Bianca Brown on Wednesday, after his work; and at her club, though he might have resisted this if there had been more time. However, there wasn't. She was having supper with a girl in another mews. This was all that she could manage, she said.

Neither—but after Monday he must avoid argument, perhaps— would she let him pay for their gin-and-lime. It was in fact a business meeting, as he had explained when ringing up. He hadn't dealt with the Pottings, and wouldn't mention them until he had. Nor was he at all sure now that even a solicitor could shift them. But he had tackled the Inspector's letter, and the form, and here they were. She thanked him effusively, and put them in her bag.

"And if there's ever anything else——"

"Oh no, Paul. I mustn't plague you. Besides, there isn't. Though you've been awfully kind."

He felt, or imagined, that he had lost a little ground. That she now regretted having consulted him, after all. And yet, for the rest of that short half-hour at the Avocado, another part of him knew that she was just the same. So it was only, perhaps, that this was different from Monday—as was pretty obvious, of course. And in the last few minutes, outside, before she drove away, it wasn't even so very different, you know.

They were laughing. There was no suggestion that she *wanted* to hurry off. Only that she must, which he quite understood. He didn't even try to detain her. He told the truth when she asked the time. Yet because this was more than the customary separation— never before had they both been going out of London—there was still some thought that was unexpressed.

Don't forget me? Well, no. It would sound blithering to say that. I shall miss you? The same objection applied. Besides, dash it, what was a week, or less than a week? He mistrusted his throat, which, at the mere notion of such remarks, was clearly threatening to seize up. If he stammered, she would drive off thinking him a fool.

So, in fact, it was quite a brisk and, to all outward appearance, a cheerful young gentleman who took his foot off the running-board, removed his hat, and expressed the hope that she would have a good time.

"Oh, thank you," she said. "And so must you."

The little car moved away, but he didn't wave or even look. It turned a corner, but he was already walking the other way. That was that, then. What had he expected? Nothing, of course. The trifling throat-trouble was forgotten. What was a week, after all? She'd be back. He'd be back. They would both have had a change. Not from each other; no, of course he didn't mean that. He was very fond of her. It had been a most agreeable two months. Or two months less a day, to be more accurate still. But, of course . . .

The chain of reasoning faded out. But it didn't matter. Nothing mattered. He preferred to feel vague. Or a sense of gratitude, without exactly deciding whether it was to Bianca or just to Life, seemed enough as he strolled back to his flat.

.   .   .   .   .

In the morning he told Spilsby that he would be going away, and Spilsby seemed gratified, too. It occurred to Paul, though he felt under no special obligation to keep on listening to Spilsby's outpourings, that he had shown more restraint in the last few days. No, he hadn't been silent, but he hadn't chattered so much. Or was this just a fancy, too?

Perhaps. But he was chattering like billy-ho now. So perhaps, again—yes, that might be it—he had his own Easter plans, all his other customers were going off, and only Paul had been standing in his way. If so, it had been a little thoughtless not to have told him sooner. But something had certainly restored his old fluency.

"Do you good, sir," he was saying, "to get away for a bit. Nothing like a breath of fresh air. Nice time of year, too—well, I mean, it might be, quite easy. I was born in the country myself, sir."

"Were you?" But Paul was only half-listening.

"Yerce." Spilsby gripped the foot of the bed; always a sign that he was settling in for a good talk. It rolled on, as Paul sipped at his still tepid tea. It was quite as dull as the weather, but it was interminable this morning. Need one respond? No, of course not. But would it give offence if one got up? Paul moved; and there was a perceptible effect.

"There, now," said Spilsby. "It's cos you're interested I kep' on, sir. But o' course—" there was even a hint of reproof—"I've got all these brekfusses to get. Yerce. Still—" at last he stood back, and the bed stopped creaking—"now you're goin' away too, sir, I shan't have no gen'lmen after tomorrow." He nodded. "That's right. Not for three days I shan't. So maybe— Well, that's it. Can't tell."

Delphic. An allusion to something that Paul had missed? Or mere Spilsbian soliloquy? One couldn't tell. Nevertheless, if all the other tenants were beating it for the backwoods, a solitary survivor would of course be a nuisance. An attempt, though hardly a serious attempt, to picture Spilsby in a sports-jacket melted, as Paul hurried into the bathroom, into a resolve not to let him pack. For on the few occasions that he had done this, he had omitted, in turn, Paul's razor, all handkerchiefs, and the legs of his pyjamas. And no amount of screwed-up newspaper, in the owner's view, could take their place when all the shops would be shut.

So he filled a suit-case himself; hastily, and even furtively, lest Spilsby should interfere. At breakfast—but by this time Spilsby was in his headlong mood, so that it became necessary to pursue him on to the landing—he secured his ration-book, though no rations. ("'S too late, sir. They're gorn"); and despite this, and because Easter was Easter, gave Spilsby a tip. And immediately afterwards—(Well, he was thinking, I'll eat as little as I can down there, though it *is* rather odd how Spilsby always says that)— he took a taxi to Cheesemonger Lane.

Maundy Thursday. And Miss Thriplow. Perhaps it would be civil, and not intrusive, to ask if *she* was going away. She looked startled. Even distressed. She said: "No, I'm not, Mr. Sunderland." He felt rebuked. He would have liked—but this would have brought something quite new into their relationship, and he had no wish to be rebuked again—to inquire what was feeding on her damask cheek.

But then, as he glanced again, though she had just sniffed, she also smiled. "Perhaps," she said, "it'll rain all the time."

Accompanied by the smile, this was a shade Delphic, too. Even the smile, on second thoughts, had been obscure. Let it go. It was his own fault for having appeared to pry into her private life; though, of course, he had only meant to be polite. He coughed; and within a few moments—though he hoped she was wrong about the rain—he was dictating, and her pencil was flashing, as of old.

"Thank you, Miss Thriplow," he said, about twenty minutes later—for the approach of Easter, as of all holidays, had already slashed his morning mail. And by then, for he still had plenty of other work, he had ceased to speculate on his secretary and her smile.

His uncle Hayward, for a senior partner can always do this, left the office for good before lunch. At about half-past four, when three other magnates had been reported absent on the telephone, and a slight moral rot was clearly attacking even the underlings here, it seemed pointless to stay longer himself. There was a train down to Greenhurst at a quarter past five. He would catch it. It was absurd to behave as if he were still at school. Both conscience and sense said Clear out.

Before he left, though, there were two reasons for having a word with old Banglewick. The first was that old Banglewick had been guarding his suit-case; and the second, more traditional, was that on the eve of any recess old Banglewick must be given a little offering.

They both knew this; just as Paul knew that it would be rejected at first, for this was traditional, too. But he had it ready, and as he took the suit-case he slipped it across. The Sergeant stiffened. But he was prepared for this move.

"Nonsense," he said, and on this occasion—perhaps because of the train—not even waiting for the actual, vocal disclaimer. "I want you to have it. For Easter, you know. And, besides—" There was at least a minor inspiration, and switch. "I've been meaning to ask you," said Paul. "How's your son?"

The old boy's pince-nez were as cock-eyed as ever. But he did an odd thing. He took them off.

"Perce?" he rejoined. He pouched the notes, which was odder still, without a murmur. "Well, sir, fer to tell the truth, we're still *worried*, you know. Me an' the missus, I mean. 'E's *gloomy*," said old Banglewick, "But 'e's no *call* to be gloomy. Why, at '*is* age——"

He seemed to realise what he had just done, after all. He began attempting to de-pouch. Paul spoke sharply.

"Now, now," he said. "Too late to argue, Banglewick. Tell him to get out more—in the open air—if he's like that. I dare say it's just the spring. We can't all be as young as yourself."

The pince-nez went back. The old warrior gleamed.

"Well, per'aps you're right, sir——"

"Of *course* I am! Is my taxi out there?"

"Yessir. The boy's keepin' it."

"Right. Well, I must be off. Good luck, Sergeant!"

Paul snatched at the suit-case, for which Banglewick was stooping. He escaped. That was a good line, he thought. Indeed, it may be feared, he thought more of the line—which, if not over-played, might be useful again—than of young Percy Banglewick's gloom.

Yet thrice, now, he had affected interest in other people's lives; and still he was unaware of his own power. That he was benevolent is beyond doubt. There was no harm in his remarks. And yet—and yet a man who is in love, and doesn't know it, is surely charged with mysterious force. Nature's intention, one would say, is that it should be beamed; not diffused. But how if he is unaware of this, too?

Of course it wasn't a Death-Ray. Quite the contrary, in fact. And yet, if there is any moral to be deduced from Paul's case, it is perhaps that it would have been safer for everyone if he had recognised his own symptoms, and used the power, like most chaps, just for himself.

.   .   .   .   .

It is to this point, in brief, that the theory has now come. Ordinary lovers, though of course infectious in a way, are such a common phenomenon, and are so frank, or careless, about revealing their state, that they are more a subject for mockery than for alarm. The rest of the race, forewarned at a glance, can take precautions, if they wish, and will be safe. But the unwitting lover can give no such clear warning. It may be that, like Paul, he is ignorant because he is innocent. Should this be so, one can hardly blame him for that.

Yet innocence is the very devil in a world where it is so rare. Furthermore, it immensely strengthens the power. As Paul Sunderland, a young gentleman virtually without vices, and whose delayed development—or thick-headedness, if anyone prefers that—in this one particular and unusual instance was so largely the result of an infernal war; as Paul Sunderland stood in a crowded railway-compartment on the short journey (for it was only about fifteen miles) between St. Pancras and Greenhurst, it may almost be felt that a case of live ammunition would have been less of a real peril than Paul.

There is no record, as a matter of fact, that, at this very short range, his condition affected the lives of the other passengers. The evidence, on the whole, is that if you didn't know him you were all right. Or that there had to be some link before he struck. Personally, he was absorbed in speculation about Bournemouth, though still there was a thick mist over the truth. But as he arrived at his uncle's house, it was the remoter past that was in his mind. He was concerned with what a little squirt he had once been.

Nevertheless, here came the Power, though there was no sign of it yet. Except—but this was the catch, for no one had known anything else—that he was looking remarkably well.

"Hullo, H.B.," he said. And a little later: "Hullo, Cranky!" with genuine pleasure, for indeed she was more than an old friend. And, finally, but this was only just before dinner: "Hullo, Prim!" And then: "By Jove—" for, dash it all, she was his cousin and a mere child—"you look a bit smashing tonight."

His cousin Prim didn't blush. Nor did she deny that she looked smashing. She said: "It's my hair, I expect."

"Eh? Oh, I see. You've had it twiddled or something. Or untwiddled. Well, it's fine from the front."

This marked the end of Paul's delicate compliments, which were sincere, but which he saw no cause to plug. He didn't say, for example: "Turn round"—which girls hate. It wasn't his custom. Any more than he stared. Naturally, he was pleased that his cousin Prim was darned pretty; though, as he recalled his last glimpse, less surprised. Good luck to her, in fact. She was one of the clan.

Yet so was H.B. Almost the pick of the bunch. And so—or, by this time, practically—was Cranky. What did she think of it all? He suddenly wondered, for the first time. He felt th tahe should have wondered before. He shot a glance at her, and was struck by another queer thought. For just as Prim was looking older—though certainly not old—so was Cranky looking younger, down here.

He hadn't noticed it at first; but it was obvious now. Had she been and done something to her own hair? He felt doubtful. Though women did. Yet he couldn't *analyse* any change. Did it mean, then—by any chance—that it was *he* who was getting old? Like that business—for his cousin Rhoda had once told him of this—of suddenly observing that there were nothing but young policemen?

But Cranky *was* young. Thirty-eight at the very most. That was nothing. The real point was that she was a pet. And a heroine. Just think of all the kindness she had shown, to himself, and to

Mark, and to Prim. And to H.B., too. He'd be sunk if she left. She must stay, then. The whole set-up should remain fixed.

"Paul! Mind your drink!"

"Sorry. Goose on my grave."

"That's cheerful," said Prim; and she laughed. "Here—I'll fill it up."

"Hi! Steady, young Prim!"

But he was steady himself now. There were no more geese, whether from Bournemouth or anywhere else, during the rest of an enjoyable evening. There was an under-current, it is true, from a dream-like world that he had once known. From a Greenhurst that was still green, before that surge of building in the 'thirties. From the period, though he had only come in for the extreme tail-end, when this had indeed been the Sunderland country.

Sad. Yet of course no sadder than what had happened elsewhere. Rather a miracle, in fact, that the little kingdom had held out so long. And the Sunderlands weren't broke, even though this was the last house left. Nor was it tragic—or in all probability—for Grannie herself that, after a long life of love and kindness all round, she should have died peacefully and at just the right time.

Yet where had it all gone to? No answer to that; even with a couple of other survivors in the room. Or three, if you counted Prim; though she was really too young. And—for such thoughts tend to play leap-frog when one is also talking and listening—if H.B. *liked* carrying on here, and wasn't haunted by something else, it was certainly a jolly nice, quiet, unpretentious sort of place. And Cranky had been jolly decent about those rations.

"What's this for?" she had asked, when Paul offered his so-called book. "Put it away. I don't want it. Please, Paul."

She had been his governess. He obeyed; though feeling guilty at first. Yet somehow, and though he had gathered that there was a very small and scratch team behind the scenes, it was a jolly good dinner as well. Afterwards, in the hall, because there was no heat in the drawing-room, he played a card-game with his cousin Prim—at which he was perhaps lucky, considering the obscurity of the rules, to find that he had only lost half a crown.

More talk. Cranky slipped off; to help the team, he suspected, if indeed not to replace them. Prim yawned, kissed her father, and left, too. H.B., unable to look out of the window at this time of night, withdrew into a dark corner instead. "Sit down," he said. "Quite early," he said. "Hrrm," he said. Now it's coming, thought

Paul. Now I'll know why I'm here. But though his uncle continued to emit a kind of aura to this effect, and though Paul continued to feel it, and was both attentive and wide awake, all that emerged was more mild, friendly talk.

About their work, though not much. About the clan. About the world. Dry, characteristic, and very sound stuff from H.B.; yet not, surely, what was at the back of his mind. He was shying off something. Or wasn't he? How on earth could one tell? Perhaps he wasn't; and presently this feeling grew less. So did the aura—the very last possibility that struck Paul was that he had one of his own—and H.B. was on the hearth-rug; which was another sign.

He jingled his keys. "Well?"

"Yes, of course." Paul bounced up. Two minds with only one thought now. Bed.

The usual patter, and responses, about breakfast and all that. Lights out. Up the stairs. Separation at the top—"No, I'm sure I've got everything, thanks," said Paul, though struggling with a yawn now himself. Another click, and more darkness, as he again said good-night. And here he was—all very nice, clean, and comfortable, too—still with four nights to go.

For that was how it took him, as he shut the door, and eyed the bed. He could no longer have yawned if he had tried. An inner click, or twinge, had said Bournemouth again. Let's see, now. About a hundred miles from London. Call it a hundred and twenty, then—so as to be generous—from here. Or less, perhaps, in a direct bee-line. But there she was. Or so he imagined. And he was here.

Curious. All he knew about Bournemouth, as a matter of fact, was that Stevenson had once lived there. He tried to picture it. He couldn't. He tried to picture Aunt Bony. He corrected the spelling in his mind. No; Aunt Boney. She was firm; or she had been. But was she kind? That was the point. Did she *appreciate* the possession of such a niece?

He ought to have inquired. An extraordinary lapse. Because if people went off to places that one didn't know—even if it was good for them to have a change and, he hoped, a rest—it put a sort of strain on other people, you see. It made it harder to think of them, in a way. In fact, it wasn't quite fair. Though he'd done it himself. But then, of course . . .

If anyone cares to call this kind of thing cerebration, then they can. It was certainly more than an oyster could have achieved.

Yet to keep it going, as Paul Sunderland did, off and on, while one
of his uncle's clocks struck eleven, and twelve, and even one, either
argues that Homo Sapiens shouldn't be trusted with a brain—
though perhaps, in the present age, this needs no proof—or, alternatively, that Paul Sunderland——

But we *know* about that. And if he didn't, poor mutt, yet lay
awake all that time, our own wisdom may say Serve him right.

.   .   .   .   .

The pattern of that visit has been experienced before, though
with varying details, of course. The visitor, that is to say, had
nothing to complain of, knew this, and even knew that he was
having quite a good, if perhaps not particularly exciting, time. The
weather remained dull, but the house—or all the parts of it that
were in use—remained warm. Miss Crankshaw, though it is unthinkable that she should have trifled with the law, continued to
provide excellent meals.

Nevertheless, there were few moments when the visitor ceased
to reflect on the mystery and passage of time. It was ungrateful,
he was well aware, to keep counting the hours. He had no wish to
be back, and utterly alone, in his flat. He was, indeed, most
fortunate to be here. And was enjoying himself. Yet still he kept
calculating, as he had once done during sermons, and, to tell the
truth, as so many visitors do.

Inevitably, also, half-time wasn't really half-time. It never
is, even in such a long thing as life. Even impatience, though he
showed no sign of it, couldn't prevent the second half from being
shorter than the first. Acceleration, though at the beginning he
could hardly have believed that it would do it again, almost whirled
him through the last twenty-four hours. Yet it is also possible that
there was a contributory cause.

On the Sunday evening, after not doing very much except
potter, walk, talk, sit, eat, sleep, and feel attached to the permanent
members of the house-party, and having still got no nearer deciding
whether H.B. had anything special on his mind or not—for whenever this idea was dismissed, something else seemed to make it
come back—the visitor (as visitors do) found himself alone in the
hall.

He had no sense of being neglected. He was quite content to
sit and smoke. He was reading a newspaper; and though he had

L

just gathered from it that delivery of the Porchester Leveret (though several improvements had been introduced) was now expected to take longer than ever, it wasn't this that made him start to his feet.

He was disappointed, that is to say, but philosophical at the same time. No, what had made him shoot up wasn't annoyance. Not the least. It was the sudden thought—though a visionary car may, of course, well remind one of a real one—that this was the moment, when nobody else was around, to put in a trunk call to Bournemouth. And then? Oh, nothing special. Just what came into his head. It seemed, indeed, that this thought had been germinating for some time, though it had only just, as it were, reached the surface.

If it was met at once, as it was, by a number of objections— such as Don't be an idiot, or Leave her alone, can't you?—it was still strong enough (for it had set off first) to get him out of the hall, and along a passage, and into H.B.'s study. For there was a telephone here. And, as befitted a senior partner, a whole collection of directories. If he could find the Bournemouth one—well, H.B. wouldn't mind. And he would be repaid. Any guest could do that.

He switched on the light. He approached the collection. If the two thoughts were at each other's throats now, he could still go this far. Except, of course, that he had omitted—like a fool—to secure the address. That Brown—if Aunt Boney was unmarried, and he wasn't actually even sure of this—was a dashed widespread name. And that——

No. Wait a moment. She *must* be unmarried. He had never been told this, but it was the kind of thing that one *felt*. Besides, if she'd had a husband, he'd have been in the photograph-album, too. Surely. Hope soared. It fell back with a thud. For she still wouldn't be listed as Miss Boney Brown; and, oh, lord—for he had got the right volume open now—just look at those columns of Browns!

Yet just because this was difficult, if not impossible, he must go on looking. The first thought seemed to thrive on opposition. Perhaps he *had* heard the address; and if he saw it, he would remember. Worth trying, you know.

He bent over the book. He began with "Brown A." His forefinger moved slowly, as he examined each address. It may be said now that, to a certain extent, he had forgotten his main object. Certainly he had forgotten that he must still decide what to say. It was the search that had become important. A Sunderland was

on the trail. And, like all Sunderlands, when they had determined to
tackle a task, he would go on till he came to the end.

Yet he didn't, as a matter of fact. He was less than half-way
through—still without having spotted any address that seemed to
click—when he sensed rather than heard someone behind him. He
shut the book. He turned round. It was his cousin Prim.

"Oh!" she said. "Oh—I'm sorry," she added.

What for? This was her home. Of course she could come in.
Even in a kimono, if she liked. Paul drew back.

"Were you going to telephone?" he asked. "Go on. Go ahead."

"But weren't *you*——"?

"No. No," said Paul. He offered no explanation of what he
was doing with the directory. But it was true enough. The second
thoughts had romped in. "Oh, no," he said. It had been a blithering
idea. Besides, he couldn't. Even if he knew the number, he had
missed the chance. "Oh, no," he repeated, slightly harping on this
point. "Not at all. I—I was only looking something up."

"Are you *sure*?" She must have just had a bath, she was so
pink. "Because mine doesn't matter. Not in the least."

"Go on," said Paul, firmly. "That's all right. I'll clear out."

"But . . ."

"Yes?"

"Oh, very well," said his cousin Prim. She looked—but this
was absurd—as if she didn't *want* to ring up. As if he had *made* her.
And of course he hadn't. (Yet perhaps he had.)

In any case that was the last of his own attempt to find a needle
in a telephonic haystack. Common sense, or what be regarded as
common sense, took over. She—he meant Bianca—would be coming
back tomorrow night, or on Tuesday morning (when he was to
return himself) at the very latest. If he had anything to say to her,
he knew her Flaxman number. He had, in fact, been rather an
ass.

Yet not such a complete ass but that something flitted across
his mind. He wondered, that is to say, in the middle of Sunday
supper—but didn't ask, because he wasn't that sort of chap—just
why his cousin Prim had come down to a cold room, in a kimono, to
use the telephone, when, as he knew, there were extensions upstairs.
Perhaps— Oh, good heavens, what *could* matter less? It wasn't
worth, and he didn't give it, another thought.

At about mid-day on Monday, or Bank Holiday, in other words, his cousin Mark suddenly arrived in a small car. He somehow formed the impression, though there was a warm welcome from all, that this had been done on the spur of the moment. H.B., for instance, said more than once that, if he had known—but trippers last year had gone off with a lot of daffodils—he wouldn't have shouted like that. Miss Crankshaw said that if *she* had known—("Oh, Cranky," said Mark, "I've only just had breakfast")—she would have switched the chicken from dinner to lunch.

Prim, as a matter of fact, only raised her eyebrows; though she gave a little twist to her mouth at the same time. Paul saw this, but attached no significance to the little twist. It was now his turn, though he wasn't exactly a host, to look welcoming, too.

"And old Paul!" said Mark, unwinding a long scarf. "The missing man. Where on earth have *you* been?"

"Nowhere," said Paul. "I mean to say——"

"Never mind. I'll tell Ma. She was rather wondering if you were alive."

"Well, you see——"

But as no one was listening, this concluded the defence; or whatever Paul had been going to say. Just for a moment he had felt as if all his clothes were coming off. But at the next moment— and, besides, that was all rot about Rhoda—he was merely as pleased as anyone else that Mark was here. The clan solidified, in the hall. They were all at their best. Mark—no, you couldn't get away from it—had some quality that was damnably enviable.

Youth? Well, not entirely. Charm? Yes, of course. Self-assurance? Perhaps. But good manners, you know. He never boasted, though he was darned clever. And in a way, all the time— No. No; self-assurance was wrong. It might even be—a queer thought, this, but it seemed to dispose of *that* kind of self-assurance— that he was a little nervous down here. Or not? Was Paul making this up?

The thing is, he suddenly decided, that I believe *I've* been overworking. He knew he hadn't; just as he was aware that this was a pretty violent *non sequitur*. He issued an order. Leave it alone. It's all right. Mark's got charm, and Prim's got charm; and so have all the other Sunderlands—not to mention kind Cranky; but as you haven't got it yourself, just shut up!

At lunch, nevertheless, it did occur to him that as he couldn't understand himself—and somehow he couldn't, these days—then of course he couldn't understand anyone else. This appeared to soothe him, and he remained soothed. Afterwards, as was only natural, Mark and Prim went for a drive. But the visit was moving so quickly by now that he could hardly remember, as he shared another and considerably less crowded compartment with H.B. in the morning, anything particular that had taken place after that.

He had been for a walk with Cranky—to look at the outside of their first meeting-place, now in the possession of a big Combine—and it was to be presumed that they had conversed as well. After tea he had first pottered and then chatted with his uncle. Mark had stayed for dinner, but then had left "because of Ma." Prim had gone to bed. Cranky had disappeared. H.B.—or was this an illusion, too?—had again somehow suggested that he was trying to say something.

But he hadn't said it. Or he had said nothing, though they had had quite a jaw, of such import that he could have thought twice before saying it. No. Look at him now; reading *The Times* over there. Dry. That was the word. Yes, and lovable, too. That was a fact, and it had all been great fun. But to have imagined, as one had, that he had been trying to talk—to a younger nephew, of all people—about something that had happened when the nephew was a little squirt, and that he never mentioned now (as the nephew knew) to a living soul . . .

No. Certainly not. Only a lunatic could have thought that. Paul plunged into his own newspaper; and as London—familiar, dirty, week-day, workaday London came sliding along on both sides, the visit dissolved, rather like cloud-capp'd towers or gorgeous palaces, into something no longer quite real. Into a memory, in fact, which might or might not be re-examined from time to time. Which each examination must also slightly fog. But which could be spared no more phosphorus now.

The mind and its group of elements must re-engage themselves with business. With the extra effort (not that business wasn't also rather fun) always required after a lengthy week-end. The machinery would be rattling and clanking a bit, until others had recovered from their own holidays. But Miss Thriplow would be running smoothly. No nonsense there. And tonight, perhaps, or tomorrow, or surely some time this week, there would be relaxation as well.

Bournemouth seemed much nearer, suddenly, now that Bianca had left it. Though it was more to the point—indeed, very much to the point—that she must now be even nearer herself.

10

DURING the next three weeks—as measured by those who took the trouble to do so—the fissure in the entity generally known as Paul Sunderland was less that between an actor and an observer, or critic, than between a couple of alternating automata.

One of them performed all the functions of a junior partner, club member, and occupant of a service-flat; and did this competently and ably enough. The other was the companion, guest, host, and telephonic interlocutor of a model employed by Michael Willoughby. Not incessantly, it is true, and has just been implied. Yet repeatedly. There can be no doubt of that.

It seemed almost to be happening of its own accord, though it is to be presumed that there was some planning as well. But there was a kind of flow, now, or rhythm, that bore him along. She had other engagements, and so had he. But the current swept past them. Or he took them in his stride. Or, again, when she wasn't there, he was someone else.

His old self, perhaps. Yet there was a change here, too. For the Paul at the office, or at his club, or in his flat, no longer argued or wrangled with an *alter ego*. He, or it, had abandoned those violent disputes, about his conduct, or motives, or creed. Whether this was an armistice or a pact can be anyone's guess; though it seems unlikely that Paul Secundus was dead. He was quiescent, however; or if he spoke, he wasn't heard. Whatever he was up to, communication had ceased.

For self-questioning was suspended, as it is when one dreams. Schizophrenia had become too complete. The second automaton, though it talked, listened, and laughed—with apparent intelligence and unfailing civility—was so distinct from the first that there was no moment when they could enter into discussion.

There were two dreams, in fact, in which Paul passed his days. Habit and practice may have concealed this. There was no hint that he was asleep. Yet for three whole weeks—according to the calendar, that is to say—there were two Pauls going around. A Paul with Bianca, or telephoning to Bianca; and a Paul when she wasn't there, or had rung off. They never met. They shared a body, in turn, but that was all. It almost sounds like the effect of some drug.

And of course, in a sense, this was just what it was. The

symptoms are far from unknown. It isn't injected, or swallowed, but it is absorbed. In the majority of acute cases, when this stage has been reached, it provokes a crisis in considerably less than three weeks. But then Paul, however foolishly, or whatever adverb may be preferred, had now been treating himself homœopathically for three months.

Friendship, he had said; which is the smallest dose of the drug. Then he must increase it; he had to, it seemed; though still, as he believed, from the same phial. When cut off from it at Easter there had been a craving, which he had controlled. But few have gained freedom like that. There is tension. To ease it, one doubles the dose. It isn't Friendship any longer. It is Love.

Yet what addict, after denying its existence, indulging in homœopathy, and caught finally by something stronger than himself; what addict, with reason all haywire by now, can bring judgment to bear on his own case? The stuff is poison, of course; though chaps have survived. But if they don't *know* what they are doing—and Paul certainly didn't—does experience suggest that they will stop?

It doesn't. And he couldn't. He was in for it now. There is no doubt that he was wildly in love. But he was dreaming as well. And the girl gave no help; though she didn't start choking him off, either.

She hadn't noticed, perhaps, that he had changed in any way; and, in fact, there was very little to notice. Automata behave as they have been told to behave, and Paul was still under his own original orders. Very polite. Very friendly. She liked him a lot. She had no idea that she was dealing with an automaton.

In her own experience—which was by no means slight, and hardly could be, with her looks and in her situation—signs of tiresomeness could be detected at once. Men turned sulky. Or soppy. Or tried to be masterful, which was even worse. Because she was kind, she tried to warn them; though without much success. For, once they became tiresome, they went mad.

Again, because she was kind (though she hadn't thought this out), they seemed to think they could repeat the whole thing. A few of them, as has been said, after several rebuffs, had married somebody else; and she was delighted. But none of them—though of course it wasn't easy in these days—had rushed off at once to shoot lions. Not a bit; and as she liked lions, this was perhaps just as well. But they didn't go *anywhere*. They came crawling back. She knew just what they were going to do. Try again.

It wasn't that she disliked them. She had explained this, of course. But it seemed to encourage them, too.

"Listen," she had said, on certainly not less than ten occasions—though it may well have been more, for she kept no count. "Listen, Brian—" or Jock—or Philip—or Godfrey—or whatever the young gentleman was called—"I'm not in love with you. I'm awfully sorry. But I'm not. If you're sensible," she usually added, "of *course* we can be friends. But I just *can't* be anything else."

Some were temporarily stunned, and she was terribly sorry for them. Some resumed their proposals at once. But even the stunned ones recovered, and often all too soon. It was nice, of course, that she hadn't quarrelled with any of them. She quite saw that it was an indication of esteem. She didn't want them to hate her. She had taken no vestal vow.

But she did *not* see why she should get married so as to oblige someone else. And she was about sick of new friends becoming tiresome in turn, and of older friends still supposing that she would change her mind. If she had been plain or unattractive she might have thought this rather fun. But as things were, it was a constant menace and curse.

One day, of course, someone *marvellous* would come along. That would be lovely; if he thought her marvellous, too. The battle would be over. They would just adore each other for ever. No one else (for, though untouched, she was deeply romantic) need then be considered at all.

Meanwhile, there was Paul Sunderland, who clearly liked her, and whom she liked; but who obviously shared her own views. She hadn't asked him, and he hadn't said so, but one could *tell* by this time. Never tiresome. Never possessive. Never plaintive—it was *awful* when they started being plaintive. Never huffy. Just sensible. And reliable. And nice.

Some girl, in fact, whether marvellous or not, would find a prize packet in Paul. He didn't realise this, which was nice of him, too; and slightly pathetic, in a sort of way. She did hope—though of course she would congratulate him, whatever his choice—that the girl would go *on* making him happy.

I shall miss him, she thought; though of course that's what'll happen. It's been fun. It's been different. I'm so glad we met. If I'd had a brother, or a cousin, perhaps, and had been allowed to pick him out, I think he'd have been awfully like Paul.

Still (thought Bianca) it's bound to happen one day. There'll be this girl. Or perhaps *I'll* suddenly meet just the right man. And then—well, there you are. But we shall still have been friends. And it's *mad* to keep looking ahead.

This was the voice of her generation, which has been planned at, but can't plan. As she spent all that she earned, plus what was left to her of the Pottings' rent; as she had no other resources; as her aunt, though more provident, in a sense, than her father, was now subsisting (sooner than starve, sponge, or put her head in a gas-oven) on an annuity; and as modelling, even at Michael Willoughby's, isn't a career that lasts for ever, it was perhaps wise to take life as it came.

Not to worry, which might have aged her, and ended her job. To be cheerful, which was good for everyone, including herself. To be firm, on her own lines, about accepting more than she could return. And never even to consider—but she couldn't, whether this was wise or not—marrying anyone, however rich, or however poor if it came to that, until absolutely convinced that she was in love.

This was rather unusual. Yet Paul Sunderland was quite right when he formed the opinion that she was a jolly nice girl.

II

DEADLOCK? Not exactly. The association went on. Neither party was conscious of strain. Beneath the surface there were, of course, all kinds of possibilities. And dangers, it may be, as well. But Paul, drifting and dreaming, in those two incarnations, was still, so far as could be detected, the old Paul. Bianca, doing neither, and still her own self, continued to see him, to talk to him, and to like him a lot; but with no gift of exclusive rights.

"Oh, Paul," she was still saying; "I'm sorry. I can't." But she didn't expect him to flare up, and he never did. Or, alternatively: "Yes, let's." But he didn't whoop. He said: "Right." Or: "What time, then?" Or something like that.

The possibility that they were on thin ice, with a raging furnace below, wasn't one of which they appeared to have thought. He still wasn't tiresome. She still used no arts. It was like Eden, in a sense, though with fewer animals and more people, so far as these two were concerned. Eventually, of course, it must go the same way. It always does. As it did the first time.

And yet, since there was no serpent, since Paul was prepared to drift, and since Bianca never attempted to egg him on, it might have lasted, in theory, for another three months. Or three years. Or a lifetime, perhaps.

But in practice it couldn't; for, again, it never does. Something would happen. That is an axiom. And, as a matter of fact, three things happened almost at once.

The first affected millions. The second, a few hundred. The third was pin-pointed on Paul. But as they all pulled together, and cracked or melted the ice, all three must be chronicled now.

On the second Thursday in May, then, the evening newspapers announced that it would be cold and unsettled; while a voice on the radio, after alluding to air-streams, troughs, belts, and wedges, plumped without qualification for strong winds, heavy rain, and an extremely low temperature.

The Climate reacted almost instantly. "Eh?" it said. "What's that? Very well, then. Here goes." With the result that by Friday morning there wasn't a breath of wind anywhere, there wasn't a cloud in the blue skies, and a delicious, balmy spell had set in— yes, we're there at last, even if it has taken a little time—which continued, as a matter of fact, for almost precisely three weeks, and transformed England, and even London, into one vast burgeoning and blooming bower.

It was spring. It was indeed more than that. It was the Poets' spring. It was soft, but not debilitating. It was all colour and freshness. It restored elasticity even to old gentlemen with gout. It intoxicated the young. It rejuvenated the middle-aged. People went about smiling, and Nature smiled, too. Birds sang. Flowers burst forth. Lungs expanded. Eyes shone. If it had lasted indefinitely there would have been complaints and an official drought. But coming, as it did, after months of dull days, it not only received a welcome from all bodies and souls not actually engaged in the umbrella-trade, but restored warmth and hope to them, too.

"There!" said the Climate. It hadn't finished, of course. Those who said that this must be paid for, as many of them did, would almost certainly prove to have been right. Yet meanwhile even

London was sparkling and green. There was a haze every morning. There was dew every night. No staleness, nor hint of staleness, as yet. All was balmy, and brilliant, and gay.

So much for the first thing, which stirred the whole land. The second was more local, and less cheery. For on the same Thursday night—and though of course it was just as well that it *was* during the night—one end of the long, ornate ceiling in the dining-room of the Junior Corinthian Club collapsed suddenly, in a cloud of plaster and black dust, and though no one was injured there was the very whale of a mess.

The black dust wasn't content to remain where it fell. It permeated through the whole premises. It could be removed, in due course, just as the plaster could be patched up. But, meanwhile— whether, as the Committee said, this was the result of the bomb that had destroyed a neighbouring building six years ago, or, as the Authorities would then say, had absolutely no connection with that occurrence—it was clear that the Club must be closed.

Only temporarily, of course. And other clubs would rally round, as they always did in the summer recess. Or as the Junior Corinthian itself would behave, when it was the other clubs' turn to close down. Nevertheless, when Paul Sunderland, who had been intending to dine here (since this was an evening, as he knew, when Bianca would be unavailable), arrived on foot (for in this weather of course he must walk) at about twenty to seven, he was first astonished to find that the front door was shut; and then learnt, since by this time there was a typewritten notice gummed on to it, that he could proceed, if he chose, either to the Combined Sportsmen or the Megalithic.

To two extremes, in other words. But why? What was up? Another member had just approached, and this member told him.

"Jolly old ceiling," he explained, "came down in the night. Thought I'd look if I could, but—" here he rattled the door— "seems I can't. Didn't you see it in the evening paper?"

"No," said Paul, for he hadn't bought one. Why should he, when he was coming here? He felt bewildered, for automata don't expect things like that. They rather rely on a stationary background.

"Good lord!" said the other member, at this point. "Look at that. Megalithic? No, thank you. Not me." He showed no gratitude to the Committee, or to the Megalithic, if it comes to that, for the hospitality that he was now being offered. "Frightful place," he said. "My father belongs. They're all over ninety, you know. Well? Coming to the Sportsmen?"

But Paul thought not. Disaster, it seemed, had forged a link with this chap, but he had no wish to carry it further. He only knew him by sight. He had never cared for his voice; or his friends; or the whole of that set. They were bar-flies. Furthermore, as he could see, or believed he could see, the chap himself was now regretting his words.

So they parted, without rancour—"Right-ho," said the chap— and as Paul now felt that he was cut off from the Combined Sportsmen, but was equally disinclined (no place for me, either, he thought) to sample the Megalithic, he went straight to the pub where you have seen him before; and thus—entirely, whatever the Authorities might say, because a bomb had blown up a fourth club six years ago —reached his flat at a quarter to eight.

It was here, also, that he met Spilsby, in the lift, with a tray. He wouldn't have seen him if he had returned when he had planned. And it was thus, once more, that Spilsby, after commenting on the weather, said: "Oh, I think there was a parcel for you, sir." And even produced it after a while, which he might not otherwise have done for several days—since when once he had accepted a parcel from the postman, during a tenant's absence, he was apt to forget this until something reminded him.

Such reminders, when a tenant was awaiting a parcel, would of course not be long delayed. But Paul was expecting nothing. It was his early return that had done the trick. Stimulated by speculation— was he going to ask for another, and unordered, tray, too?—Spilsby's memory was jogged. And at about a quarter past eight he reappeared, and handed over the parcel.

"Oh," said Paul. "Thanks." He couldn't think whom it was from. But he opened it, as soon as Spilsby had withdrawn, and saw that there was a letter inside.

"*Dear Paul*," he read, standing by the window. He glanced at the signature. Looked distinctly surprised. And returned to the beginning.

"*Dear Paul,*

What on earth do you think? Rex was grubbing about in the cellar at his office, and he found this. Just like a publisher, though of course he hadn't joined the firm then—in fact I think he was at school with you—not to know what he's published! So he brought it home, and he says if you want any more copies he'll sell them you cheap, as it doesn't seem to have gone very well.

Here you are, though, anyhow. I saw Bianca last week, when we were both in a queue, and she told me she'd been seeing you, which is more than we have. Ring up soon. I'm going to have another baby. Isn't it thrilling! Pa-in-law is still at it—thanks to you. But he's a bit slow. Rex says it all comes of giving a party on St. Valentine's Day, and if so we must always do it.

Good luck and all that,

Lulu."

Despite the warmth and even intimacy of this communication, Paul—or as much of Paul as wasn't now wrenching at more paper— still stuck to it that only Parky was his real friend. It was a fixation, if you like. It is how some bachelors' minds work. Nothing yet—not even a letter like this—could convince him that he had gained another friend, too.

However, as he tore at the inner wrapping, he gave a start. Both the Parkinsons passed clean out of his head. For he was holding a book. Not that this made him start; since he had known it, even before reading the letter, from the general shape and weight of the parcel. But now he had seen the plain jacket. *Poems, by Alured Brown.* He dropped the paper. He began reading again.

He read the title-page first, with the imprint and date. 1930. Yes, he had just gone to school. That, in fact, helped to explain why he hadn't heard of it at the time. He should have been relieved; but he felt rather wrought up.

Dedication. *To the Memory of my Wife.* Oh, poor *child*! He had known. But to see it in print! He trembled slightly.

But he still read on, as he sank (for support) into a chair. The Table of Contents—hardly distinctive, though clearly lyrical in tone. Thirty-three poems in all. Mostly short. Yet thanks to generous margins, large type, thick paper, and a process once known to the trade as "bumping-out," it was quite a solid sort of volume to hold.

Paul held it, and continued reading, with close attention and care. Not only was he seeking for some clue here, though he perhaps hardly knew what; but he *wanted* to sympathise, and admire, and understand. Few readers, it may well be, of *Poems by Alured Brown* had approached them with a greater wish to discover their beauty and truth.

He didn't hurry. He took pains. If criticism raised its head, he slammed it down, and looked stern, and went on. Some secret, he still felt, must be contained in these lines. He would extract it, if he had to read them all twice. Bianca's father was speaking. He had produced Bianca. And she had adored him. Very well, then; she must be somewhere here, too.

Outside, the exquisite spring evening turned slowly to dusk, so that presently he switched on a light. But the stern look had changed to an almost permanent frown. He moved uneasily. His judgment was refusing to be suppressed, and he was engaged in a real fight with it now.

It wasn't that the poems didn't scan. They did. It wasn't that they weren't poems. They were. It wasn't, again, in his opinion, that they weren't infinitely better than the poems of Ella Wheeler Wilcox, though it was possible that they lacked some of her assurance. But that was just it. They were woolly, as well as weak. They expressed nothing, though they expressed it with reasonable skill. All they revealed was the character whose photograph he had seen. Kind, ineffective, doomed to failure in life. A figure, he suddenly felt—and almost writhed at this point—of appalling and infinite pathos.

He couldn't stand it. He shut the book. He lurched to his feet. And in a flash—for such was the effect, after all, of these poems—it was Bianca who was so unutterably pathetic. Her courage. Her loyalty. Her silence about that Shelter. Her risky, impossible life. Her laughter. Her own kindness. Her beauty. Her Rules. Her generosity. Her——

He couldn't go on with the list. For there was a second flash; and a huge lump in his throat.

He swallowed, with some difficulty. He stared into the night. He began speaking, aloud, to himself.

"Blind!" he announced. "And half-witted as well. I'm always happy when I'm with her. I'm never happy—I never *have* been—when I'm not. Friendship, indeed!" said Paul Sunderland, with a ghastly sneer. "What nonsense. What absolute rot! It's *far* more than that. I've been in love for three months."

He considered this. And nodded. He was tingling all over. It also struck him that he had wasted three months. A wild look of impatience, despair, hope, misery, terror, and beatification passed over his face in a third flash. Thus it was that the late Mr. Alfred Brown's one book of poems, which would never have been published if he hadn't paid for it himself, of which only thirteen copies had been sold, and which, also, had represented a considerable disappointment to him until he was removed suddenly and (let us hope) painlessly to Paradise, achieved, nearly seven years after his death, an effect beyond all that he could have surmised.

It was they, not the hidden furnace, that had demolished the ice. And not because they were good, but because they were bad. Or poor, at the very best, and quite uninspired, as poems can be though a poet has given all to them. For it is not enough, or so it seems, to refuse to be a civil engineer, to marry for love, to lose your wife, to be adored by your daughter, and to be so gentle and muddle-headed that you also lose most of your money—unless the Muses approve and assist.

It isn't enough to die suddenly, by a kind of double mischance. Real poets must do more than that. Even changing your name from Alfred to Alured—though as a matter of fact, and as we have learnt, this was really another accident—may still leave you on the lower slopes of Parnassus. Yet in certain circumstances—and here they were—a spark may spring from a distinctly mediocre book of verse, and produce an almost overwhelming result.

.　　　.　　　.　　　.　　　.

Is this to say that Paul Sunderland would never have caught fire if Mrs. Parkinson hadn't sent him that parcel? Of course not. At any moment he might have burst into flame; another case of spontaneous combustion. But the weather, his early return—so that he read the book at once—and the book itself, all acted together at the same time.

Sleep avoided him that night until past three o'clock, for the first time in many years. His thoughts, and condition, in the morning have long since been described, and may be found at the beginning of Part One. He was anxious. Dashed anxious. He even felt, as chaps do, that it would have been better, in many ways, if one could put the clock back.

But this was only because he was so nervous. If he had been offered the chance, he would have refused. Besides, it was impossible; unimaginable; and absurd. He knew what he wanted. It was, of course, a million to one that he wouldn't get it. But he must go on now. He could neither pause nor retreat.

He could never remember how he got through the forenoon; though as a matter of fact, among other apparently quite normal activities, he dictated eight letters to Miss Thriplow. But it was Saturday. At a quarter to one he rushed out, and this time bought a pound's worth of flowers. His next appointment with Bianca, as planned, was for tonight; when they had arranged to dine, not at her domicile—for they had done this on Thursday—but somewhere near, and go on to a film.

It was all fixed, in fact. But at two o'clock he rang up. There was no reply. He tried again, three times—not intending to declare his love yet, but in the hope of an earlier and personal opportunity of doing precisely this thing—before she finally answered, at about five.

He was then momentarily struck dumb. Yet he rallied. He spoke.

"Oh, Paul," she said, "yes, do come in sooner. Only I must have a bath first—the water was *stone*-cold this morning; so could you get here about six?"

He could. He did. He was ten minutes early, for he had never known such an interminable hour. He had the flowers, too—at last. He hadn't faltered this time. Though as she opened the door to him he suddenly thrust them behind his back.

"Hullo," she was saying. "I thought it would be you. Come in, then—and I'll give you a little drink."

They were in the sitting-room now.

"No, thank you," said Paul. "I——"

She turned round, looking surprised. She saw the flowers—they were red roses, and might have cost perhaps five or six shillings before the war—for he was holding them out. And she looked still more surprised.

"What——" she began.

"They're for you," said Paul.

"But——" She was drawing back.

"There—there's a reason," he said. "Bianca—— Oh, well." He put them down. "Are you listening?" he inquired.

"Yes, of course; but——"

"All right. I—I shan't take very long. Look here—to start with—I—I told you a lie once."

Rather a queer start, too. But she only stared. He ploughed on.

"Yes," he said. "That first time I—I met you outside your shop. I told you it was an accident. Well, it wasn't. D'you see? I—I was waiting on purpose that night."

There! said his expression. Now at least I've come clean. But she still looked surprised—until she laughed.

"Oh, Paul—you look just like a funny little boy. What does it matter? Why on earth are you worrying now? Do you mean—" she glanced at the table—"that *that* was why you brought me a present? But you needn't. You shouldn't. Though of course they're awfully——"

She stopped. She was puzzled again, as he began fumbling in an inner pocket.

"Paul! What is it?"

He was opening his note-case. He had extracted, and was exhibiting, a book of stamps.

"But, Paul, I don't *want* it. I bought some today. You *mustn't* be so—so silly about nothing. As if it mattered—*months* afterwards——"

"But it *does!*" he burst in. "And it isn't nothing. And I'm only *showing* you. Don't you see? It's the little book you gave *me*. That time I paid for the drinks. At your club. Don't you remember?"

"Well, yes, but I—I don't understand."

"I kept it," said Paul. He slid the book into the case. "I've never used it." He returned the case to his pocket. "*Now* do you understand?"

It hardly seemed, though, that she did.

"All right," he resumed at once; "I'll go on. I've been blind, you see——"

"*Paul!*"

"No, not like that. Wait a moment."

"But what do you *mean?*"

"I'm telling you," said Paul. "Gimme a chance. Those roses come into it, too, of course. I bought 'em because I lul-love you. And I kept the stamps because I love you. But I didn't *know* I loved you, until something suddenly happened. Well, that's why I came early—because as soon as I knew, I couldn't wait. And, look here, don't think I *haven't* loved you all this time; because I *have*; only——"

"Oh, no, Paul—*please!*"

"Eh? I haven't finished. Where was I? Oh, yes. Well, you see, Bianca—darling, darling, *sweet* Bianca—I've never done this before —and of course I'm doing it rottenly—and I'm not *suggesting* you've ever encouraged me. But I've suddenly found out. It—it's changed the whole world; though I was *mad* not to see it before. All your kindness. All your sweetness. I've never thought of anything else since the second I saw you. I've got about twelve hundred a year,

M

by the way," he suddenly threw in. And even added: "Net," as she tried to speak.

But then again he was off; not looking at her now; and astounded, in a way, that it was so easy. Perhaps not looking at her helped. Or a disregard for mere syntax, as he babbled of love, blindness, madness, stupidity, unworthiness; though also, and unquestionably —for there must be no misunderstanding about this—of how he was offering her marriage.

It was an exhaustive if, at times, a confused performance. Occasionally he gesticulated, though not always with much bearing on the text. Sometimes he shouted, sometimes he was hoarse, but he never paused. At the very worst—and the very worst was now well on its way—he was sensible of unmitigated relief. For the occlusion had dispersed; and his heart, though it was also pounding a bit, was at last telling the truth.

And all the time the object of his declared affection stood there. Almost motionless, except when she again tried to speak, and the flood swept her aside; or except, just once or twice, when she glanced at the sheaf of flowers with a strange, frozen look. Her lips parted. She got as far as saying "Oh, Paul—" But he was determined, it seemed, to make his meaning quite clear. Though he had already done so, and without a vestige of doubt.

Yet he could feel the end coming. Or he had heard the sound of his own voice. He was forcing it, and it was resisting. He became tangled in such a sentence that it was impossible to proceed. He jerked his hand—as if to show that it was cancelled, and that he was starting afresh. But there was a pause at last, all the same, as he gulped and took a breath. And Bianca dived into the gap.

"Oh, Paul," she was saying. "Please. No. *Don't* go on!"

"What? But I haven't——"

"*Please*. Oh, Paul, it's no use. I *was* fond of you—I *am* fond of you; but I—I thought you were *different*. I thought for once, I thought at *last* you were someone who *understood*. It was stupid, I suppose, but you *were* different, Paul. I—I trusted you more than *any* of them!"

"Eh?" said Paul Sunderland. "Any of whom?"

"*Men*—can't you see? All doing the same thing. All pretending they're friends. And then suddenly— But it isn't *my* fault. I can't explain before they start. How *can* I? That would be ridiculous. It would be conceited—and rude. But there's something wrong with me——"

"No, there isn't."

"I seem to *make* them go mad. Oh, Paul, what can I do? I can't go into a nunnery—it isn't that, in the least. I'm quite ordinary——"

"No, you're not."

"I *am*. That's just it. But I want to wait, till it *really* happens. I must! Perhaps I'm backward——"

"I don't think so."

"—but I'm *honest*. That's all. I—I try not to accept things. Perhaps you've noticed——"

"Yes, I have."

"—but even that—" and here she looked mournfully at the roses again—"doesn't seem to work. But, Paul, I'm not awful. And then, you see, I had a shock. I've never told you. But something happened to poor Daddy."

"I know," said Paul. "Mrs. Parkinson told me. I ought to have said something, perhaps——"

"Oh, I'm so glad you didn't. And that's nothing to do with it, either. It never made me want to die, or to think of no one else. Paul, I swear it hasn't made me abnormal. And you mustn't think—because some people do—that it's Dorothea. Of course we're friends still, and she never really let me down. But it all happened just when another man—not as nice as you, but awfully nice until *that* started—simply wouldn't leave me alone. It was too much at once. And then she took his side. But, Paul, if I didn't love him, how *could* I?"

"Of course not," said Paul, in a bit of a whirl. "Have I met him?" he suddenly asked.

"Yes."

"But you're not going to marry him?"

"No."

"Well, that's something," said Paul, "I suppose."

She didn't answer. She just stood there, looking pale and distraught.

"Would you say—" a cad's question perhaps, but it was out— "would you say you were fonder of me?"

"Oh, Paul, don't be cruel!"

"I like that," he said. "Though of course I'd no business to ask." He shrugged his shoulders, though it was rather as if they had done this themselves. "Well," he added, "perhaps I'd better go, then."

"If you think so," she said.

"I shan't—well, I'm afraid I can't come back."

There was a faint, tragic smile. It contained less than contradiction, and there was even a trace of pity. But of course they all said that; and, so far, only one thing—which one shouldn't mention, and still less, of course, recommend—had succeeded in keeping them away.

"I shan't," he repeated, again like the rest. "And it isn't temper, or sulks." This was a shade more original, but only a shade. "It's just— No, how *can* I? I can't!" He gave a milder, and perhaps more conscious, shrug. "I—I've made rather a mess of all this, I'm afraid. I suppose you'd say that I *have* let you down. But I couldn't help it," he must still explain. "It's Love." A ghastly smile. "What they call the Real Thing. It—it sort of blew up, don't you see?"

"Yes, Paul. I'm sorry——"

"Oh, never mind that. But I wasn't *hiding* it—except from myself. And I'm terribly grateful——"

"Oh, *please*, Paul——"

"All right. Though I *am*. Well—" He seemed to choke, but he tried again, with more success. "Well, I'd better clear off now. Good-bye. Unless," he suddenly added, in a muffled voice, as he picked up his hat, "you—you think you could change your mind."

"No!" It was a sound of agony; and he was in agony, too, for that rash appendix had pierced his own pride. If he had suppressed it, he thought, as he left the flowers, and let himself out, and went slowly down the outside stairway, he would still be suffering; but far less than this. For it was just exactly, or so he had gathered, what the other chaps did. She had even warned him, by mentioning the fact.

It was no use saying that he had been too quick, for that wasn't true. On the contrary, he had been much, much too slow. He didn't claim that other chaps mightn't have found better words—they probably had—for their own declarations. He was inexperienced. He had babbled. But he had been polite. He hadn't whined. He had remained reasonable, or almost reasonable, until the very last second. He had received the blow with immense self-control.

He might almost, indeed, have been a third party looking on; even if, in a sense, this was how he had felt. But he hadn't lacked decency, or even dignity of a kind—until suddenly he had blurted that out. The echo pursued him as he slouched up the street. "Whipped cur," he remarked, to a lamp-post.

"All over," he muttered. "Though I suppose," he growled, "I

shall want to come crawling back, too. But not yet. Because I can't. Even if she asks me, I can't. I—I've got to get over this first. . . .

"Though of course—" he shook his head—"I shall never do that. I'm finished. I love her, you see."

As he neared the King's Road he was still conducting this monologue, and still occasionally shaking his head. However—this is a fact, as will be recognised if one stops to think—the streets of London, and indeed of all cities, are so full of people going about muttering to themselves, testing imaginary conversations, or arguing with invisible adversaries, that he attracted no special attention.

Nor did he actually hit any lamp-posts, though there were one or two narrow escapes. His feet bore him on. His eyesight still worked. It saw the other citizens, though they were all a bit blurred, and still kept him out of their way.

And then, at the last corner, it saw something else; and, as it did so, became focused again. There was a public-house here, as there often is. Its swing-door opened as he approached. And out came—though again this was perfectly natural, and nowhere more so than on a Saturday evening in Chelsea—the "artist" with the beard and the blue shirt.

He wasn't drunk. Of the two, it was Paul who had been less steady; though he was in complete equilibrium now. And in complete despair. For this was a sign, don't you see? He didn't know the chap's name, he didn't even know that he *was* an artist, nor could reason have furnished any significance. But he had seen him first at that party, when he had first seen Bianca. He had seen him again on that night when she had taken him to the opera. And now, this third time, it was clear—all too clear—that he was a symbol, as he had been all along.

Of Fate, in each case. But of Finality now. He might not know it, but Paul wasn't fooled.

First appearance: Here she is. Second appearance: You're friends. Third, and last: Now you've lost her for good.

An awed numerologist—but of course the poor fellow *had* just had rather a facer, and wasn't really more of an idiot than anyone else who is in love—saw a taxi; hailed it; stumbled into it; asked the driver to go to the Junior Corinthian; remembered, half-way, that the dashed place was shut; scrabbled at the sliding window; and, amending his original request, asked the driver to go to the Megalithic.

For he couldn't face Spilsby; or that gosh-awful flat. The

rollicking sound of the Combined Sportsmen was too much. So he chose the Megalithic, and indeed he chose well. For on a Saturday evening, when it is nearly always as good as empty, its vast rooms and pillars, its mid-Victorian furniture, its waiters like mutes, and its general air of utter depression, might almost have been created for a young gentleman crossed in love. Who wished to be alone with his own Stygian thoughts. And whose last wish on earth was to be cheered up.

PART THREE

I

BECAUSE she liked roses, even more than she liked lions; because, whether she had liked them or not, she could never have maltreated any living thing; and because it was out of the question to return them—as she might have done with a less perishable gift—to the donor, Bianca Brown lifted the sheaf from her gate-leg table. Removed the paper. Savoured the scent, which was undeniably enchanting. Filled a glazed-earthenware jug at her kitchen sink. Put the paper in the dust-bin. Placed the roses in the jug. Returned with it to the sitting-room. And having first set down a small cork mat—owing to a well-known property of all such vessels—put the roses back on the table.

They were dying, of course; though they would have died in any case. The rose's age, as it has been said, is but a day. Nevertheless, they drank. Not yet had a petal fallen. She bent over them, as she was surely entitled to do, and once more drew in their sweet smell.

"Lovely," she murmured, but with a quite expressionless face. "Oh, bother!" she added, with a little frown. She turned away, with a delicate shrug of her own. She stood motionless, for a moment or two. It had just struck her that, as well as having been through a rather painful and also far, far too familiar experience—here, it must be admitted, the frown changed to a slight flush—she was left high and dry about supper.

It wasn't the solitude that she minded. Just at present it would have been her choice. She even hoped that no one else would ring up. But if you live alone in an upper part, and cater carefully, as she did, a Saturday evening is the wrong time to be caught short.

She was all right for tomorrow; but tonight she was to have dined out. The loss of the film was immaterial. She was in no mood for films; though if she had been, she could still have seen one alone. But now she must either go to a restaurant by herself—and somehow or other she loathed this idea—or eat what she had got in for Sunday evening.

"Bother!" she said, again, with a renewal of the little frown. Yet she wasn't hungry, it now crossed her mind. On the contrary— here she darted a look at the jug—she wasn't sure that she didn't feel faintly sick. She put her head out of the window—from which, as she had once said, one could just see the river; though not now, with the leaves on the trees—and drew in some deep breaths. She felt better, though she still avoided the jug.

"Sardines," she observed. Well, later, perhaps. Or if there *were* any, but she wasn't quite sure. Or the loaf. Or perhaps nothing. She would see. After all, it was supposed to be a good thing—or so some people said—to miss an occasional meal.

And definitely she wasn't hungry. Though of course she was upset. She always was, after one of those scenes. Besides, this one—though she *knew* she had done the right thing—had come as such an awful surprise. Should she, or *could* she, have guessed that it was on its way? She, too, turned her thoughts to the past. No, she decided. It was just madness again. He *had* been different from all the others—until today.

And she had relied on him, too. And she had *never* set snares. If it were her last moment—and she hoped it wasn't—that was the truth. She had only *liked* him, and believed that he was what he pretended to be. But now; or now, *again*——

Oh, *dear*! thought Miss Brown. It's a sort of *plague*—and one fears that she was alluding to Love. It's a sort of *Curse*. And it *wasn't* my fault. I've had enough of it—and she meant this. It *ruins* all one's friends. And now either he'll go and marry the next girl he meets—because he *is* attractive, but if he isn't happy I shall feel awful—or else he'll start ringing up, and explaining, and trying to make me change my mind. Like Godfrey. And Jock. And all *those* ones.

But I shan't.

"I won't!" said Miss Brown. It was decisive enough. "I *won't*!" she repeated; and looked stubbornly at the telephone. The telephone said nothing. It didn't even ring. And yet, at this moment, either it or the past, or perhaps both, put a thought into her mind.

Dorothea. By dialling her number one might, as it were, recapture some of the more distant past. Hampstead, it was true, was a long way away. But if one saw her one would be seeing someone totally unconnected with Paul Sunderland. Someone, in fact, who didn't know that he existed. Not only might this be soothing, not only was there a standing invitation to go up there whenever one liked, but solitude was, suddenly, a kind of vacuum to be abhorred.

A crowd of thoughts wished to fill it, and they were now

unbearable, too. Though she knew she was guiltless, she could *feel* what they would say. They would reproach her. They would attack her. They would make excuses for Paul. And though she had forgiven him—for no one should be blamed for going mad—they could still start a headache.

She put her hands to her temples. She moved nearer to the telephone. But then—and perhaps she had been a little mad herself not to have realised this sooner—there was a kind of vision and echo of the character whom she still chose to think of and to describe as Hopgrove. He might answer. Or if he didn't he was unlikely to be out; unless, of course, Dorothea was out, too.

Marriage, in other words, had balked even this hope. The distant past couldn't help. It was extinct. Just for a moment she quivered. But she wasn't a coward. She bit her lip, and dismissed the idea. Furthermore, now that she had done so, she called on fresh strength. The very last threat of tears ebbed away.

I'll do some mending, she thought. Or I might wash my hair. After all, there had been very few free evenings lately, and they weren't half bad fun, in a way. She felt as if she had gained something. She began to relax. Though this was quite unnecessary, for only Mrs. Blankett had a key to the upper part, she bolted the front door.

Yet this strengthened her, too. It was symbolic, perhaps. And though it seemed, after some search, that she was out of sardines, and though an odd sense of fatigue made her decide not to wash her hair, she found an apple, and she made some fish-paste sandwiches, and a pot of tea. And she brought in her mending, and supped and sewed. And felt calmer, particularly as the telephone kept quiet, until presently—with several shoulder-straps re-anchored, and a really very successful bit of darning done as well—she left the sitting-room and went up to bed.

She slept. In the morning she was still sorry, but not upset. Time, she felt, had behaved well during the night. It was being helpful, and though of course she must still be prepared for more trouble sooner or later—since she was now convinced, on further thought, that Paul wouldn't rush off and marry someone else—she was also far more convinced that she could cope with it.

He had startled her, but this was something that he couldn't possibly do twice. Henceforth she would be armed, and alert. She would manage him, in fact, or at least keep him at bay. She would of course be kind, but, like her aunt, she would be firm.

That was it, then; and he would probably lie low for a few days. It was the custom; and he had now shown that he was like the rest. Poor Paul, by all means, if *he* was upset. It was an awful pity, and he'd really been awfully sweet. But it would be worse now—far worse—if she'd been weak.

So the beautiful Miss Brown, for she was still certainly that, and the gentle Miss Brown, for she must always be this, too, passed a peaceful Sunday, with some friends near Burnham Beeches, to which she went and from which she returned in her little car. They laughed. No one teased her, except as she liked. And there was a baby in the house, who laughed, too. Heavenly weather. "You *must* stay for supper," they said. So she did; and drove home by herself.

Just as she was getting ready to start out on Monday morning, Mrs. Blankett clocked in with her key. Her voice was heard from the little kitchen.

"You don't seem to have eaten *anything*, miss," she said.

"No," said Bianca, without alluding to Saturday night. "I spent all yesterday in the country."

"Did you bring back these roses, miss?" said Mrs. Blankett, who had now got the lid off the dust-bin. "It does seem a shame they're all dead."

"Oh," said Bianca, from the landing. "No. That was something else. But of course they didn't last. They never do."

Then she left for her work. And Time still rolled on. After several days she did begin wondering, faintly, if anything had happened to Paul. But of course she couldn't ask. She still had her Rules, and a very strong one was to stir no man up.

Yet after several more days, when Mrs. Blankett—again with a slight resemblance to Juliet's nurse—suddenly asked if Mr. Sunderland had gone away, even the beautiful and gentle Miss Brown displayed a momentary touch of testiness.

"I've no idea," she said. She even added a challenge. "Why, what makes you think that?"

Mrs Blankett—less Shakespearianly—dropped the subject at once. It wasn't, of course, that Bianca missed him; or not as had been implied. Yet it was strange that, after a week now, he should still be lying low. It was what he had foreshadowed; what she had accepted; and it was no doubt better this way. But quite apart from its being just a little unfriendly, it showed a flaw in her knowledge of Life.

She had plenty to do, though. Lots of work. Lots of dates. Or if she chose, as she sometimes did, to do things by herself, this meant nothing; except that it was her choice.

2

ON the same Saturday evening that Bianca Brown opened the little jar of fish-paste, Paul Sunderland ate a three-course dinner.

He had no appetite, it is true. Psychologically, he was still stunned. But he had come to the Megalithic—so vast, so oppressive, so legendary, so grim, and even today (though a car-park had been established outside, excess items from which were constantly being shooed away from its front steps by the under-porter or a policeman) so reeking, as one might say, of the age when it had been built; and having come, and having been admitted (for his own hall-porter was now installed at a little table), and having slouched in its huge, sombre smoking-room for a while, he fell under a further influence, too.

Not of hunger. Indeed not. He was through with all that. Yet as he slouched, almost alone, and as time slipped by, he must have twitched, or perhaps groaned, or ground his teeth.

The effect was instantaneous. The smoking-room waiter, though well stricken in years, had long been trained to interpret such sounds. He was accustomed to grunts, and queer signals or signs. In this case, if not always, he guessed what they meant. But in this case he inferred, though in fact he was quite wrong, that his temporary guest—who had been so lifeless until a moment ago— wished to order his dinner.

At the Junior Corinthian, of course, this is a much simpler business. One went into the dining-room—if the ceiling was still there—and behaved almost exactly as in a restaurant. But at the Megalithic one either tottered to a mahogany desk, mumbled over the menu, and slowly and painstakingly scrawled one's demands on a printed slip (which was then wafted away, but would reappear later on, with the prices and total added, wherever one was now seated), or—what a refinement, and glimpse of the past!—one chose and ordered without leaving the smoking-room.

Suddenly, therefore, a uniformed patriarch was standing rigidly in front of Paul with the programme. It was even framed. And as it was forced rather than passed into his nerveless hand, he not only realised what it was, not only realised in another moment that (thanks to the State) there was precious little to choose, but was so scared of the patriarch, and of the Megalithic, and of doing the wrong thing, that he in fact ordered soup, sole, and cheese.

"Very good, sir," said the ancient, as he scribbled himself. "And to drink, sir?"

Again Paul gave in. He didn't answer, that's to say, or not immediately, for he had forgotten the names of all drinks. But when the ancient said: "Very nice hock, sir," he nodded—not that he wanted it, but he was quite powerless to say so—and felt at least that he wasn't yet quite disgraced.

"In about a quarter of an hour, sir?" said the waiter, at this point as if the Megalithic had never heard of such a thing as an electric hot-plate, or, alternatively, as if no gentleman could ever hurry. Paul registered instant submission.

"Very good, sir." Another scribble. "And—" a civil, aged little cough—"the name, sir, if you please?"

For a moment it almost looked as if Paul had forgotten this, too. But he made an effort. It came back to him. He supplied it.

"I'm a member," he began explaining, "of——"

"Yes, quite, sir. Of course." As if, was the very clear implication, I should be speaking to you if you weren't. Yet, again, as Paul shrank, the old waiter piped up; and perhaps as if bygones were bygones.

"And a glass of sherry, sir?"

"Oh," said Paul. "Er—" He hated the stuff. He always had.

"Very good, sir," said the waiter, and shuffled off.

But *he* didn't forget. So that, as a result of pure nerves, Paul drank not only nearly half a glass of sherry—(no offence, though; quite the contrary; for of course the waiter finished it off)—but the best part of a bottle of hock. And again, though he had meant to peck, and even doubted if he could do that, there was another waiter in the dining-room who kept an eye on him, or so he felt; so that in the end it was as if he were back in the nursery.

Otherwise, of course, there was no resemblance at all. Yet if he had consulted a doctor, and if the doctor had been wise, there can be little question that food and drink would have been pre-scribed. Well done, the Megalithic. And it was curiously cheap. For the very old are no longer, necessarily, the very rich.

A few of them loomed, and pottered, and coughed. And Paul wasn't tight, but his strength was maintained. Any notion that he might have formulated of starving himself to death could hardly survive such a start. Too late now, in fact. He must continue to face life. But though physically—and this was very unlike poor Miss Brown with her fish-paste—he had now done the best for his frame, morally and mentally he was still in the depths. And here, though the Megalithic did nothing to rasp, it would have been astonishing it it had even attempted to cheer.

After dinner, as he still felt distaste for his flat—which he had left with hope, as he now knew, so that, when he returned, it would be exactly as if Paul Secundus were awaiting him, and would slap him on the back, and shout "What luck?"—he explored rather more of the Club premises.

This was action, in a sense; a slight drug for his thoughts; though he couldn't have done it if the place had been thronged. But on a Saturday or Sunday night—and, as he would learn later (owing to its size, the great age of its members, who preferred congregating for lunch, and the almost unanimous decision of the Junior Corinthians to become temporary Combined Sportsmen), on most other nights, too—there was a certain likeness, it must be confessed, to the tomb.

Ghostly, white statues confirmed this idea. Even the architect seemed to have been inspired by Mausolus. It was larger, that is to say, than the ordinary tomb. More decorative, too, in its own grim way. But as Paul ascended the extreme edge of the gigantic stair-case—for it would be impious as well as dangerous to use the middle—and peered into one great chamber after another (in most of which there was no sound but the ticking of a clock, though in some there was a little coughing and muttering), he still knew that if he must live at all, and make use of a club, the Megalithic at least matched his mood.

On the second floor, it is true, he received one short, sharp shock. Opening a door, he beheld a group of clearly choleric old buffers engaged in wrangling about a game of bridge. Since apoplexy appeared imminent, he quickly withdrew, and made a note not to intrude here again.

Descending, however, he came on a much larger door. He

pushed it gingerly. It yielded softly. He was in an immense room lined with books. Shelves all round. Shelves so high that they must be reached by a spiral stairway. Books in bays. Books on tables. Books beneath them.

There seemed more than a hush here, as the door quietly closed. As he held his breath—for the Library at the Megalithic virtually demands that one should do this—he saw not only that it was deserted but that there were printed cards here and there, each of which bore the single word SILENCE.

He resumed breathing. No word could have been more to his present taste, as he tiptoed towards one of the low chairs. He sank into it. It was rather hard, but it had arms and a back, and even a book-rest, though he thrust this aside. It was in a recess, so that he could only be approached from in front. It was a refuge, a kind of sanctuary, at last.

He made no attempt to read, though. He just sat and thought. Gloom engulfed him; but Silence as well. It was here, in fact, during the next phase in his life, that Paul Sunderland spent much of his time. The chair, which had been sat on for at least eighty years, gradually adjusted itself, slightly, to his form. Sometimes there were rustlings—and coughings, of course—but for the most part he had this Library to himself. It called him when he was away from it. It didn't, and indeed couldn't, ease his pain. But one point was that it was wholly unconnected with the past—or his own past, to be more scrupulously accurate; while the other was that it might have been built for dark thoughts. And furnished, and as good as labelled, as well.

So he thought darkly, though he can no longer remember for just how many nights. And the weather remained glorious, and he was without hope.

Things happened, of course. He still did his work—without laughing, but then no one expected him to laugh—and still went to bed in his flat. It was here, because he couldn't sleep, that he at last took up the novel which his cousin Rhoda had so kindly given him; and flung it aside, for what did *it* know of Love?

It was here, too, though not in bed, that he chanced to observe—but what the blazes did it matter, anyhow?—a strange absence of ebb in his whisky. He had grown so accustomed to its oozing away, and had guessed why—though he had always preferred, for some reason, to say nothing and to replace it—that for a moment there was a further, faint shock. If it came to that, and now he thought of it, Spilsby was still a little glum. He no longer chattered. Good lord! Had *he* guessed something, too? Was it possible—however nauseating—that he was showing tact?

Paul baited the sideboard with a second bottle, and drew the cork. There was no sequel. For though it is a fact that neither bottle was touched, he also forgot what he had done. It was unimportant, you see. Or his better self disapproved. Or, again, he was so glad not to be pestered with conversation, that he had now accepted this new Spilsby, too. There was some reason, no doubt, why he neither prattled nor sneaked nips. But Paul, now convinced that he *couldn't* have guessed, let Spilsby pass right out of his thoughts.

Something happened at the office. In fact, several things happened. The first was that Miss Thriplow—but it never struck him that this could be tact—seemed slightly more silent, too. Not that *she* ever chattered. And perhaps, on second thoughts, it was because he was more silent himself. This was natural, when he was so wretched. It was even an effort to dictate. But as she, too, must suspect nothing, he made an attempt to draw her out. Only one. She looked so startled, and even alarmed—though he had merely mentioned the weather—that he feared she might suspect after all.

He dried up. She calmed down. They went on with their task. Either he had imagined that she was more silent—and, dash it all, if one was completely *raw* one could imagine anything!—or, as he had supposed, it was his own fault. Let it go, though. Again, it was inconceivable that she should have guessed. And Heaven knew he didn't *want* her to talk.

It was at the office, again, that he fell in with Prim, and Miss Crankshaw, in the corridor, near the lift. Prim was looking radiant, and he forced a false grin. But the odd thing was—"No," he had said. "Mustn't stop. Wish I could. But" (though this wasn't quite true) "I'm simply *plastered* with work;" the odd thing was, as he returned to his own room, and hastily created some extra work, so that, even if summoned, he would have a genuine excuse; the really remarkable thing, don't you know, was that Cranky—yes, *Cranky*—had looked pretty.

As he wasn't summoned, he was able to speculate on this point. Of course, he thought—as he still shuffled some papers, and frowned —she had never, at any time, been a monster. She was so nice, too, that of *course* she had an awfully nice face. But something had happened to it; or to her; or to both. She had looked so *young*.

Honestly, you know, and though of course she wasn't old, it was the most extraordinary change he had ever seen.

Why, she was practically a Beauty. Good gracious. What next! He had half a mind to say something to H.B. about it. Or not? For perhaps this was imagination as well. Another effect of his own state of mind. And though H.B.—(well, that's another thing, unless I'm making it *all* up)—had been curiously mellow this last week, sometimes, also—there was no doubt of it—he had been edgy and abrupt. In fact, it was as if he had changed, too.

"Rot!" said Paul, at this point. "It's me. It's the strain. I'm all taut. I'm half cracked. And it gets no better, you know. It gets worse every day. The wonder is——"

He broke off, as the third thing occurred. The sudden entrance— unusual, though he leapt hospitably to his feet—of old Whichery, of the firm's firm of solicitors.

"Are you busy?" he wheezed.

"No, no," said Paul. "Come in. Er——"

"Just been seeing your uncle. Oh, a private affair—that's why I came round here. But I thought, if you're not busy——"

"No, no. Please go on."

"——that I could tell you the result of—hrrm—our inquiries, on your behalf. Briefly . . ." said Mr. Whichery, and became anything but brief. He sat down—though Paul had naturally offered him the best chair—he put on his spectacles, he blew his nose, he produced some notes from his leather case. He was discursive, he was long-winded, he was irrelevant, he was slow. But the long and short of it, and the reason that had brought him into the room, were that careful consideration of all aspects of—hrrm—your friend Mr. Potting's position showed that no power on earth could turn him out.

"Unless," said Mr. Whichery, "he should *decide* to surrender the lease. Or unless—for, as I always say, one must never overlook that— your friend Mr. Potting should—hrrm—decease."

"I see," said Paul. It would appear, in fact, that in putting the problem to the old codger he must have been a little less lucid than he had supposed. Yet of course it was extraordinarily good-natured to have gone into it so thoroughly, and to have reported like this, whatever the charges might be.

"I see," he repeated. And: "Thank you," he said, without explaining that he had never seen Mr. Potting. Gradually, also, and with some resemblance to a retreating thunderstorm, Mr. Whichery recapitulated and faded out.

"Always delighted," he said, "to do anything for any of you." He looked so penetrating for a second that Paul felt hideously transparent—until he recalled that it was a professional trick. It was a sign, though, that he had finished. His client accompanied him to the lift. They shook hands. And Mr. Whichery, who had not only as good as given the same opinion more than a month ago, but had unquestionably, on this second occasion, drawn it out to the 'utmost possible length, nodded briskly, and sank down the shaft.

Lawyers, thought Paul; though it was decent of the old boy (for a cog had slipped in his own mind) to have come round in person like that. Jolly decent; if quite unnecessary. "Your friend Mr. Potting." He twitched. He twitched twice, as he re-entered his room. For a fleeting moment he had thought: I could ring her up now. Or write.

But then he knew that he couldn't. It wasn't pride. More like funk. It would hurt so horribly if he heard her voice, or even penned a few lines. Besides, though, if there had been anything helpful to pass on, one might have argued, perhaps, that it was one's duty, there was nothing. Or nothing new. It had been a footling idea. His only hope—and what a hope!—was to forget.

So he sat thinking of Miss Brown, with a lump in his throat, and an ache behind both of his eyes. It would be a relief, in a way, if he could burst into tears—even here, at his desk in the City. But it seemed that he was too old, and that it was too long since he had wept. He remembered vaguely, moreover, that it only made one feel worse. A wan, tortured smile. A sharp and self-delivered kick in the mental pants. And Paul Sunderland, or quite enough of him for the purpose in hand, plunged stubbornly back into his work.

3

I⊤ will have been seen, though, how Fate couldn't leave him alone; though indeed it need hardly have troubled. Morning, noon, and night still—and as this infernal fine weather still went on—there was always something to rack his poor soul. There were constant reminders, whatever he did. They leapt out suddenly, from a newspaper, from a sound, sight, or scent; from a careless word that some blundering ass dropped.

They didn't *mean* anything, of course. He fully realised that. And he seldom gave more than a slight start. Although his hide was still thin, he was acquiring a mask. Sometimes it laughed, for no reason, and seemed to startle them, too. Or sometimes *they* laughed, and it remained blank.

But if his hairdresser (and even Paul was still clean and neat) began talking—though he had never done this before—about music, and actually mentioned what he described at *Boheem*; or if his tobacconist (for even Paul hadn't given up smoking) spoke of the Chelsea—help!—Flower Show; or if some idiot of an actor announced that he was reviving *The Taming of the Shrew*; or, dammit, if a dashed errand-lad *would* come sauntering past one with a sheaf of red roses—well, how could one *ever* forget?

One wasn't meant to, perhaps. One didn't want to, in a way. One was weak. And of course one was half-mad. But when one was braced—as in the presence of one's partners—there were no reminders. It was when one relaxed—and, dash it, one couldn't *always* be on guard—that reminders sneaked up from behind.

Drink? Quite ineffective. One *knew*, without trial. Besides, one had quite lost the taste.

Time? Well, of course people *said* that this helped. But it wasn't moving. It had virtually stopped dead. And even reason didn't see—though of course one would never really get over this—that anything less than about ten years could ease such anguish. Time, indeed! If it *wanted* to help, it would turn back. It would give him those three months again.

And he'd bungle them again; for somehow (is it possible to respect him for this?) he mustn't picture a *complete* second chance. But he'd be with her. He would be happy. He wouldn't *know* what lay ahead. And perhaps—though this was certainly against all experience—he could make them seem longer that way. . . .

Thus, once more in the murky Library at the Megalithic—while Miss Brown, whatever her thoughts, was in fact barely a quarter of a mile away, at a playhouse—thus did Paul chew the bitterest cud. Some, indeed, had been so thoroughly masticated by now that it would be surprising, if he weren't in love, that it was still there. Or possibly, again—for even ungulate ruminants, with any number of stomachs, must eventually nibble as well—it was the tenuity of this acrid pulp that called for a fresh line of thought.

It had been waiting, no doubt. He was still far from unique. To many chaps it has come almost at once. Even as they take the blow, some reaction suggests that the girl herself can provide someone else.

Not that they *want* anyone else. But they are reeling. They are lost. Though they know, perfectly well, that there is only one girl like that, she only, they feel, can produce another. They have been known, as the blow falls, to whine such an appeal. "Can't you," they bleat, "find somebody for me just like you?"

You don't believe this? But it's true. And a kind of compliment, in a way. And nice girls, like Miss Brown, never laugh. They pretend to think, though they can guess that even a twin wouldn't do. Besides, they have learnt—if they are like Miss Brown—that if the chap *does* switch his aim, it will almost certainly be directed at their precise antithesis.

Instances, indeed, of a girl saying at once: "Yes—what about Susan Hammersmith?", and of the chap instantly saying: "By Jove—yes, of course!" and fairly hauling such a substitute to the altar, are so rare that they can be disregarded. Or we have never heard of a case. Generally speaking, the girl breaks it, as gently as she can, that she feels unable to supply a stand-in.

Generally speaking, again, the chap faces this fact. He may even regret, as he looks back on that harrowing scene, that he ever made such a blithering suggestion. Nevertheless, if the prop of his whole being is knocked away, if he is left plunging, as it were, into a vast, vacant void, any chap may still have moments—for he is still alive, after all—of the instinct of self-preservation.

It is this, we should say, that accounts for the inquiry which Paul, as a matter of fact, hadn't put. Yet the thought, or something not unlike it, was approaching him now. He knew, that is to say, that he was finished with Love—in the sense that he could never love anyone else. Even if this were possible, he didn't wish to. It was a loathsome idea. But for three months, and all the time with diminishing gaps, he had *relied* on his meetings with Miss Brown.

He had counted on them. They had become part of his innermost self. So had she. So had the result, as he now saw. But he had lost her. For ever. He would remain a bachelor for life. And in these circumstances, with such an ache and a hole in his heart, and with absolutely no intention of even smiling at another girl—not, dammit, that he could smile if he tried—it might help, just a little, if he took one of 'em out. Like jumping into another kite after a crash.

The thought hovered. He was disgusted. But he must think of himself. Of his nerves. And how he *must* bring them round.

No question, just at present, but that he would be a singularly poor host. His guest might suffer. It was perhaps a good deal to ask. But then, dash it all, girls were used to dull chaps. They couldn't *always* expect a good laugh. It might be brutal; but he wouldn't be mean over the bill. And if—(here one sees how the thought developed, as it sometimes does, to the next and almost definitely brutal phase)—if she irritated him, and he hadn't much doubt that she would, this *might* be like caustic on a wound.

He could hardly hope that it would cure him. He didn't, in fact. But if, for only five minutes, he disliked one of 'em enough; or if, for the same period, he could feel that a girl was only a girl—well, possibly—or perhaps . . .

It was all rather obscure. Loneliness, misery, and some desperate remedy, were all involved, as he sat there and scowled. Yet inaction was over. The thought lured him on. It would be a frightful sort of evening, but it was the right thing to do. He had been refused; and he would *never* love anyone else. But it wasn't cowardly. It would be no worse for the girl than for himself. And it might sort of have some effect.

·   ·   ·   ·   ·

We offer no opinion on this decision, such as it was; nor on the logic, if any, that had evoked it. He was slightly mad. Leave it at that. Or he was in love, and had been refused. Some chaps, as the first numbness begins to pass off, hurl themselves into violent activity. Some turn into bores. Some still merely mope. It has been observed that there are many types in this world.

But Paul Sunderland, at this particular moment, left his book-lined retreat; edged down the huge staircase; passed diagonally (avoiding pillars and statues) towards another recess; and entered one of the solid, old-fashioned, mahogany telephone-boxes of which genuine Megalithics still make such infrequent use.

It was equipped, though. A bulb lit up, as he closed the door. There was a telephone. There were slots for coins, and two buttons. There were all four volumes of the current directory. They were even stacked, if you can believe this, in the right order.

For a moment, since the extraordinary notion had just come to him of selecting the girl Ariadne as victim, his hand strayed towards Volume II. Hobson, he recalled, was her incongruous surname. Yet not only must there be many Hobsons, not only had he no idea where she lived, and not only was it at least doubtful if she, too, had a flat of her own; but, dash it, he hardly knew her; it was a preposterous choice. Besides—he shuddered—even to see her would be more than he could bear, owing to her painful connection with his lost love.

So he recoiled. But he didn't withdraw from the box. For suddenly—well, of course—there was someone else. He had neglected her, disgracefully, but there was no connection here. Or it was so slight that he *ought* to be safe.

The very girl, in other words, for whom in fact he now craved. As a companion. Or perhaps a pain-killer. But that was all. He snatched at Volume IV. He held it beneath the light. He turned the pages, and found what he sought. And even if, at this point, it was largely a conviction that she was bound to be out that served to strengthen his will, nevertheless he inserted twopence, and dialled.

He listened. If the number were engaged, it would be a sign. Button B, then, and no second shot. Or, again, if there were no reply, after four or five double-trills—for they had started now—this, too, would be a sign, and he would stop. Quite half of him, indeed, was now hoping for escape. But the third double-trill was cut short.

"Hullo?" said a feminine voice, from about two miles away.

"Oh!" said Paul. And lost his head. Or at least forgot Button A. "Is that—Are you—Could I——"

"Hullo?" said the voice again. "Hullo? Yes? Hullo?"

He took the point. He jabbed the button. The coins fell with a clank.

"I beg your pardon," he said. "Is that Mrs. Vaughan?"

"You want Rosemary?" said the voice; automatically, one might judge. But of course it was perfectly right. "I'll call her," it added; for mothers, whether dull or otherwise, all know better in these days than to ask who anyone is. Paul, who had begun saying, simultaneously, that he was sure she was out, and indeed was even wishing and almost praying that she was out, was left babbling for a moment alone.

But then, for it would seem that not only the Parkinsons and his uncle Hayward went in for extensions, and as Mrs. Vaughan (one might imagine) continued calling to her child, here was Bubbles's voice in his ear.

"I'm here," it said. "Here I am. This is me. All right, Mummy!" it cried. "Yes, I'm here!"

"Bubbles—" said Paul, in a slightly faltering tone.

"Good heavens! It's Paul. Well, no wonder you sound nervous."

Had she heard, then? Had somebody guessed, or found out? He very nearly dropped the receiver.

"I—ah——"

"Oh, don't twitter like that. Of course I'm not angry. How are you?"

"I'm afraid," said Paul—but in fact the worst of his fear had now left him, for of course his dark load was still private—"I'm afraid I've been rather dashed rude. But——"

Luckily, since he had no explanation prepared, she interrupted him.

"Oh, my dear Paul, as if I *ever* worried about that sort of thing! I know what life's like." She laughed, though it was a brief kind of laugh. "One dam' thing after another; and it isn't as if——" She broke off, and began again. "Well, you've only caught me," she said, "because I've got a headache."

"Oh, Bubbles, I *am* sorry. I——"

"Don't mention it. I think it's better. I'll be all right tomorrow, I'm sure."

"Oh, I do hope so——"

"That's very nice of you."

"Because, you see, it's like this. I mean, I apologise. I *have* been *frightfully* rude. But you did say——"

"Yes?"

"Well, could you forgive me?"

"Oh, Paul, what *is* the matter with you? I'm not touchy. You ought to know that."

He knew it. It was the truth. And she was doing him good. Why *shouldn't* he say what he then said?

"Well, look here—could we have our evening, then? After all. I mean, in spite of my rudeness."

"Of course!" said Bubbles.

"To-morrow?" he urged. "You see——"

Again it was perhaps lucky that she suddenly said "Yes." And then: "Oh, do let's!" as if denying all doubt now. "I mean," she went on, "there's a sort of party—but I could look in late. And I'd really much rather— Oh, Paul, that'll be lovely. Yes, do let's do that. I——"

"Yes?" said Paul, for she had stopped.

"It was nothing," she said. "But, look here, don't let's dress. Let's just meet. Well, where?"

Not Belloni's. And of course not the Serene, if they weren't to dress. In fact, nowhere—and there was quite a long list of such places now—that might bring on fresh pangs. Yet his mind was at work, and suddenly he knew. The connection, of course, was his cousin Rodney. Or the link. For Roddie had said something about Bubbles that Sunday, and had cracked up some restaurant, too.

He'd got it! For once the old brain did its stuff. Antonetti's. In Soho, somewhere, but he could soon check that up. Meanwhile, because it would be polite, and because he hadn't checked up, he would (so he announced) fetch Miss Vaughan from her home.

There was a little argument, but she yielded. Half-past seven was fixed. Civilities were exchanged. They rang off.

Paul emerged, feeling hot, and exhausted, and strained. Nice girl, of course. Couldn't be nicer. But of course he had been mad. He didn't want her, as a companion or anything else. All he wanted was to sort of hide under a stone. Weak? Very likely. There had never *been* anyone so weak. But ill-mannered? Well, no. Perhaps not.

He must go through with it, then. He had been quite rude enough. It wasn't *her* fault that he happened to be off his nut. He felt sorry for her. He also felt sorry for himself. Yet once more habit, or something, got him through the best part of another twenty-four hours—during the course of which he tracked down Antonetti's, and again telephoned, and booked a table; and at half-past seven, sharp, on the following evening (which was now the last day of May), he arrived at the Vaughans' block of flats.

He was clean. And quite sober. He asked the taxi to wait. And this, though quite wrong in suspecting romance, which it had often found highly profitable, the taxi consented to do. He spent not more than two minutes with Colonel and Mrs. Vaughan in their little drawing-room; though, again, this was quite long enough to confirm his opinion that they were the two dullest parents on earth.

Then Bubbles came in, like a breath of fresh air, though she looked just a little tired, too. He didn't say so. In fact, he forgot it at once, as she brightened, and said: "Hullo, Paul."

"Hullo, Bubbles," he said. Yes, an awfully nice girl. And he'd really been rather a cad.

"Have a drink?" she said.

"Well," said Paul, "I've got a taxi."

She was intelligent. She knew where hospitality must draw the line. In fact, it was rather marvellous how she never fussed.

"Oh, well," she said, "in that case . . ." And was ready, it seemed, to start. "Good-night, pets," she said to the two stuffed figures who had so unaccountably combined to produce her. She didn't say that she had her key, because of course she had her key. No fluff-pate, in spite of her curls.

"Good-night, sir," said Paul. "Good-night, Mrs. Vaughan."

The stuffed figures looked, if possible, duller than ever as he withdrew. Was one sorry for them? Not particularly. They were used to all this. They were so dull that they probably preferred being alone. Yet Paul envied them, for a moment, which was an odd thing to do. Until he forgot them as well.

"Where are we going, Paul?"

"Eh? Oh, a place. Haven't been there before. But they say it's all right. 'S a matter of fact— Oh, I say. How's your headache?"

"All over, thank you."

"What, all over your head?"

"No, no. I mean, it's gone. I—I'm perfectly well."

She laughed, too—as someone else had once laughed, now and then, at words that weren't meant to be funny. He twitched. Then he scowled. He *must* fight this mood. He commented on the extraordinarily fine weather.

"Yes, I know," said his fellow-passenger. "And yet I *don't* know. Doesn't it make you sort of want to get away?"

"I can't," said Paul.

"Nor can I, if it comes to that. Never mind, though. I'm glad you rang up."

"Well—" said Paul. But he could feel that she wasn't listening; and she was right. He was only going to have been as dull as the old Vaughans.

He tried again, with more success. He kept things going in the cab. Or perhaps she was helping him, too. There were pauses, there can be no doubt; but of course they were old friends—I'm really *fond* of her, he thought, more than once, as they sped along—and old friends needn't chatter like apes.

"Here we are," he was announcing. "At least, I think we are. Yes, that's it. I hope it's all right."

He paid off the taxi, with a generous tip. He advanced into the little restaurant. And Antonetti—if this *was* Antonetti— seemed delighted to see him. Bowed, fluttered, was full of succulent suggestions; each of which proved remarkably sound. They had cocktails. And a wicker bottle of admirable wine. The waiting was first-class. The accoutrements were spotless. It wasn't stuffy, and they had been placed on the most comfortable banquette. There weren't even bright lights in their eyes.

The only thing, in fact, that was wrong—and Paul didn't mind— was that they virtually had the place to themselves. A couple of diners left within a few moments of their arrival. Another couple, and then a trio, drifted in later on. But that was all. It seemed, indeed, unless this were a very abnormal evening, that fashion had somehow eluded this haunt of Roddie's. Not, of course, that it invariably throngs where it is treated best.

Rather tough, thought Paul. Once or twice, after a while, though conversation was swinging along easily enough now, he glanced into the street—for it was still daylight, and the wide plate-glass window was only screened by a flimsy net curtain; saw a wayfarer pause; and mildly willed him to come in.

But without effect. Either the wayfarers *wanted* a crowd, or else they had already eaten elsewhere. And though he felt for Antonetti, or his proxy perhaps, he was not only disinclined to go out and act as a tout, but had his own worries as well.

Once, indeed, he missed a chance. The door opened abruptly. A figure shot in. It even hesitated—but all this was in the tail of Paul's eye, and he happened to be talking to his guest—before turning and at once shooting out. It was the kind of thing that the tail only reports when it is all over. I *might*, he was thinking, have looked encouraging or something. After all, they're doing *us* pretty well.

But it was too late now, and, of course—however tender-hearted this shows him—attracting custom wasn't really his job. Forget it, he thought. And forgot it forthwith. Though not only would he be reminded within forty-eight hours, but, with prescience extending to no great distance beyond that, would have been justified in shouting for joy.

The trifling incident, in fact, was of such supreme importance— marking, as it did, the beginning of a chain which, nevertheless, must be described link by link—that it was almost clearly inspired by St. Valentine. But the figure *wasn't* St. Valentine. Nor a small, winged, blind boy. Nor, again, did Paul Sunderland fall madly in love, either now or on any subsequent occasion, with his extremely attractive guest.

He just talked to her, and she talked to him, as they sat side by side. As they ate. And as each gathered calm. Paul, of course, knew that his own couldn't last. Miss Vaughan might still have one more headache. There were no confidences, no confessions, or not a millimetre beneath the surface. Yet somehow they were attuned, in Antonetti's little restaurant.

It was quiet. So were they. They were apart—in the sense that there wasn't another patron within five yards of them—and yet they blended. Paul didn't notice—though his thoughts, it must be admitted, were often far, far away—that Bubbles's smile came in starts. And if Bubbles observed that he was sometimes slightly *distrait*, it may be that this suited her, too.

Neither of them said: "Tell me—what's on your mind?" Neither mentioned the names that were on their own. They clung, without touching. Absorbed in themselves. Yet grateful and glad for this hour.

They were alone now, for, in fact, it was more than an hour. The waiters had vanished. The woman at the *caisse*—and if she had a moustache, she had a charming expression—was yawning, and crocheting, too. Antonetti (on the assumption that he wasn't called something else) would of course do nothing to unsettle his remaining clients. When he moved, it was as softly as a cat.

Yet Time, no less cat-like, still treads its own path. It says nothing. It knows us by now. It is, in fact, inescapable, and has no need to speak. Paul sensed it; and glanced at his watch.

"By Jove!" he said. "Not that *I* want to go. But didn't you say something about a party?"

No subterfuge here. Just the tidiness, as it were, with which he viewed anyone's pledges. But of course he had broken the brief spell.

"Oh!" said Bubbles. "I rang them up. I—I said I was tired." A tidy girl, too, one might gather. "But I think—" she seemed to take in the emptiness of the room—"that if you *don't* mind—well, I ought to get home."

"Of course!" said Paul, earning a smile—but he wasn't looking—

for this example of his characteristic candour. "I do hope, I mean
to say——"

But his eye had caught Antonetti's. Here was the bill, on a
plate. He disbursed. The woman with the moustache sprang to
life. His change was produced. He picked up his own share. As he
pushed, his host pulled at the table. It slid away. He stood up.
And Bubbles was standing up.

"I say," he suddenly suggested, for indeed it had all been remarkably quick; "have I rushed you?"

"Oh, no! You've been an angel."

"What rubbish!" said Paul. "The fact is——"

He stopped short, as if on the brink of a precipice. The putative
Antonetti faded in.

"I 'ope-a you an' ze lady—'ave everyzing you like?"

"Rather!" said Paul.

"Delicious!" said Bubbles.

"Ah, you say too motch. Joos' tonight—" the sad, southern
eyes rolled like olives in oil—"ees not vairy full. Bot anozzer time,
many peoples—yess? So you com'. You com' again. Maybe soon?
Olways   pleast.   Good-night,   sair.   Good-night,   mees.   Zees-a
way!"

"Poor chap," said Paul—for there had been a prowling taxi
outside, and he was in it, and so was Miss Vaughan. "Must be
ghastly when no one turns up. I wonder if they ever do."

"I'm going to *make* them," said Bubbles. "I think he's too
sweet."

"Well, "said Paul, "you're not short of friends."

She didn't answer. Could she possibly have objected to this
great truth? He turned his head, but she was looking out of the
further window.

" 'Friends,' " said her voice. She seemed to shiver, miles away.
And then, suddenly, she just touched his arm. "Anyhow," she said,
"you've been awfully kind."

"Oh, rot."

"And I was awfully dull."

"You weren't!" said Paul. "*I* was, if you like. I *am* dull, you
see. Though of course——"

Good heavens, and sakes alive! He bit his tongue. He had so
nearly concluded "you must be used to that"—in all too clear and
quite unpardonable reference to her parents—that he broke into a
cold sweat. Mad, of course. Not tight. Just mad. Because of what

had happened a fortnight ago. No, dammit, he was well into the third week.

But still, you see, he was at least half off his head. And why not? What else could anyone expect?

He didn't groan in the taxi, but he was certainly dull. Or remote, if that comes to the same thing. Once, when his companion said: "Oh, Paul, are you taking me back first? You shouldn't *really*!" he replied with a brief statement that he always did.

Perhaps this silenced her, too. Perhaps she spoke, and he didn't hear. Or perhaps she had now said all that she had to say. They just trundled, not exactly like ships that pass in the night; for they weren't at sea, and were both going the same way.

Then they stopped, and he came alive, and skipped courteously out. She thanked him, and he must have heard this, for he again said: "Rot." But he had forgotten her entirely as soon as she was out of sight. His companion was the ghost of another girl now, as he sat slumped, with his hat well down over his eyes.

"It's getting worse," he growled. "It's getting worse and worse. If it goes on like this, I—I shall *crack*!"

Yet though Paul Sunderland must still suffer, and acutely, for a while; if, indeed, for a while, his suffering must even increase, he had just—though he didn't know this—punched a hole in the dark cloud. And we should all know with what such clouds are lined.

4

THAT evening at Antonetti's (and, by the way, the latest news of this little establishment is that it has doubled in size, is invariably packed out, and, alas, if also perhaps consequently, is now no better than anywhere else) saw the last of the month of May; with the fine spell, as has been said, still going strong.

On the same evening Bianca was entertaining her friend and colleague Ariadne; so that Paul, even if he had persisted in his original, wild impulse, could not, obviously, have done so, too. They were in the upper part, with both windows of the sitting-room wide open, because of the heat, and with the remains of a simpler meal on the gate-leg table.

One of them—and anyone who has studied this record at all carefully should know which—was smoking, and had already filled a large ash-tray. The other, curled up at the end of the sofa, was merely looking attentive; and decorative.

"Of course," said the deeper and huskier voice, "I should hate it if you felt I was letting you down. I mean, I know how you're fixed. Well, *not* fixed, I mean. And how you were let down before. But, you see . . ."

The speaker frowned. She had said all this before, too. She had received not only attention, but sympathy, encouragement, and—when it was at all clear what she wanted—gifts of moral support. Yet still, so it appeared, she must do her thinking aloud, and still on the same well-worn track.

Bianca, though still manifesting extraordinary patience, could and must relax slightly at times. Or enough to allow certain thoughts of her own to run parallel with her colleague's remarks. Yet she said: "Go on," as Ariadne paused. And Ariadne at once went back.

"You see, darling," she said, for about the seventeenth time, "the whole thing was such a *surprise*. I'd never thought of him like that. I'd never dreamt of such a thing. There we were, I mean—well, *you* ought to know—just wage-slaves, and—and rather laughing at him sometimes. I thought, when he started changing, that he was just worried about business. And *I* didn't want to be sacked, so I tried to be rather nicer. Do you think that sounds awful?"

"No," said Bianca. "I told you I didn't. I expect—" but this was an addition to the usual reply—"I should probably have done the same thing."

"Well," said Ariadne, "I'm jolly glad you didn't. Because you're far more attractive than me."

Bianca crinkled her nose. "He doesn't think so, thank goodness."

"Why do you say that? Don't you think *he's* attractive?"

"Yes!" said Bianca, with perhaps a shade too much emphasis; but after all this was the sixth time she had been asked. "I think," she hurried on, as she saw her friend's expression, "that he's very nice, and very kind, and you're extraordinarily lucky. No," she must at once add. "I don't mean you're not good enough. I think it's marvellous. But, darling, it *is* your affair. I don't count. And I *swear* I'm not jealous."

"Oh," said Ariadne. "I rather hoped perhaps you were."

"But *why*?"

"I suppose just because I'm a beast. But, you see, he's never *looked* at anyone else. We'd have known. Isn't *that* rather frightening?"

"No," said Bianca. "It's part of your luck. And another thing. It's just nonsense—such nonsense that you *must* be in love—to pretend that he'd lose all his customers. If he's happy, he'd probably do better than ever. There's no *law* against men in his job having wives. I know they don't, as a general rule. But you could help him, you know."

"What, by going on modelling?" Miss Hobson actually put down the latest and still unlighted cigarette.

"No, of course not! But by giving him more confidence in himself. I mean, when he's *not* in the shop. It's what he needs more than anything. Can't you see it?"

Miss Hobson's mental processes were slow, and not always sure. For a moment it almost seemed that she did take this point. But she was quite a hundred per cent feminine, too.

"Why," she suddenly asked, "are *you* so keen on the idea? You— you didn't sort of *plan* it. Did you?"

"Of course not. I was just as——"

"Well, it's all very odd," said the visitor, shaking her head. "Because I can tell you just when it all started. It was that evening —what's happened to him, by the way?—the evening that that friend of yours—Paul Something-or-other—came to fetch you, and ran into Michael. I saw them, through the doorway. I've never thought of it till now. But that was the night he rang up. Not Paul. Michael. He said he wanted to talk. He did, too, for about half an hour—about nothing—while my supper was all burning. I thought he'd gone nuts. But the next day he was all respectful, suddenly. And since then he's been sort of darting forwards and shying back, and making me wonder what on earth was the matter—until yesterday— Oh, darling, I *adore* him, you know. At least, I think I do. How does one tell?"

"Well," said Bianca, a true friend even now, "supposing you heard something had happened to him."

"What do you mean?"

"Well, for instance, that he'd broken his leg——"

"I should die!" cried Ariadne, and leapt to her feet. "I couldn't bear it! Oh, darling, how cruel! But I see what you mean—oh, dear, I felt quite *sick* for a second. I say—shall I ring him up—now?"

"If you like," said Miss Brown. But her own bell rang first. Something passed across her face. It seemed to flicker, for an instant, between at least three different expressions. But then she reached over, and the sound ceased.

"Hullo?" she was saying. "Oh, Brian." A faint sigh. "No, I'm not—but go ahead. . . . Oh, I'm sorry; I can't. . . . No, nothing's the matter, but . . . No, I can't do that, either, I'm afraid. . . . Oh, all right. . . . Very well . . . No, I haven't seen it. But, Brian, I—I mustn't be late. . . . Yes, yes. I'll be there. And thank you so much. Good-night, Brian. No, I *must* hang up now."

She did so. There could be no doubt that she had at least cut him short. But, of course, she should have been firmer still. She didn't *want* to see that film; or Brian Cairns, if it came to that. He'd rushed her—because she was thinking of something else. But all she wanted, and craved for, was—what?

She didn't know. Not Paul; for, wherever he had gone, she just *couldn't* start all that again. Never. He'd spoilt things. And played the lowest of games. He'd pretended he was different, he'd made her *believe* he was different. And then—— Yes, but what was he doing *now*?

She was worried. Or puzzled. Even baffled, for once. Because, honestly, though of course she'd been perfectly right, if somebody just *disappeared* like that——

"Hullo!" said the guest, who had been teetering round on her very high heels. "I say, haven't you *changed* something here?"

" 'Changed'? What do you mean?"

"Well, there used to be a picture—just there. I never new what it was meant to be. I suppose I'm not clever enough. But— I say! They've *all* gone! Well, that *is* an improvement. Don't you think so? I say—what have you done with them?"

"They're under my bed," said Bianca. "I—I agree. I suddenly ——"

But she couldn't explain more. It was a week ago since she had yanked, abruptly, at all the Brickfields, and had carried them upstairs, and stowed them away. But whether this was because she was sick of them, because her taste had advanced, because she had recovered from the shock of Dorothea's treachery, or because a constant visitor had quietly yet invariably avoided looking at them himself, she still neither knew nor was prepared to say.

She just stared at the marks. She shrugged, and gave up.

"Well, Mrs. Blankett never liked them," she finished, feebly.

"Oh, Bee—you are really the most extraordinary girl! Just fancy— But, still, it's a 'normous improvement. I hate things I can't understand. Well, I'm a fool, I know. But you've been awfully sweet. I might have dithered for weeks if you *hadn't* been so sweet. But I do love him—(Where's my bag? Oh, yes; that's it)—though I shan't tell him tonight. I—I want it all to myself, for a few hours. But I *will* be kind to him; and if the business goes bust——"

"It won't," said Bianca.

"Well, I shouldn't mind. I'd see more of him if it did."

"You're a baby," said Bianca.

"I know. It's such fun! Well, darling, thank you ten thousand million times for everything—including my supper. I know I ought to have washed-up, but I'm just a shade cracked. I'm happy, you see. I'm so terribly happy. Let me know if you want your screw doubling. *I'll* fix it! I'll be beastly to all the others——"

"You won't," said Bianca.

"Well, p'r'aps not. But I think I'll kiss you. Good-night."

In actual point of fact it was another quarter of an hour before Miss Hobson got to the foot of the outside stairway, still accompanied by her hostess, because of all that she still had to say. Then at last she slunk off. And Bianca climbed aloft. And shut the door, and carried debris into the little kitchen.

She didn't mind washing-up. It wasn't envy that made her sigh. Nor did she regret that Ariadne—who, as it now appeared, had put quite as much ash on the floor and chair as in the ash-tray— must now be finally written off as a lodger. *That* didn't matter. Nor anything else. So long as people were happy, and kind.

But it really *was* a bit thick—well, unlike him, you know— just to vanish. To skulk. To go off in a huff—when *all* that she ever done was to be honest. It was——

Bother! Why on earth had she poked a fork into that onion? Transference, perhaps, a psycho-analyst might have suggested. Yet the properties of a pierced onion are notorious for their effect on the eyes.

5

THE glorious 1st of June, as it is known in one connection, brought no glory—though still there was that blazing blue sky—to the youngest partner in Messrs. Sunderland & Co. Any temporary peace that he had found last night had long since ebbed away. Again, he must awake with the old pangs, and a muffled groan. Again he must at once cough, so that Spilsby should be deceived. And though Spilsby, as matter of fact, was more scatter-brained than ever on this occasion—not only arriving with a teapot containing nothing but hot water, but returning a little later with another resident's trousers—one must still remain wary. And glum.

"Thanks," indeed, was all that Paul said, when he was eventually supplied with the right garment. He made no reference to the teapot, so as to avoid further speech. Besides, *he* didn't care what he sipped. He didn't care, if it came to that, what, or whether, he ate; though perhaps, once more, it would be suggestive if he ate nothing.

So he rammed down some breakfast, with a certain disgust. He left by the stairs, because he could see Spilsby—*blast* Spilsby!—coming up in the lift. And then, so far as possible, he merged with the morning crowd; sinking his identity—or at least slightly hunching his shoulders, and looking particularly blank—until, by such means, he had done all he could to turn into an automaton again.

As such he worked. As such, though punctilious in putting a little false life into his features, he conferred with his relations. As such, in due course—but his expression could go hang now—he went back to the Megalithic, took steps (though Heaven knew why) to maintain his metabolism, and then edged up the stairs into the Library.

This is better, he thought. But it wasn't tonight. Either it resented last night's break in his routine, or else more than twelve solid hours of automatism were as much as his system could stand. It was as quiet and as deserted as it had been all along. But it failed to soothe. He was in anguish, and hideously conscious who he was. He felt flayed. Not for a moment could he escape from himself, and from all the thoughts that produced fresh despair.

Round and round they went; and backwards and forwards; and, periodically, slap through his heart. No relief here. He knew it. Nor anywhere else. Furthermore, don't you see—yes, he'd got this at last—every time that he dodged or eluded the pangs, they merely returned with more strength. They were tireless. It was *he* who was wearing himself out. And yet, perhaps, if he *really* wore himself out; physically, that's to say . . .

This, anyhow, was the evening—though he would never know afterwards where, exactly, he went—when Paul Sunderland set out walking, and walked and walked, until well into what are known as the small hours. His sturdy and, if he had known this, not unpleasing figure passed through miles of modern Babylon at a spanking pace; avoiding others, it might be deemed, by chance rather than care, though towards the end he had whole streets to himself.

Yet he still hadn't escaped. Every memory came too. He still groaned as he strode through the night. He was seeking muscular fatigue, but he was so extraordinarily fit that it was something else that at last slackened his course.

For no post-war sock could stand up to such work. One of them split. He was menaced with a blister as well as woe. And on the advice of a head and shoulders protruding from a manhole—sole representative at this point of the human race—he made his way to a junction of strange, cobbled roads, and was picked up after a while by an all-night bus.

It took him within reasonable distance of his flat. He reached it, unblistered, though at much reduced speed. And then—well, it would seem that he had done the trick after all; for he not only fell asleep as he lurched into bed, but still slept after Spilsby had come and gone.

It was nearly nine o'clock, in fact, when Nature, and renewed pangs, woke him up. Yet he *felt* that it was late, and grabbed at his watch. "Blast Spilsby!" he repeated, though indeed even a much better manservant might well have assumed, after more than a thousand callings, that there was no need either to shout or to shake him.

Then he shot out of bed. Beat all records in the bathroom. Beat others in dressing. Bolted his breakfast without troubling to sit down. Seized his hat and rushed out—it was another lovely morning, but he couldn't bother about that—and, churning with pangs and exasperation, with misery and annoyance, virtually ran all the way to the Tube.

But he was nearly half an hour late, though the Tube did its stuff, and though he ran just as fast at the other end. Did this matter? Not the least, or not for once in a way, in a world where so few are on time. But Paul had a conscience. He had let himself down. Besides, he was rattled and racked. So when Sergeant Banglewick sought to accost him as he flew in, he didn't pause, but merely used some of his old skill on the football-field to dodge round him and dash up the stairs.

" 'Morning!" he cracked; and was gone like the wind; though in fact, for the lift was just coming down, it would possibly have been quicker to wait. But he didn't. He couldn't. He bounced into his room. Flung his hat on the hook, and, again without sitting down, used considerable force on the bell-push.

As near as a toucher, and though no one could conceivably have arrived with more promptitude than the admirable Miss Thriplow, he would have done this again. But here she was. He subsided, though still a little out of breath.

"Sorry, Miss Thriplow," he yet managed to remark. "Not like me, I know, but—well, I'm afraid I'm a bit late. Well, the fact is—most unusual thing—that for some reason or other— I beg your pardon?"

"I didn't say anything, Mr. Sunderland."

"Oh. I thought you were going to. Well, in that case——"

"Oh, I'm sorry, Mr. Sunderland. But there *was* just one thing."

"Eh?"

"Mr. Rodney rang up."

"Oh," said Paul, who had been convinced that it was something really important; for it *would* be, of course, when he was late. "What did he want?" he asked, more calmly.

"He didn't say. I thought—well, just for a moment, Mr. Sunderland—he sounded—well, just a little excitable. But he wouldn't leave any message. He said he'd ring back."

"Oh," said Paul, again. Just his manner, he thought. He'd probably called Miss Thriplow "old fruit," or something Rodneyfied like that. Perhaps she'd liked it. Who knew? But no action seemed required. "Well," he said, "let's get on with the mail."

It had all been opened, of course, and arranged on his desk, with the appropriate files waiting, too. Trust Miss Thriplow, though he was so accustomed to trusting her now that the thought never entered his head. Nor did it occur to him that he might have postponed ringing the bell until he had at least glanced at his correspondence.

But he had been impatient. It was an attempt to regain that half-hour. And, in fact, he was pretty sharp off the mark.

"Ah!" he exclaimed, tearing the guts from a rather long-winded communication, and seeing at once that they were just what he had surmised. "Now we've got 'em," he said. It was from a Ministry, of course. "*Now* I'll quote what they wrote us in March!"

He inhaled. It is just possible that there was another trans-ference here; that the Ministry had become symbolic of his private sufferings. Yet there was absolutely no question that he'd got 'em stone cold. And though there wasn't a hope that he could ever get through their hides, he was pulling no punches today.

"Um," he observed. "Yes, that's it. Off we go. 'Dear Sir——' "

The larger of his two telephones rang.

"Dash!" said Paul. "Would you mind?" he appealed. "Say I'm busy, unless it's someone——"

The admirable Miss Thriplow had already obliged. "It's Mr. Rodney again," she said.

"Oh. Very well." Paul took over the hand-piece, and re-deployed a few brain-cells as well. "Hullo, Roddie," he said. "I'd no idea you were——"

"Whoops!" interrupted an almost deafening voice. "I *am*, though. And isn't it grand to be alive!"

Of all possible statements this was the one, perhaps, with which Paul Sunderland found himself least in agreement. He recoiled, and not merely from the blast in his left ear. "Is that," he inquired, after swallowing twice, "what you wanted to ring up and say?"

"No," said his cousin. "It just struck me. That's all. This marvellous weather, and all that. By Jove, I feel terrific! I could take on six heavy-weights. I could——"

"Roddie!" said Paul, sharply. "You're an awfully good chap——"

"Thanks, old boy. Same to you—with large knobs."

"—but I'm a bit behindhand this morning——"

"Aha! That's just it. But you won't be in a jiffy. Paul, you old cold-blooded huckster—stand by for the big news. Paul—and to think I jolly nearly shied a brick at you the last time I saw you; Paul—you inanimate lump of tinned brawn—listen to this! I'm ——"

The line suddenly went dead. As it often does, of course, for various technical reasons; if seldom, somehow, when you are hitched on to a bore. Paul rattled; but nothing happened. He rattled again. The girl at the firm's switchboard said she thought he had been cut off. He quite agreed; but though his cousin Rodney *might* come through again—that was to say, unless a couple of doctors had now spotted him, and done the right thing—he had no idea where he was.

Besides, he hadn't got time. Besides, Roddie was cracked. He speculated, admittedly, as to why the blazes his cousin should have contemplated shying a brick at him. But for the rest——

"Cut off," he announced, sinking back. "Sorry, Miss Thriplow. Perhaps— Well, let's get on. If you could just . . ."

" 'Dear Sir,' " said Miss Thriplow.

"Oh. Was that all? Well, let's try again. Hrrm. 'Dear Sir—er— In reply to your letter dated 28th May and received today . . .' " He nodded, though he didn't actually know whether he had scored off the Ministry or the Post Office. "Er—" he added, but of course Miss Thriplow didn't take this down. He tried to concentrate. He felt frantic, as the right words slipped away. What the deuce had Roddie——

"All right! I'll take it!"

For the bell had trilled again. But this time he was too quick. For some other technical reason, not unfamiliar to subscribers, his speed had defeated the ingenious mechanism. All he could hear was the dialling tone.

Then it stopped, and the same girl expressed the view that he had been cut off.

"Thank you," said Paul. "Very much."

He replaced the hand-piece. He resumed the letter. The bell rang once more. This time he was more cautious. He could hear Roddie's voice. But it was accompanied by a constant series of loud clicks.

He yelled. Roddie yelled. But no complete phrase came through. The effect was like a chorus of castanets. Then, abruptly, they ceased. "Ah!" said Paul. "Go ahead." But now—and, of course, it is really a marvellous invention, but it has never quite got over the war—Roddie's voice was so faint, and so squeaky and small, that it was as if he had been changed into a mouse.

"Speak up!" roared Paul.

"I *am*!" said the mouse. "But this is hopeless. Tell you what, though. I'll come right round."

"No!" shrieked Paul. He was far too busy. But he was also too late. He had meant to explain; to suggest that they should meet when he got away. But even that first, poignant negative—

as he knew, from a final click—had almost certainly stopped at this end.

Dash, then. And blast! Not his cousin—who presumably had *something* on his mind, and was still undoubtedly the best of good chaps; but *things*, which had first made him sleep like a pig, and then wouldn't let him catch up.

He shrugged heavily. Yet Miss Thriplow still seemed undismayed. And though of course—or so he imagined—*she* hadn't been walking about all night (like an ass!), he felt rebuked by her patience and poise. He even glanced at her face. He caught her eye. That was queer. Once again, for an instant, it occurred to him how little he really knew about her. Not, of course, that her private life was his concern.

" 'Dear Sir,' " he resumed, with fresh, stubborn attack. He got going again, more or less. Yet somehow these sentences weren't —and he knew it—either as terse or as brilliant as he had planned. They lacked power, but he couldn't help it. He'd been put off his stroke. Or he was hurrying—well, naturally, with that threat of further interruption. He even split an infinitive once.

"I beg your pardon," he added, quickly. "Wash that out." He changed the words. But really, you know, after a night like last night, and on top of everything else, to transact *any* business, with Roddie, in all probability, half-way here by now——

The threat, and the dictation, were both checked by another sound. His door was opening. Good lord, was this Roddie already? He swivelled. He prepared to say: "Just a second, old man." Then he leapt to his feet. For it was Prim!

"Hullo!" he gasped, in the utmost surprise.

"Yoo-hoo!" said his other cousin, from the doorway.

"Eh?" said Paul. "Why? What for?"

"Just yoo-hoo. I just thought I'd pop in. Good-morning," she added, with a charming smile for Miss Thriplow. "Is he as busy—I mean, *really*—as he's trying to look?" But she didn't wait for any answer. "Never mind," she went on. "Oh, Paul, I'm so excited, you know!"

"Eh?" said Paul, again. So was Roddie. Had something happened? What was it? He gaped like a fish. And then, suddenly and, after all, not unreasonably, he asked: "Why?"

"Aha!" said his cousin Prim. She pirouetted by the door. "Well, *one* thing is—if you haven't heard—that Cousin Charles has come home. Isn't it thrilling! He flew in this morning, you know. I—

they didn't think he'd be here for another week. But then everyone started telephoning, madly—so here I am."

"Yes, but *why*? I mean to say——"

"Oh, Paul, aren't you *dense*!"

"Am I?" said Paul, densely. "I should have thought——" He was about to say that, in his own view, Rhoda was the one to be exhibiting all this pleasure, when some earlier conjectures burst in. "I say," he began again, "is it something to do with Roddie? He rang up just now, but——"

"Of course not!" said Prim. She drew nearer, as the admirable and tactful Miss Thriplow slipped away. "Oh, Paul, you are a juggins! Oh, Paul, you are *blind*. Oh, Paul—shall I give you a kiss?"

"Why?" said Paul. And then: "Help!" as he was violently kissed. "Good heavens!" he added. "What on earth's the idea? Do you realise that my secretary——"

"Yoo-hoo!" said his cousin Prim. "Here, take my little glass; you're all covered with lipstick."

"Yes, but——"

"Please! Or she'll see it—and perhaps she won't understand."

"Well, *I* don't," said Paul, though he accepted the little glass and rubbed vigorously with his handkerchief. "You—you mustn't *do* things like that!"

"Not even today?"

"What's that got to do with it?"

"Everything!" said Prim. "It's the most marvellous day! But I'm off now. Stay there. I shan't tell you just yet. I'd love to, I mean—if you're such an idiot that you can't guess. But they're all talking about it, in Daddy's room—that's why I came out—and he's got to *pretend* to think it over."

"I don't——"

"No, poor Paul. But you will. Very soon. May I have my little looking-glass, please?"

"Oh, yes, certainly. But——"

"There, there. It's all right. And, besides, Paul—" she paused— "well, 's a matter of fact, *you* helped *both* of us, too. In a sort of funny, extraordinary way that we can't explain. But we *know* it— and that's why I kissed you, of course. And now you can get on with your work."

She vanished. As he was balked by the desk, he had to shout.

"Yes, but, Prim! Here! Hi!" He was round the end of the desk.

"Prim! Wait a second!" He again felt insane. Or he *must* get to the bottom of this. *"Prim!"*

She hadn't quite shut the door, and he wrenched at the knob. In another instant he would certainly have been out in the corridor, and very possibly repeating his cries. But there was an impact, and not with the cousin who had just left. He reeled. He might even have fallen on his back, if two hands hadn't clutched at his arms.

" 'Prim'?" said a deep, hearty voice. "I'm not Prim. Are you crazy? I'm *Roddie*. Siddown!"

6

PAUL was sitting. Sometimes he blinked as he sat. For his cousin Rodney was not only still employing the most emphatic language, but was marching around, too. So that sometimes his cousin Rodney (who, as usual, was attired in a rather striking mixture of old and once vivid raiment) was very near, large, and loud—and even bent over the desk, so that almost anyone who was behind it must have blinked; while sometimes, as he plunged towards the opposite wall, the blink was in a sense one of relief.

It was rather, in fact, as if a vocal and extremely active thunderbolt were in the room. It destroyed even the remote possibility of going on with one's dictation. Yet gradually, from a vast number of broken sentences, self-interruptions, and tangled fragments of slang —not to mention a concurrent tendency on the part of his cousin Rodney to emit short bursts of lunatic laughter—Paul picked up a point here and there.

Roddie, it seemed, had been telephoning from a public call-box, and had only observed, after the baffling experiences that had ensued, that there was a notice on the door saying that it was out of order.

"That just *shows* you," he added, "the sort of state I was in. And still am!" Here, again, he had leant right over the desk. "But, dash it all, it's a marvellous state! And I *had* to explain, because if it hadn't been for you—yes, *you*, of all chaps— Well, there we are. Most extraordinary thing 've ever known. Took me right in the wind. 'Good golly!' I said. 'Look at Paul!' Eh? 'Dash his buttons! I said to myself. And then the whole business broke loose! It was like—it was like a sort of biff on the snout. Here I am, though. By Jove! I was doing forty in Cheapside. But I *had* to come round here. Eh? What?"

Paul attempted to speak, but was again shouted down.

"No!" said his cousin Rodney. "Get it right off my chest. I misjudged you, old boy. Though, by George, if I hadn't! Paul—don't you see? It was Fate. *You* were Fate."

"I was? But, Roddie——"

"Slap-bang in the slats. Makes one laugh, eh?" And Rodney laughed. "Darkest hour before the dawn, though. And she *likes* you. Don't worry about that, old man. Tell you what." Here he loomed. "We must all get together." He turned. "Yes, that's it. You must meet her. We'll all hit it up. *That'll* show you. I say—shall I tackle her now?" He turned again, and bore down on the telephone. "Or not? What d'you say? Shall I leave it till lunch? Do you think— Well, what's the time? Mustn't rag her, you know. I mean, of course she's an angel——"

"*Roddie!*"

"Wossa matter?"

"You *haven't* explained. Who the deuce are you talking about?"

"Eh?" For a moment Rodney Sunderland appeared stupefied. Is it possible, said his expression, that old Paul's lost his wits? But then it seemed to strike him that he must be patient, at least. He started speaking again. There was a momentary hitch. He overcame it. He said: "Rosemary, of course!"

" 'Rosemary'?" said Paul. "But—but, Roddie—who's that?"

"Oh, all right, then. Bubbles, you ass. Only I've decided—we've both decided—that I'm going to *call* her Rosemary. In future."

"But—but why?"

"Because, dammit, we're engaged!"

"Oh," said Paul. He was delighted. It was like a knife in his heart. "Con ——" he gasped—"gratulations," he said. "I—I didn't know that," he mumbled. He wrenched some muscles, and grinned. The grin faded. "I—I think you're darned lucky," he said. "But ——"

"Wossa matter, then?"

"—but you said something about if it hadn't been for me——"

"Well, of *course*—bless your soul. It was *seeing* you there."

"Where?" said Paul, wildly.

"Antonetti's, old boy. Night before last. Just come down. Just going to pop in for a bite. Suddenly spotted you. Caught me right in the teeth. 'There!' I said. 'I've put this off, because I thought I could wait. And I knew she was popular, but it never worried me before. Well, safety in numbers, and all that.' But *then*," said Rodney Sunderland, "when I saw *you* on that sofa—looking all earnest—well, dreary, if you like—I thought to myself, 'Golly! He's pinched my best girl'—because *she* looked so serious, too. I'd never seen her like that. She'd always been cheery. I thought— well, you must forgive me, old boy, but you *are* a fish—that she *couldn't* be there, and as solemn as all that, unless— Well, I went nearly *mad*!"

"But, Roddie, I *swear*——"

"That's all right, old cheese. Everything's all right. Tore round there first thing in the morning—after the hell of a night, though— and put it to her straight. You or me. And——"

"But, Roddie, I never——"

"I know. She explained. I—I can hardly tell you what she said. But—well, here it is. She said it had *always* been me. And she was just depressed because she thought—poor little thing—that I preferred machines. And she was waiting. And *I* was waiting—till I got this big scare—though I've never even looked at another girl. Bubbles! I mean, Rosemary. And *you* pulled it off. I'm so darned happy— Well, of course, I had to tell you first. I mean, as soon as I came round. I'm *engaged*, old boy. I'm over the moon! I say— you're quite sure you don't mind?"

Another gulp.

"Of cuc-course not. I——"

"That's fine, then. And nor do her parents. They've been charming! You know, I'm awfully fond of them, too."

Paul choked on a kind of gasp. But he took the point. This was Love. Even the extraordinary dullness of Colonel and Mrs. Vaughan was swept from its path as by fire. It was true, also, of course, that old Roddie wouldn't have to live with them. But——

"*What?*" He had gasped again. He was even touched, as well as tortured, by the vision that arose; of a church somewhere; of his cousin washed, polished, and in the most unusual attire; and of himself standing by with a ring. He could hardly imagine an experience that would give him more pain, or that would underline a more horrible contrast. But he couldn't say so. And Roddie was over the moon. He must remain there, at whatever cost to oneself.

"I mean," he stumbled on, "I shall probably bungle it——"

"No, you won't. *I'm* the one who'll be shaking like a leaf. But if *you're* there, old stick, I'm bound to get through. You'll keep your head. You always do. It's a bet?"

"It—it's jolly kind of you," croaked Paul. What a statement about his head! "If you really——"

"That's fixed, then. Good work! Gosh!" said the joyful Roddie, and began marching again. And gesticulating. And crashing into the furniture. "It's marvellous!" he kept on saying. "You don't know what it's like. There was I, simply wasting my beautiful youth. And then—bingo!—you—*you* put the wind up me suddenly. 'Straordinary. You've no idea what I went through that night. But then—bingo, again!—up goes the balloon. Away go the horrors —there's never been such a girl, you know—and everything's jake. I feel tremendous!" With an illustrative movement he flung out both arms, and knocked three books off a filing-cabinet. "But what we *must* settle—" he kicked them aside—"is when you can *meet* her, you know. I *want* you to meet her——"

"But—but Roddie—I've known her for years."

"No, you haven't. You don't know how brainy she is. I want to *show* you— Hullo! Did *I* do that?"

"No," said Paul, whose left hand had reached out at the buzz. "It's the intercom. Just a second." He unhitched the smaller desk-telephone. He said: "Yes?" He said: "Right." He hung up. And rose, as he did so, again. "Sorry, Roddie," he said. "But H.B. wants me now. We generally have a sort of pow-wow, about this time, you know. And generally, if it comes to that, I've at least *read* my letters. Mustn't keep him. But don't run away."

He even meant this, perhaps; as a clansman, if so; though as a clansman he had also duties that came first. But Roddie declined the invitation at once.

"What!" he said, and thumped his chest like a gorilla. "Stay here all alone? On this marvellous day? Couldn't do it. No, no; I'll go round to where she works. That's better than ringing up, don't you think? No, wait—just a jiffy——"

"Oh, Roddie, I *can't*!"

"Eh? But, look here—are you going to tell 'em about *me*? Or ought I to do it myself?"

"Just as you like," said Paul, trying to pass him. "But Roddie— honestly——"

"Oh, all right, old hermit. I won't spoil your fun. Besides—

whoa!—I've just remembered they want to tell her grandmother in Scotland before anyone else. I mean, *you* don't count. Well, you *had* to know. But keep it under your hat till the old girl waves back. I'll ring you. I'll——"

"Right—thanks," said Paul, and rushed off. Scarcely, perhaps, in the fittest frame of mind to give the whole of his attention to a business conference. And having utterly forgotten, though there were reasons for this, not only Prim's statement that quite a different sort of conference was in fact going on, but even that he had seen her at all.

He just paused, in other words, to assure himself first that his cousin Rodney was really taking his leave, and secondly that he turned the right way. And then, having noted his egress, and having informed him (as proved necessary) that the lift was to the left, he turned the handle of the main avuncular door.

So far as there was anything in his mind now—apart from turmoil, and a kind of mixture of envy and shame—it was picturing the large, quiet room that he was about to enter, and knew so well; with the dry, yet reliable and always lovable, H.B. in his customary chair; and with his cousin Clinton and his uncle Oliver also in readiness for another normal discussion.

They would probably, he thought, be looking towards the door, since he was perhaps thirty seconds late. So that he opened it quickly, with an apology on his lips. And stopped dead. For not only was his entrance quite unobserved, but there was no question of the room being quiet.

It even seemed smaller, owing to the quantity of occupants. They were chattering. They were laughing. There was no suggestion of business. H.B., it was quite true, was ensconced in his chair. The other partners were undoubtedly here, too. But so was Charles Medway. And Rhoda, by Jove! And Prim—here, of course, certain memories rushed back. And young Mark. And even Cranky. It was like a dream.

It was still more like a dream—though of course it *couldn't* be a dream—owing to the fact that no one, as yet, seemed to see him. He felt invisible, as well as puzzled, as he paused where he stood. And then they all seemed to see him at once.

"Ah—Paul!" said H.B.

"Hullo, Paul!" said his cousin Rhoda.

"Paul!" said old Charles, though he was looking younger than for years.

"Come in, Paul," said his cousin Clinton and his uncle Oliver, simultaneously.

"Yoo-hoo, Paul!" said his cousin Primula.

"Paul, by Jove!" said his cousin Mark.

"Here's Paul," said Miss Crankshaw, summing up.

Then they all laughed again, perhaps partly at themselves, or at the swift unanimity of their chorus. But Paul himself merely stood there, with his mouth slightly ajar. And though this, for some reason, produced another burst of laughter, he still looked bewildered and blank. And then a trifle indignant.

"I say—what's the joke?"

"*You* are," said Prim, at once, and laughed again.

"No, he isn't," said Mark. "Don't rag the poor chap."

"All right, darling. Shall I tell him?"

"Go ahead," said Mark.

"I can't!" said Prim. "It—it's his face. I feel shy. Oh, won't somebody else——"

A kind of uproar broke out. And then Prim's voice, again, over all.

"No, Daddy," she was shouting. "Daddy darling, you *must*! Come on, Daddy! Now, Paul. Flap your ears."

This, of course, was something that Paul Sunderland couldn't even attempt to do. Yet he directed his gaze—as did everyone else—on the senior partner. And H.B., having first cleared his throat with a loud "Hrrm," embarked on the following speech.

"Well, Paul—" he said. "If you'll just close the door. Ah—thanks. The fact is—and I don't wonder you look surprised—" ("Go on, Daddy—*please*!" said Prim)—"for I was surprised myself—but these—ah—young people—well, they've rather rushed us, you know. But they seem quite decided." ("That's right," said Prim.) "They even say they've been waiting; for—hrrm—Charles to return. But then they caught him in the middle of the night. And they caught *me* before breakfast." ("Poor Daddy!" said Prim.) "And there's no question, of course, that they're both far too young—ridiculously young, if I may say so—" (but he was smiling). "Absurdly and—hrrm—preposterously young. But Mark's not a fool." ("Oh, *thanks*, sir," said Mark.) "And Prim—well, I suppose she's grown-up." ("Yes, I am!") "And times have changed, of course. I mean to say, what difference would it make if I *did* put my foot down? If it comes to that, Paul, why *should* I?" ("Hear, hear!" from Paul's cousin Clinton.) "You see, *Charles* hasn't!" ("I was feeling too sick," said Charles Medway. "I wouldn't let him," said Rhoda, at the same moment.) "And Charles—well, I've the greatest respect for Charles." ("Thanks, H.B. Same to you.") "Not at all. So there you are," said the senior partner, contriving in some manner to look both beaten and bucked. "That's what's happened. Of course I can't do any work. But I tell you—to be quite frank—it's rather grown on me in the last hour." ("*Angel* Daddy!") "So I thought—well, you'd better know, too."

Applause from Oliver Sunderland.

"Know what?" said Paul; though these words, for he wasn't a complete fool, either, had rather lagged, as a matter of fact, after his thoughts.

"Idiot!" said Prim. "Mark and I are *engaged*! Why, I practically *told* you just now!"

"Good gracious!" said Paul. He was there. But he was sunk. Two cousins in one morning—no, three, by gum! All wallowing in happiness, and he was jolly pleased, too. But to expect him— He rose, with a fearful effort, from the depths. "Congratu——" He tried still harder. "—ulations," he said. And then fiercely, and all at once: "Congratulations!"

"How sweet of you!" said Prim.

"Thanks *awfully*," said Mark. He approached. He was looking purposeful. And of *course* Paul was pleased. But if Mark tried to place any responsibility on him—like Roddie, and Prim . . . He stiffened. It may be he warded this off. But he was quite unprepared for what came.

"I say, Paul—" Here the hubbub was renewed, but Mark approached nearer still. "I say—I've no idea when this thing'll be coming off. Early days, in a way, and all that. But I *do* want to ask you—and Prim wants it, too—if you'd mind signing on as Best Man. You see—" Paul felt exactly as though an earthquake were rocking the whole building, and even his vision was momentarily obscured by what appeared to be wreaths of volcanic dust— "we both feel you're the best chap for the job. And, besides—well, that day we were all at Greenhurst, you know. Easter Monday. That was the day I—I sort of asked her, and she said Yes. And you *helped*——"

"Mark—I *didn't*!"

"Yes, you did. You kept H.B. out of the way."

"Did I?"

"And Prim says you've been a mascot all along. I've felt it, too,

Paul. I kept thinking, *Paul* ought to get married. He's cut out for it.
And of course—well, one's always really thinking of oneself—I sort
of decided I was dashed if *I'd* put it off; quite apart, I mean to say,
from being loopy about Prim. So you see . . ."

No, Paul didn't. Nor did he hear any more. Yet if it were true,
and it was, that *he* was always thinking of himself, here at least—
not, of course, that he could possibly refuse—was a chance to be
less abominably egoistic.

"Right you are," he broke in. He didn't *look* very noble. He
looked more as if his mouth were full of wormwood. Yet Mark's
gratitude—just for the moment—produced a faint, twisted smile.
And as Mark almost immediately merged in the throng—but first he
had either banged his prospective supporter on the back, or *something* had made him totter and clutch a chair—he could now relapse
into the role of a spectator again. Which, in turn, allayed some of
his pain.

For really, you know—(Oh, help! Be a man. Don't give the
whole show away!)—it was a most extraordinary scene in a place of
business. Relations all gabbling as if drinks were going round—or
as if all taxes had suddenly been halved. Yet in fact because of
Love, which had no use for him, but was yet so powerful that it
could do even this.

Yes, Love, thought Paul. As arbitrary as it was absurd. As cruel
as it was patently unfair. The world's biggest nuisance. Mankind's
greatest pest. It grabbed you, and either you were whirled to the
heights, or plunged into pitch-black despair. There was no sense in
it. It was a menace. But once it grabbed, there you were. It was a
hook that there was no wriggling off.

"Love!" he growled, perhaps more audibly than he had either
intended or supposed. For: "That's right," said his cousin Rhoda;
and as she smiled, he must smile back. For he was dashed fond of
her; as, in fact, he was still fond of the whole clan. So that now—
though it is always possible that no one would have noticed this,
anyhow—he, too, began gabbling away. Or, dash it, one *must* be
polite.

It was at about this point that Mrs. Kelsey came in, and offered
her liege-lord an envelope. But though in ordinary circumstances—
for it was quite clearly a cablegram—he would have opened it at
once, he just pocketed it, and told *her* what had happened.

At first it rather looked as if this would start the whole thing off
all over again; for Mrs. Kelsey—though she never forgot her real

rank—had long been virtually accepted as a sort of Sunderland. But though her interest, and felicitations, left nothing to be desired, she yet somehow still symbolised work.

This was felt; and the feeling spread. Charles Medway, who hadn't yet, so it appeared, been to his own office at all, said he *must* just look in before lunch. Cousin Clinton and Uncle Oliver seemed struck with like thoughts. Rhoda was leaving. Mark and Prim must leave, too. For though the former had been granted, or had taken, a day's absence, both were pledged (as was now revealed) to a celebration at the Serene—another pang for Paul here—and the room was suddenly full of good-byes.

"I suppose," said the youngest partner, shuffling slightly, and reflecting that, on a day like this, it was perhaps waste of time to raise the query; "I suppose," he suggested, "you won't be wanting me any more? Well, not this morning, I mean, as it's so late."

"Eh?" said H.B., turning back from the window. But he didn't say anything else, and as the continued presence of Miss Crankshaw —(I say, you know, it's *amazing* how young she's taken to looking)— seemed to hint that there was to be some private or domestic business, the junior partner slipped out; and returned to his own room; and found, though this was quite in order, that Miss Thriplow had gone to lunch. And as this was so—though he did make a few pencil notes—he presently oozed out himself.

His own lunch, which in his view was more tasteless, if not actually nauseating, than ever, took longer than it deserved; if only because, as usual, there was a shortage of staff, and a horrible crowd in the place. Yet of course he must pay. And to pay he must get a bill. So that he must wait. And, as he waited, he suffered afresh; owing to what was going on in his mind.

It seethed. It rushed round like a rat in a trap. Other people were happy, it was constantly pointing out. He wasn't. And though perhaps this was quite a simple idea, there was no limit to the varieties of its presentation. If he retreated from one aspect, he merely crashed into another. "Gar!" he muttered, sometimes. And: "Ow!" And: "Oh, hell!"

Yet at last he was permitted to discharge his account, and to return, through a jostling City, to his office. Once more, as he re-entered, he was vaguely sensible of an impression that Sergeant Banglewick would have addressed him if he could. But though he nodded, it was just out of the question that he should chat. "Some other time," was the signal that he transmitted as he sped on. And the grizzled warrior, who would certainly have hobbled after him if it had been anything of an official nature, fell back and retired to his glass box.

Once more, also, or as soon as he was again seated at his desk, he pressed the bell-push that summoned his secretary. She appeared. He eyed her quickly; but there was nothing to suggest, whatever the staff might have made of this morning's irruption, that Mrs. Kelsey had broadcast since then. He relaxed slightly.

"Awfully sorry, Miss Thriplow," he said, "about those interruptions this morning. But I think we can get on now—" he was gathering up papers, and a proportion of his wits—"if—ah—you don't mind stopping on a little late."

As Miss Thriplow had never failed to oblige him in this way, it is to be feared that he neither looked at her nor awaited her answer. Had he looked, he might have seen just a trace of distress, before it vanished again behind her mask. But she made no audible protest, and in another few moments he was again doing his best to dictate.

It wasn't easy. He had seldom shown less command of the *mot juste*, or less ability to come to the point. He havered. He boggled. He kept changing his mind. He cancelled sentences, and started again. Never once, though he wasn't watching her, did Miss Thriplow exhibit even a hint of impatience. Yet his conscience kept saying, You're wasting her time. And it was all too clear that he was wasting his own.

At about half-past three his cousin Rodney rang up. But as Miss Thriplow, in response to an almost agonised grimace, had taken the call, he begged her, hoarsely, to say that he was out. She did so. His conscience informed him that he was a cad; to make her lie, and to be so cowardly himself. His reason retorted that he knew just what old Roddie was after, and that he was dashed if he could face either him or his prize; let alone two such love-birds together.

But it was no help to his dictation. Nor, when exactly the same thing happened about a quarter of an hour later, did he feel any the better for that. In fact, he felt worse; as was perhaps morally just. But when, at about four, a point arose on which it was really essential that he should consult his uncle Hayward; and when, having buzzed him, he was told by Mrs. Kelsey that he had telephoned, after lunch, to say that he wasn't coming back at all, then— well, it would be an exaggeration to say that his mighty heart cracked. For it didn't. It was still ticking over.

Yet he rose, nevertheless, as if pierced by a pin. Why the blazes, he was asking himself, should I hang on here—making a mess of every darned thing I touch—when I'm feeling *ghastly*, and all this'll have to be torn up, and it won't make a pennyworth of difference to anyone if they don't get their answers till Monday?

He began babbling again, swiftly, before his conscience could chip in.

"Look here, Miss Thriplow—just remembered—awfully sorry—but got to clear off. Leave those letters—and everything. I'll have to do 'em again. And clear off, too—if you want to, I mean. Absolutely no point in— Eh? Who's that?"

Half-way to the hat-hook he had heard the telephone ring. He paused. Miss Thriplow spoke, and—admirable as ever—placed her hand over the mouthpiece.

"It's Mr. Rodney again," she said.

"I've gone!" blurted Paul; rammed his hat on his head; and transformed this remark into the truth. He raced down the stairs. He hurtled past old Banglewick—too rapidly this time even to observe yet another attempt to stop him—and darted right out into the street.

And walked. And stumbled. And dodged. And kept on. Still, and ever, in search of escape. Yet his thoughts still milled round, and in the intervals of again deciding that he was cursed, doomed, and damned, and of realising that nothing short of extinction could provide escape from himself, it also struck him that if he went either to his flat or his present club, he would merely be a sitting target for his cousin Rodney.

He knew his energy. His tenacity. He'd go *on* ringing up. Wrenching himself—ow!—from his loved one's embraces, a chap like Roddie would think nothing of telephoning all night. At the flat there would be an incessant and insupportable tinkling. At the club—where it was understood that one would be protected from women, but where it would be thought suspicious if one went on refusing to speak to a man with the same surname—there would be a constant procession of page-boys.

So at about twenty minutes to five, and having by this time reached the neighbourhood of Piccadilly Circus, Paul Sunderland plunged impulsively into a large, darkened building, full of tobacco-smoke and electrically amplified speech, and sat there, while huge human shadows mopped and mowed on a screen; not at peace, but at least (if no one in the film industry will misapprehend this) in asylum.

At first it was enough that he was alone, and sitting down. His eyes and ears were as good as switched off. He did some quiet, solid churning, in something of a trance; for the conditions in such buildings, especially if one's eyes and ears are switched off, are distinctly hypnotic.

But then a particularly loud voice or an unusually large face impinged, and aroused some of his attention. It grew. At about a quarter to seven he was gazing sourly at a screaming farce. At about a quarter to eight—for the thought of food never entered the wreckage of his mind—he was following the Big Feature which he had disregarded when he came in. And with growing attention again.

For there was a chap in it who had received the brush-off in the first reel. And after that—though he was rather an ass, in a way—there was a whole series of incidents in which he appeared in the wrong light, so that the heroine curled her nostrils at his very name. It was perhaps too much to say that Paul identified himself with this chap. Yet there was something faintly consolatory in his incessant misfortunes; until—at about half-past nine—a shower of treacle seemed to pour over the picture; all explanation was dispensed with; and chap and heroine were clearly going to clinch.

It was borne in on him, in other words, that here, too, he had merely been attending a manifestation of Love. Already, in fact, he was struggling to get out. And then his eyes, which after the best part of five hours in the dark had become like a cat's, or an usherette's, suddenly showed him something else.

All over the huge, sloping floor of the auditorium, heads were leaning together, arms were cuddled round shoulders, and hands—he had just separated two by treading, in his haste, on their cognate feet—were entangled and entwined. Love, again! And he apologised. But though the rest of the spectators were still awaiting the last lingering, sciagraphic nose-to-nose, Paul Sunderland raced up the aisle at full speed; his one wish now to escape from this agapemone.

It was still daylight. The momentum took him almost to his flat. And there—well, dash it all, even Roddie would probably have stopped ringing by now; or, if not, one could just let him ring—he completed the journey, and entered the lift, and passed once again into his alleged home.

He wasn't hungry. He dismissed the thought of food with disgust. But he was exhausted. He had been through the hell of a day. And though of course he had no intention whatsoever of getting tight, this was a moment at least—or so it struck him—for a fairly stiff peg. It might help him to sleep. He had heard that it did. And, dash it, he felt dashed near collapse.

He advanced to the sideboard. He picked up the whisky bottle. He uttered a terrible oath.

Spilsby! It was all too clear. He'd started helping himself again. The fluid was right down to the label. Fresh disgust overcame the unfortunate Paul. It was unthinkable now that he should drink what Spilsby left; or that he should drink at all, for that would reduce him to the same, vile level.

"Ugh!" he observed, and put the bottle back. But in the morning—after another abominable night—it still seemed more important that he should grunt at Spilsby, so as to stop him chattering, than that he should attempt what, in fact, he had never done yet. For whether Spilsby confessed, or defended himself, he would *talk*. So Paul grunted. And grunted again. And though Spilsby made several attempts of his own—seldom, indeed, had he *looked* more loquacious—the grunts did him down in the end.

"Will you be dining in, sir?" was his final, and feeble, remark.

"No," said Paul; and seized his hat, and shot off.

7

To the City, of course, on this still peerless morning of Friday, June 3rd—though at last, and because all forecasts had plumped for No Change, a few faint wisps were approaching the sun. To the City, by Tube, in the customary jam, for he was five minutes early today. But duty was duty. Where else could he go? Moreover, as he must now cram two days' work into one, at least *some* other thoughts might pipe down.

He still looked grim, though, rather than jaunty, as he entered Cheesemonger Lane, and passed up the well-known steps through the well-known door. For the fourth time Sergeant Banglewick stepped forward as he saluted, and with a distinct air of being charged with a few words. But Paul, on this occasion, was hardly

more than a blur. He said " 'Morning," for it was a custom, but he
didn't pause as he dashed by. He went straight into the lift, and
was taken up.

Grim, too, or at least grimmish, was the Paul Sunderland who
stepped out. Concentration was on his brow, and, indeed, not only
there, as he neared his room and a double dose of agenda. He opened
the door. He hung his hat on the usual hook. He went round behind
his desk, twitched his trousers, and sat down. His vision, to some
extent, was still clouded by cogitation, though he was just aware of
something strange within its range.

Before, however, he could achieve a very simple analysis of this
effect, the door opened again, and he turned his head.

It was Miss Thriplow. He hadn't rung. Still less, if it came to
that, had he invited her to enter darting and almost skipping. He
looked faintly surprised. He concluded that he had been mistaken,
for she was quite steady now. A touch of giddiness, no doubt—for
which Heaven knew there was more than enough cause—must have
deceived him.

On the other hand, as she *was* here, the sooner they got to
work——

"Oh, excuse me, Mr. Sunderland," she was saying, clearly
enough. "But Mr. Rodney——"

"I can't speak to him!"

"But, Mr. Sunderland, that's just it."

"Eh?"

"He rang up—just now—to say would you forgive him——"

"What on earth for?" asked Paul. "I beg your pardon. Yes?
Yes?"

"—but he said he was taking Miss Vaughan—I *think* that was
the name—to see his old school today. He said he'd ring up this
evening. He said he hoped that would be all right."

"Oh," said Paul. What a rum sort of treat for poor Bubbles.
Though of course if she *liked* it—or liked Roddie enough— There
was another aspect. It meant that the siege had been interrupted.
He breathed more easily. "Yes, perfectly all right," he went on.
"But as you *are* here, Miss Thriplow, and as I've got a lot of . . . "

The vigour trickled out of his voice. All sound ceased. Slow as
he had been to detect the precise difference about his desk this
morning, he had not only spotted it now, but was as good as
flabbergasted.

He stared. He stared again. He drew back in his seat.

"What——" he began. He passed a hand across his eyes. But the red geranium in the little flower-pot was still there. "Who——" he tried again, as he pointed at it with a shaky hand. "Who the——"

Luckily, for there can be little question that the next word would have been lacking in consideration for the fair sex, his inestimable amanuensis broke in.

"Oh, Mr. Sunderland," she was saying—and he could hear her—"*I* did. I *had* to, Mr. Sunderland. I just *had* to, you see. I mean, I know it's not *nearly* good enough for you—after all you've done——"

"Whoa!" said Paul. He could sense sentiment. He had heard of secretaries who suddenly did this. He was appalled. But she was still rushing on.

"I don't mean all your kindness. It's *far* more than that. Well, you see——"

"Pup-pup-*please*!"

"—I was *awfully* upset. It was my friend——"

"Eh?"

"—well, I knew he was fond of me, in a way. But he was shy. So was I, Mr. Sunderland. We only met in the train; and hardly ever going home, because he gets off earlier than me. He's in a Government job, you see. And how *could* he say anything in the mornings—in all that crowd?"

"I dunno," said Paul; all attention, and distinctly ashamed of himself now, but still in a considerable fog.

"Oh, Mr. Sunderland!" Miss Thriplow was looking positively arch. "You're just teasing me, I *know*; but I *am* so grateful. Because yesterday, you see—all thanks to you—there he was in the same compartment. And it was before the rush-hour, so we were quite alone after Stratford. And then the engine broke down. And—oh, Mr. Sunderland, isn't it wonderful! I shall be leaving you!"

"But you can't!" was Paul's instant and violent retort.

"I can! I *must*! Mr. Sunderland, I—I'm engaged! So of *course*," said Miss Thriplow, who now, in some unaccountable fashion, looked almost glamorous for a moment, "I had to buy you that plant—because I'm so happy. I mean, if you hate it——"

"I don't," said the gallant Paul. Never could he hope for such a secretary again. And he felt sick, though he most certainly wasn't jealous. You, too! was the theme that once more shook his soul. Love was loose now, it seemed, like a tiger or an epidemic. He appeared to cower. Yet he not only expressed the greatest admiration for the red geranium, but even added—if with a few extra syllables, as was becoming habitual—his congratulations.

"I think," he declared, "he's very lucky indeed. I—I'm sure—" A wave of nausea seized him again. "I mean—" He couldn't make it. But Miss Thriplow had sat down. If she were simpering, as he suspected—but he was dashed if he'd look—it might yet be gathered that she still regarded herself as a stenographer.

"Um," said Paul. And: "Oh, yes." And emitted further such sounds. But then—for after all there is great power in routine—he did actually get back to business. He was slower than usual. There were more pauses as well. Yet by half-past eleven he had broken the back of his dictation, and towards the end at increasing speed.

His desk was undoubtedly looking tidier again. There was a pile of files ready for removal by Miss Thriplow. One or two he had kept back, for they must still be discussed. But considering everything, he had almost caught up. Good! he thought, though there was still plenty of work to be done. "I think that's all, just for the moment," he announced.

Then he rose, as his secretary picked up the files. To stretch his legs? Or as a tribute—for, to tell the truth, he didn't generally rise on these occasions—to Miss Thriplow's new status in life? He shook his head, as Miss Thriplow slipped out of the room. He sighed profoundly. Or, rather, he started to sigh. And stopped, and stood glaring at the geranium.

Seldom, one would say, can any innocent plant have received a look of such absolute venom. For not only must it remind him of some flowers that he had bought himself; not only was it again pointing the contrast between other people's happiness and his own utter despair; but, dash it, it represented a further and outrageous idea that he, Paul, was a professional pander.

At this Shakespearian word—and "marriage-broker," in fact, would have been much more apt—he advanced on the geranium with such a frightful grimace as to suggest that he was about to hurl it against the radiator.

"You blank!" he began. "You——" He stopped. He span round. The office buzzer had just buzzed, and the plant was saved.

"Hullo?" he said, sharply. "Oh, yes. Right you are." And business came first, after all. He snatched, that is to say, at the remaining files on his desk. He hurried from the room. He turned, as he had turned almost exactly twenty-four hours ago, to the right. And in another moment he was in the presence of the senior partner.

But this morning H.B. was quite alone, at his own big desk. Nor, as yet, was there any sound as Paul drew nearer.

"Are the others coming?" he asked; referring, of course—since he had supposed that there was to be a conference at last—to the two intermediate partners.

"No," said H.B. "Not just yet. Will you shut the door?"

Paul shut it. And then, as he looked round again, there was H.B. right over by his favourite window. Gazing out of it, too. With his back to the room. Still in silence; until he suddenly said: "Paul."

"Yes?" Paul decided to put the files on this other desk. "Here I am," he continued, "H.B."

"Ah," said his uncle. "Yes, I wanted a word with you. You see—well, she was your governess first. She's very fond of you, too."

"You mean Cranky, H.B.?" Well, obviously. Of course. But H.B.'s back seemed to wriggle a bit.

"I wish," he said, though still addressing the window, "you wouldn't call her that. After all . . . "

"I beg your pardon, H.B." And yet *Prim* called her Cranky. And Mark. What the——

"Thank you," said the senior partner. "You see—well, to tell the truth, I've been rather exercised about her future. For some time."

"Have you?" said Paul. "But——"

"Never mind about that. The point is that your cousins' engagement—but don't think that I'm not truly delighted—has rather brought things, as one might say, to a head. It—it has changed her position. I foresaw this, in a way. I even discussed the—ah—financial aspect with Whichery. I've said to myself, more than once: If Prim gets married, what will happen to Elvira?" Paul goggled, but said nothing. "I mean, she's young. She's attractive. She's——"

"Oh, rather!" said Paul. "Yes, I've noticed it, too. I mean, it's marvellous, in a way, how she's come on since she left school."

"Eh?" said H.B. "Who are you talking about?"

"Prim, of course."

"Well, I'm *not*," said H.B., with some emphasis. "So please don't interrupt."

"I'm sorry," said Paul. But he was still extremely bewildered. "Who——" he began again.

"Now, Paul, if you *please*. The whole situation—this is what I

wish you to understand—has changed entirely since yesterday.
First there's this engagement, of which I—and Charles and Rhoda,
too, I'm glad to say—thoroughly approve. Then there is the
problem: What happens to Elvira? I was troubled. But for Prim—
Well, perhaps you see what I mean. But without her it became at
once more acute. I was deeply troubled. I have for some time,
whether this surprises you or not, felt more than respect for Elvira.
Are you listening?"

"Y-yes," said Paul. "But——"

"Then kindly," said H.B., still staring out of the window, and
with a sound less of authority than of appeal, "allow me to proceed.
I had known, as I say, for some time what would make me very
happy. Curiously enough—" he almost turned here, but not quite—
"this was particularly borne in on me during your visit at Easter.
Since then, in fact—though I can't quite think why—I have
somehow *associated* you with the idea. But until yesterday,"
resumed H.B., after a brief and still mysterious pause, "I had
regarded it as impracticable, if not impossible. I'm old-fashioned, I
suppose, though I am still, whether you realise this or not, on the
right side of fifty. But marriage—I beg your pardon?"

"I—I didn't say anything," said Paul. But he took out his
handkerchief, and wiped his forehead.

"Ah. Nevertheless, in my view it is a sacred contract. It is true
that, to oblige your aunt Nita, I took steps to dissolve our union.
Well, she was very determined, and I should have had no peace
from her if I hadn't. To be frank, I must admit that we were quite
unsuited to each other. And she seemed to have no affection for
Prim. Yet still, while she was alive, I somehow hesitated to re-marry.
I don't know whether you can understand that at all?"

Paul felt—among other feelings—that, in the case of H.B., he
could quite clearly understand it. It was H.B. all over, with his
unparalleled set of principles. He admired them. He was an uncle,
and partner, in a million, of course. But why—(had he just had
some news that he was trying to break?)—had he used the words
"while she was alive"?

"H.B.!" This was going to be dashed difficult you know. "Do
you mean that—that Aunt Nita——"

"Just a moment, please, Paul. Yesterday—as I must explain
—I took Elvira out to lunch." (And why the deuce does he keep
calling her that?) "It was quite natural. She had come here at my
special request. Prim had gone. It—it was my duty, in a way."

"Absolutely," said Paul. "But——"

"*Please* let me explain. I felt a little emotional—well, perhaps you can understand that, too; but I had complete self-control. She was looking very delightful. She has always been pleasant. Yet I was conscious—being so concerned about her future now—of considerable strain. I fidgeted. One does. I put my hand in my pocket. I felt an envelope. I took it out. It was a telegram, my dear Paul, which I must have put there without thinking—no doubt owing to the crowd in this room. I said: 'Excuse me.' I read it. Paul——"

"Oh, H.B.! I do *hope* it didn't hurt. I——"

" 'Hurt'?" H.B. echoed, swinging right round at last. "It was from Nita——"

"Oh!"

"—from some place in Nevada——"

"Eh?"

"—to tell me—and it was so like her to cable instead of writing, and then to save perhaps a shilling or two by using our telegraphic address; to tell me that she had just divorced Hiram Curtis—for mental cruelty, she said, though he was the kindest fellow I've ever met—and that she had married another man—an American, I take it—called Otto J. Stark. She even added—she's an extraordinary woman, you know—that this Stark was 'worth,' as she put it, forty millions. Dollars, I imagine. But that's not the point."

"Isn't it?" said Paul.

"Tchk! Not the money, I mean. It was the *effect*, my dear boy. How *could* I feel bound to someone like that? It came to me, in a flash, that I was now only one of *three*. And it isn't the same thing, you know. I felt released. I didn't show Elvira the telegram—or not at the moment—but I asked her to marry me. It solved everything, you see. I—I love her, what is more. And *that* isn't all. She loves *me*!"

"Good heavens!" said Paul.

"Why not?" said his uncle Hayward. "Do you think—though I know I don't deserve such a woman—that she would be capable of even a trifling prevarication? She *told* me. She said it had *grown*—do you hear that? Of course—owing to my situation—it means a ceremony before a registrar. But, Paul, she said herself that you *must* be there, too. Besides, I have this feeling that you have *helped*, in some strange way. So will you, as it were, be Best Man?"

A mixture of agony and light-headedness, of pleasure and blank amazement, tend to tangle up anyone's tongue. There was a kind of splutter from the junior partner. Half a groan, and a sort of crow. But he was nodding. His hand was being wrung, and he wrung back. "Of course!" seemed to burst through a slightly clenched jaw. "Congratu—I—I'll be *delighted*!—atulations!"

Then a mist descended, as it was almost bound to descend. He was as much attached to Miss Crankshaw, and to his uncle, of course, as to any two such characters on earth. He hoped sincerely, and also believed, that they would be extremely happy. That his uncle's loneliness would be ended, and that Cranky (though he quite saw that he must now stop calling her that) would be blessed among ex-governesses from now on.

He even spared a thought for his ex-aunt Nita, in Nevada, and for her second and third husbands as well. Let 'em *all* be happy, so far as *he* was concerned. Perhaps they would be. More than likely, in fact.

But for himself, once again, there was a ghastly mockery in this news. For though people, so it seemed, were getting married right and left, and no less than six of them had secured his services for their weddings, he, the wretched outcast on whom Fate had frowned, couldn't even be allowed to forget!

Bianca, he thought. He felt giddy. And sick. He was also convinced, more than ever, that he was cursed. Love! He all but snorted. It was a *horrible* thing. Why the blank couldn't it have left him alone?

But it hadn't. And in addition to ruining his whole life, it must keep bobbing up on all sides. One ought to laugh. But of course he couldn't. Any more than it would be correct to scream. No. He must just bear it. And go on suffering like hell. And congratulating—bah!—everyone in sight.

So he forced further creases into a face that felt like stone. He emitted words that, whatever the actual sound of them, were at least apropos. And either his uncle Hayward was in a condition where he failed to notice strange convulsions and hollow undertones, or else Paul was more successful than he supposed.

Gradually, also, he was adjusting himself to this fresh shock. And presently, though not until Messrs. Clayton and Oliver Sunderland had again been summoned, and had offered their own sincere felicitations—for no Sunderland would ever dream of criticising any other, and both were naturally devoted to Miss Crankshaw; presently—if not until about a quarter to one—the meeting broke up, once more without any business, in the ordinary sense, having been transacted at all. And Paul tottered back to his own room.

He also saw the geranium. But he was too numb to do more than blench. He was also too numb, or so it appeared a little later, even to contemplate staggering out for lunch. With an air, though possibly a false one, of sudden and brisk determination, he buzzed for a minor underling, ordered sandwiches to be brought in, and sat munching and working, and occasionally sipping water, while the rest of the staff ebbed and flowed.

He was still working, though he had now long since finished both the sandwiches and the water, at about half-past three, when Miss Thriplow skipped back through the door. He eyed her with something of the mien of a bilious bloodhound. But of course he knew why she was here.

"My letters?" he suggested.

"Yes. Mr, Sunderland. I've been as quick as I could."

"Thank you," he growled. And she had been accurate, too. Though he sighed as he began signing his name. At each signature the still admirable Miss Thriplow whisked the letter away, and blotted it. Quick, indeed, was the word. He had never known her so quick. And suddenly, either because of this, or an inference that he sensed, or because of misery, or languor, or plain fatigue, he became aware that he just *couldn't* stay on here himself. And gulped. And achieved further speech.

"Look," he said, though in fact he meant "Listen," of course. "It's Friday, after all. Rather a special day for you—" another gulp, but he mastered it—"what's more. Just leave everything else. Take the rest of the day off. I—I think, 's a matter of fact——"

"Oh, Mr. Sunderland—may I really?"

"Yes! Run along. Catch the same train again."

"Oh, *thank* you, Mr. Sunderland. I——"

"Hi! Take the letters!"

"Oh, I'm sorry, Mr. Sunderland—but *really*, you know . . . "

She fluttered, she was girlish, and again Paul felt sick. But now she had gone, and, by Jove, he was off, too! He needed air. A long walk. To get away from that darned geranium. IIis two uncles and his cousin could whistle if they wanted him—though in all probability, since the office had become a love-nest, they, also, had thrown in their hands; but today, and *now*, he was getting out of this place. He had had enough. He quelled his conscience, and as it collapsed he stood up. "I'm *going*!" he announced. And he went.

Out of the room first, of course, and along the corridor, and down in the lift, and across the hall. But here at last—for he wasn't looking, and had no chance to dodge—Sergeant Banglewick was waiting firmly in his way.

"Mr. Paul——"

"Eh?"

"—if you've got a moment——"

"What's the matter?" said Paul. But he had stopped. He could hardly knock an employee down. "Well?" he inquired, a shade sharply.

The frosty veteran, as he now observed, was unbuttoning an outer pocket. Then his pince-nez—of course!—slipped, and there was more delay.

"Look here," said Paul, registering a certain impatience with his own fingers, and feet. "Is it anything important? Because——"

"Important, sir?" The old fellow was like a ramrod again, though the angle of the pince-nez was still oblique. "Couldn't 'ardly be more 'ighly—" he sucked a tooth—"as I think, sir, you'll agree." He glanced at whatever he had taken from his pocket. He looked up, and with anything but a frosty smile. "It's my boy, sir," he said. "Perce. You remember the advice you give 'im?"

"No," said Paul, which was indeed the truth. "I—I've never seen him," he pointed out.

"That," said old Banglewick, "don't make no difference, sir. 'E took it. I passed it on. If 'e'd took it a bit sooner, it'd 'ave spared 'im—an' 'is mother, and me, too, sir—a lot of worry. 'Tell 'im to get out more,' you said, sir—" here he not only beamed, but gave a chuckle—"an' it's all led to this. That's why, sir——"

"Just a second," said Paul, who was neither beaming nor chuckling. "Led to what?"

"Ar!" said the old sergeant. "We was worried, too. Mopey, 'e was. Orf 'is food. Proper miserable, if you like, sir. 'Is mum kep' saying as 'e ought to go to the orsepittle. But 'tween't that, sir—though, mind you, 'e never let on. No, sir. It was all doo to a young lady!"

"Oh?" said Paul, rocking slightly. But he was too civil to rush away. "Really?" he tried to croak, as he was interrupted.

"Yessir. An' a very nice young lady, too. But Perce thought she was orf 'im. 'E'd no *confidence*, you see. But this very last Sunday, sir—when 'e was moping something crool—I says to 'im—thinkin' of *you*, sir—'Why dontcher go out? Get some air,' I says.

'There ain't nothing like air.' In fack, sir, I almost pushes 'im out. But 'e goes. An' there's the young lady—she only lives down the road—a-startin' out, too. 'E can't 'ardly avoid 'er. They goes all the way to Epping—not as they meant to but I was young meself once, sir, an' you know 'ow it is. An' whether it was the fresh air, or—" another chuckle—"maybe the young lady 'erself, 'e plucks up 'is courage; and in course she says Yes; and 'e's so 'appy, sir, now—an' so's 'is mother an' me—for we've always liked 'er— she ain't like some of these gurls; there's such a change, sir— Well, jes' look at this!"

"Eh?" said Paul, though he was aware that something—it felt like a postcard—had just been forced into his hand.

"They 'ad it took sir. Out at Epping, you see. An' *don't* they look 'appy?"

"Oh," said Paul, and in turn forced his eyes on to the portrait. It represented one of the plainest young women that he had ever seen, in close company with a young man who, whatever his virtues, not merely resembled an anthropoid ape, but one that had shaved all the hair over its ears, while the rest stood erect in a thick tuft.

Of happiness, as he understood it, he could detect no sign at all. Yet he could believe that they were happier than himself. For not only was old Banglewick chuckling once more, not only was the work of alfresco photographers notoriously unflattering, but he— Paul Sunderland—had just been charged with another crime. Or, to be more accurate, was being thanked for it again.

"No!" he protested, and thrust the portrait away.

"But it's *true*, sir. We've all drunk your 'ealth. 'I'll tell Mr. Paul,' I says. 'That's right,' they all says. But I didn't seem to get no chance—well, not till jes' now. Can't I give 'em a message, sir, back?"

Yes, thought Paul; you can tell 'em— But no. He must play the game. It was fantastic to suppose that he had really brought this about; but if they shared this increasingly loathsome illusion, or, indeed, in any case, he must observe the code.

So that again he had a short, violent struggle with his vocal organs. And triumphed so far that when he spoke there was for once no hitch.

"Yes," he said. "You must give 'em my congratulations, of course."

"You don't mind, sir?" The old Sergeant peered up into his face. "I 'aven't taken a liberty, sir?"

"No!" said Paul, though this was purely in reply to the second point. Then he lied. "I'm *delighted*," he said.

At this stage the mist returned so thickly and overpoweringly that he never quite knew whether he had really slapped old Bangle-wick between the shoulder-blades or not. Though perhaps he had, for one might do anything in a nightmare.

And a nightmare it was—the whole world, that's to say—as Paul Sunderland strode through the streets. Of all the innumerable characters who were now talking and muttering to themselves, few can have said more, or have pulled quite so many faces, as he cannoned not only off lamp-posts, pillar-boxes, parked vehicles, and pedestrians, but from one thought to another that he couldn't bear.

On this occasion—he is almost certain—he entered no cinema. Nor does he believe, though he has some vague recollection of gazing gloomily into the Serpentine, that he ever sat down. His route, it may therefore be judged, was circuitous; though he was never lost in the sense that he had lost himself two nights ago.

It is known, however—or he knows—that he left the office at about twenty minutes to four, and that he reached his residence at about ten minutes past six. As to *why* he fetched up here, rather than anywhere else, there is a comparatively simple explanation. It was the Climate.

He hadn't noticed, at first, that the sun was now obscured. Or he may have felt that this was purely subjective. But at about half-past five a kind of soft drizzle began (rather resembling the Quality of Mercy); and though for a while he was as unconscious of this as of where he was, it was then gradually borne in on him not only that he was getting damp, but that he was becoming saturated by a strong, steady downpour.

The fine spell, in other words, had at last come to an end; though quite gently, and with no explosions of thunder. And even if pneumonia or rheumatic fever might, in his present view, be rather welcome than otherwise, there is no one on earth who likes wearing wet clothes. So he must change them. And as there was only one place where he could do that, he made for it, dripping and splashing along. And arrived. And hurried straight into his own flat.

8

He made no attempt to enter quietly. He fairly shot into the tiny hall. But then, though it had been his intention to proceed direct to his bedroom, he heard a sound, and veered off to the right.

If the sitting-room door had been shut, he would have heard nothing. But it was open, and he was inside in a flash. Spilsby, he was thinking. I must ask him to dry these things. But though he was right, up to a point—for it was certainly Spilsby—he was quite mistaken in that forecast of his next remark.

"Good heavens!" in fact, was what he actually said. "What on earth are you up to? I say!"

Spilsby, who was still holding the whisky bottle in one hand and a half-filled tumbler in the other, developed several expressions. Servility was the least obvious. There was perhaps a faint dash of shame. But annoyance and even resentment were far stronger than this. While strongest, if also most unjustifiable, of all was an extraordinary air of elation.

For a second or two he remained silent as well. But then, just as Paul was about to repeat his inquiry—and though he was still holding the bottle and glass as before—a certain trace of the old Spilsby emerged.

He said: "Tchk! You're wet through, sir."

"I know that," said Paul. It might even—but of course this was a dialectical point—have been supposed that he liked it. "But what I *want* to know," he resumed, almost at once, "is why the blazes I come in here and find——"

"Oh, sir! I—I just *had* to!"

"Eh?" said Paul, taken aback. Was the fellow ill, then? Or was he drunk? This second speculation made him tauten some muscles. Then he relaxed, for there was nothing actually threatening in Spilsby's face; though it certainly looked very strange. He reverted to the first theory. "What's the matter? Are you feeling faint?"

"Oh, no, sir. Thank you, sir. It's not that, sir. I'm just so happy!"

"*Are* you!" snapped Paul. The second theory revived. It was also quite intolerable that even Spilsby should be happy. "Would you," he asked—and if there were a touch of irony here, it may possibly be excused—"mind telling me why?"

"Oh, sir, I was going to. I was meaning to, sir. I said to myself—just now I said——"

"Buck up! And put that drink down."

"Eh? Oh, *thank* you, sir."

The translated Spilsby poured the spirits down his throat—which, of course, wasn't the least what Paul had meant—and smacked his lips.

"That's more like it," he announced. "It's very good of you, sir. But then you *'ave* been good." He seemed to note the missing aspirate, and then to brush it aside. "I look on you, sir—if you wouldn't mind such a remark—as being my reel lucky star."

Paul, who had been trying to get a word in, stopped trying; for it was clear that the man was mad. He advanced, though far from sure that there wouldn't still be a fight. But Spilsby, whose countenance was now wreathed in smiles, stood his ground. He also finished the glass.

"There, sir!" he said. He set it down, and the bottle as well. "And the best of good luck to you, sir, too. Mind you," he rambled on, or this was rambling to Paul, "I've given the stuff up, altogether. You see, *she* didn't like it. Well, that's good enough for me. But last night, sir, I admit—well, Dutch courage, you know, sir. 'Course I'd made up my mind, but I was *scared*. And then, sir, just now—when I thought what she'd said—well, I 'ad just to celebrate, once."

He raised a hand, as if for silence, though Paul could still only gape.

"But that's the end, sir," he continued. "That's the last drop I touch. For when," said Spilsby, "I think of my future 'appiness—and 'ow it was *your* whisky, sir, that gave me the pluck—and 'ow it was *you*, sir, goin' away at Easter like that what 'elps me, as you might say, over the first 'urdle . . . Ah, sir," proceeded Spilsby, now rolling his eyes, "I reckon you never guessed those times you saw me coming back—for she's a 'ousekeeper, sir, in some flats in Conduit Street; I reckon——"

"Spilsby!" It burst out at last.

"Beg pardon, sir?"

"What are you *talking* about?"

"Love, sir," said Spilsby. And Paul Sunderland drew back. "I'm 'ooked, sir. 'Ooked proper. It catches me *'ere*." He patted his black waistcoat, and Paul again could have shrieked. "It's orl what they say, sir. It fair alters one's 'ole life. But I still say as but for you, sir——"

"Shut up!" cried Paul. At the same moment the telephone

started ringing. "Blast!" he added. Of course this was Roddie again. "Go on—answer it," he gibbered. "Say I'm out!"

"Very good, sir." Not a hint of impetuosity now. For a moment at least—(Lord! I *must* change, thought Paul)—man and master were back in their old relationship. Click! went the instrument. "Yes, madam, but I am afraid he's out . . . Very good, madam . . . Thank you, madam." And the concluding click.

An extraordinary, fantastic, and miraculous idea had just shot through Paul's mind. It was Bianca. She wanted to see him again. He ought to have dashed forward, but——

"Quick!" he gasped. "Who was that?"

"Mrs. Parkinson was the lady's name, sir. Was that all right, sir?"

"Grrh!" said Paul Sunderland. No inward query as to *why* Mrs. Parkinson should have rung him up; though an avoidance, so far as possible, of the thought of a certain book of poems. He looked stony. "Here—" he thrust it violently aside—"I'm going to have a bath. I'll chuck these things out, and you might just— Oh, hell take it, congratulations, I mean, Spilsby. Of course. But I'm sopping!"

"Very good, sir. And I'm very obliged, sir, I'm sure. And you do understand, sir——"

"Yes, yes," said Paul. Hell, in fact—though there wasn't much left now—could take the whisky, too. And Spilsby, with that repulsive tremor in his stupid voice. Ugh, again, in short, as— already with his back turned, and crossing the little hall—he began unbuttoning, and wrenching at his sodden tie.

A little later he hurled everything that he had been wearing out of the bathroom. And when he emerged himself, at least persuaded that he had now conquered any chill, the clothes had gone. And so, thank Heaven, had Spilsby.

With further mutterings and mumblings, and plaintive or injured sounds, he jerked at drawer-knobs in his bedroom, unhooked another suit, dived for a pair of shoes, and, shortly before seven, was once more fully dressed. Yet pledged to go out now, in spite of the rain. For not only, as he remembered, had he said that he would be dining out, but he was dashed if he could stand any more Spilsby.

It was still possible, of course, just to sit here and brood. But no. In point of fact he was rather hungry by now; as he well might be, after that light lunch and long walk. Moreover—and though he could only hope that this would wear off presently—the air of the sitting-room was soiled. Spilsby banging his waistcoat like that. Spilsby trembling and throbbing—and mocking him, too. Revolting. It was unthinkable that one should remain in such a room. Once more—it was as if the Furies were after him—there was only one word. Escape.

So he seized his raincoat and a dry hat—he was of the generation which, for some reason, seems to have abandoned the use of the umbrella—put them on, and shot out of the flat. Down the stairs— he was too impatient to wait for the lift—and out on to the pavement; where, as it chanced—and it *would* chance, for Fate must of course show, or attempt to show, in this sort of way, that it was really (pah!) quite a kindly old thing—another tenant was just alighting from a taxi.

"Do you want this?" the other tenant even asked. And Paul growled: "Thanks." He addressed the driver, for it would seem that there was only one place to go. "Megalithic Club, please," he said.

Then he embarked, and slammed the door; and the cab rolled away, with the rain drumming on its roof, and streaming down its windows. It was at just about this moment that Miss Brown—as arranged on the telephone three nights ago—having partaken of a light meal at the Avocado Club (for which she paid) with Mr. Brian Cairns, having "managed" him so far (though he had already been rather tiresome once or twice), and having driven him in her own little car to what proved to be the best available parking-space, was proceeding on foot (and, owing to the rain, Mr. Cairns could hardly be told not to take her arm as he hurried her, protectively, along) to the cinema that had been selected.

But Paul didn't know this, as he swished through blurred streets. Still less did he know that it was the same film that he had himself seen. Nor could he tell, though he was certainly thinking of Miss Brown, how its theme might affect her companion.

He just sat looking grim, until the taxi drew up. Then he paid; and, after an absence of about forty-six hours, once more entered the grim Megalithic.

9

As it was still a bit early to start eating, perhaps, or possibly because his appetite was again quailing after a glimpse into the huge dining-room, he turned—or as soon as he had disposed of his hat and coat—to the gloomy smoking-room on the other side of the hall.

As usual, it was almost empty; but he didn't mind that. He eluded the aged waiter, by skirting some of the mammoth furniture —for even a stimulant, it would appear, was rather more than he was prepared to face—and sank into a deep chair in the furthest corner.

Here he mused for a while—though some thoughts hung on so long that they almost ceased to be thoughts—and concluded, again, that he was doomed and damned. But then—whether this was automatic, or a form of defence against the waiter—he picked up an evening newspaper, which another member had discarded on the little table just beside him, and focused his eyes, more or less.

Its front page, again as usual, announced domestic and foreign crises. He read, but as it was inconceivable that he should feel more depressed—and, besides, like so many others, he was largely inoculated against this stuff—there was no particular effect on his frame of mind.

The second page was for the most part financial. He skipped that. He knew it all; or all that mattered he already knew. The third page was a gallimaufry, from which he acquired, but almost immediately forgot, certain facts. And among them—but there comes a point, or so it is said, at which one can feel no more pain— that delivery of the Porchester Leveret had not only again been postponed, but that the price had been advanced by ninety pounds.

He wasn't surprised. He merely shrugged, and passed on. What the deuce did *he* want with a car? Once, of course, he had imagined . . . But that was all washed up. Forget it. He couldn't entirely do this. But he turned, rather rapidly, to the next page.

Something struck his eye, as it prepared to hesitate between the leading article and the other columns. There was no cartoon tonight, but there was a half-tone block—or, to be more precise, its impression—which for a moment made him think: That's rather like someone. Who? He had no idea, as he gave it a second glance. Nor did the caption—or again, to be more precise, the line of print underneath it—add much to his information as yet.

"She Wore His Frocks," it said, perplexingly and somewhat teasingly. He knew now—for still there was that faint suggestion of *someone*—that somewhere, among all the cross-headings on this page, the same words should be lurking again. This was the custom. And he found them.

"The announcement," he began reading, "of a romance in the world of *haute couture* is bringing widespread congratulations from a large circle of friends to good-looking, debonair Michael Willoughby—" something here about dollars, but Paul had palpitated and passed on—"and tall, slim Miss Joan Hobson (see today's picture above)—" here Paul's pulse regained most of its rhythm—"who has been employed as a demonstrator of his creations. Miss Hobson, keen on sport like her fiancé, tells me that her marriage, which is expected to take place shortly, will end her career as a mannequin. 'I shall be a housewife,' she said, laughingly, 'and the two jobs don't mix.' 'That's right,' said Mr. Willoughby, when I spoke to him, too. 'Ariadne'—for it is thus that his bride-to-be is more generally known—'will look after my home for me.' But he added that part of the honeymoon is to be spent in Paris, where pleasure, as he put it, can be combined with business."

Paul read this paragraph two or three times; and, of course—for there they were, or, rather, weren't, in the illustration—he remembered those lips now. Yet curiously enough, and though there had been a momentary, wild pang, he neither groaned nor flung the newspaper away.

He saw, clearly enough, that this was Fate at the same game; that it had *hoped* to push him right over the edge. But it had failed. Or it had gone too far. He *couldn't* suffer any more. Besides, though he knew both parties, they hadn't told him themselves. Nor, again—but here, of course, he was in complete ignorance of what Miss Hobson had told Miss Brown—had either of them claimed that he was responsible.

He was conscious of slight relief. He felt he had taken this pretty well. He might even drop a line to Ariadne. Or not? He appeared to test certain nerves, and shook his head. No. It was quite unnecessary. He hardly knew her at all. And he wasn't as invulnerable as all that.

Nevertheless, there was no doubt that a stab from Fate had as good as missed; or that he had received too many to react to a mere prick. It didn't occur to him—yet why should it?—as he rose, laid the newspaper down, and began moving slowly towards the dining-room, that Fate is never so deadly as when it *seems* to ease off. That it knew just what it was up to—for, unfortunately, it always does. Or that its whole intention, in delivering this comparatively soft blow, was to weaken his defences against a wallop.

In utter ignorance of this, too—though there had been a warning, if he had only known—he passed through two pairs of swing-doors, and chose three courses. And consumed them, in the remote company of about six other members. Drank half a pint of beer, which in these days, though expensive, can have no other effect. Rose again. Paid his bill. Made the ascent of the wide stairs. And edged once more, like a ghost, into the Library.

This was the result rather of absence of decision than of any plan. Or it was just a habit, despite the breach in it last night. But the room was still empty. There was no one in his niche. He sank down. He was jolly tired, as a matter of fact. He was still in torment, notwithstanding his recent yet, alas, only brief sense of calm. But he did lean back. And he did close his eyes.

Did he sleep? It is thought not. Or it was a prolonged cat-nap at most; for there can be no doubt that he heard that click from the heavy door. His eyes re-opened. He was annoyed at this invasion of his private gloom. Or had it, perhaps, been somebody going out?

He half-rose, to make sure, and leant forward as well. Dash! He was looking straight into an old buffer's face. And—dash, again!—he had identified it, too. It was coming nearer. He continued to rise, because he must. But of all things—in this Library—to encounter someone he knew! He clutched at a shelf for support.

The huge head and immense upper lip of Sir Edmund Parkinson —or of Mr. Justice Parkinson, if that is more correct, though in business hours (which is so confusing) he was addressed as My Lord—came right into the recess, and pulled up.

"Ha!" he exclaimed, in total disregard of all the notices that said Silence. "Young Sunderland—heh? I didn't realise—I was unaware—hah!—that you had joined our number."

Well, thought Paul, if *he's* going to talk here, I suppose I can't very well just make signs at him. Besides, they were quite alone, if it came to that.

He began explaining. "I'm not really a member, sir," he said. "But——"

"Heh?" A forensic frown. A distinct air of tut-tut.

"——I'm a sort of guest. From the Junior Corinthian."

"Ah." There was no necessity, then (it might be gathered) to

summon a tipstaff. "I see. Hum. Curious. Very curious indeed."
A portentous nod. Yet at the same time—though why?—the
strangest dawn of a most uncharacteristic look of jollity. "The
fact is," said Sir Edmund, "that I very seldom come here now
myself."

He paused; still erect, so that Paul must stand, too. But if
there had been anything funny about that last remark, he was
totally unable to perceive it.

"Really?" he said, as it appeared to be his turn. A hand was
raised as if he had tried to interrupt.

"Most curious," said Sir Edmund. "But——" He broke off,
with a sudden look of suspicion. "Have you been talking to Reginald
—today—heh?" he asked.

"No, sir." But Mrs. Parky—oh, all right; Lulu, then—had rung
up. Paul recalled this. Were they in trouble? Was a child ill? Or
what? With a little more time, he might have rejected this idea;
for who bothers a bachelor about croup? But the huge face and the
long lip made him nervous, of course. "Has—has anything happened?
he gasped.

And again he was astonished, for the old boy's mouth seemed
to be struggling with a kind of smile.

"I should think it *had*," he replied; "though— Well. Hah. But
that's just it. Most *remarkable*—finding you here."

"Is it?" said Paul, feebly.

"I've just said so. Very queer. For, as I say, it was the merest
chance that I decided to dine here. I—I was feeling a little restless,
you see."

"Oh. I'm sorry, sir."

"Heh? No, I'm perfectly well. I've never felt better in my
life."

"Oh," said Paul. "That's good. Er——"

"But, you see, *you* were there. In fact—hah—I might almost say
if you *hadn't* been there——"

"Where?" asked Paul, half-convinced that the old boy was
bats; though he certainly felt bats himself.

"Heh?" The solid figure took a grip on the same shelf; and
slightly lowered his head—like a bull. "Just," he said, "cast your
mind back—if you'll be so good—to the early evening of February
14th."

Paul did this at once, with no difficulty at all. He had been
doing it for three and a half months. But *he* didn't smile. He looked

wretchedly strained. And still more so—as many a witness had looked—when Sir Edmund's free forefinger shot out and pointed straight at his midriff.

"Have you got it?" he boomed.

"Y-yes, sir. I remember."

"You broke a glass."

"Yes, I know, sir; but——"

"Just a moment," said the Judge. "I'm not claiming for that."

"Oh, th-thank you, sir."

"I'm very glad, now, that you did it."

Paul's eyebrows went aloft. "I—I don't quite follow, sir," he said.

"I hope you will, though, my boy," said his persecutor—for there was really no other word for him now. "I hope you will," he repeated, with almost staggering geniality. "A young fellow like you—well, you *ought* to get married. Why don't you? Heh? What? Look at *me*!"

Paul looked. He was hemmed in. The face was larger than ever. He jerked a volume right out of the shelf.

"Leave it!" barked his lordship. Paul straightened again; though, with no prop now, he all but gave at the knees. "Never mind about that. This is much more important. Paul, my boy—" this was a form of address that he had eschewed since the war, so that the object must again blink and start—"there'll be no secret, from anyone, in—" here he glanced at a marble clock—"in less than twelve hours. But I want *you* to know *now*; tonight! You remember me poor wife, too. And Gerry, poor lad. I've been lonely. But, Paul, this is great news, you know. Edith Gourlay—and I'll admit that she turned me down nearly thirty years ago—has promised—" the full diapason now—"to become my wife!"

There! said his whole being, from about two feet away. But even then he must drive home the last shaft.

"Thanks to *you*, Paul," he said. "It was that glass that brought it off. It was hers, you see—charming woman, don't you think?— and I set myself to replace it; and I did! It gave me the opportunity — Well, well, I dare say this is fanciful in a way. But dear Edith— poor child, she's been a widow for twenty years, but she'd only just come to London—has frequently mentioned it, too. The Lucky Glass—ha, ha!—we both call it now. So you see, when I find you— most extraordinary coincidence . . ."

And a lot more, very likely, from this enamoured old Judge,

though only fragments now penetrated Paul's ears. He did, that is to say, gather—if not actually for the first time—that Parky and his cheerful wife were bucked, too. He even gathered, and was mildly shocked—yet perhaps it was a good thing—that "dear Edith" had been left a packet by her deceased spouse.

Frankness, indeed, fairly bubbled and poured. Such was the flow, and so essential was it, apparently, that it should be unchecked, that at one moment, when a second buffer (who in fact, though Paul didn't know this, was a member of the Committee) entered the Library and seemed about to protest, he received such a glare from the babbling Betrothed that he vanished as if he had been blown out.

But the horror for Paul—well, it should be obvious where it lay. Fate knew. It had only pretended to lay off. But that a *grandfather*, with three grandchildren—no, dammit, nearly four!—should come in here, into this place of refuge, and start twaddling like a loopy adolescent about *his* happiness and the state of *his* heart. That a lean and slippered pantaloon (though in fact Mr. Justice Parkinson was both well-covered and well-shod) should buttonhole and cackle, instead of thinking of his latter end. That he should affront a decent, harmless, and unfortunate chap by parading his own grotesque and almost infantile glee—it was *this* that was indeed the last straw.

No sympathy with his situation had yet touched Paul's soul. Others might possibly have been affected by those allusions to his dead wife and his dead son. But not Paul. Or not yet. It was his *age* that was the offence. One might concede that one's contemporaries, and even H.B., weren't barred altogether—however tactlessly and inopportunely they might have done this—from pairing off.

But that a man in his sixties—not to mention a woman who must be at least in her fifties—should carry on in this contemptible way. That they should conspire, deliberately, to ape what they should have long outgrown. That one of them—and one of His Majesty's Judges, too!—should be so lost to decorum that he was now behaving like the brutes that perish. And that instead of doing this quietly, or with even a slight sense of shame, he should come charging into a library, and boasting of his folly—it was *this*——

Or no, it wasn't. It was much worse than that. It was *Love* that was so shocking, and so odious and foul. It was a monster. An ogre. It didn't care twopence who fell into its jaws. Age or aspect meant *nothing* to it. All it wanted—this ravening, imbecile power—was to turn men into nincompoops, to paralyse their reason, and to drive them, like hogs, into a stock-yard where they were at once stunned; by the thousand; or by the million, if it could.

All over the world, in fact, couples on whom this truth hadn't burst—as it had just burst on Paul—were simpering and ogling, like zanies and louts, while Love—pah!—just looked on and laughed. He saw it, for the scales had at last dropped from his own eyes. And though, for a few seconds, he also felt as if the floor had given way, he then recovered—or such was his personal belief—and *knew* that he had torn off Love's mask.

Nevertheless, however remarkable this achievement might be—or however bracing, perhaps, a little later on—he still had no wish—in fact, less than no wish—to play stooge to this foolish old man. Civility, which (it appeared) he hadn't entirely sloughed off in this new incarnation, still restrained him from just walking out. But he picked up the book. He even tried to interrupt. And then—was this also chance, or a fresh feat of strength?—Sir Edmund faltered, and half-turned, with another glance at the marble clock; and forthwith interrupted himself.

"Good gracious!" he exclaimed. "I'd no idea it was so late. Will you excuse me, my dear boy? The fact is—hrrm—you see, that Edith couldn't get out of a little dinner-party this evening; but she said she'd leave early, and I—ah—promised to look in. So if you'll forgive me——"

He was half-way towards the door, but turned again.

"May I offer her your good wishes?" he asked.

Paul looked like thunder, though only for about as long as a flash of lightning. Civility, it seemed, must still prevail.

"Oh, rather," he quacked. "Yes, certainly. I—I mean, of course. And if it comes to that——"

But it didn't come to that. The five- or possibly six-syllable word was for once neither mangled nor fluffed; nor even uttered at all. For Sir Edmund couldn't wait. Sir Edmund had gone. There was just a hiss, from the apparatus at the top of the big door, and the softest of little thuds as it shut.

Paul backed towards his chair. He appeared about to sit down. But he couldn't. For though again he was quite alone in the large room, he had just realised that it would now never be the same. It was sullied, it was haunted by the scene he had been through.

Echoes clung, or so he felt, to all those books. Never again—and, as a matter of fact, he was perfectly right—would it serve as a place of retreat. It had turned against him. Yes, old Parkinson had deprived him of even this. For though still quite decided that Love was a noxious plague—here he, too, began advancing towards the door—he was dashed if he wanted constant reminders.

No. He was less certain, as is perhaps natural at a re-birth, of *where* he would pass the evenings henceforward. But not up here. Because he couldn't. He *loathed* the darned place. In fact, but for a sudden apprehension that if he rushed down the stairs he might easily overtake that old buzzard, there can be little doubt that he would have fled at top speed.

But he remembered. He lagged. He heard a boom from below— "Good-night, Boniface. No, my car's waiting, thanks." And then, as the sound ceased, he tiptoed lightly towards the hall, and made his way to the sparse assortment of hats and coats.

    .   .   .   .   .

It was at this precise juncture that Bianca—lovely creature— approached a much larger assortment of considerably larger objects that were drawn up in ranks just outside. The rain had paused, but only a short while ago, so that the roadway was still full of puddles. The Climate, it might be judged, was merely taking a slight rest—after some absence of recent practice at this particular form of weather—before resuming, and pelting all night.

The sky, in other words, was one immense, dark-grey cloud, though technically and officially it was still day. And she was alone. For though she had stayed until the very end of the film, not only had Mr. Brian Cairns—or Moustache, as another character had once privately called him—developed an increasing tendency to lean heavily against her; not only had he also developed a no less heavy and distinctly ominous type of breathing; but as they emerged, and though the rain had quite obviously stopped, he had again tried to appropriate her arm.

She had removed it, gently enough. He had tried again. She had said: "Oh, Brian—please don't." But whether he had been affected by the film, by his own imagination, or by her unquestionable charm, he had preferred, or had felt compelled, to grasp it firmly this time. And to start repeating a rather wearisome declaration.

"Oh, *please*, Brian," she said. "You *can't* do this here."

"Yes, I can," he had replied. "No one's listening."

"But they will. And you *mustn't*." She had jerked her arm free. "Brian!"

"Hullo?"

"You must behave—or I shall have to leave you. *Brian*—" for he still seemed to miss her clear point—"I've told you—again and again—it's no good. I've *never* encouraged you. And I *shan't* change my mind. Now will you just, please, kindly *stop*!"

"No. I hadn't finished. Besides, it's just about time——"

"Oh, it isn't! Not for this."

"Well, let's have supper."

"I don't want any."

"Well, come on. I'll see you home."

"Oh, please not. I'm tired."

"Here—I say—can't a chap——"

"No, he can't. And I—I think I'd better say good-night. No, Brian, if you try and follow me, I shall scream. I've had enough! I——"

And here—though one would wish it to be known that this was a very poor example of her "managing" tactics—as he recoiled, just for a moment, at what of course was an absurd threat, she darted across the pavement; she dodged behind a bus; she dodged, in the other direction, so as to avoid a van and a Rolls-Royce; and, still running like Atalanta, she continued to dart and dodge, until at last she slowed down and looked back.

There was no sign of pursuit. She had won, for the time being. Or perhaps she had done even more. For though of course she had behaved like a child or a complete fool—and no one was more conscious of this—it is yet a fact that very few young gentlemen, however passionate for a passing phase, like to chase pretty girls through the streets.

They can lean, they can breathe, they can hang on to arms. They can even, or so it seems, start proposing in public. But if they chase, they will be conspicuous. The thought of dignity returns. And they might, at about half-past nine, in the neighbourhood of Piccadilly, quite easily be run over as well.

So that although Mr. Cairns knew just where his ex-companion's little car was parked, for he had assisted to align it himself, he would appear to have concluded that his dignity was now involved; and that if he walked there he would certainly arrive too late.

Thus he fades out of the story, and into a bar, as a matter of fact; where he may be left, for he was never one of Bianca's worthiest friends. And thus Bianca herself, no longer panting, but still put out, reached the car-park; tipped the hobbling attendant; slid, gracefully, on to her own front seat; wound down the windows; and felt in her handbag for her little key.

Bother! she was thinking, though she had found her little key. That was awful. I can't stand it, you know. And what's more (she was thinking), I must be losing my grip. Why didn't I stop him sooner? Or why did I ever say I'd go? He's just a nuisance. A big booby. I knew exactly what he's like; and with everyone else, too, if it comes to that.

But I was tired, she was thinking. And I half-forgot he was there. That was the trouble. I don't know if I'm sickening for something, but . . . Oh, well. Come along. I must get to bed.

She thrust the key in, and turned it. The starter worked, and the engine roared. "Right you are, miss!" said the attendant, beckoning her forward, though he was directly in her path. She twisted, and he side-stepped, but he had made her take too wide a curve. She braked; or she would have scraped the kerb-stone. She must reverse now. She did nothing of the kind. Paul Sunderland—unless she was absolutely insane—was a yard away, carrying a coat, and with a hat in the other hand. And the look he gave her was such a look as she had never seen.

Not only, in fact, had she never seen it from Paul. She had never seen it from anyone on earth. It was cold. Almost contemptuous. It set up prickles in her spine. He was glaring at her, as if one at least of them were Medusa. And quite silently. He had the air of a young gentleman who was transfixed. What did it mean? For three weeks, all but a day, she had *known* he would come crawling back. And had been ready. But never for *this*.

The prickles surged. It was the most extraordinary sensation that she had ever known. They were like a rocket that seemed to burst in her head and heart. He detested her. That was obvious. But what had she *done*? And what—oh, what *could* she do now?

I've lost him, she thought. He was the one all the time. I was *mad*. And now he hates me. I shall die!

"Paul!" she gasped.

He stepped nearer. Yet the car might have been an aquarium, and she a fish, for any vestige of human feeling in his face.

"Good-evening," he observed, bowing slightly from the waist, "I hope you're quite well, and all that."

"No, I'm not!" she almost wailed, as tears welled into her eyes. "Oh, Paul, what's the matter? And where've you *been*?"

"I've been dining at my club," said Paul Sunderland. He amended this. "At my temporary club, that's to say. And you?" he inquired; but not the least as if he cared.

Yet she must keep him, at all costs. "I—I've been at a film. Paul——"

"A good one, I hope." He was stepping back.

"Paul!"

"Eh?"

"Paul!"

"What?"

"Come here! Oh, Paul—*please*!"

He seemed to hesitate. Or to be considering if he need answer at all. He looked up. And received a raindrop, smack in his left eye. In another instant it was pelting again.

"Paul! You'll get *soaked*!" She leant across, and flung the door wide open. *"Please* come in!"

"Oh, well . . ." There was still the code; and he bore no personal grudge. Besides, it was cats and dogs now—or like Tennyson's warrior's widow's tears—and even a raincoat, if he put it on, would be no protection for his shoes, shins, and ankles. He did, that is to say, just glance round; for there might be a taxi. But, of course, there wasn't. And it was unthinkable—here, indeed, he looked sterner than ever—that he should go back into the Megalithic.

So he executed one of his shrugs. Rain like this, he may have believed, couldn't possibly continue for very long. There was no need to explain what he had discovered about Love. That could and must be his private affair. But for a few moments, perhaps, as a reasonable man . . .

He shot forward, for the water was now pouring down inside his collar. But he had forgotten something; and as his skull hit the roof with a violent bang, he not only yelped *"Ow!"*, he not only fell rather than sat, but he was athwart the driver, just for a moment. He could feel her softness, and scent her fragrance. A very similar brand of rocket exploded in his own breast. And he was now clinging to her, as she clung to him, too.

"Paul—*darling*—are you *hurt*?"

"No—not in the least. Oh, Bianca——"

"You don't hate me?"

"I *can't*!"

"Oh, Paul—has it been *awful*? I—I've been *such* a fool!"

He had found her lips. They were more responsive than anything he had ever dreamt. But they slightly delayed his reply. Then, however—but he was still kissing her neck—he spoke again.

"You haven't," he said. "It was *all* my own fault. But you did—I say, you *did* call me 'darling'?"

"Yes, darling."

"*Darling* Bianca!" said Paul, in return. A positive kaleidoscope of visions whirled round this main thought. The Pottings shot by, and didn't matter a curse. And Dorothea, whom he had never seen, either; but nor did she. And the man in the blue shirt; but that had never meant anything. And the Porchester Leveret, but that was equally unimportant; though one day, perhaps . . . It whizzed away.

He beheld fragments of his own agony, and of past happiness as well. But the former shrivelled; and present rapture swamped all. Why—he began to chuckle—if they married quickly enough (and not for a moment, as they kept on kissing, could he doubt that this was what she meant) he might even escape being three Best Men.

She said: "Darling—why are you laughing?" He began to explain. But though she listened, as he began, it seemed sheer waste of time. He petered out, and she didn't suggest that he should go on.

"Other people!" she was saying, in the old, enchanting voice. "What *do* they matter? Oh, Paul—think of *us*!"

So he did this, exclusively, and there was still much that they had to say. His arm was round her, and still they must pause to kiss now and then. But how they talked! And as it was growing darker, owing to the rain and the gathering dusk; as the rain made the few passers-by scuttle on; and as even the attendant was seeking shelter more than fifty yards away, they had almost as much privacy as if indoors.

Nor did the steady downpour seep in through the roof, as they continued to sit beneath it, and talk. Nevertheless, the little car was still at an angle to the kerb, and on a spot where—though frequently put to this use—it was strictly forbidden to park. The porter at the Megalithic didn't mind. It was too wet.

Besides, there was still space to draw up. But presently a policeman, in a glistening cape, strolled along—for all we know it was the same policeman who had once lurked outside Belloni's, and perhaps it was, for this was only the next beat—and saw the obstruction (as he deemed it), and padded softly to its side. And stooped, to peer under its dripping roof.

As it happened, however, he was just in time for a fresh embrace. Long, lingering, and intent; but no more. He straightened slowly, and turned away. All objection was withdrawn. For he was so familiar with its converse that he knew innocence at once. It reminded him, rather pleasantly, of his own courting days. "Ah, well," he muttered, gently, as he splashed through the rain, "I reckon it makes the world go round." And who shall say that the policeman was wrong?

THE END